Pinkie Promise

SAPPHIRE HALE

Copyright © 2024 Sapphire Hale

All characters and events in this publication, other than those clearly in the public domain, are fictitious and any resemblance to real persons, living or dead, is purely coincidental.

'American Elite' is a fictitious college cheerleading championship created by the author for the purposes of this novel.

All rights reserved.

No part of this publication may be reproduced, stored in a retrieval system, or transmitted in any form or by any means, without the prior permission in writing of the publisher.

ISBN: 9798871718780

ALSO BY SAPPHIRE HALE

The Phoenix Falls Series

Where We Left Off
Where It All Began
Where We Go From Here

The Carter Ridge Series

Pinkie Promise

CONTENTS

Playlist	i
Prologue	1
Chapter 1	7
Chapter 2	18
Chapter 3	27
Chapter 4	36
Chapter 5	46
Chapter 6	51
Chapter 7	58
Chapter 8	67
Chapter 9	76
Chapter 10	84
Chapter 11	100
Chapter 12	109
Chapter 13	119
Chapter 14	135
Chapter 15	147
Chapter 16	156

Sapphire Hale

Chapter 17	170
Chapter 18	181
Chapter 19	189
Chapter 20	202
Chapter 21	214
Chapter 22	221
Chapter 23	229
Chapter 24	242
Chapter 25	267
Chapter 26	281
Chapter 27	289
Chapter 28	304
Chapter 29	314
Chapter 30	330
Chapter 31	342
Chapter 32	347
Chapter 33	356
Epilogue	367
About the author	378

Sapphire Hale

PLAYLIST

Crown On The Ground – Sleigh Bells

Mess It Up – Gracie Abrams

The Good Life – Three Days Grace

Bad Liar – Selena Gomez

It'z Just What We Do – Florida Georgia Line

Dutton Ranch Freestyle – David Wallis

Son Of The Dirty South – Brantley Gilbert ft. Jelly Roll

I Can See You (Taylor's Version) – Taylor Swift

Wild As Her – Corey Kent

Clean – Pale Waves

Somewhere In A Small Town – Conner Smith

I Wouldn't Mind – He Is We

Spin You Around – Morgan Wallen

Wow. – Post Malone

In The Bible – Morgan Wallen ft. HARDY

Supermassive Black Hole – Muse

Ceilings – Lizzy McAlpine

Sapphire Hale

Nonsense – Sabrina Carpenter

I Deserve A Drink – Morgan Wallen

Feels Like – Gracie Abrams

Tennessee – Conner Smith

Let It Snow! Let It Snow! Let It Snow! – Dean Martin

I Think He Knows – Taylor Swift

LOCO – Machine Gun Kelly

Take It Slow – Conner Smith

Body Like A Back Road – Sam Hunt

Paper Rings – Taylor Swift

One Of Them Girls – Lee Brice

22 (Taylor's Version) – Taylor Swift

180 (Lifestyle) – Morgan Wallen

Sidelines – Phoebe Bridgers

Good Girl Gone Missin' – Morgan Wallen

Wonderland (Taylor's Version) – Taylor Swift

Me To Me – Morgan Wallen

Outlook – Morgan Wallen

Sapphire Hale

PROLOGUE

Fallon

No fall is too high to get back up from. That was the advice that my high school cheer coach gave me back when I was a junior. My parents didn't grant me endless hours of freedom for my one afterschool extracurricular so my coach knew that, for me to keep the top of our pyramid shining, we had to practice fast and thorough if we were going to make it to the junior league nationals.

For me though, it wasn't just about the junior league nationals.

It was about securing the top *score* at nationals so that the colleges which bestowed sports grants to the athletes who could help take their cheer squads to the annual American Elite tournament would give me one simple look and say, *that's the girl for us.*

Because whether or not my parents were Olympic champions still rolling in the spoils of international success, they made sure that their daughters would learn life the hard way.

In plain terms: if I didn't get a sport scholarship, I wasn't going to college.

My sisters had already managed the feat so I knew that it was doable, even if their sports of choice weren't exactly the same as mine, but it wasn't sibling rivalry or competitiveness that drove me to physically *need* that college grant.

It was the fact that there wasn't a chance in hell I was going to stay at home with my parents.

After spending my childhood being the perfect daughter only to realise that I was never going be good enough for them, I took matters into my own hands and decided to get my praise from another avenue instead.

A+. A+. A+.

100%. 100%. 100%.

Books taught me every joy that my parents never did and that's why I have no intentions of leaving academia yet – as long as I can retain my funding and keep my place at Carter U, one of the best colleges in the U.S. for Division I athletes, set in the heart of Carter Ridge.

An undulation below my feet instantly brings me back to the present.

I glance hesitantly down, my composure slipping as the cheer basket beneath me starts to ripple slightly.

I have always been confident in my ability to perform. It's other people that I know not to trust.

If there's one thing that I'm grateful for where my parents are concerned, it's that they taught me that self-sufficiency is the key to success. Motivating yourself to be the best at whatever it is that you're doing means that you will never have to rely on other people to pick up your slack, and you're never disappointed when they don't meet your level anyway.

But that's not exactly why I've instilled that advice so deeply into my soul.

For me, I refuse to rely on someone – to let them in –

and then have the rug ripped from under my feet.

If you never let anyone good in, then you'll never have to go through the pain of losing them.

And if my own parents didn't want to be there for me, why on earth would anyone else?

It's the first week of my year as a college senior and the cheer team tryouts came and went three days ago, meaning that we now have a number of new girls currently getting to grips with our pre-American Elite regimen. But if the girl gripping my right ankle doesn't lock her arms in the next two seconds, we are very much about to topple the hell over.

"Blair?" I say warningly, because obviously I remembered Wobbly Arms' name. She's a freshman who should definitely *not* have made the team but we all know who her father is so she got a place regardless. "Um, Blair, please could you maybe–?"

In the next second we're all screaming as Blair completely releases my leg and shoots away from the inevitable fallout. My body tilts to the side and, just before my left foot is yanked out of the socket, my roommate Aisling O'Malley shoots over from where she's watching us and shoves me back into position so that we don't end up in a heap on the floor.

The three girls that are now holding my legs re-stabilise my position and, after a shaky inhalation, I plaster an American Elite smile on my face, kick one leg up at a one-hundred-and-eighty degree angle, and throw my arms out wide as the routine finishes.

Aisling is our team's captain and coordinator, so she puts on a brave face as we regroup on the plush red cheer mats.

"Okay, that wasn't so bad," she says to the room, her ponytail swishing in full-on cheer mode. "But, uh..." She flashes me an *I am so sorry* look before saying, "We need to do the double pyramid before the practice is out, so..."

I shoot a hasty glance over to Blair who is carefully avoiding my eyes, and then I focus on my sparkly manicure until I can get a one-on-one moment with Aisling.

"Ash," I hiss, as the rest of the girls rearrange themselves further back on the mats, getting into their starting positions. Seeing as there are so many of us on the comp team we're using the stunning white gymnastic suite, whereas the separate cheer events squad tends to use the spaces at the Carter U gym.

Without me needing to explain anything Aisling rests a hand on my arm and says, "Fallon, I know, I'm going to talk to her dad. But we can't have them cut our funding otherwise we won't be able to go to Elite next year and…"

And if we don't go to Elite then I won't be able to get the sports grant to fund my Master's.

I nod in understanding and give her one of my crazy cheer smiles, making a laugh burst out of her as she elbows my waist.

"We just need to survive a couple more sessions with her," she says easily as we make our way to the rest of the girls. "You can do this, Fallon. You've gone through worse."

We share a secret look of support and solidarity sparkles in my chest.

Aisling is the only girl who I've gotten close to since starting Carter U and our bond is based on similar childhood distrust. The O'Malleys are one of the richest real estate families in the entire country, meaning that Aisling's formative years were full of the anxiety of not knowing whether someone really liked her for her, or if they were using her for money and status.

The song that we've had blaring on loop starts up again and I re-tie my ponytail, getting myself in the mood.

I can do this, I can do this, I can do this.

I cartwheel my way into my start position in order to get my inner-rhythm flowing, and when I get to my spot in front of Blair I give her a cheery *you've got this* smile, even though I don't quite believe it myself.

Regardless of the hurt that I experienced as a semi-pro child athlete with ruthless Olympian parents, I'm not a hater. If Blair wants to be on the comp team, and especially if she's going to be one of the girls keeping me suspended in the air, then I'm going to give her all of the support that I never had when I was starting out.

Even if I would secretly much prefer it if she wasn't one of the girls holding onto my ankles.

She gives me a wobbly smile in return, which is not exactly reassuring, but I swish around without delay and we start up our routine again.

At the second chorus, when the tempo has drowned out all of the thoughts in my brain apart from what my next move is about to be, I'm tossed back onto the higher pyramid, so that Blair and Whitney can secure my ankles.

Or at least they're supposed to secure my ankles, but Blair is having trouble maintaining her own balance as it is.

There are three pyramids in our formation and ours is the only one that's starting to go sideways.

"Blair?" I shout again as I feel her fingers clamouring desperately around one of my cheer socks.

It's funny what you focus on when the world slows down in front of you.

We haven't got this year's competition outfits yet because we knew that we would have a couple of new girls on the team, and we need everyone's measurements before we send off for the pieces. Being in charge of everything, Ash already knows what colours we're having this year, but one of my favourite things about being a cheerleader has always been getting my new bow.

For two years in a row we wore our Carter U colours – a stand-out blue, with red and white accents – and today for practice I decided to wear that particular comp outfit, so that the new girls could get a feel for how things tend to start looking when tournament season is upon us.

So now, as Blair's slippery hands grapple desperately around my ankle, all that I can think about is how much I enjoyed wearing this particular outfit at that particular tournament. The sock goes to just beneath my knee and the body of it is blue, with red and white sparkling diamantes wrapped around the rim in two thick stripes.

It's a shame that it's about to be ripped clean off my body.

I know that there's no way that Blair is going to catch me after they shove me into the highest flip in our entire routine, but I do the flip anyway because this is what I've been trained to do. I tuck and spin before landing back in Whitney's awaiting hands, but Blair's hands?

They're nowhere to be seen.

"Blair!" I scream, shooting my arms out as I try to regain my balance, but as I look down into her eyes it's way too late.

I'm already falling.

Whitney screams a second later because, although Whitney is strong, she's not strong enough to keep me from falling all on her own, and in a matter of moments my leg shoots straight past the place where Blair's hands were supposed to be, gravity yanks me down, and after less than three beats the world goes black.

CHAPTER 1

Fallon

Two weeks later

"They've arrived!" my roommate Aisling says excitedly, pink hearts shimmering in her eyes as she hip-bumps the front door to the condo closed, setting the inconspicuous brown box down on top of the coffee table in front of me.

I slide my eyes over from the screen of my laptop, allowing myself to soak in the sight of the little package, as if I didn't specifically orchestrate this uncharacteristically early morning study session for this very precise purpose.

"They were arriving today? I didn't know," I say weakly, my tone as casual as I can manage.

"Should I open them now?" Aisling asks, her fingers brushing adoringly over the paper.

Them, I think, a small splinter cracking in my heart. *As in, there's more than one this year.*

Holding back my sad little gulp I nod my head and hold my breath.

"You know what? I'll model them for you," Ash decides, much to my absolute horror. "You wait here, and I'll be back in, like, ten seconds."

"Ash," I begin, in a voice that clearly translates to *dear God no*, but she's already speed-sashaying into her bedroom, a vision of petite cheerleader perfection.

I drop my gaze back to the unfilled grant application on my screen and the ever-growing pinch between my brows burrows a little deeper. Did I really want to spend my senior year at college applying for the most hotly contested arts scholarship available at Carter Ridge University? No. But I also didn't expect to get benched from the cheer team after three years of being their perfect, unbeaten top-of-the-pyramid flyer, meaning that the graduate sports scholarship I have been not-so-secretly praying for?

Yeah, not gonna happen.

Thoroughly distressed by the empty state of the document at my fingertips, I shut down my laptop and set it down on the glossy table, sighing inwardly at the fact that, without funding, this is one-million percent about to be my final year in the safely suspending arms of my academia haven. My final year of being enveloped in this condo, researching my latest Lit essay and obsessively plotting my secret just-for-fun dream manuscript, whilst thinking that this is what life could have been, if I had only worked hard enough. Not having to fear the prospect of heading indefinitely back to my parents' house and disappointing them further because I don't want to go pro with my sport.

As much as I love doing cheer, I don't want to be ogled for the rest of my life on the field of every NFL game.

But it isn't just about doing the work, my mind reminds me. *It's about having the money.*

Which brings me back to my original point: not being on the cheer team means not getting another sport scholarship, and not getting another sport scholarship means not getting to stay on at Carter U for the Master's degree that I've always wanted to do. And if I can't stay on at Carter U to do my Master's, then I'll be sacrificing my studies – my only form of genuine validation in this world – not to mention my secret manuscript, for the kind of job that will pay my bills but will never leave me enough time to accomplish my real dreams.

Or even worse: it will result in me moving back home, without an end-date in sight.

The irony of this situation is that I purposely cleared my schedule of all non-academic working arrangements this year so that I could ensure that Carter U's cheer team would excel at Elite. But now that I'm benched from the comp team I'm desperately seeking a last-minute extra-curricular job because I *really* need to amass as much money as possible if I'm to stay on for a graduate year without getting into debt.

The issue with this plan? There are zero jobs to be found in the campus radius.

Although, my brain reminds me, *there is that one job...*

I do a full-body shiver and quickly lock that thought away.

I'm going to hold off on that possibility for as long as is humanly possible.

With slightly shaking fingers I reach down to pick up my coffee, and I'm momentarily semi-balmed by the small illustration of Baby Yoda being picked up by the Mandalorian on the mug.

I take a sip and look up at the ceiling, picturing the intergalactic galaxies beyond.

The Mandalorian would never drop Grogu, I think to myself.

"Ta-da!" Aisling announces herself in her bedroom doorway, her hip cocked up and one hand behind her beautiful chocolate brown hair.

Then she turns around and I get the full force of it.

I let out a little gasp and clutch at my heart.

"Super cute, right?" she asks with a grin as she looks

back at me over her shoulder.

There's a brand new cheer ribbon affixed in her hair.

"They finally let us pick lilac," I whisper. I take a shaky sip of my coffee.

"It gets better," she says, before unfolding the hand that she'd hidden from view.

"Oh my God." There are literal tears in my eyes.

"I know right!" She holds up the second ribbon, a big red one with tiny icy crystals embellishing its centre knot, and she twirls over to the mirror between the windows so that she can admire it for herself. "So the purple one is for nationals, although we still have last year's red-and-blue one as back up if we choose to stick with the whole 'rep the college colours' thing, and *this* one is for" – she gives me a naughty conspiratorial look – "that *thing* that I can't tell you about yet."

As well as being one of the most important athletes on the squad, Aisling runs the executive committee, meaning that she has intel on the cheer calendar that no-one else but the Carter U board has access to.

"Technically," I say quietly, dropping my eyes from the beautiful cheer ribbons of my dreams, "technically you *could* tell me what the event is, now that I got kicked off the team and all."

I'm hyper-twiddling with the end of one of my blonde curls but I can still feel the moment that Aisling's gaze zaps over to me, the sudden understanding dawning on her from across the room.

She sinks down onto the couch, legs crossed and facing me directly.

"You weren't kicked off the team, Fallon," she says, her eyes wide as she mentally face-palms herself. "It wasn't even your fault that you were… that you were…"

Benched. That I was benched. Because the coach wanted to give a freshman girl a chance but when she started making blunders I was the one who took the fall. Literally.

One too many times.

I rub my head, remembering the seemingly never-ending series of falls that took place during our first two weeks this year of pre-season training.

So now I have not only no job and no money, but also no extracurricular.

This is going to look *so good* on my grant application.

Aisling pushes on, determined to drag me out of this rough patch. "You're still the best flyer Carter U has ever seen and maybe this re-shuffle will only be temporary."

I sustained two concussions in under two weeks so it's not going to be temporary, but Ash already knows that. Carter U might value me as an athlete but there's no way that they're going to keep me on their public competition team when the repercussions of continued brain trauma could literally kill me, and without being officially on the squad I'm unable to apply for another full Carter U sport scholarship. Which I need. *Desperately.*

"Also," she continues, this time giving me a sparkly hopeful look that piques my curiosity. "Close your eyes."

I want to scowl at her but, at the end of the day, she's my best friend. And there's also the fact that Aisling's family owns this entire block of stunning pool-topped condos and they let me live here rent-free, meaning that I am low-key the O'Malley family sugar baby.

So I close my eyes.

I hear the sound of Aisling springing free from the couch, the whack of her full-body-slamming into her bedroom doorframe, the small howl of pain followed by one-footed hobbling noises, and then she's back in front of me, placing something in my hands.

"Open them," she says, the smug lilt in her voice telling me that she is very pleased with herself.

I wait a beat and then I peek one eye open, squinting down to my lap so that I can see what she's handed me.

When I see the two beautiful ribbons that she's ordered

for me despite my not being on the comp team anymore, I almost burst into tears.

I throw my hands up to my eyes and set my elbows on my knees as I try to rein in my overflowing emotions.

"Fallon," she coos, a sad concerned wobble in her voice as she wraps her slim arms around my head. She pats my hair affectionately as I regulate my breathing. "We'll find a way so you don't have to go back home, okay? We'll find a way to keep you at Carter U. And, you know, you have your secret manuscript..."

I shake my head because I don't think that that will be possible – staying at Carter U, getting the arts funding, *or* doing anything with my manuscript, if I ever even finish it – but I keep my mouth shut because I hate being a burden, especially to someone like Ash who deserves a fun uncomplicated friend who she can study and party and cheer with.

I lift my head and she gives me a sad smile.

"It's fine," I say shakily. She offers me her lip-gloss and I accept the glittery doe-foot.

I roll my lips together as she sticks the applicator back in the tube and then I swipe my fingers over my cheeks as a knock sounds on the door.

Aisling immediately rolls her eyes, knowing exactly whose fist is pounding on the wood.

"Go away," she calls out loudly just as it swings open.

"Hey, gorgeous. You ready?" Aisling's two-hundred-pound, soon-to-be NFL star, hunk of a brother is leaning just inside the doorframe, a pleased-with-himself smirk on his face as he looks me up and down.

Connell is Aisling's twin but they're fraternal and total opposites.

Admittedly, Connell is another perk of being the O'Malley family sugar baby. Having slept with most of the female population that Carter U has to offer, Aisling has forbade him from going anywhere near me, but that doesn't mean that I can't enjoy accepting rides in his car to my lecture halls and his ridiculously hot outer-packaging. He's a safe zone for someone like me who needs to put all of her concentration into her grant application but doesn't mind some harmless flirting in the meantime.

"Ugh, no way," Aisling says, giving her brother a palm-out *be gone* gesture before climbing up onto the back of the sofa so that she can affix one of the new cheer ribbons into my hair.

"Ash, it's okay, you don't need to…" I begin, but then she's halfway through lacing my first top-plait so I cut myself off and send Connell a slightly guilty look. "This might take a minute," I tell him as Aisling moves onto the second plait.

He gives me a cocky grin. "Take all the time you need."

Aisling scoops up the two plaits with a little more vengeance than she usually would, making my head pull back. I release a tiny mewl and Connell's eyes get a little darker.

"Connell, we live five fucking minutes away from Fallon's department," Aisling growls. "Have you seen her legs? They're super long. That means that she can walk to class real fast."

"I've seen her legs," he grins.

Aisling's lip-gloss goes flying across the room.

Connell catches it in his hand and gives me a self-satisfied smile.

I laugh and roll my eyes.

Aisling fluffs up the portion of my hair that she's left down and un-plaited, and then she releases me to go and perfect it myself in the mirror. I'm wearing the pretty lilac bow and it's so fun and girlish that it makes my heart hurt.

I give my roommate a sad look through the glass.

"I would've looked so good in the purple costume," I tell her and she nods knowingly, looking as devastated as I feel.

"Don't let a good costume go to waste," Connell says casually, tossing the lip-gloss back into his sister's lap and strolling up behind me so that he can envelop me in his thick arms.

Aisling throws a fuzzy cushion off of Connell's bicep before stomping loudly over to the kitchen.

Nothing will ever happen between Connell and me but sometimes Connell likes to pretend that he doesn't know that information.

"I'm serious, Connell. She doesn't need all of these lifts that you keep giving her."

When Aisling turns to grab a mug from the cupboard Connell smiles at me in the mirror and gives me a squeeze. Connell is obviously ten-out-of-ten attractive and he's also horny twenty-four seven, so being around him helps to fulfil my guy-related oxytocin curiosity. I'm pretty sure that he thinks that I'm hormonally just a really, really, *really* late bloomer, but regardless of what his conceived notions about me are, he always looks out for me and I trust him when it comes to this sweet, teasing, friendly kind of affection.

He's hot, he knows what he's doing, and he doesn't plan on settling down for the next five billion years, so there can be no miscommunication about his intentions.

When his sister turns to look at us again Connell turns us around and starts walking us towards the front door. I stoop to grab my laptop and my canvas tote, and we all pretend that we don't hear him groan when my hip bumps against his groin.

"She isn't going straight to class, she's heading to the gym," he says to Aisling, pulling up a rolled-up bundle of flyers from his pocket that he told us he'd get printed.

I thump my palm against my forehead and make an anguished sound. "I'd forgotten about that," I grumble dejectedly, and Connell gives me another reassuring squeeze.

That's right. I've gone from being Carter U's cheer team's star flyer to being the girl who literally *delivers the flyers*. I pluck one of them from Connell's hand and glance at the text, an advertisement for the cheer team's car wash on Frat Row next week. It's a fundraiser for next year's costumes, wherein any overspill cash gets donated to charity.

I still haven't decided if I'm going to participate now that I'm not on the comp team.

Then my brain gives me a little nudge. *Maybe it'll be good practice for that job you were thinking about–*

"Please tell me that you aren't doing the wash," Connell says to Aisling from behind me, to which she gives him a vicious smile. Aisling is undeniably one of the most beautiful girls at Carter U which means that she gets a *lot* of attention, regardless of her having a boyfriend at a different college and a brother who lives in her building. And that's saying something, considering the fact that Connell is a six-two bulldozer with biceps that are bigger than the football he throws around.

Like, guys are willing to *die* in order to flirt with Aisling.

While Connell groans in misery above my head I point towards my mug on the coffee table and ask Ash, "Please can you rinse that for me? I'll wash it when I get back, but I don't want Baby Yoda staining."

She gives me a cross-eyed look because she thinks that I have OCD but then she nods her head, so I blow her a lip-gloss kiss.

"Are *you* doing the wash?" Connell asks me quietly, a smile in his voice as he tucks the flyers back into his pocket. He ignores his sister as she evil-eyes him out of the door.

I shrug against him and he squishes me tighter. "I need to do a car wash for *me*. For *my* funds," I tell him.

"We can give you cash, Fallon–"

I shake my head as I begin attempting to slip my laptop into my tote. Connell and Ash are the only people who I've confided in about my money troubles and, as lovely as he is, I know that he doesn't get it. I've *earned* everything that I've ever gotten and I refuse to rely on anyone to get to where I need to be. "I'm not taking your parents' money."

"But—"

I glance at him over my shoulder and take in the sight of him. His strong jaw and golden hair, his eyes authoritative and commanding.

The face of a man who has all the money in the world.

"Connell, it's okay. I trust you and Ash with my life but I don't want to be in your debt, if I can help it. There's no way that I'm going back to living with my parents but, even if I don't get that grant, I'm going to claw my way to getting that money. I'm not taking your charity just because I'm, like, some sort of pet to you."

Connell hums low and thoughtful above my head, pressing the elevator button in the dark ruby hallway.

"Okay," he says, his voice quiet and deep. I know that he hates it when I talk about money but I don't want to lie to him just so that he can think that everyone has his level of privilege. He scratches at the back of his head, probably trying to calculate how little I have in my bank account if I can't afford one more year of college tuition. "If you wanna go forward with this grant thing then fine," he finishes, walking us into the elevator and then settling into silence as we ride down to the luxury garage in the basement.

When the doors slide open we head over to his car and we both slip inside without saying anything.

Once I'm buckled up I wait for him to kick the engine to life but instead he rubs his fingers over the gear stick, obviously contemplating something. I roll my eyes at his *can't handle the truth about money* rich boy confusion and I brush invisible lint off my skirt, crossing my legs just for something to do.

He looks briefly in the rear view mirror, checking that we're alone, and then his eyes move to mine, burning with that look that he sometimes gets when it's just the two of us. I raise my eyebrows at him, saying *uh, can I help you?*

Connell's eyes catch on the bow in my hair and he reaches across to tweak it. Then he settles his arm around the back of my headrest, eyes on my lips, my little jumper, and then finally on the short hem of my skirt.

Then they're back on mine.

He swipes his tongue over his lower lip and makes a low sound in the back of his throat.

"My football practice doesn't start for another thirty minutes," he says gruffly, splaying his thighs a little so that I can't help but notice the size of them. "You wanna, uh… wanna make out?"

Okay, so maybe the whole this-is-a-platonic-friendship thing is a little one-sided. But I know that Connell doesn't do it with bad intentions: he really is just *that* horny all of the time. I'm sure that he does this with all of the girls that he gives rides to, only they're probably more hormonally sound than I am and they probably actually take him up on his very generous offer.

I lean over the stick shift and Connell's eyes widen slightly, blinking quickly as I reach an arm around his abdomen. Knowing that I never do anything with anyone, Connell is suddenly breathing like he's in the middle of doing cardio.

"Connell," I whisper, smiling up at him.

"Yeah?" he grunts, his hands gripping into his seat.

I rip the flyers from his pocket and he groans in disappointment when I smack them hard across the expansive breadth of his chest.

I throw myself back against my headrest and I give him a wily grin of my own.

"Nice try, quarterback. Now shut up and drive."

CHAPTER 2

Hunter

I study Coach Benson from across the office desk, a dark expression on his face as he looks at his page of notes.

His right hand is going for broke on a little stress ball that's shaped like a hockey puck.

Doesn't bode well for me.

"Right," he says, dropping the stack of papers and pinching roughly at the bridge of his nose.

In the three seconds that he keeps his eyes squeezed shut I take a glance down at what he was reading and deduce the fact that they're notes from the first 'friendly' game of this semester. I know this because there are a lot of words like *'NO'* and *'FUCK'* and *'SHIT'* written on it. During the game, the team and I were too busy winning to realise that Benson had suddenly lost ten years off his life, but straight *after* the game when we went to the locker room for our debrief the whole team took the bollocking of the century.

Now it's time for our one-on-ones.

"What I want to know," Benson rumbles in his rough drawl, "is why during our first *friendly* game of the season – let me reiterate that so that you're clear, Wilde: the first *friendly* game of the season – the top scorer on my team decided to get himself the most time in the sin-bin, out of everyone else *combined*."

I roll my shoulders and shift on the seat.

I've never needed to be a player who watches his step, mainly because I made myself ineligible for NHL drafting when I was eighteen meaning that my balls were never in that vice. I've also never exactly been a dirty player. I mean, I can't help it that sometimes when I return a swing to a guy who hit first he goes flying across the ice because I'm two hundred and twenty pounds. But now that I'm thinking of signing as a free agent, and also since Benson thinks that this year I'll be able to break the record as Carter U's top hockey scorer of all time, Coach has started making a real big deal about keeping our games completely clean.

This isn't what I wanted to listen to at nine in the damn morning.

"We won," I say simply.

"You were the most penalised player of the whole damn game."

I stick my tongue in my cheek, spreading my knees a little wider, because yeah, okay, I can't argue with the facts. Maybe I did play harder than I usually would but none of my game was unwarranted. Our 'friendly' competitors were a total fucking nightmare.

"You were there, Coach. You saw how they were playing."

"I did see how they were playing, but I also saw how *you* were playing. You think you're all noble dishing out justice? That's the ref's job. Not yours, Wilde."

He's right, which riles me up even harder.

"Why is this a big deal all of a sudden?" I ask, my leg beginning to bounce up and down.

Benson gives me a disbelieving look. "Because you're

the *captain*."

I grunt. *He's got me there.* "It was… my first time in that position. Being their captain. Being that responsible." I look across at Benson and he's watching me intently. Listening to me. He gives me a subtle nod to continue and I feel the tension in my chest loosen slightly, relieved that he's letting me explain myself rather than benching me for the rest of the fall.

Even if talking about this is really fucking awkward.

"I'm really, uh, proud to be the team's captain. To be trusted with that title is…" I look out of the window towards the mountains of Carter Ridge, the vastness of the small town landscape grounding me a little. "It's an honour. And because of that, when our opponents were body-slamming the shit out of us, I didn't wanna be the asshole who passively let that happen."

"To an outsider it's just gonna look like you're hankering to get involved in every fight you see."

"I wasn't fighting back," I grunt. "I was taking the hits."

"Being the captain means that you need to consider what's best for the whole team. Being Captain-less isn't it." Benson shuffles his papers, then longingly eyes his stress-puck. "No more taking the fall so that the other guys don't suffer. You hear me? It's fucking ice hockey. Every guy on the team is going to suffer."

I clear my throat. "It's my duty to—"

"You think that they can't fight for themselves? As their captain, you should have more faith in them."

I feel my jaw harden. Sometimes Benson is a real prick.

"If you're still in the same mindset that you were in last year, wanting to get signed as a free agent for when you graduate, then I want to see no more of this interfering shit. All that that's gonna do is jeopardise your season, and jeopardising your season is going to jeopardise you getting signed. And I'll make damn sure of it because if you don't fall in line, I'll bench you."

I open my mouth to protest but he cuts me off with a *don't even try it* look.

Last year we got the Rangers all the way to the national championship finals only to lose the game in the last period. There's not a chance in hell that Benson is going to let a victory like that slip out of our gloves again, especially considering the fact that this year's Frozen Four final is taking place *right here* in Carter Ridge.

"We're taking the NCAA title this year, and you're breaking the record as Carter U's top goal scorer. You got that, Wilde?"

Benson levels me with a stare until I let out a deep exhale and nod.

"And one more thing," he calls out as I stand to leave. I look down at him, my hands tucked into the front pockets of my jeans so that Benson can't see how violently they're flexing right now. I need to release some energy. I already trained this morning but this conversation has grated me so hard that I'm going to redo the whole fucking set. "I know that you weren't just taking the hits out there, Wilde. You're a big guy. You could do some serious damage."

I grimace. "We're all big guys."

Coach breathes out a wry laugh. "Don't give me that shit. You spend all of your free time training and you've still got that much pent-up energy? Sort it out before it becomes a problem. I'm being serious. You need to blow some steam."

We stare at each other without speaking because I'm trying to work out if he's saying what I think that he is. Benson doesn't generally get involved in his players' private lives, but I'm pretty sure that he's hinting at the one thing that my team loves more than playing hockey.

Coach Benson has one rule: no dating during game season. With the exception of the few guys who came to college with a high school sweetheart, if you weren't already loved up back home then you don't get to start that cushy shit once you join the team. It's a rule that works for most of the guys given the fact that, once they're off the ice, they like to play the field.

Heat begins to spread up my cheeks but I hold Benson's eyes because I'm not tapping out until he does. Yeah, like most hockey teams we have a pretty colourful reputation – something that Benson knows about – because we *are* big guys with certain big needs. But there's a reason why I'm one of the best players at Carter U: I dedicate my free time to staying on top of my sport rather than staying on top of anything else.

"Right," I say gruffly, wanting an end to this conversation, stat. I know what he's implying when he says *blow some steam*, and I am more than capable of taking care of my–

Benson jerks his head at the door, silently telling me to get the hell out of his office.

Fine by me.

I'm busy thinking about how much I definitely do not need to find a chick to blow some steam with as I exit Benson's office and then shove my way straight through the next set of doors, only to suddenly hear a yelp and a thump as the wood slams forwards.

"Ow!"

My chest halts on a huge inhale the second that I realise that it's too late to catch her, the girl who was on the other side of the door already down on her ass and rubbing roughly at her forehead.

Wait, why the hell is she rubbing at her forehead?

"Shit, shit, shit," I say in deeply rasped succession, settling quickly on my haunches in the wide gap between her thighs. "I'm so sorry," I rumble, desperately searching her face for signs of blood. If Coach Benson finds out that I'm mowing people down off the ice too then I don't doubt for a second that he'll bench the shit out of me.

Fear grabs me by the gut when I realise that there's a

small pink mark in the middle of her forehead, right beneath her soft curling calfslick.

I take a shoulder-heaving inhalation and look down to meet her eyes.

They're big and round and surrounded by beautiful black lashes, and they're sparkling up at me in a way that almost makes me choke. There's a purple bow in her hair and she's wearing a matching purple jumper, that's so well fitted that I can see exactly what's going on underneath it. Two perky curves and the tight cinch of her little waist. Fuck, she's petite. My gaze trails down to where she's splayed wide right in front of me and suddenly my jaw is going slack, my body growing rigid.

A low sound that I'm not fucking proud of rumbles deep in my chest but it suddenly turns into a pained grunt as something hard and heavy is launched straight against my head.

"What the hell?" I mutter, looking down at the object in front of me.

"I. Am. *Sickofthisshit!*" she growls, shoving herself to her feet at the same second that I do. I glance briefly down at the ground between us to check out the paperback that she just smashed off my forehead. It has a cute illustration of a couple making out on the cover. I breathe out a laugh and settle my gaze back down on hers.

When she was down on her ass I thought that she was petite but now that we're standing I can see the full extent of it. Like, this chick is seriously fucking small. I give her another reluctant once-over and then I cross my forearms over my chest.

"Who the hell opens a door like that?" she exclaims, frowning up at me and mirroring my folded arms. "If I end up getting another concussion I am *seriously* going to lose my shit."

My body instantly stills.

What does she mean by another *concussion?*

"Come again?" I ask, dipping forward slightly.

She flips a curl over her shoulder, as if people get concussions all the time.

"Look" – she narrows her eyes as she reads the name on my team jumper – "*Austin*, I–"

"Austin?" I say, confused, and I glance down at the stitching over my left pec.

Aw hell, she's right. I'm wearing my teammate's damn jumper.

I knew it felt tight.

"That's not my name," I say, looking quickly back down at her. "I'm–"

She turns a sharp one-eighty and quips, "Tell someone who cares."

Christ. "Look, I'm really sorry. Let me make it up to you."

She's walking real fast so her hips are swishing like crazy, and as I glimpse at her little skirt something heavy twists in my abdomen. I look around the clean white hallway of Carter U's sports building to make sure that no-one else is here, worried that the thoughts suddenly pounding in my head are going to be written all over my face.

Maybe I took the book to the head harder than I first thought because I should not be getting hot for the chick who just hit me with it.

With her cute nose raised high in the air she makes a little sniff and asks, "Why are you following me?"

I clear my throat hard and glance back over my shoulder. "Why were you standing behind the doors?" I ask, frowning slightly.

She looks up at me over her shoulder.

Her eyes are really pretty.

"Weird way to say 'sorry'," she says defiantly, although her voice is softer now.

I take an inhale so deep that my chest brushes against

the back of her head. Her eyes widen momentarily, then she picks up the pace of her little speed-walk.

But I'm 6'4". This is my regular pace.

"I already said that I'm sorry," I say as I reach around her to push open the next set of doors, gently this time.

My conversation with Benson is still ringing in my ears. *You're a big guy. You could do some serious damage.* Maybe this is the kind of shit that he was talking about – my strength transferring in a way that isn't positive.

I glance down at the girl's perky bow because, yeah, I am still following her, and my muscles flex in protest when I realise that I could have actually hurt her.

"If there's anything that I can do–"

She turns on her heel so damn fast that her chest presses flush against my abdomen.

I momentarily go blind.

Hot damn. Not so petite after all.

"You know what you can do, Not Austin?" she says, giving me a cute head tilt that says *I'm the one in control here, sucker.* "You can leave me alone, I have stuff to do."

This time when she spins around and storms away from me I think better of continuing to chase after her, so instead I run a hand through my hair and give it a rough tug as I watch her go. But when I see her check that I'm still here just before she rounds the bend my hands flex by my sides, wishing that I was still right next to her.

My eyebrows rise instinctively at the wounded-kitten look in her eyes.

Hell, did she *want* me to keep on chasing after her? If she did, then she had a damn unusual way of showing it. But what do I know – maybe she's having a rough week.

Her words from a moment ago ricochet through my mind.

Another concussion.

I narrow my eyes. Maybe she's having a *really* rough week.

When she finally looks away from me and struts out of sight I turn around and immediately head back to where we came from. The bottom of the corridor is like a little crime scene, and I scoop down to pick up the book that she'd forgotten in her haste. I flip through the pages until I get to the point that she's bookmarked. I give it a brief scan and then I move my attention to the bulletin board in front of me.

Suddenly I'm in a really good mood.

I see the words *cheerleaders* and *car wash* and now I know exactly what she was doing behind this door.

So she's a cheerleader. I can't help but breathe out a disbelieving laugh because, in all of my years at Carter U, I've never met a chick who's on the cheer squad.

Having a D1 hockey team and a college rink means that the Rangers are meant to have a good connection with the cheerleaders. We have a whole gymnastic mat set-up at the head of the rink which was meant to be where our home girls could do pre-game cheer performances. Show a little home support and get the guys extra pumped.

At almost every college that we've travelled to for away games they always have their girls put on a show before we hit the ice, but during all three years that I've been at Carter U we've never been able to secure them for a game.

I mean, God knows that we've tried to get them down to the rink, but the damn D1 football team is hell-bent on keeping them to themselves. The cheer girls have always been too booked up to make it to our games and I haven't got a doubt in my mind that this year will be exactly the same.

I tuck the paperback under my bicep and pull down one of the flyers from the board.

Carter U Cheer Squad Car Wash, this Sunday!

I roll my shoulders and almost smile as I slide the flyer into my pocket, right next to the keys to my truck.

Good thing that I've got a car.

CHAPTER 3

Fallon

You know what's even crazier than hosting a car wash on Frat Row?

Hosting a car wash in the fall.

While it's raining.

"Hmm," Aisling says, cocking her head to one side as we observe the scene in front of us from the opposite side of the road.

It's a stormy Sunday afternoon meaning that we were originally going to cancel our fundraiser, but nothing motivates the frat guys like the prospect of unabashedly staring at cheerleaders. They've set up a portable gazebo-canopy for each car to drive through, one at a time. It means that the team can wash the cars without getting pneumonia, while the frat boys sit on the sidelines, watching open-mouthed and soaked to the bone.

I tilt my head as I watch one guy snuggle up under a wet Carter U blanket.

Aisling switches the umbrella that she's holding over us

from her hand to mine, and she snaps a picture on her phone to post on the team's Instagram page. I have to physically restrain her from hitting the post button when I see that she's captioned it *Cum rain or shine!*

Technically I should be over there with the rest of the squad right now, but I'm still feeling a little sulky over getting benched.

Although working this wash would kind of be good practice, my brain suggests. *For when you go for that job at the—*

I quickly shake the thought away, bringing myself back to the present.

"The queue for the wash is like thirty cars long," I say, staring in disbelief down the block as another vehicle joins the queue. And these are really nice cars because the majority of Carter U's student population typically doesn't struggle when it comes to money.

Aisling must sense my vehicular lusting-slash-daily neurotic finance spiral because she starts adjusting my bow and stroking my hair, her usual caretaking methods of choice.

"You know that no-one else knows the situation that you're in, right? You don't need to worry about... image, or whatever," she says to me quietly as the current car leaves the canopy and is immediately replaced by another. These cars are so expensive that I feel like I'm in a Formula 1 fixing pit.

I know that no-one other than Aisling and Connell are aware of my money troubles. Or my grant troubles. Or my at-home troubles. And that's exactly the way that I need for it to be. Some people say that a problem shared is a problem halved but I know the reality of the situation: people either use your weaknesses against you, or you become a burden that they need to rid themselves of.

This is why I try to never bring them up to Ash, but she always seems to know exactly what I'm thinking damn it!

"Ooh, this one is *huge*," she says suddenly, and both of

Pinkie Promise

our attentions divert from the row of dazzled frat guys to the large truck currently driving up the wrong side of the road.

I blink at it in confusion as it heads straight towards us.

It isn't brand new like most of the other ones. It's big and gnarly and I think that I like it the most.

"Uh, do you think that they're trying to cut in?" I ask, raising an eyebrow as the truck begins to brake. I glance briefly across the road, grateful to see that the frat guys haven't noticed yet.

An oestrogen-shimmer radiates out of my roommate. "I hope so," she purrs, entranced by the prospect of a live scuffle.

I'm about to hair-swish and selflessly say "I'll deal with it" when the truck parks up right in front of us and I finally see who's sat in the driver's seat.

Reading *my book*.

"Oh my God," I whisper, as I watch him cock up a leg and flip to the next page. I catch sight of a pink sticky-tab through the rain-washed window and my fingers fly up to smother a gasp. "Ash, please can you go back over to the tent while I get rid of this, um, this…" I gesture vaguely toward the death-trap in front of us, while handing her the umbrella again.

Aisling streaks across the road. My eyes don't leave the truck.

Sat in the driver's seat is the guy who almost knocked me unconscious when I was flyering in the sports building at the start of this week. He has dark messy hair and shoulders the size of Colorado. And I know that they're the size of Colorado because that's where I'm from.

I attempt to pretend that I'm not impressed, but truthfully he's the most attractive man that I have ever seen.

I narrow my eyes on him and bang hard on the glass.

He looks up at me and grins. Rolls down the window.

"Hey," he says in a deep voice, eyeing me up and down.

"Great day for a car wash."

I try not to shiver as his eyes linger on my cheer top. He gives me a smirk and closes the book resting in his lap.

I take a big swallow. "That's… that's my book," I say thickly, the rain beginning to make my cheeks pinch pink.

He gestures over his big shoulder with his thumb and I notice that his hair is dripping wet, like he's just had a shower. "Is this what you do? You're a cheerleader?"

"Please tell me that you didn't read it," I continue, my eyes boring a hole through the front cover.

Realising that my attention isn't on him he tosses the book onto his passenger seat. I make an alarmed sound, fearing that he might crease the pages.

"Why're you standing over here in a pair of jeans instead of getting suddy with your friends? Is your bit done now? Get in the truck. I'll take you home."

My eyes practically roll out of my head. "Absolutely not, stalker. Give me back my book."

"If I pass it to you now it'll get ruined in the rain."

Damn it he's right. And doesn't he know it.

He leans back in his seat, pleased, and I try not to stare at his wide abdomen. Then he shifts his belt buckle and I go a little cross-eyed.

"Look," he says, pulling his car keys out from the slot before holding them through the window like an offering.

I pretend to look down at them but really I'm looking at his hands.

Very, very big.

"Hold onto these for the next three minutes so that you know that I can't drive off with you. You can get yourself dried in my passenger seat and I'll give you something to use so that you can wrap up your… uh, porn book."

I gasp, "That is *so* inappropriate." *And completely accurate.*

Then I scowl, grab the keys from his hand, and round the hood of his truck at a fast clip.

He reaches for the door handle from the inside but I

manage to grip it first and pull it open.

I slide inside the truck as he leans back to his side and I shiver dramatically from the sudden surge of heat.

"Did you have the heating on?" I ask absently as I lovingly pick up my book and look around for something to wrap it in. I drop his keys onto the dash as I consider what I could protect my paperback with.

"Here," he grunts, pulling his jumper off in one fluid rip. "And no. Didn't have the heating on."

I stare blankly at the jumper that he's holding out to me, a little scared by how much warmth seems to be radiating out of it.

"Er, what do you want me to do with that?" I ask.

He pushes it onto my lap and my mind goes blank.

"It's for your book," he says, as if giving me his jumper is perfectly normal.

I look up at him and my cheeks begin to burn. Partially because he's secreting heat like an animal, and partially because he's so big that he can barely fit in his seat. His biceps are bulging out from the short sleeves of his shirt and his chest is swollen, rising heavily up and down in the confined cabin of his car.

"Nice bow," he says gruffly, jerking his chin at my hair. Today the cheer squad is wearing last year's competition ribbons, which are in Carter U's red and blue colours. "Name's Hunter, by the way. It's written there, on the jumper."

He jabs a thick blunt finger at the embroidery that I've just uncovered. Underneath his name are the words *Hockey Team Captain*.

"You ever been to a hockey game?" he asks, his eyes burning into my skin.

My mind flicks back to him smashing a door into my forehead. "I think that I got a live preview on Monday."

He immediately winces. "Fuck, I'm so sorry," he says, shifting in his seat so that he's fully facing me. "I had no idea that you were behind that door. How's your forehead?" he asks, looking anguished. When I don't respond he continues with, "When I saw that you'd left your book, bringing it back to you was the least that I could do."

I'm actually amazed that he didn't burn it. Throwing it at him was not only out of order but it was also completely reckless, a clear indication that my brain has been all over the place recently.

This is why you need to focus harder on getting the arts grant, I remind myself. If I start making headway towards securing another year at Carter U then I won't have to stress about moving back home. I'll be able to focus on refining my dream manuscript and giving myself the life that I've always wanted.

That's why I quietly admit, "I… shouldn't have thrown it at you. Playing karma like that was really dumb."

When I feel him tense up beside me I give him a fleeting glance. He's frowning slightly, like I said something that resonates. But then he recomposes his expression and pulls a flyer out of his back pocket, dropping back down to his seat with a low grunt.

"I know it isn't Halloween yet but there's this thing that me and the guys are going to next weekend. There's like a corn maze and stuff." He breathes out a laugh and his cheeks begin to turn a little ruddy. He swallows hard as he passes me the flyer and says, "I never do this, but I was wondering if… if you'd wanna come. You don't have to come *with* me or anything, but it'd be cool to see you there." He scratches at the back of his head and adds with a growing grin, "Maybe we'd even get around to you telling me your name."

I stare at him, speechless, and he gives me a kind of smug eyebrow raise. It reads, *how about it, baby?*

Did taking the door to the forehead leave me with serious brain damage? Is this an extensively prolonged hallucination? Is this actually happening?

Pinkie Promise

The captain of the Carter Ridge Rangers is asking me out?

"Unless you were already going... which you probably were," he adds, looking at me a little deeper like he's trying to push his way into my head.

There's a whole host of new sensations tingling in my body, and I'm not sure that I want to give any of them the time of day. Behind us outside I can hear the window-muffled sounds of low frat-boy voices and the spray of multiple hoses. The rain isn't torrential but it's pattering steadily on the roof and washing the common sense straight out of my head.

Why am I enjoying this guy's attention? Why am I feeling it deep down in my belly? Now is *not* a good time for me to get myself a distraction. I should be thinking about research and staff endorsement letters and finding somewhere else to live if Aisling's parents kick me out of the condo.

"Is this a guilt thing, because of the head injury?" I ask. "Because if it is, don't worry about it. It happens more often than you'd think."

If I thought that that would give him the relieved get-out that he needed, I couldn't have been any further from the truth.

"What does that mean?" he asks, his irises aflame.

I clutch my now-jumper-wrapped book against my stomach, successfully ignoring how warm and soft it feels, and I shake my head at his aghast expression. No time to explain the disastrous end to my show-stopping cheer career.

"It doesn't matter."

"But–"

I pass the flyer quickly back over to him and scooch on my seat. "My roommate told me about the Halloween night and I would... kinda like to go. I'm not sure if I'll have the time though." I hug my jumper-book a little tighter against my body and Hunter's eyes flick down to it, his forearms flexing. "I just have a lot on my plate right now."

I turn to face the passenger door and I'm a little horrified to see that I've completely steamed up the window.

"Hey," he says, his voice low as I turn back to face him. He jerks his chin at me and for some reason it makes me blush. "I understand. I usually work the whole weekend too. But the guys and I have to throw in occasional social sessions so that we have off-rink team-building opportunities. I have to be there." He holds my gaze for one long, heated moment and then he leans across my body to click open the door. When he notices that I've stopped breathing he flashes me his grin again, warm humour returning to his sparkling eyes. "I'll be looking out for you."

"Uh…" I stare at him even as he pulls back to his side, studying me so unabashedly that I simply stay still. "I…"

His phone suddenly buzzes on the dashboard and his eyes flick lazily over to it, tipping the screen so that he can deem its worthiness. He checks it for a beat and then throws the device into his glove compartment. I try so hard to not care that dozens of Carter U girls will be hitting Hunter up all day, every day.

But it's exactly the kind of grounding that I needed.

"Thanks for returning my book," I say, "even though this is kind of grounds for stalking."

He flashes me a grin, eyes on my hips as I slip out onto the blacktop.

As I'm about to unceremoniously slam his door shut we both hear a shout of "Yo Hunter!" from behind me, meaning that the frat guys have finally clocked him and are now vying for his attention.

Great. This is exactly what his two-hundred-and-twenty pound ego needed.

Hunter laughs at whatever he reads in my expression and I thump his door closed extra hard.

He winks at me through the window and mouths *see you*

Saturday.

Letting out a shaky breath I turn on my heels and run across the road, heading for cover from the rain under the car wash canopy. I don't give Hunter the satisfaction of watching him drive away but when the wash is over and I'm shot-gunning in Ash's car I do unravel my paperback and flick to where I'd last left off.

Something warm and tingling stirs in my belly when I notice the fact that I now have two bookmarks.

One is the receipt from when I purchased the book.

And the other is a scrap of paper with Hunter's number on it.

CHAPTER 4

Hunter

"Well," I growl through gritted teeth as I smash the puck into the top corner of the net for the tenth time this practice session. Our goalie, Austin, gives me a *come on, man* look from behind his helmet and he drops his arms dejectedly to his sides. Tanner snickers as we reposition ourselves on the ice, already knowing where I'm going with this. "I gave her my number."

"And she's clearly been blowing you up all week," he says dryly, his eyes sliding over to mine. "What's her name, again?"

I give him a *go fuck yourself* smirk because, yeah, I don't know her name yet, and then Coach sounds his whistle – the worst thank you gift that a player ever got him – and we shoulder-bump it out as we make our way off the ice.

I've managed to keep my mouth shut about my one-sided cheerleader situation but it's been five days since I slipped my digits into her cute romance book and the silence is starting to make my quads tense up. If she liked me she would call. It's as simple as that.

We clip on our blade guards and trudge down the narrow corridor to the locker room, pulling off our helmets and shaking out our hair. I drop down onto the bench and splay my thighs, giving myself a second to recoup before I start stripping for the shower.

"Do you know what classes she takes? 'Cause I don't recommend stalking her at cheer practice," Tanner says as he rotates the combination into his locker and pulls it open.

I let out a low groan and mumble, "Don't give me ideas."

"Did you invite her to the Halloween thing tomorrow?" he continues, pulling off his jersey and unfastening his shoulder pads.

I nod as I begin to take off my boots. I played way too hard during our rink-time today and this time it had nothing to do with defending the players on my team. I'm just stressing the hell out about a chick who isn't interested.

"Maybe she's playing hard to get," Tanner offers, pulling out his phone and scrolling through a very, very, *very* long list of contacts. He finds the one that he's looking for and taps on her photo, turning the screen in my direction. "Like this one. I've been waiting for a text back for three fuckin' years."

I stare at the picture and then give Tanner a look. "Tanner. Aisling O'Malley has a boyfriend."

He gives me a grin before I get back to removing my gear, knowing about Aisling O'Malley's situation because I have classes with her brother. Tanner chucks his cell back into his bag, and I head over to the stalls with my towel because my muscles are dying for some heat relief. I squeeze into one of the cubicles and immediately hit the tap, swallowing down a grunt as the spray scolds the valley between my shoulders.

This is what I need, I think to myself as I brace one palm on the wall and run the other through my hair. *Get on the ice and sweat her out of your system. Doesn't matter if she doesn't show up tomorrow. Getting signed is what's important.*

I hose myself off, knot my towel around my hips, and then I walk back to the benches where Tanner is waiting for me. We're two of the only guys on the team who were born and raised in Carter Ridge, going to the same small town high school despite having different economic home lives. Tanner's parents are low-key rich as fuck, hence the pricey SUV that he unlocks when we get out onto the lot. He also doesn't have that many siblings, whereas I'm the oldest of six.

Our other roommate Caden is leaning against the SUV's side panel, his cell to his ear as he says something in a hushed voice. He has black hair, thigh tats, and he's built like a tank. He's also only twenty. He's living with us even though he's a sophomore because he has a girlfriend from home and he fucking hated his freshman year. At least when he's living with Tanner and me the passage of chicks in the apartment is much more discreet.

"I'm heading to my parents' tonight, and I'm gonna be working in the garage until late tomorrow," I say as Tanner pulls off onto the main road. My dad is a mechanic and my mom owns the local diner, so I usually spend Saturday in the workshop and Sunday in the diner's back office.

"You still coming tomorrow night?" Tanner asks as he indicates.

"Yeah, but it'll be close," I say, wondering if I'm even going to have time to shower the car grease off my fingers before heading to the corn maze. Then I think of the girl that I may or may not bump into and with a little more steel in my voice I finish with, "I'll be there."

Tanner snickers as he takes the turn at the junction and he mutters a dark, "I bet you will."

*

Pinkie Promise

Every year on the outskirts of town, Carter U hosts a big Halloween party out in the corn fields. Tanner and I have been sneaking into it since we were fifteen, so we're more than well acquainted with the set up.

I lift the beer bottle to my lips and take a seat in the open-air booth, scanning across all of the pumpkins and the hay bales to see if the girl that I'm looking for has arrived yet. If she's going to be showing up at all.

I just have a lot on my plate right now.

Hell if those words didn't make my jaw clench tight. She seemed so serious when I saw her at the wash, even when I was trying to keep it light and teasing. What's got her so stressed?

I'm about three-quarters of the way through my beer when I catch sight of something in my peripheral vision. The fuzzy halo. The bunched white leg-warmers. The tiny pleated 'skirt' that makes my jaw drop to the table.

"What the hell?" Tanner shouts, and my eyes flash over to him. It takes a second for me to realise that I just poured the rest of my drink on him.

I set the bottle on the table and run a hand through my hair. Then I curse because, yeah, I do still have black car oil all over my fingers.

"Am I hallucinating?" I ask, jerking my chin in the direction of the cheer squad.

Tanner follows my line of sight and suddenly he no longer cares about the beer on his shorts. "Jesus," he grunts, getting to his feet so quickly that he knocks over every other bottle on the table.

"That's what I thought," I say, and suddenly the whole team is in motion.

She senses us before the other girls do and her eyes widen the second that she sees me. Smile-creases cut into the sides of my cheeks as I look her up and down, taking her in.

After a beat of hesitation, she bolts straight to the back

of the pack.

I shake my head as I round her squad and she stops her little jog after a couple of laps.

She mutters something frantic under her breath and then looks up at me with her big sparkly eyes.

"You found me," she says, her voice slightly breathless.

"Yeah I found you, because I have fucking eyes," I tell her teasingly, flashing her a grin before I give her outfit another little once-over.

"I see you didn't wear a costume," she says, as she takes in the fact that the whole team came in our hockey gear. The guys also have war-paint smeared on their cheekbones, which works great for me seeing as I was already covered in oil from my hours under the hood of a customer's truck.

I jerk my chin at her halo and say, "I see you didn't either."

Her cheeks flush pink as she realises what I'm implying. I fold my arms over my chest, satisfied as hell.

"You really didn't need to wear all of that..." She gestures vaguely in the vicinity of my arms. "You know, your shoulder pads and stuff."

I give her a confused look. "...I'm not wearing shoulder pads," I say to her.

Her pupils immediately dial out and it's so damn sexy that a grunt rumbles through my chest.

"Wanna do the maze?" I ask her, rolling a shoulder backwards in the direction of the lit-up corn fields.

For the first time ever I hear her laugh, and something warm immediately spreads through my chest.

"Seriously?" she asks, curiosity twinkling in her eyes. "Isn't that, like, for kids?"

I feel my neck get hot and I glance over to where Tanner is dog-tailing Aisling O'Malley. Although this set-up is for Carter U students only, I guess that the maze is kind of childish – which is probably exactly why it was our favourite part of this night back when we were fifteen. But I didn't have a girlfriend when I was fifteen, so I hadn't had to think about how mature I needed to be acting.

That realisation makes my neck get even hotter because, having never had a girlfriend, how mature exactly am I supposed to be acting now? Am I supposed to just… jump right in? Because if she wants to, I can get real mature real quick. I glance back down at her and let myself imagine doing just that. Laying her on my mattress and getting down to work.

"Uh…" I rasp, scratching roughly at my stubble. Then I swipe a hand across my forehead, worried that she'll be able to see what I'm thinking. "We don't have to do the maze," I say hoarsely. "We could, uh, we could just–"

"Pairs, right?" Tanner says loudly, clasping a hand around my shoulder. "First team to reach the middle gets, I don't know, seven minutes in heaven or something. Hunter's going with you," he orders to the angel in front of us. Then he tips his head to the side. "I'll be going with her."

"Uh, no you will not," Aisling says, rolling her eyes as she breezes right past him.

Tanner stares after her for a long beat and then his eyes trail down to the girl that I haven't been able to stop thinking about all week.

"She's cute," he murmurs, way too fucking loud.

"Christ," I groan as I hear her little laugh again. "I'm gonna grab another beer," I say to her as we start to pull away from the group. "You want something?"

She stares at my chest for about twenty seconds before looking back up at me and saying, "N-no, I'm not thirsty."

I grin. "Right."

I grab a beer and then gesture with my chin for her to lead the way, pissed at myself for not scrubbing ten layers of skin off my hands before I came here tonight. No way can I touch her little angel outfit when my fingers are charcoal-grey with damn engine fluid. I look down at her perky ass and swallow back a groan.

"Thanks for coming tonight," I rasp as she leads the way into the field, my eyes raking over her hips as they tick from side to side.

"You're welcome," she laughs, "but no way when we win this thing are you getting seven minutes in heaven with me."

I choke on my beer and then swipe my palm down my jaw as I try to decide which part of that bollocking I enjoyed the most: the fact that she's so competitive she's certain that we'll reach the centre first, or the fact that she remembered the line that Tanner threw out to us and is bold enough to put me in my place about it.

My eyes burn into hers when she glances back at me over her shoulder. Or maybe she's just checking that I'm still here with her.

Don't worry, baby. I'm not going anywhere.

I clear the gravel from my throat as she picks which direction we're going to walk in next and I say, "You're real confident. I like that."

Then we walk in silence for so long that I'm starting to think that she didn't hear me. Or that all of the glances and the blushing were in my head and she isn't into me at all. Or that maybe she's bringing me further into the maze to get some more finite revenge on the door-to-the-forehead situation.

My eyes settle back down on her sexy behind and I drain the rest of my beer in one long pull.

"What else do you like?" she finally asks me.

My eyebrows rise because I hadn't been expecting that question, but hell if I'm not about to take this opportunity to state my intentions loud and clear.

I give her an appreciative once-over and say, "Long hair. Big eyes. Short as fuck."

She flashes me a happy nose-scrunch and something heavy twists in my gut. I've stepped so close to her that my

Pinkie Promise

pecs are almost pushing into her back as I finally demand, "Tell me your name."

She stops in her tracks and I bite hard into my fist when my hockey shorts brush up against her skirt for half a second too long. I take two big steps backwards, almost crashing into the handful of students who are taking the same path as us.

She turns around to face me and crosses her arms over her chest, head tilted to one side as she makes me sweat it. She doesn't need to. No other chick has ever made me wait two weeks to find out her damn name.

"Fallon," she says with a small smile.

My chest practically doubles in size.

"That's beautiful," I say, stepping forward, and she takes that as her cue to begin walking me again.

"You drink a lot of beer?" she asks me, not rude but with a slightly worried edge to her voice. Understandably, probably because she doesn't want to be in the middle of a corn maze with a guy she doesn't know when he has an unspecified amount of alcohol pumping through his system.

I don't want to mention that I only picked up this beer so that I'd have something to occupy my big dirty hands with, so instead I say, "When I'm with the guys."

"You aren't with the guys right now," she points out, sending me a look.

Fuck. True. I change the subject. "What do you wanna win if we reach the centre first?"

"*When* we win," she purrs. "What can you give me?"

I grunt hard and start ripping the paper off the bottle. "Uh," I rasp, trying to think of something normal that I can offer her. I'm convinced that she didn't mean to say that provocatively but my brain is immediately in the fucking gutter.

I look down my torso and an idea snaps into place.

"Come to my game," I blurt out.

She slows down her speed and then readjusts her halo.

Fuck. "Are you... offering me, or telling me?" she asks with a knowing laugh.

I hunch down a little so that she's not snapping her neck to just get a look at me and I say, "I'm offering you, Fallon. Do you wanna come to one of my games?"

Her eyes get a little wider before dropping completely. Her lashes cast shadows on the warm apples of both her cheeks.

So damn pretty.

"Um," she says nervously. "What's the date? Of the game, I mean! I'm not saying th-that this is gonna be a date."

My palms are starting to sweat. *We can call it whatever you want, baby.*

"Next Friday," I tell her. "Our first home game of the season is next Friday."

Her expression glitches and my stomach instantly drops. That's a 'no' if I've ever seen one.

"I can't make that day," she says, looking almost embarrassed. "I have... work on Friday."

I look at her for a prolonged moment, trying to figure out why there's a slight tremor in her voice.

"But... maybe I could come to another one?" she suggests. "To your second home game?"

"Yeah," I grunt, even though I feel like I'm missing something. I pull out my cell from the side of my boot and say, "Give me your number."

When I see her raised eyebrow I add on a rough, "Please."

As she begins tapping her digits into my phone a hand thumps hard on my back and I turn to see Tanner standing right behind me. He's looking down at Fallon, a blank but determined look on his face.

Sensing him, she glances up as she hands me back my phone. I snicker when I see the book emoji that she's typed in next to her name and we momentarily share a secret smile over her little taunt.

"Your roommate's looking for you," Tanner says to her.

Fallon's expression turns briefly concerned. "Why? What'd you do to her?"

Tanner's eyebrows rise. "…Nothing," he says slowly, his eyes narrowing for a beat. "But she said that your team is heading to a sorority house or something. They're waiting for you."

I try not to look too pleased about the fact that they aren't going back to Frat Row tonight.

"Okay," Fallon says, equally dubious. She sucks in a breath and then turns her big eyes on me. The heavy muscle in my shorts thickens like a motherfucker. "I guess I'll… maybe see you at one of your games," she says, laughing a little as we share a smile.

"Rink-side, Fallon. Your tickets are gonna be rink-side."

I pretend not to hear Tanner's mumbled *"ah Jesus."*

"Okay," she says, her voice breathless as we watch each other. "Bye then… Hunter."

I run a hand down my jaw. *Hearing my name on her lips is my new favourite thing in the world.*

"Bye Fallon," I rasp, soaking in every last second of her.

"And *bye Tanner*," Tanner says obtusely, staring at her as she brushes between us, but she keeps her sparkling eyes on mine until she disappears around the corner.

CHAPTER 5

Fallon

I'm fifty-two minutes into trying to focus on researching my upcoming assignment when Whitney, my top-of-the-pyramid replacement, takes her second fall to the mats.

Luckily for Whitney, the whole pyramid was already beginning to wobble when she did that high-kick, which means that the rest of the squad had already began panic-squatting, foreseeing the inevitable which just took place.

"What the hell!" Whitney shouts, staring across at Blair who could no longer hold her up. I drop my eyes back to my work, not wanting to watch another screaming match.

"I think that they should call it time."

Connell's voice sounds behind me, and he gives me an affectionate squeeze across the clavicle with his big footballer forearm. Living one floor down from Aisling and I, Connell is our post-cheer ride back to the condo.

"Get off me, Sweaty," I say to him, mock-clawing at his arm. Usually I wouldn't mind his brotherly post-training physical compressions but today is different because this evening I have my first shift. I take a little gulp to try and calm the bubbling in my belly.

Connell laughs but removes his arm, and then he's standing in front of me with his arms folded over his chest. He's staring down at me with the kind of omniscience that isn't great if you're keeping a secret.

"What is it?" he asks, his eyes narrowed.

"It's just the grant thing," I lie, tucking my notes back into my bag.

He waits for a few seconds before he says, "Fallon."

I decide to add some truth to the lie, to make it more believable. "Although I *did* finally hear back from Dr. Ward, so that means at least I don't need to worry about my referral anymore!"

Connell's face scrunches up. I see some minor cat-fighting going on behind him. "Dr. Ward? As in Parker Ward? Isn't she renowned for being an ass to her students?"

I vehemently shake my head but Connell doesn't even look slightly convinced. "No, not at all! Well, technically yes, but I really need her on my team if I stand any chance at securing the funding."

"Why?"

"Because she's, like, best friends with everyone who's at the top – all of the people who make the big money decisions eat right out of her palm. She's respected, she's listened to. Plus, she did teach one of my requirement classes last year and, okay, she was my hardest grader, but I still came out on top, and you just can't argue with the numbers," I say with a shrug.

"Fallon, don't you think that maybe you should…"

I stare up at him with big pleading eyes, the message that they're transmitting to him being *please don't tell me to find another faculty member. I messaged seven former tutors and Dr. Ward is the only one who even got back to me.*

Connell seems to understand what I'm saying because

he nods and then gives me another hug. I pretend that I can't feel his pity seeping into me.

"Maybe don't mention the Dr. Ward thing to Ash," I whisper to him just before he pulls away.

When he does pull away he looks down at me, concerned. Then he links his arm back around my shoulders and we walk in silence all the way to the lot.

*

I shoot a shifty look left to right before I finally put a heel down on the rain-slickened road.

I probably look like I'm about to try and shift some drugs. I clip as quickly as I can without snapping an ankle and then I take a deep bracing breath as I look up at the neon signage above me.

Rodeo Bar is situated on the outskirts of Carter Ridge, with a clientele of grizzled small-towners who want a little entertainment. It's early evening but the place is already buzzing, with one waitress walking across the counter and pouring shots from a height, while another side-saddles a mechanical bull and sends flirty eyes to the guys leaning over the barrier to watch. The women who work here are confident with their sex appeal, and the guys going slack-jawed over them are rough-around-the-edges hot.

I don't feel as at ease here as I did at the wash on Frat Row but it has some small town charm that I'm hoping I can run with.

"Ford?" a woman asks, and I turn around to face her.

She has chocolate brown hair scraped back into a ponytail and sharp cat eyes that seem to bore into my soul. She also has 34DDs that have me questioning my sexuality and a blood-red "Hello My Name Is" clip-tag which simply reads *Don't Ask*.

"Hi," I gush, giving her my best cheer smile and holding out my hand for her to shake.

Pinkie Promise

She looks down at my hand, dismayed, and then her worried eyes flash back to mine.

"*You* applied for the vacancy? To dance on my bar? To shimmy around my tables?"

Okay, so I take it that this isn't a hand-shaking kind of establishment. "That would be correct," I say, smile wavering only slightly.

"How the hell old are you?"

"I'm twenty-one."

"Yeah, me too. ID?"

I hand her my ID and she looks as though she can't believe her eyes. She shakes her head and hands it back to me, settling a hand on one of her hips and leaning back against the pool table.

"You're a dancer?"

"Cheerleader."

"Are you sure you wanna show your skills here?"

I look around the warm room and see that eyes are already on us. I blush slightly and Don't Ask says a prayer under her breath.

"Ever ride a bull?" she asks.

"Er…"

"Or pour a drink?"

"Well–"

"Ever *had* a drink?" she continues, her eyes wide with concern.

"Ijustreallyneedthemoney," I say quickly, hoping that that will be explanation enough for her to stop the inquisition and give me a tray.

She looks at me for a long moment before nodding and turning on her heel. We walk to a door that belongs in a high-security prison and she punches in the code. Then we both go inside and she settles down in a chair.

She pulls on a pair of sexy cat-eye glasses and rummages through a desk full of paperwork. When she finally finds a blank contract sheet she hooks a pen around the top and passes the document over to me.

"You can read through this out there. Sign it if you think you can cope with the attention."

"I can cope with—"

"With *this* kind of attention, Ford. You know what I'm saying." Before I leave she adds on, "It's in the paperwork but working here requires a strong stomach. You'll be dancing to drunk guys, and they aren't always cuties. You'll be riding the bull. You don't have a boyfriend, do you?"

"Why would that be—?"

"Because boyfriends don't like other men going after their girlfriends. Any guy-trouble and you're gone. That rule is hard and fast."

"I don't have a boyfriend. Your bar seems... really nice."

She pulls her glasses off and cocks an eyebrow at me. "You really don't have to do this. I'm sure that there are more" – she gestures vaguely at my cardigan – "*you* jobs out there."

I take off the cardigan and her eyebrows rise a little higher.

That's what I thought.

I've been wearing cheerleading outfits since I was back in high school – I know how to pull off a mini-skirt and a crop top.

"I did not peg you for the double-denim type," she says, a little impressed.

I almost smile. Maybe this won't be so bad after all.

CHAPTER 6

Hunter

This is bad. This is real bad.

I can barely see, let alone walk straight, so when the guys push me through the doors to Rodeo Bar I blindly hand Tanner another wad of tens so that he can grab the team our tenth round to celebrate over.

Winning our first home game of the season always means celebrating hard on home turf, but tonight it's turned into a captain's initiation. Which isn't usually a problem except for the fact that, one, I have work at 8am tomorrow and, two, *I'm* the captain. We started out at the hockey house so that the guys who aren't twenty-one yet could drink with us, but it's been a few hours since then so now we're off campus and drinking Carter Ridge dry.

"Where the fuck are we?" one of our defence-men asks, his jaw so slack that he looks like he's dislocated it. There's a chick somewhere to the right riding a mechanical bull and I have zero intentions of watching her work it. I don't want to get hot and bothered in public just because I haven't been... unloading the way that I need to.

But there's a chance that things might be different this year.

I shift heavily on my seat as my mind strays to a certain cheerleader. Those big taunting eyes. That petite waist that I could span both of my palms around. I let my vision cloud over until the neon lights behind the counter are a big red blur, and I picture seeing her at our next game, wondering if she'll want to see me again.

"Keep it in your pants, man." Tanner grimaces over to one of our teammates as he sets the beers on the table, four in each hand gripped by the stems. "Waitress is bringing the rest," Tanner slurs as he thrusts another bottle into my fist.

I take a long pull of the liquid, and then shove myself to my feet. "I'll get them," I decide, taking another drink from the bottle as I wonder if Fallon will let me watch her cheer. Then again, considering how hard I get at just the thought of her, maybe watching her high-kick in a mini-skirt isn't such a good idea.

I readjust the situation getting heavy in my jeans as I trudge roughly between the tables. Jesus, it's dark in here. I finish off my beer and slide it onto a table before raking a hand through my hair and momentarily closing my eyes.

That feels good. That feels way better. And with my eyes closed I can pretend, even for the briefest moment, that Fallon is–

My body smacks into something small and soft, and my eyes fly open just as I hear her squeal. I lock my forearms tight behind her, shoving her upwards before she hits the floor. Her head smacks off my pecs and I hear a little moan of anguish.

Then I look down to see who I just crashed into.

I must be *way* drunker than I originally thought.

"We have *got* to stop meeting like this," Fallon says breathlessly, her hands gripping into my shoulders and her lips mere inches from mine.

She's really here. In a chicks-dancing-on-the-tables bull-riding dive bar.

And so am I.

I'm way too drunk for any of this to make sense. *Why am I here? And why the* hell *is she here?*

Was this the job that she was talking about? This was what she wanted to spend her year doing?

Not happening. That is *not* fucking happening.

"Fallon," I grit out. "What the hell are you doing here?"

When she starts wiggling in my arms I realise that I've still got her crushed against my pecs, but if she thinks that I'm gonna expose the little outfit that I can feel beneath my fingers to this bar's clientele, then she can well and truly think again. I walk her to a side-booth at the corner of the room and then I pull away slightly, finally revealing what she's wearing.

"Oh Jesus," I say hoarsely. So much for not needing to beat one out in public.

I think I stare down at her tits for three minutes straight, the little strip of her bare belly making my hands flex into her back. She looks small and soft and like exactly what I've been waiting for, but then her little gasps finally penetrate my lust-fog and my eyes shoot back to hers.

"What?" I grunt. *How the hell is she this pretty?*

"You're… it's… you need to…"

I blink down at her. "Huh?"

"It's on my belly," she whisper-pants, her irises going black. "I know that you're drunk but–"

The second that I realise what she's talking about I almost lose my damn mind. I'm fully-erect and I'm embedding it straight into her stomach, a chick who barely knows me and is in the middle of a damn shift.

Which brings me back to my original question.

"Fallon, why are you in here?" I ask, dropping a palm onto the dark table behind her to stop myself from falling over. The movement causes me to thrust against her, and a sound leaves her throat at the sensation of being impaled.

"I-I'm working, this is my new–"

Suddenly she pauses and the fingers on my shoulders begin biting in harder.

"Why are *you* here?" she demands, eyes narrowed and blazing.

Hell if I know. I lift and drop a shoulder and then vaguely say, "Hockey."

Her eyes narrow even further. "So this is what you do after your games, is it? Come to a place like this for a little post-game relief?"

I can't think straight and my balance is getting worse by the second. I see a patron needing to squeeze between us and the rammed table behind me so I clutch Fallon tighter, pinning our hips tight against the table's edge.

Her eyes roll into the back of her head.

"If this place is so damn bad, then what the hell do you think that you're doing here, Fallon?"

"I need a job, Hunter. Something that rich hockey boys wouldn't understand."

"I'll help you get a job. It doesn't have to be something like this."

"Why not? Seems like you're into it."

I duck down to her level and look her hard in the eyes. "You keep this job and I'll be here every night, baby."

She tries to shove me off of her but I hold her tighter. *God, it feels so good to just hold her.* I drop my forehead to her shoulder and swear that I almost fall asleep.

"Hunter," she whispers, maybe realising how gone I am. "You still need to… to…" She squirms her belly a little so that I'll understand what she's talking about.

I groan into her neck as my erection thumps against her. "That's not helping, baby."

"Oh God, d-don't call me that, I'm not your… your *baby*," she whispers frantically, and she starts steering us away from the booth. I don't know where we're going but I'll happily go along with it if it means that I get to stay

Pinkie Promise

wrapped all over her.

I pull back and everything is spinning. She's the one thing that I can focus on in this neon red blur.

"You could be," I rasp, hooking my forearms around her neck from behind. She ignores everything that I'm saying to her and throws apologetic smiles to the tables we weave through, clearly steering me towards the front door.

When I catch a guy smiling back at her I promise him a long slow death with my eyes.

I'm aware that she's trying to politely kick me out but, without knowing it, she's actually taken me back to the hockey table. Most of the guys have stilled on their seats, jaws in their laps as they watch Fallon's colleague going to town on the bull. Tanner's on his phone and he glances up as soon as he senses us.

He raises his eyebrows at Fallon and she grits out, "Don't. Even. Ask."

"I wanna get you a different job," I murmur, resting my stubble-coated jaw in the soft curve of her neck. "I can tell that this is what had you stressin' last week."

"Stop it," she hisses. "I need you out of here, now."

"Why?" I ask, pulling her around so that I can look down at her. "Let me take care of you."

"You don't even know me," she says desperately. "I can't lose focus right now, Hunter. I have too much going on to let myself have a distraction–"

"Jesus Christ, Ford. I told you: no boyfriends."

Fallon claws her way out of my arms and I steady myself on the table behind us. She has a pleading expression on her face as she walks over to the woman who just called her Ford.

"He's not my boyfriend, I swear–"
"That is not what it looks like, Ford."
"I'm trying to get them out of here, but they're–"
"You're trying to get rid of my clients?"

Fallon's hands fly up to her hair and she looks frantically

around.

The sight of her looking so small, alone, and out of her depth punches through my alcohol haze and clenches something tight in my chest. I shove myself off the table and plant myself behind her like a damn tree.

"Everything alright over here?" I ask, hooking my fingers through the belt-loops of Fallon's denim skirt.

"Swell," the older woman deadpans, and then her eyes flash back to Fallon. "Look, I don't think that this is the fit for you. I'll pay you for tonight but... I want this shift to be your first and your last."

Fallon keels forward slightly and I rein her in by the loops.

"Are you – firing me – on my – *first shift?*" she gasps.

The other woman looks up at me and the guys who have all congregated around Fallon.

"I don't hire students. This is literally why. Your boyfriend here? He looks like he wants to murder me. Take this as a compliment when I say: you do not fit in here."

Without another word she turns around and leaves us. I hear one of the guys mutter something about an Uber back to a frat house and the guys begin draining the rest of their drinks.

Fallon hasn't moved a muscle and she's staring unseeingly straight ahead. For the briefest moment I swear she whispers, "*I never fit in anywhere.*"

"Fallon," I begin, trying to twist her around to face me.

She flashes me a *drop dead* glare over her shoulder and I remove my hands immediately from her skirt.

"Did I just get her fired?" I ask Tanner as Fallon storms away, one palm rubbing down my jaw and the other gripping the back of my neck. "Did I just... get her fucking fired?"

Tanner winces and avoids my eyes as we lumber over to the entrance.

"I need you to do something for me," I say to him as I

crane my neck for one last look at Fallon. "I need you to do something for me because I'm not gonna remember this tomorrow. I need you to tell me to get Fallon a job."

"How're you gonna get her a job?" Tanner asks, rolling his eyes.

He clearly doesn't understand the kind of obsessive psycho that he's dealing with.

"I've got it covered," I rumble vaguely. "Don't worry about the little details."

Tanner pulls his phone out of his pocket and ten seconds later mine is vibrating. I check the screen and it reads: *you fucked up and got your gf fired. fix it, loser.*

"Jesus Christ. Thanks I guess."

We hunch down into the Uber and he slides his phone back into his pocket, smirking. "Any time."

CHAPTER 7

Fallon

I get a little sparkle in my belly when I hear the *ping* coming from my phone.

After checking my surroundings I slip my cell from a tiny side pocket in my leggings and I anxiously tap the bubbles on my screen. The message from Ash that has just popped up almost makes my heart burst with joy.

AISLING: *Fallon!!! This is so good, I'm swooning!!*

My eyes practically spill with happy tears.

Really?! I type back to her, and I get an immediate, *Yes my queen.*

I clutch at my chest and sniffle back a watery smile. *Thank you Ash.*

Getting hired-and-fired at Rodeo Bar six days ago has been the catalyst for my nervous-wreck productivity bender, meaning that I managed to finish my first essay of term a whole week early, and I don't even need to worry about my thesis right now because I already wrote the first draft over the summer. It's times like now that have me wishing that I could talk to my parents the way that other people do in the hopes of receiving a little familial appreciation, but I know to think better of it so I keep that Messages page as blank as it's always been.

So instead of doing more coursework that I'm already caught up on or guilt-tripping myself into attending cheer sessions that I'm technically still banned from participating in, I treated myself to a rare moment of one-on-one time with the little document on my laptop titled "Dream Manuscript". Only this time I took it one step further.

I shared the first chapter with Aisling.

I know the impossibility of ever doing anything with the words that I've written but, after three years of trauma bonding, it feels like a weight has been lifted off my shoulders now that I've shared something so close to my heart with the only girl on campus that I genuinely consider to be a real friend. One of the reasons why I want to stay on at Carter U after senior year is because I love the gratification of receiving academic validation, but in reality there's also the fact that I have no idea what I'll do when I graduate. Being an author isn't even on the table because I know how slim the chances of getting a publishing deal are – that's why I've spent years writing for fun, but sharing my dream with Ash today has made me feel kind of amazing.

I take a screenshot of our messages and then stash my phone at the bottom of my gym bag, a warm kindling of hope flickering in my belly.

And then another thought pops into my head and I roll my eyes, almost laughing as I reach back into my bag to turn the sound off on my cell.

Aisling aside, there is one other person who has been single-handedly blowing up my phone.

HUNTER: *Fallon? Hey, it's Hunter.*

HUNTER: *I'm so so sorry about the other night.*
HUNTER: *I wanna talk to you. Please can we talk?*

I stupidly opened Hunter's first few messages with my read receipts turned on and, as soon as he realised, he sent me a little smiley face because I'd been caught red-handed.

Now I'm getting daily updates. As in, when I go to turn the sound off on my phone right now, I literally have *another* update.

HUNTER: *Currently at Carter U gym. D'you train on campus?*

I stare at the new message before glancing up at the Carter U gym right in front of me.

Darn it.

I ignore the text and shoulder-bump my way through the first set of sleek glass doors, heading towards the locker rooms situated across from the main training area. I probably won't see him in here anyway. Carter U's gym is truly gigantic and I would put good money on Hunter being in the WWE section at the back, an area that I have never and will never step foot inside.

When my phone vibrates in my hand again I can't help but peek down at the screen.

Photo attachment.

I frown, suspicious, before unlocking my phone.

Then I come to a complete stop, choking on a halted inhale.

It's a picture of Hunter sat back on the weight bench, his solid thighs planted on either side of the long black seat. His hair is a goddamn mess – dark, tousled, and dripping with sweat – and his cheekbones are flushed beneath the deep tan of his skin. Swollen biceps, giant chest. His masculine face is hard and emotionless but when I zoom into the area between his huge thighs–

I whack my forehead against something hot and hard, and big hands grip my waist as I immediately stumble backwards.

"Something caught your eye?" a deep voice asks from above my head.

I squeeze my eyes shut. *You have got to be kidding me.*

"Oh my *God*." I disentangle our bodies and scowl up at Hunter, shoving my bag back up to my shoulder and folding my arms across my chest. It would be easier to be grumpy with him about aiding my speedy firing from Rodeo Bar if he wasn't looking at me right now with such a dark smouldering expression. When his eyes flash down to the phone screen in my hands I quickly press the top button to hide the incriminating evidence.

"So you do train on campus," he says, his voice raspy with post-gym exertion. Then a sexy dimple cuts playfully into his cheek. "I've been hoping that I'd bump into you."

I give him a look. "You bump into me everywhere. That's the problem."

He's too preoccupied with staring at me to register the words that I'm saying to him. His eyes trail down my body and he rubs a hand over his jaw.

"You always wear this sort of stuff when you train?" he asks, chin tipping at my outfit. I'm wearing a matching set, sports leggings and a long-sleeved top, both in a soft and subdued shade of lilac. My hair is scraped up in a ponytail and my curls are bouncing all the way to my lower back.

"Yeah," I say, my eyebrow rising even higher. *Has he never seen a girl in sportswear before?*

He grunts low and tight before he asks roughly, "What days do you train? In fact–"

He pulls his phone from his shorts and then nods to himself as he pockets it again.

Before I can ask if he just checked the date and time to co-align our workouts, he runs a hand through his hair and flashes me another devastating smile. "Did you like the pic?"

I take a shaky breath. "Um…"

"I've never taken a photo like that before," he rumbles, "but I'd do it again if you like it."

The honest confession takes me by surprise and my cheeks heat up like *I've* just done a workout.

He grins knowingly so I huff right past him.

"Wait up," he says, easily matching my pace. When we reach the girls locker rooms I give him a victorious smile of my own.

You can't come in here, my expression reads smugly.

He makes a low sound as he wars with himself against the threshold.

"When are you next free?" he asks, his tone deep and demanding.

I give my ponytail a swish. "Not for a billion years."

He grips the back of his neck and says, "Fallon, I'm so sorry about what happened at the bar."

I exhale a small weary sigh. "Honestly, you were so drunk that I'm surprised you remember any of it."

His eyes momentarily drop to my belly as he mumbles, "How could I forget?"

Our gazes catch for a split second and I quickly look away, remembering how Hunter's body felt pressed up against my stomach. I let out a shaky breath and remind myself never to come to this gym again.

"I want to make it up to you, Fallon. Let me fix this."

"No," I say stubbornly.

"Fallon, I promise–"

"I don't want your help."

Hunter looks deep into my eyes and hurt flashes through his irises.

Suddenly I feel like the worst person in the world.

This is why I don't try with people anymore. This is why I don't let myself develop the bond of comfort and familiarity. I don't want to secretly cherish their attention only for it to be swiftly ripped away because I can't be perfect twenty-four seven.

I need to calm down so that I can rationalise my feelings. I'm stressed because this is probably my last year of college and my imminent future is still yet to be decided. All I know is that I can't speak to my parents and I *won't* go home, which means that I need to do something so that I can safely remain at Carter U. I want that funding so freaking much and it's eating me up not knowing if I'll get it.

Hunter shuffles his large body on his feet and the move is so self conscious that my heart aches in my chest.

Feeling overwhelmed and guilty, I tuck a loose curl behind my ear with slightly shaking fingers, wishing that I could tell him, *Hunter, you're so beautiful it's crazy, and I can't believe that you think that I'm worth talking to, but I'm scared that if I let myself start to like you, you're going to end up hurting me like my parents did back home.*

Instead I opt for, "I'm… sorry, please let me start over. You're really kind, Hunter. But I can't ask you for your help because I don't want to be a burden. It's, uh, kind of a sore spot for me." I rub my hands up my arms until I'm anxiously gripping my elbows. "I need to be able to take care of myself. I need to be able to…"

Hunter takes a small step forward, a concerned pinch between his brows. I look up at him with wide eyes, half expecting him to laugh and say *yeah, you're a mess.*

Instead he says, "Fallon, you're not a burden."

I never knew until this moment how much I wanted to hear someone say those words to me.

A small kindling stirs gently in my belly and I press my hand over it, as if Hunter might see it if I don't.

He takes another step forward and I don't back away. He braces one arm against the doorjamb and looks down at me.

"You didn't need to apologise, I'm the one who's been

messing up. But I'm gonna push my luck anyway seeing as I've finally got you standing in front of me." He rolls his right shoulder and then braces that arm on the doorframe too. It's heavenly here in the cage between his biceps. "I want to go out with you, and I want you to say yes."

I can imagine saying yes to a lot of things that Hunter asks of me.

"I'm still job hunting," I say, "so I'll need to find a good job before I let myself have any downtime." Now is not the time to explain about getting benched from the cheer comp team and the arts grant that I now need if I want to stay on and do my Master's.

There's something burning in Hunter's expression, like he's fighting with himself to offer me something. He's straining with the effort to keep himself from saying it.

Let me fix this.

For the briefest of moments I wonder what he meant by that.

He swipes his tongue over his lower lip before finally nodding and saying, "You'll get one soon. A real good job, Fallon, I promise."

He's so unyieldingly confident that I can't help but think, *no wonder he's the team captain – you can't disobey a man who is this sure of himself.*

"Okay," I breathe out, feeling a little dizzy.

His mouth lifts up at the corner, pleased with the resolution that we have managed to come to, and he moves in so close that we're almost touching.

"Go out with me, Fallon," he repeats, his eyes burning into mine.

I'm about to say yes when the glass doors behind him swing open.

"How's it going?" Connell calls over to me with a grin, eyeing me up and down like he's never seen a girl before. Hunter glances at him over his shoulder and his tongue pokes roughly in the side of his cheek.

Pinkie Promise

I feel like I'm having a fever dream.

Connell catches Hunter's gaze and says cheerfully, "Hey, man. Didn't know that you knew Fallon."

Hunter stares at him for a long beat before replying with, "Uh, I didn't know that *you* knew Fallon?"

Connell holds a palm out for Hunter to clasp and Hunter reluctantly drops an arm from the doorframe, drowning me in a quick wave of his post-workout heat, before smacking his palm roughly against Connell's. I can tell that it was rough because when they finally let go of each other Connell shakes out his hand and his fingers crack.

"Fallon and I go way back," Connell says, leaning against the wall beside the jamb and flashing me a quick smile. "We're practically roommates."

"Is that so," Hunter says dryly, his knuckles turning white.

They're talking like they actually know each other which I find greatly disturbing.

Connell jabs his thumb at the gym entrance and says to me, "Wanna stay for an hour and then dip?" He gives Hunter a look and adds on, "I'm her ride."

I remain strategically silent. Hunter gives me a long heated look.

Connell must finally register Hunter's hulking stance and the muscle rolling angrily in his jaw because, after retying his trainers, he finally asks, "Were you two in the middle of something?"

I think that Hunter and I have been in the middle of something since the first moment that we met. He's looking down at me with such blatant interest that I don't even feel embarrassed when I reciprocate the stare.

Hunter's chest swells as he watches me watch him and then he says hoarsely to Connell, "Yeah, we are. But, actually, I kinda need to talk to you about something too. Meet you in the locker room in a minute, okay?"

Wait, what?

They clap hands again and I look between them in alarm.

As soon as Connell opens the door to the guys' changing room I flash my eyes back up to Hunter and ask, "How do you two know each other? What do you need to talk to him about?"

"We're in the same classes," he says on a shrug, disregarding my second question entirely. "I have a game coming up and I want you to be there. Can I text you the details?"

My eyes stray briefly to the bulging vein in his large bicep.

"Yes," I say, a little raspy.

He smiles at my tone and gives me a savouring once-over.

"I love this outfit," he murmurs gruffly. "When you come to watch the game please do not wear it."

I blink in surprise and a small laugh bubbles out of me. "Why not?" I ask, smiling even though I'm confused.

"Because I have to keep my eyes on the puck if I want to win, Fallon."

My lips part open and Hunter shoves his body backwards off the wall, tucking one hand in the front pocket of his shorts and jostling it slightly as he gives me a final once-over.

I take my bag off my shoulder and clutch it against my chest.

"Bye Hunter," I say.

He tips his chin at me before heading down the hallway after Connell.

"Bye Fallon."

CHAPTER 8

Hunter

I tap my thumbs against the steering wheel of my truck and stare ahead at the diner in front of me.

I know it in my bones that I have completely overstepped the mark but as I watch Fallon retie the bow on her apron and give my mom a nervous smile, I can't bring myself to feel bad about it.

Fallon needed a job, and I had two.

The second that Connell approached us in the gym and said that he was Fallon's ride home, I knew exactly how to fix her job dilemma. Fallon had said that she didn't want me to get involved, that she wanted to sort out her situation herself, but she seemed so stressed that I *wanted* to fix it for her. Never mind the fact that I was responsible for getting her fired in the first place, she'd been in a state of panic since the first time I laid my eyes on her and I couldn't see that go on any longer. So I briefly mentioned to Connell that I'd seen a job advertised for the diner in town, carefully avoiding the fact that it's my *mom's* diner and that it's *my* job.

Connell's eyes had shot to mine and he'd asked, "You didn't tell anyone else about this job, did you?"

I remained impassive. Told him no.

Then he said, "Do me a favour and don't mention it to anyone else? I know a girl who could really do with getting it."

So now Fallon is wiping down the small booths that I spent my high school years doing homework at.

I've been working at my mom Willa's diner every Sunday since I can remember but, as soon as I turned eighteen and got into Carter U's hockey team, I wouldn't let my mom pay me the hours that I worked anymore. I still get a cheque for working my dad's garage on Saturdays but when it comes to working with my mom I don't feel comfortable accepting cash from her pocket. Especially now that I'm ninety-nine percent sure that I'm gonna go pro with my sport – a sport that has an embarrassingly high signing figure. So when I told my mom that I needed to stop my shift at the diner because I knew someone else who really needed a job, I was confident that there would be enough cash to give Fallon a good salary, seeing as I've been free-labouring for the past three years. Plus I said that I'd do an extra day at the workshop with my dad, no strings attached, so I've successfully covered all of my bases. My mom and dad have me working the same amount of shifts, and Fallon's about to start getting a nice steady income.

I'm fucking exhausted but I don't care. I couldn't watch Fallon stress out about money troubles that *I* could solve for one more minute without doing something about it.

As long as she doesn't realise that I've set this whole thing up behind her back, everything is going to be fine.

Tanner clears his throat next to me and jerks his chin towards the windshield.

"Are we just gonna sit here and watch her or…?"

I run a hand through my hair, still wet from the shower.

"Give me another minute," I grumble, rubbing my

knuckles against my jaw.

My stubble makes a harsh scraping sound and I suddenly wonder if Fallon likes stubble on the guys that she dates. I mean, she's a girlie type of chick – she reads romance books, she does cheer. It's safe to take a punt that she probably doesn't like rough-around-the-edges types of guys.

I try to picture her going on a date with one of those pastel-wearing yuppies from Frat Row and suddenly I'm throwing myself out of the truck and slamming the driver's door after myself.

"We're just picking up the takeout and then we're leaving," Tanner instructs, even though I want to spend the next two hours sitting in a diner booth so that I can watch Fallon waiting tables. But Tanner is crazy successful when it comes to chicks so I'm going to do what he's suggested and try to not lay it on too thick.

With my mom in the back office, Fallon is the only staff member now out on the floor, and she's pouring a coffee as we make our way over to the counter.

I look her right in the eyes as she glances up at us, trying to gauge her reaction to seeing me in here. I'm playing with fire even stopping by, seeing as half of the diners in here already know me as the owner's kid, but I'm giving them major *do not fucking talk to me* vibes as I head straight towards Fallon.

She looks a whole lot surprised to see Tanner and I in here but as soon as we're right in front of her she can barely contain her smile.

She lets out a nervous laugh and says, "Surprise! I got a job."

I bite hard into my bottom lip to stop my own grin from spreading.

"Knew you'd find one," I tell her, my voice sandpaper rough. A satisfied feeling spreads in my chest at the knowledge that I'm secretly responsible for this – this new financial safety net for her, the happy sparkle in her pretty eyes. It seems like a weight has been taken off her shoulders, her movements lighter and her demeanour more soft. And the look that she's giving me... it's a green light. Like the storm is over now and she's ready to be open to me.

Then she says with a cute little nose-scrunch, "It's all because of Connell really. He's the one who told me about it."

Tanner chokes beside me.

"Connell's a great guy," I grit out.

"Anyway, what can I get for you guys?" she asks as she lifts up the counter door, coffees on a tray as she takes it over to a table behind us. I turn to watch her and my eyes fall to her behind as she bends over to set down the drinks. My jaw goes slack as I let my mind wander, picturing her in nothing but that apron as I take her from b–

Tanner shoves me in the shoulder and I quickly turn back to the counter.

My cheeks are damn near on fire.

"Hunter," he hisses. "Calm that shit, now. You don't even know if she wants you like that yet."

I run a palm down my face and nod once, curt. I'm getting way ahead of myself but damn if it doesn't feel good. Finding a chick that I can't get out of my head and finally being in a secure enough position to actually do something about it.

When Fallon slides back to the other side of the counter Tanner nods his head towards the boxes in the heater and says, "We ordered takeout."

Fallon's expression falls slightly, her eyes flicking over to mine. "Oh. You aren't eating in?"

"No," Tanner says, while I practically growl, "Yes."

He shoots me a look and glances back down at Fallon. "We've got plans tonight. Maybe another time."

"Okay," she says, avoiding my eyes now as she heads to

Pinkie Promise

get the takeout boxes. Like she's upset. I shoulder Tanner hard in the back and, if anything, the prick looks smug.

Fallon brings over two takeout boxes and this time *I'm* the one looking smug.

"Uh, Fallon," I say, tilting my chin back over to the heater.

She looks back at it confused and then lifts her eyes to mine. "Yeah?"

I give her a smile. She raises her eyebrows.

"They're all for you guys?" she asks, shooting a startled glance over at the other five boxes in the heater. "Are you serious?"

"We're serious," Tanner says.

She retrieves our other boxes and begins piling them into paper bags as I take my card out of my pocket and wait for her to key the order on the reader.

"Give me a minute, I'm new at this," she mumbles after handing Tanner the bags and looking nervously down at the cash screen.

"Take your time," I murmur.

She gives me a small grateful smile. Tanner makes a subtle retching sound.

"So, uh, do you come here a lot?" Fallon asks, tucking a curl behind her ear and glancing up at me under her lashes.

"Yeah, I come a lot. I mean – fuck – I come *here* a lot!" I swallow hard and grip the back of my neck. "I come here, like, a normal amount of times."

My voice is so deep right now that I barely recognise myself. Fallon hides a small smile as she submits our order in the reader so that I can pay and then she turns around to grab our receipt from the printer. I turn a full one-eighty to stop myself looking at her perfect little ass again.

Tanner looks like he's praying for strength. When he catches my eye he mouths, *for the love of* fuck, *stop saying the word 'come'*.

Fallon turns back to us with the receipt and she holds it

out with a warm glow on her cheeks.

"Well, see you, I guess," she says, looking up into my eyes.

Yeah, I'm more than a little gratified that she isn't paying Tanner a single second of attention.

I take the receipt and clench my jaw when her soft fingers brush against mine.

Tanner clears his throat and I look at him, although all I can think about is Fallon's hand in mine. He raises his eyebrows like I've forgotten something. It takes me a good fifteen seconds to get my brain in gear.

"Fuck, yeah," I rumble, and I quickly stash the receipt in one pocket while pulling the paper wristbands out of the other. "Here," I say to Fallon, thrusting the two blue bands towards her over the counter.

She looks down at them and then back up at me, a question in her eyes.

"Our next home game. Thursday. There's a QR code on the band that y'all have to get scanned on the door." Not all colleges are strict about having an accounted for audience, but Carter U likes to ensure their players' privacy and safety.

"There are two bands here," she points out, and this time her eyes slide over to Tanner.

He looks behind himself as if he has no idea that she's addressing him.

"Am I supposed to bring someone?" she asks.

Tanner shrugs and says to the floor, "Can if you want. Bring a roommate or something."

Fallon makes an interested hum before sliding the bands off the counter and into her apron pouch. My eyes wander over the tight cinch of her waist before roaming up to the soft mounds of her chest. For a petite chick I'm surprised by how… full they look. I remember seeing her at the car wash in her jeans and her little cheer top, and she looked so damn hot that every window in my truck steamed up. I take a second to imagine seeing her in her whole cheer outfit and the cords in my neck instantly tighten.

I need to get back to my room and work on spraining my fucking wrist.

"We should go," I rasp, my thickness straining against my zipper. I can barely meet Fallon's eyes as I rake my hands through my hair and grunt, "See you Thursday."

Tanner mumbles an equally gruff goodbye and then we muscle our way out of the doors.

When we're both inside the truck I stare blankly out at the diner windows. I'm borderline panting. Tanner covers his face with his hands and muffles a low groan.

There's no denying it. Fallon is really fucking hot.

"You need to beat it out of your system before you even think of asking her on a date," Tanner says finally as I pull into a space outside of the hockey house. "I can see the way that you're looking at her, like you're already picturing her in a wedding dress."

I stifle a grunt. *Great.* Now I really *will* be spraining my wrist tonight.

"I know what I'm doing," I tell him, even though I don't have a damn clue.

I'm still telling myself that I know what I'm doing as I throw a takeout box down on my bed and lock my bedroom door. I pull off my shirt and exhale deeply as I settle my body on top of the duvet, my muscles bunched tight.

I pull my phone out of my pocket and click the Apps button, typing in 'Instagram' and then hitting *download*. I'm not a social media user but the Carter Ridge Rangers have a team page, and damn if I don't know that password.

I open the app as soon as it downloads, typing in the username and password and waiting for it to connect. Once I get my bearings on the app, I find my way to the search section and type in Fallon's name.

I scroll a little until I find her and then I tap on the tiny circle with her picture.

I swallow hard as I open up her account. The little picture of her is bigger now, showing her smiling as she crushes a huge trophy against her cheek. She's got her cheer bow in so I guess that it was taken at a previous competition.

When I realise that the rest of her pictures are hidden because her page is private, I tap the button that says *follow* and stare anxiously at the 'requested' symbol.

I inhale a deep calming breath and flick open the top button on my jeans.

Then the page refreshes and suddenly I'm in. *Jesus, she must have just accepted the request.* I sit up on one elbow and scroll quickly down the page. There are, like, at least twenty different pictures of her on here. I click on one where she's wearing a white halo and I instantly recognise it as the outfit that she wore for Halloween. Then I scroll one picture further and my mouth goes dry.

The muscle in my jaw flexes, then turns rigid.

It's a close-up photo that she took of herself, hair splayed against her pillow and a secret smile on her lips. She's wearing a pyjama tank top and *no fucking bra*. My thumb jerks accidently on the image and a red heart pops up out of nowhere. Don't know what the fuck that means, but I go with it anyway. The jerk of my thumb also means that I've scrolled farther down the picture, and now I can see a text caption beneath it. Why the hell anyone would read a caption when the picture looks that good I do not know, but I read it anyway and it says: *Trust the process. Good things are coming.*

It's the kind of ethereal cryptic shit that I would expect from someone as enchanting as Fallon. Positive with a stressed-out undertone. Intriguing and unpredictable.

I gently move my thumb on the screen so that I'm back on the picture and I slowly ease down the zipper of my jeans.

I groan at the instant expansion and carefully shove

Pinkie Promise

down my boxers. Then I wrap my fist around the base and begin frantically stroking.

I've got this all under control.

CHAPTER 9

Fallon

I spend Wednesday on the couch, huddled under a fuzzy purple blanket with my laptop balancing on my belly. I have my hoodie drawn up over my head and the sleeves pulled down so that only the tips of my fingers are visible. They're a sparkly lilac blur as I tap away at the keys.

I'm more than a little amazed that my thesis supervisor, Dr. Sloane, emailed me this morning with her first run-through of my initial thesis draft. What with it only being the very start of November I hadn't expected her to be so prompt, especially when she has twelve other senior students that she's supervising this year. She told me that I'm her only student who has completed their first draft, a fact which was so gratifying that it motivated me to get halfway through my second draft too. Then I spent the time after my thesis-blitz trying to find every potentially relevant document that may be of use to Dr. Ward – the professor who's going to be my grant referee – seeing as I got an email from her at crazy o'clock in the morning asking me to re-send the grant documentation because she couldn't find my previous email in her inbox.

Her recommendation only needs to be between one-hundred and three-hundred words long, so I'm surprised that she hasn't rattled out something easy and generic instead of asking me for further details. As I send her the documents a nervous tremor surfaces in my stomach, thinking back to what Connell said when I mentioned that she was my reference of choice.

I mean, it's only been a month since she told me that she would be my referee and she will have obviously been very busy, but then I think about someone like my supervisor who is getting back to me weeks *ahead* of schedule, and suddenly I'm wondering if maybe I *did* pick the wrong faculty member for my grant submission.

I log out of the college server and then treat myself to a peek at my manuscript. I scroll through the chapters, rereading bits here and there, and then when I get to the part that I'm now up to I drum my nails against the keys, wondering if any words will come.

I type slowly, cautiously, for the next half an hour, pausing every now and then for a sip from my Baby Yoda mug.

I write a little over the next forty-five minutes, and then I get a text from Aisling and I put my laptop aside.

AISLING: *Where are you? We have cheer, like, five minutes ago.*

When I look at the time I realise that it's way later than I originally thought.

So yeah, I'm skipping cheer, but it's only because I'm no longer on the squad. When I remind Aisling of this she instantly responds with:

AISLING: *Participating in Nationals isn't the only reason to be a cheerleader — we aren't just a comp team, remember? We have an events squad too... ;)*

I slowly sit upright because she's being alluringly suspicious, making my heart beat a little faster in my chest. *Why else would I come to training if I wasn't flyering at Nationals?*

Is there a chance that I can still spend my senior year doing cheer, even if it isn't with the comp team?

AISLING: *Get your tush over here now, Fallon!*

I grin, grab my things and bolt out of the door.

*

I scooch my way along the plastic seats, looking for the one that corresponds to my wristband, and when I realise how close to the rink I am my cheeks go a little pink.

I'm practically on the ice. In fact, I think that I'm actually *in* the sin bin. I've never been to a hockey game before so I wasn't sure what to expect but, just in case, I've dressed for Antarctica. Giant scarf, knit jumper, thick woolly tights. I huddle the scarf around my face and slouch further into my seat, slow-chewing my way down a candy cable while I anxiously wait for the players to appear.

The lights go down, the music goes up, and after a five minute countdown both teams are flying onto the ice.

I thought that it might be difficult to determine which player is which but Hunter's body is so big that he's impossible not to notice. Hunter begins stretching out his thighs, warming up for the first period, and the second that he sees me he gives me a heart-stopping smile.

I glance over my shoulder to check that he isn't smiling at someone else and when I turn back to look at him his grin gets even bigger. Then he slaps down the shield at the front of his helmet and slides around to face his team so that they can have a quick pre-game discussion.

With the large expanse of his back facing me I see the name WILDE written across it in bold red capitals.

I don't take a breath for the entire game.

Hunter is fast, ruthless, and borderline brutal. He hits the puck so hard into the back of the net that the severe strike reverberates down to my core.

If I wasn't so amazed I think I would be terrified.

Hunter gets sent to the sin bin on one obvious occasion and I'm pretty sure that he did it on purpose, mainly because when he shoved into a guy with the thick swell of his shoulder the puck was literally on the other side of the rink. As soon as he's in the sin bin he knocks on the board in front of me and, panting hard, he gives me a once-over and a wink.

"Oh my God," I whisper, trying to cover my crimson cheeks with my scarf.

"What do you think?" he calls to me, smirking like a total hotshot.

"Hunter, do not tell me that you just got sent into the sin bin so that you could come and talk to me right now."

He smiles sheepishly at his gloves, his cheeks almost as red as mine. "We're already winning, Fallon. Wanted to make sure you were having a good time."

Something warm and painful tightens in my chest. When he looks up at me from under his beautiful black lashes I can't help but give him a small lip-biting smile, because I simply cannot believe that he just did that for me.

When the final whistle is blown and Carter U's team has finished celebrating their win, Hunter pulls away from the group and quickly skims the ice over to me. Now that the game is over his movements are light and graceful.

He swerves to an easy stop in front of the sin bin and leans a palm on the board, his other hand gripping his helmet so that he can pull it over his head.

His hair is dark and sweaty, and his cheeks are flushed.

"Hey," he rasps, excitement and adrenaline making him breathless. His voice is low and muffled on the other side of the glass. "I'm gonna be five minutes in the showers. Can we talk after? Can I meet up with you outside?"

I nod up at him and he breathes a sigh of relief, shaking out his hair and then doing a nod of his own. I make my way slowly out of the sports building, not wanting to wait outside in the cold, but just as I'm about to breach the back exit I hear footfalls pounding behind me down the long corridor.

"Hey," Hunter pants, catching up to me in a matter of strides.

He must have been less than three minutes in the locker room and, from one glance at him, I can tell why. His hair is now drenched and his clothes are only half on. His jeans are unbuttoned and his shirt is clinging wetly to his abs.

When we get outside we keep to the side of the building, and I rest against the wall as Hunter tosses his gym bag onto the blacktop. I watch in wide-eyed disbelief as he positions himself in front of me, pulling up the zipper on his pants and then leashing a belt through the loops.

As he feeds the tongue through the buckle he glances at me from under his lashes. His chest heaves in quick weighty pumps as he explains, "Didn't want to keep you waiting."

Don't mind me. I let out a little laugh, cross my legs, and squeeze.

"What did you think?" he asks, crouching down slightly in front of me so that he can grab a hoodie from his bag. He has a hopeful smile tugging at his mouth which makes something warm and fuzzy tingle in my belly.

"It was… fast," I tell him honestly, and a low laugh rumbles out of him.

"That a good thing?" he asks, pulling the jumper roughly over his head. He flashes me a dark inch of happy trail in the process and I'm suddenly very lightheaded.

"Uh, yeah," I squeak. "Although I think that I missed

every single goal. And it was… more rough than I expected. Like, you had blood on you at one point."

Hunter nods down at me, gauging my reactions cautiously. "Yeah," he says, like he knew that there was blood. Like he thinks that that's normal. "Wasn't my blood though," he shrugs, and I choke out a small laugh.

Hunter laughs at my reaction and gives me a guilty smile. "Sorry, I didn't mean to say that to freak you out. Hockey's rough, that's why I tried to ease up today." When I blink at him, not fully understanding what he means, he clarifies by saying, "That's why I played gentle tonight."

"That was you… playing gentle?" I ask hoarsely.

Hunter drops his head and smiles, gripping at the back of his neck.

"I, uh, I usually get sent to the sin bin a lot. Only needed to stop by once tonight." He grins down at me and I can't help but return the smile.

"Oh, I just remembered," I say quickly, grabbing the jumper that he leant to me at the car wash from my bag and holding it out to him. "Thank you for letting me… use your jumper."

Hunter looks down at it with a frown, his hands stuffed resolutely in his pockets. "You can keep it," he says, gruff and succinct.

I look up at him from under my lashes, almost shivering at the intensity in his eyes. "Oh, I couldn't possibly. It gets… cold in Carter Ridge. You might need it."

He gestures to his hoodie and says, "I'm covered, Fallon."

"Hunter," I argue, willing him to take it.

And not because I want him to. I want him to take it back because I *don't* want him to. Hunter wanting me to wear his soft hockey jumper just feels so intimate, and the sparkly feeling in my belly is scaring me down to my toes.

He swipes his tongue over his lower lip, studying me for a moment. Then he seems to make some sort of decision and nods, tentatively retrieving the garment.

He grins at me when my fingers cling onto it for a millisecond too long.

"Okay, I'll take it back," he says slowly, giving me a lazy smile as he stashes the jumper into his bag. "Guess I'll just have to find another excuse to give it to you again."

I breathe out a dazzled laugh as the door to my left slams open, and a hoard of hockey guys come pouring out of the building. They're Hunter's teammates, and a few of them give him quick jerks of their chins or hold up their phones as if to say *we have plans, remember?* Hunter's friend Tanner catches my eyes and I swear that he looks a little hurt. Then I remember the fact that he clearly wanted Aisling to come to the game with me – hence the extra wristband – and suddenly I feel bad for him.

There's no way in hell that I'm going to tell him that the reason why she couldn't come is because she was spending time with her *boyfriend*, but maybe if he stops by my new job at the diner again I'll give him a to-go coffee as my treat.

Hunter waits a beat so that we're no longer directly in the eye-line of his entire ice hockey team and then he takes a step towards me, propping a forearm on the wall above my head.

To my surprise he looks as nervous as I feel. His cheeks are slightly red and his eyes are down on our feet. The small crease between his brows tells me that he's having a complicated internal conversation with himself right now.

I give his boot a little nudge and his head snaps up, eyes burning.

"Sorry," he grunts, shoving his free hand through his hair. "I know I'm holding you up from, uh, a cheer social or something."

It's actually very sweet of him to assume that I have a social life. Since being benched from the comp squad I haven't really been going out, although, after what Aisling told me yesterday, my cheer career may be about to take a new direction.

Hunter quietly clears his throat before he finally asks, "Wanna go out with me sometime?"

The toes of our boots are still touching. Nothing in the world could stop me from smiling right now.

But before I can answer him one of his teammates calls over from the lot, "Yo Cap, come on!"

Hunter's eyes remain on mine for a good five seconds before he glances over his shoulder and precisely mouths the words *fuck off*.

I laugh out loud and Hunter flashes me his handsome smile.

I feel giddy and excited for the first time all term. I feel the way that you're *supposed* to feel at college. Maybe meeting Hunter was exactly what I needed.

Maybe I don't mind taking a few falls if where I land leads me to him.

So I tuck a curl behind my ear and ask, "What did you have in mind?"

CHAPTER 10

Hunter

I rap a fist against the door and then tuck my hands into the pockets of my jeans.

Fallon buzzed me into the building and now I'm waiting outside of her condo, heart thumping fast in anticipation of our first date.

The door opens up a crack and Fallon peeks around the door.

"Uh, hi," she says, smiling and sounding breathless. Her cheeks are a little pink and she's got an embarrassed look on her face. For one quick moment I instantly think the worst. *She's hooking up with a guy, right this second.* But then she shakes her head and opens the door a centimetre wider, explaining, "Ash had me do a one-on-one cheer session and it overran by, like, seven billion hours. I need five minutes to clean myself up before we can go."

After a moment of contemplation she decides to open the door all the way and my jaw about hits the floor when I see what she's wearing.

"You can wait on the couch if you'd like? I can power-shower in three minutes, tops."

I tear my eyes away from her sweated-up cheerleader outfit and look as far away from her as possible. "Don't worry about it. I'll wait on the couch," I rasp.

I can hear the little smile in her voice when she says, "Hunter, you can look at me you know."

The one second glance that I got of her before turning quickly away is already seared into my brain for life. I let out a nervous laugh, shoving a hand through my hair as I say, "Fallon–"

"Hunter."

Something about her sultry tone makes my eyes drop down to hers and I'm instantly aflame as our eyes meet and lock. Getting the green-light from Fallon makes my chest swell and heave, and I take a deep swallow before letting my gaze rake down her body.

It's so much fucking worse the second time around. Her top is moulded to her chest and her skirt doesn't even begin to cover her thighs. She wears this shit in public? Other guys are gonna see her high-kicking in this? My body moves forward instinctively and I knock the door shut with my shoulder as I enter her condo, jaw muscles rolling as I take my fill.

"What do you think?" Fallon asks, gesturing vaguely to the condo behind her.

I could not tell you one detail about that condo if I had a gun pointed to my head.

I trudge forward and Fallon back-steps until the backs of her thighs hit the side of her couch. Then I root myself on the spot so that I don't do anything stupid, inappropriate, or unfuckinghinged.

"It's a… nice outfit," I grunt.

"Oh, you like it?" she asks innocently.

My eyes slide up to hers and I see that she's still smiling. She's messing with me. She can tell how hot she gets me, and something about that makes her even hotter. I give her a *yeah, I'm an idiot* grin and scrub at the back of my neck, dropping my eyes.

"Hilarious," I say to her. "Go shower and change before I do something stupid."

"Like what?" she teases, stepping a little closer. My eyes are back on hers, the air between us on fire. My brain knows that she's just innocently teasing, but tell that to the muscle getting long and heavy in my pants. Every inch of my torso is thrumming with heat, and it gets even worse when she gives me a fucking three-sixty.

I feel my pupils dilate and I drop heavily onto the couch, spreading out my legs and scraping a hand over my mouth.

"Please go and shower," I manage to say. My eyes are still roaming over her long bare legs and if I stare at her for one more second I'm going to lose my damn mind.

Noticing my fixation Fallon squeezes her thighs together, and I give her a warning look as she looks down at me from her standing position.

"Fallon, please get ready, or I'm gonna take the low-road and ruin the surprise."

Her eyes sparkle, like this is as new to her as this is to me. "But I'm… enjoying watching you look at me," she admits, her candid honesty making her sound so damn young.

I bury my head in my hands and mumble, "We're going to the movies."

When I spread my fingers over my eyes so that I can look up at her through the gaps she's watching me with an expression that's so stunned my heart skips a beat.

"I've been… wanting to go to the movies," she says, her eyes unblinking.

I swallow hard. Yeah, I know that she's been wanting to go to the movies. I get notifications whenever she puts up one of her Instagram stories, and she keeps on sharing photos from an action flick that's just been released.

Pinkie Promise

"Yeah," I say, trying to not sound too much like a stalker.

She stares at me for a long scrutinising moment before saying, "Was it... was it you who followed me from the hockey account?"

Fuck, I wish she had some clothes on. Those soft little thighs are murdering my ability to think straight.

I give her a jerk of my chin and her eyes sparkle brighter.

"You liked every single one of my Instagram photos," she breathes.

I nod again. "Yeah. Isn't that what you're supposed to do?"

She laughs and cocks her head to the side. "What d'you mean?"

"Like, when you see a picture that you like, you click the heart. I've never had the app before but it seems pretty obvious to me."

She raises her eyebrows and says, "You downloaded Instagram so that you could follow me?"

God, this room is warm. "Yeah," I say gruffly. "I did."

I can tell that she's pleased from the lip-biting smile that she's giving me. "Which picture was your favourite?"

Not exactly gonna tell her that I like the one where she's flat on her back and I can see the outlines of her nipples. Instead I clear my throat and say, "They're all... really fuckin' nice."

She narrows her eyes playfully, still smiling. "Hmm, no, I think you'll have a favourite. Don't worry though, I'll get it out of you."

I spread my thighs wider on the couch. *You've been doing that, alright.*

I tug at the collar of my shirt, trying to angle the subject of this conversation away from my extracurriculars with Fallon's Instagram. "Okay, I'm giving you four minutes or I'm gonna have to drag you out of here dressed like that."

"Why four minutes?" she pouts. "I told you I needed five."

"Your skirt just annihilated ten years off my life, Fallon. I don't have time to waste."

She breathes out a laugh and mock-groans, "*Fine.*"

I watch her bare feet pad across the floor, catching her eyes again before she closes the door to the bathroom.

I immediately throw my shoulders against the back of the couch, shoving one fist in my mouth and the other down to the front of my jeans. I fumble with my belt buckle and quickly flick the top button on my pants. My fingers breach the waistband and I slide my palm under my boxers, grunting hard into my fist as I grip the solid root of my cock. It's borderline impossible to jack off when you're being constricted by two layers of clothing but God loves a fucking tryer so I give it my best shot. Just enough to take the edge off sitting shoulder to shoulder with Fallon in a dark confined space for the next two hours.

I tighten my hold on my shaft and give it three fast tugs, my jaw bunching hard as a spurt of moisture shoots out of the tip. I swipe it quickly with my palm and then stroke it down my length.

Then I hear the shower spray begin to pound and I almost come on the damn spot.

I remove my left fist from my mouth and grip it into the top of Fallon's sofa, although I keep my other hand in my boxers to try and alleviate the deep pulsing ache.

After one godforsaken minute I decide that staring like a serial killer at Fallon's bathroom door isn't helping my cock come down from its high, so I slowly extract my palm from my pants and begin buttoning myself back up.

She's naked in the shower right now. Her hot slick body is dripping with warm water.

The cords in my neck tighten as I slide my belt back into place and then I lumber stiffly to her kitchen, bracing my palms flat on her counter.

Pinkie Promise

Did she even lock the bathroom door?

It's none of my business. NONE of my goddamn business.

Seven and a half minutes later Fallon is breezing out of her bathroom with a big towel wrapped around her body, and she's slipping soundlessly into her bedroom without meeting my eyes. I white-knuckle her kitchen counter for the next fifty seconds while hearing the sounds of drawers opening and zippers closing, and then she quietly exits her bedroom in a cute knit jumper and a pair of ass-hugging jeans. She has the scarf that she wore to the game around her neck and her hair is down, reaching just below her waist.

"I brought my truck," I tell her as I carefully manoeuvre my body back around the counter, and she nods her head at me as she pulls her key from her jeans pocket. I trail my eyes down her body while she locks up the condo and then I decide that it's for the best if I just don't look at her for the rest of the night. *How the hell is she still getting me going when she's covered from neck to ankle?*

"Do I get to twenty-one questions you while you drive us to the movies?" she asks.

Something poker hot strikes in my abs when she uses the word 'us'. I follow behind her as she walks towards the elevator and she gives me an encouraging smile over her shoulder when my silence breaches the ten-second mark.

I clear my throat hard. *She can do whatever the hell she wants to me while I drive.*

"Yeah," I say as we descend to the ground floor, the elevator going at lightning speed. "This building's fucking insane."

Fallon remains quiet for a beat and then, as we step out into the lobby, she says, "My roommate's family owns the whole complex. I, um… I don't pay rent." Then she shakes her head and quickly adds on, "Of course, when I finally get a long-term job I will absolutely give them the money that I owe them. They haven't asked me to, but I have this really big thing about paving my own way."

I reach around her to shove the door open as she scans her key-fob against the electric lock.

The more time that I spend with Fallon the more evident it becomes that money is a real issue for her. I'm not sure how she's made her way through college, and I'm even more concerned about what she's going to do after she graduates.

"Is that why you've been looking for a job? To pay back your rent?" I ask her.

She lets out an embarrassed laugh and says, "That's actually so that I can stay on at Carter U for another year. I know that working a Sunday job won't pay for a Master's, but it's more about amassing cash in case I don't get the grant that I'm applying for. All grants are really hard to get and I literally don't know what I'll do with my life if I don't secure one. I guess getting a loan, but I'm not exactly crazy on that idea."

I unlock my truck when we reach it and I pull the passenger door open for her.

She looks at the interior of the cab and says wistfully to the passenger seat, "We meet again."

I breathe out a laugh, glad that her spirits have lifted now that we're at my truck. I close the door gently once she's tucked her legs inside and then I round the hood to the driver's door and hunch down under the roof. I shut the door after myself and click the belt into the mechanism.

I kick the truck to life and battle with myself about whether or not I should push her further. I settle on asking one more question and then vowing with myself to mind my goddamn business.

"What about your parents? Can't they help?" I ask, and instantly I feel her body stiffen at my side. Right. So there's my answer to that question.

When we approach the red light I glance over at her and she gives me a little nose scrunch.

That nose scrunch speaks a thousand words. She doesn't want to talk about it, which means that, whatever the situation is, it isn't good.

"I'm sorry, I shouldn't have asked," I admit, my tone low as I ease the truck back up to speed. "I won't ask any other shit like that."

"It's fine," she says on the weariest sigh that I've ever heard. "Maybe it's good that you know. At least it explains why my emotions have been all over the place lately."

My eyes flicker down to her lap where she's currently wringing out her hands. Fuck. My right fist flexes on the wheel, wanting more than anything to lock my fingers right through hers.

"What about you?" she asks, twisting slightly to face me. I would do anything to hit another red light right now, just so that I could look at her again.

"My parents are fine. They work me like a dog though."

She breathes out a small laugh and I flash her a grin.

"You know the war paint that I had on my face when we were over at the corn maze for Halloween? Mine wasn't from a paint bottle. I'd literally been under a car all day. My dad's a mechanic so I spend my Saturdays grinding at the workshop." I think for a moment and then quickly add on, "And Sundays too. I work… both days at the shop."

Definitely do not mention the fact that you used to work Sundays at the diner.

"Busy guy," she comments as I pull up outside the cinema.

I shrug, shaking my head. "It's nothing. Just work, classes and hockey, and then shooting the shit with the guys."

"And the girls?" she asks.

I smirk and shake my head. "Ain't no other girls, Fallon."

She lifts an eyebrow and tries not to smile at me as she crosses her arms over her chest. "That's how you're going to play it, huh, Captain of the Carter Ridge Rangers? You're six-four and built like a truck. I'm not an idiot. You must get girls all the time."

I unfasten my seatbelt without meeting her eyes. I don't know if it's best to correct her assumption here and now or ignore it completely until she forgets that she ever mentioned it. If Tanner was here he would tell me to definitely not fucking address what she's hinting at, so I get out of the truck without saying a word, reaching her door before she can let herself out.

Her eyebrow is still cocked and she's looking at me like I'm a serial fucker. I jerk my chin at her, my cheeks turning beet red, and say, "Out, or we'll miss the trailers."

She slides out of her seat with a heated look in her eyes. "Well we wouldn't want that," she says as she brushes right past me.

I lock up the car and tail her into the building.

I already know which movie she's hankering to see so I slap down two tens in front of the guy on reception and point to the poster that's framed in the Now Showing section above his head.

Fallon watches our exchange with wide observant eyes and when she sees me looking down at her she gives me an almost ashamed looking smile.

"Thanks," she says, her fingers agitatedly plaiting a tiny piece of her hair.

I pocket the tickets and get her walking by bumping my chest into her shoulder. "Don't mention it," I tell her, hoping she understands that I mean that literally. It's only a cinema ticket – it barely merits a thank you, let alone that sad shimmery look that she's got going on in her eyes.

When was the last time that someone took her out? When was the last time she was treated the way that she deserves?

I walk one step behind her as we take the stairs down to the smaller screening room, but my front thumps into her back as she pauses by the snack counter. I peer down at her over the top of her head and watch as she stares hungrily at a bag of candy cables.

"You want some of those?" I ask, and she scrubs at the button of her nose nervously.

"Uh, no, it's fine," she says, and then she starts moving again.

As if I'm not about to buy her the whole damn counter.

I hook my middle digit in the loop at the back of her jeans and grab five bags at random before pulling my card from my wallet.

"We'll take these," I say to the woman behind the till, at the same time as Fallon hisses at me, "What are you doing?"

I don't know if she's talking about the finger-in-her-belt-loop thing or the wanting-to-sugar-her-up-like-a-spoiled-princess thing so I ignore her question by shoving all of the candy into her arms. She cradles them against her chest and shoots me that surprised wide-eyed look again.

"Want a slushie?" I ask, already knowing the answer.

"Uh..."

I'm guessing that the red is strawberry and the green is apple or grape. I don't have a fucking clue what the blue one is supposed to be and I don't believe the woman behind the counter for a minute when, reading my mind, she gives me a bored look and drawls, "It's raspberry."

In what universe is the blue one goddamn raspberry?

I give Fallon's loop a little tug to encourage her to pick, but this time she shakes her head, flushing a little.

"Not today," she says, immediately looking mortified with herself.

"Why not?" I ask. "I'll buy you whatever you want, Fallon."

"Oh, no, it's not that," she amends. She glances between me, the slushie machine, and then back to me again. "It's, uh..."

She looks really embarrassed. Why's she looking so

embarrassed for?

She drops her voice to a whisper and says, "I don't want, um… they make your tongue change colour. I don't want, like, a bright pink tongue."

My eyes dip to her lips and suddenly my chest is pumping a little harder. There's only one reason why she'd be thinking that deep about a slushie, right? Does she… does she expect me to make out with her in there?

Am I gonna spend the next two hours making out with her in there?

I can't think of anything other than the now imminent prospect of making out with Fallon, so after pocketing my card I immediately start shoving her towards the cinema doors again.

"Sorry, that was, like, really forward," she says, clutching the candy tighter as if she's cringing real hard.

I shake my head and steer her into the back row where we finally drop down onto the red velvet seats. I turn to face her and she's avoiding my eyes, pretending to be fascinated by her bags of candy.

"I didn't bring you to the movies to make out with you for eighty minutes straight," I tell her. Although, actually, if no-one else comes in through those doors then we will literally be the only people in for this showing. "I knew that you wanted to see this movie so I thought that maybe we could do it together. Nothing formal like dinner and roses before I know if you're… interested in me like I'm interested in you, and nothing lame like asking you to meet me at a frat party."

"I am, by the way," she says quickly, still burning holes through the packaging of her Jelly Babies.

"…You are what?" I ask.

"Interested." She takes a hasty swallow and wets her lips. "I've had a crappy month and, whether I like it or not, you've kind of been there with me for all of it. But I'm hoping that things are gonna get better soon so… I don't know, I'm probably pushing my luck with the Universe but I... um, I would like to... with you... if you'd want to."

My mind fills her blank spaces with terrible, awful things.

"Yeah, I want to," I rumble and she finally meets my eyes, just as a staff member closes the door and the lights lower into blackness.

The air between us gets a hundred degrees hotter.

The trailers start to play on the screen but all that I can focus on is what's happening in my peripheral vision. Namely, Fallon's chest rising and falling in double time as she lets out these shaky little exhales, like she's as nervous and excited as I am. I shove a hand through my hair and try to calm the hell down.

Focus on the trailers. Just focus on the trailers.

A small rustling sound breaks through my lust and I take a wary glance down to see Fallon poking around in one of the candy bags. I can't help but smile when she looks up at me, silently offering me some of her candy.

I lean closer so that I don't have to raise my voice over the trailers. "I got them for you, Fallon," I murmur.

"You don't like movie snacks?" she asks, looking a little hurt.

The movie snack that I want is sitting right next to me. I'll do anything that Fallon wants me to though so I breathe out a laugh and shove my hand in the bag, but before I pull it back out the bag tears down the front completely, and in the next second Fallon has a lap full of Jelly Babies.

"Shit," I grunt, instantly pulling my hand back from Fallon's lap.

"Sorry!" she says, her voice high-pitched. "I guess you won't want to eat any now."

I bite down hard on the inside of my cheek. I've never wanted to eat a Jelly Baby so much in my damn life.

She drops them back into the broken bag and then lets out a nervous laugh as she tucks some hair behind her ear.

"Sorry," she whispers again, and then she curls up on the seat, her small shoulder resting gently against mine.

The movie starts and I stare blankly at the screen, my chest pumping heavily as I try to keep my shoulders still. But every small shift of Fallon's body has my abdomen flexing, the need to just get her up on me almost making me sweat.

By the time that we reach the film's one and only make-out scene I'm ready to go into cardiac arrest.

"Are you okay?" Fallon whispers, probably because I'm no longer looking at the screen. I do not need a thirty-foot by fifty-foot reminder of what I want to be doing to the girl who is curled up right next to me.

Bracing myself, I look down at her and she's gotten so cosy up against my bicep that her cheeks have flushed with warmth.

I run a palm down my thigh. *She's flushed with* my *warmth*.

My eyes drop to her lips and I imagine giving in. Gripping a hand in the back of her hair and pulling her gently up to meet me, whilst sliding my other palm beneath her jumper and squeezing a rough palm around her–

"Hunter?" she whispers.

I clear my throat and look away. I'm not going to get one minute of sleep tonight.

"The photo you took of yourself," I suddenly rasp. Yeah, I've just gone from one stupidly hot subject to another stupidly hot subject.

"What?" she asks, her attention split between me and the movie playing out in front of us.

"My favourite photo? On your, uh, page? It's the one you took of yourself. You're in your bed" – hang on, I hope to *fuck* that she took it in her own bed – "and you're wearing this sort of flimsy-strapped tank top, and your hair is all…" I swallow hard. "Uh, thick against the pillow, and you have this kind of secret smile going on, and–"

Something small and soft reaches my hand, enveloping

it in warmth although the tips of her fingers are still cold. I flip my palm so that it's facing upright and the second that her touch resettles I lock my fingers right through hers, squeezing her gently before looking back down at her. Her attention is all on me now and hell if that doesn't make me the happiest guy on the planet.

"I don't do this a lot," I murmur, quiet and honest.

She gives me a teasing smile. "What, hold hands?"

I breathe out a laugh. "I never hold hands. What I mean is I don't…" I look down at our interlaced fingers, hers spread obscenely wide due to the thickness of my digits. The sight of it, the comparison between us, catches me off guard and I distractedly murmur, "You're really small."

She glances down at our hands and brushes her pinkie against my knuckle. "Sorry," she says. "I know it's weird."

I frown and stare down at her, confused by her reaction.

"It's all the gymnastics from when I was a kid – the repeated pressure on my joints kept me kind of short, and now that I'm an adult I don't look… I should be more…" She glances up at my chest and her eyes roam across the breadth of it so damn longingly that my cock begins to strain. "Like, you look like a man. A grown man. Whereas I…" We both look down at her body, so petite that she's managed to curl up entirely in her seat.

I rub my free palm down my stubble and bring our interlocked hands higher up my thigh.

"Fallon," I say, raspier than I should be for a guy who hasn't even taken her to first base yet. "I really, *really* like the way that you look."

She rolls her eyes and tries to pull her hand out of mine. Nice fucking try but that's not gonna happen.

"You're a guy," she huffs. "You'll say that to anyone."

"Fallon, look at me," I say, gripping her hand a little tighter. "I like that you're petite. It's cute, and I like it."

She could be 5'1" or 5'11" and my feelings for her wouldn't change one bit.

"This was a really bad idea," she whispers, beginning to look around, getting flustered. "Maybe I'm just not cut out for this. Dating and stuff—"

"Fallon. Listen to me. I haven't dated while I've been in college."

Fallon stops herself mid-sentence and her eyes suddenly lift up to meet mine.

"I haven't been on one date and I'm in my senior year. I saw you and I liked you. You're the only one."

Her lips keep opening and closing, and after a while I have to stop staring at them. I should be more embarrassed by what I just told her but for some reason I feel like it's exactly what she needed.

"You don't date around?" she asks, her voice shy and hopeful.

An explosion goes off on the screen. She doesn't even glance at it.

"No, Fallon. I don't date around."

Her brow twitches a little as her brain goes into overdrive. "So you… you just sleep around," she mumbles. "Not that I'm judging," she says quickly. "You're a big guy, I know that you'll have, er, needs to fulfil."

My neck muscles tighten. As subtle as I can I give my groin a two-second grip and then, looking away from her, I grit out, "Yeah. I have needs."

"I have a lot going on right now," she says quietly, as if she hasn't tried to warn me away from her before. "I'm really probably not the best option."

"Fallon, you aren't an option, you're the only girl who I want to spend my time with. I wanna date you. Repeatedly. And you're the only person that I wanna do that with."

"Are you sure?" she says, so concerned that she's almost wincing.

"I'm sure."

"Are you sure that you're sure?" she asks, but now she's laughing nervously and I can't hide the smile on my face.

Pinkie Promise

I bring our hands to my mouth and press a hard kiss to her tiny pinkie, looking up at her beautiful face from under my lashes. "I'm more than sure, Fallon," I murmur. "I promise."

CHAPTER 11

Fallon

Once Hunter got his hands on me he simply couldn't let go.

When the movie finished he waited for me to stuff the candy packets into my jeans and then he led us out the door, his hand never leaving mine. By the time that we reached the foyer he was walking right up behind me, his palms gripping into my hips, hard, heavy, and firm.

We reach his truck in the lot and he pulls open my door, his front warm and solid against the back of my jumper.

I glance at him over my shoulder and he tips his chin towards the truck's interior. "Get in," he says huskily.

I bend forward and slip inside and he waits by my door until I've strapped myself in. Then he quietly shuts it, rounds the truck, and heaves himself inside.

"You like the movie?" he asks as he gets the truck's engine going.

"What movie?" I ask, and he flashes me a lazy grin.

"You're a real funny chick," he says, shaking his head. "I like that."

Suddenly I'm thinking of all the first-date questions that I haven't yet asked him so I curl up on the passenger seat, rummage around for a stray Jelly Baby, and ask, "Where are you from, originally?"

He rolls his shoulders and says, "Carter Ridge through and through, baby."

My eyebrows rise. "Seriously? You're from here?"

He grazes his teeth into his bottom lip like he isn't sure if he should be telling me this, but I can't imagine why it would be a secret that he's local to the area.

"Yeah, Tanner and I were both born and raised around these parts."

"You guys seem like brothers," I tell him.

"He isn't by blood, but he is in the way that counts. We got into hockey together, that kind of thing." Then he laughs and says, "I have a fuck-tonne of siblings, but I don't wanna scare you."

I get comfy in my seat. "Tell me."

He grins at the road. "You sure?"

"Why would I be scared?" I laugh.

He flashes me a smirk. "I'm one of six, Fallon."

My hands instinctively move to my belly. *That is a lot of babies.*

Hunter glances down at my stomach before refocusing on the road.

"My mom has one girl and five boys. I'm the oldest. The youngest is Wren, then Archer, Ryder, Gunner, and Colton. Then me. The babies are real cute but Colt's kind of my favourite. He's in high school now and he's getting all moody. He has, uh…" He laughs and shakes his head. "He's a little obsessed with the chick who lives next door."

"Sounds like a romance story," I murmur with a smile.

He smiles back at me. "Maybe you could write it."

I try to hide my dimpling cheeks as I turn to look out of the window, my neck getting warm and my belly feeling fuzzy. *Maybe I will.*

"You got siblings?" he asks, and my smile instantly drops. "Shit, wrong question," he says quickly when he notices my expression. "I'm sorry, Fallon. I won't mention your family again."

I shake my head but my voice belies my emotions. "It's fine, I'm sorry," I say, trying to brush it off with a little laugh. "It's honestly not even a big deal."

He makes a low unsure grunt but he thinks better of fighting me on it. Instead he takes his right hand off the wheel and holds it out for me to hold. I place a Jelly Baby in his palm and when he looks down at it he laughs out loud.

He throws it back into his mouth and then he shoves his fingers straight through mine.

I have to stifle a small gasp as I say, "You have really big hands."

"Hockey player," he says by way of explanation.

"All those years of gripping the stick?"

He chokes on his swallow. "Among other things."

When adjusts the stick-shift he makes us do it with our hands still entwined, and the action is so cute that it makes me giggle. In my defence, I try my best to suppress the sound.

"You got a driver's license?" he asks.

"Nope. You?"

He sticks his tongue in his cheek, trying not to laugh again. "You are so fuckin' weird," he murmurs.

His tone is so fond that I preen and snuggle further into the seat.

"What do you study?" he asks as we approach the road that takes us toward the dark and sexy O'Malley condo block.

"Guess," I say to him.

He smiles to himself. "Shoulda known," he murmurs. "You're an English Lit chick, right?"

"Congratulations Detective," I say, and he rewards me with a hand-squeeze.

Then he surprises me by saying, "My major's Engineering."

I should have known that seeing as he already mentioned that he knew Connell from his classes, but for some unknown reason I hadn't put two-and-two together. "It sounds intense," I comment.

He shrugs. "Same as yours. Just a different flavour."

"Why Engineering?"

"Right now the plan is to play for the NHL, but after I finish up my hockey career my brothers and I will be taking over our dad's garage. Not that he'll step down – we'll just be handling more than we used to so that he can spend some time with our mom." He contemplates something for a moment and then grins. "In my second year at Carter U I took a Physics module because at the time one of my brothers was all crazy about space. Thought I'd learn some shit that could blow his little mind."

I scrunch up my nose and laugh. "That's really cute."

Hunter's smile widens. "Yeah, I'm super fuckin' cute," he drawls dryly. "Honestly, I'm only at Carter U because of Tanner. He said I'd be kickin' myself in four years if I didn't, because at the time I wasn't sure if I wanted to go pro with my sport."

I'm in awe of Hunter's down-to-earth honesty. I think that it's a small town thing and I'm a little bit in love with it. "Hold up," I laugh, leaning slightly closer to him. "Are you saying that you didn't want to go to college?"

He smirks and says, "Hell no I didn't wanna go to college, I wanted to do car shit with my dad. I don't mind doing hockey though 'cause it's still something physical. And the pay..." He swallows hard. "I'm not gonna lie, the pay is... good."

"Did you get to pick the number on your jersey?" I ask, remembering the big number 9 on his back.

He flashes me a grin. "Yeah. Sometimes colleges can be weird about it but Carter U was fine with us picking them, as long as they weren't already taken."

"Is nine your favourite number?" I ask, smiling when he breathes out a laugh.

"I mean..." He looks away from me for a beat, his cheeks flushing a little. "Considering my number of siblings... and at the time I knew that my parents were, like... God, this is gonna sound weird as hell but, I knew that they were trying for a girl so..."

"So...?" I prompt, secretly loving the fact that he has something as cute as a favourite number.

He shakes his head as if he can't believe that he's telling me this and then his beautiful sparkling eyes meet mine.

Warmth spreads through my belly and I try not to spontaneously combust.

"So I guess nine and eight are my mom and dad, then seven to three represents my baby siblings." He rakes a hand through his hair, flashing me the swollen curve of his bicep. "Guess that makes me two."

We stay silent for a few seconds, breathing heavily as we watch each other.

"So," I say finally, my voice a whisper, "if your family represents the numbers from nine to two... who's the one?"

Hunter swipes his tongue over his bottom lip and rasps, "I guess we'll see."

After putting the car in park Hunter looks down at me as I unbuckle my seatbelt and, when our eyes meet, the cabin of the car gets instantly warmer. I watch him as he swipes his tongue over his lower lip, but then he clicks open his door and heavily dismounts to the road, the truck groaning loudly in protest as he comes around to open mine.

He doesn't lock up the truck as he walks me to the entrance of the condo, showing me that he doesn't expect an invite inside.

Small town guys, I think to myself, a golden sunshine

feeling in my belly. *It's always the small town guys who act like gentlemen.*

When I get to the front door of the building I can feel Hunter's warm body right behind me. I fumble to get my key out of my pocket and, in the process, a bag of candy slips free from my jeans. Hunter catches it before it hits the sidewalk and then suddenly we're both very still.

Hunter's chest is right up against my shoulders and we're in a kind of purgatory, well aware of what usually happens at the end of a good date, even if it doesn't go so far as to the bedroom.

A deep rumble reverberates through Hunter's chest and then, after a heavy inhale, he reaches around me and begins tucking the candy back inside the front of my jeans.

I stop breathing completely.

Hunter's right hand moves up the sleeve of my jumper, rubbing me firmly until he reaches my clavicle.

"Thanks for spending your evenin' with me," he says quietly, his left hand still wedged in the front pocket of my pants. Warmth spills over in my belly as I feel the powerful press of his thick fingers. The hand that was stroking my collarbones slowly climbs the column of my throat, before gently tangling itself up in the back of my hair. Hunter's breathing gets heavier as he murmurs, "Is this okay?"

It's dark out here, outside of the building, and the glossy black exterior is swallowing every trace of light. I nod my head subtly and Hunter's mouth moves slowly against the lobe of my ear.

"Did you have a good time?" he asks me quietly as he presses his pecs harder against my shoulders. His chest swells on the impact and then he moves his lower body against me too.

"I had a good time," I whisper. "I don't have a clue what happened in the movie."

I feel him laugh against my cheek and then the hand in my hair carefully tugs, pulling me backwards. I turn my head slightly to face him and he's flushed and breathing erratically.

"Gonna let me see you again?" he asks as he slides his hand out of my pocket and begins roaming it up towards the waistband of my jeans. His irises are dark and smouldering, darkening further when his fingers reach the bottom of my sweater. They pause there but hold firm while he awaits the answer to his question.

I answer him honestly. "I don't usually have a lot of free time."

Between writing essays, organising my grant documents, and now working the diner, I don't give myself a whole lot of downtime. Now add on top of that the juicy information that Aisling told me regarding cheer, and I'm not so sure that I'll have any free time at all.

"I'll work my schedule around yours," he says quietly, pressing harder against my behind and strangling down a groan when my body yields to his. "We can make it work if you want us to. I definitely fuckin' do."

"Are you sure?" I ask, looking up into his eyes.

He glances behind us over the swell of his shoulder before pushing us harder up against the side of my building.

"Fallon, I'm gonna make so much fuckin' time for you."

The warm hand that was teasing my waistband suddenly slides up beneath my shirt and a gasp catches in my throat as he pushes it hard against my belly.

"Is it too soon to kiss you?" he asks, dipping his forehead down so that it's resting against mine.

His body is warm and hard and I can't help but submit to his welcoming enveloping. When he feels me lean exhaustedly against him a rough sound rumbles in his chest.

"Christ," he mutters. "This is way too fucking soon."

I turn around so that we're chest to chest and now he's grimacing like he's fully in pain. His hand is still up my shirt, only now it's gripping tightly into my lower back. I tentatively wrap my arms around his shoulders and he lets his hand climb higher until he's leashed his fingers into the back of my bra.

"We've known each other for a month," I whisper. "By a lot of people's standards, they'd think that we've been taking it pretty slow."

He shakes his head, staring longingly at my lips. "Don't care what other people think. I only care what you think. You hated me not two weeks ago – I don't want to go ahead making out with you and then, two days down the line, you feel that way about me again."

I bite back a small smile. His honesty makes my heart hurt.

"Hunter," I whisper, and he presses his forehead imploringly against my temple.

"Yeah?" he groans, his fingers gripping desperately at the lace of my bra.

I tilt my head back so that he can meet my eyes and I give him a secretive smile. "I don't think that I ever hated you, Hunter."

His mouth crashes down on mine with so much force that we stumble against the building, his hand immediately protecting my head from the impact. I moan, cupping my hands around his strong jaw, and he releases a deep sated sound from somewhere in the depths of his chest. He pulls his palm from underneath my jumper so that he can grip his fingers around my chin and he tilts my head further backwards so that he can take me from a different angle.

His chest is moving in big unsteady pumps when he finally pulls back to look at his handiwork.

"I'm gonna text you, Fallon," he rasps. "And you're gonna start replying."

I'm too weak to laugh properly so instead I breathe out a little wheeze.

"You wish," I mumble tauntingly, and to my delight he kisses me again.

"You're so difficult," he murmurs against me, his tone

almost adoring. Then he kisses at my cheeks, his mouth warm and soft.

"Fine, you can take me out again," I say when he pulls back, saying it like it's a treat for him.

He grins down at me with that cocky smirk of his and says, "Well, don't sound too excited about it."

"Fine, you can take me out again, *Captain*," I rectify, and his eyes go from charcoal grey to not-a-single-star-in-the-sky black.

I win this round, I think to myself smugly.

"Are you gonna let me go to sleep now?" I ask him after twenty seconds pass and he's still nuzzling into my neck, massaging his palms into my body.

I don't want him to go but I may have read one or two relationship guidebooks, and I know that you're supposed to keep a guy on his toes.

"Are you gonna post some more photos on your Instagram?" he asks hoarsely, watching his hand as he grips it around my hip.

"Why?" I tease. "You need some new material?"

His deafening silence makes my cheeks turn crimson. He doesn't meet my eyes as he finally takes his hands off me.

"Okay," I squeak, my chest pumping even faster than his. "M-maybe I'll post some more photos on my Instagram."

CHAPTER 12

Hunter

We have ten more minutes of practice before we have to vacate the ice, and Benson's absence from the stands today means that I have to play the role of Coach as well as the role of Captain. We start up a final drill of high-speed puck-passing and by the time that it's five to the hour the whole team is starting to look borderline nauseous.

"Think I've got whiplash in my head," Tanner groans before throwing up the guard on his helmet and bending at the knees.

"Four more minutes," I shout to the guys.

"I'm never complaining about Benson again," Hughes, one of our defence-men, growls after a painful sounding gag.

After two and a half more minutes of back-and-forth sprinting up and down the rink, I take a look at my crawling teammates and decide to call time.

Tanner limps over to me, trudging hard across the ice.

"Motherfucking fuck," he mumbles, tossing his helmet

down next to us. I remove my helmet too and nod at the guys as they make their way to the changing rooms.

Although Tanner is acting like he's dying I know that it's just a front for whatever shit is actually going on in his head. If I hadn't been chosen as this year's captain then Tanner would have been in the role for the second year running. He's a machine on the ice when he's not stressing over chicks.

Our roommate Caden pulls off his gloves and skates over to us, never lifting a blade from the ice. He removes his headgear and shakes out his dark spiky hair.

"You played like the fucking Terminator today," Tanner acknowledges as Caden stows his helmet under his bicep. Tanner's eyes then slide over to the one person sitting in the audience and he adds on dryly, "I wonder why."

Caden rolls his neck and snickers. "You jealous? You're lucky that I'm even wasting my time over here talking to y'all given the circumstances."

I glance over to the stands where Caden's girlfriend from home is sat, her knees tucked up under her chin. Her pink hair matches her flushed cheeks.

"I wanted to make sure that you've got the shit ready for this weekend," Tanner says, puffing out his chest as he crosses his arms in front of his pecs.

It's safe to say that Tanner is not the jealous type, but given his recent dry-spell he hasn't been on his friendliest behaviour.

"What shit do I have to get ready?" Caden asks with a grimace. "I'm not twenty-one. I can't get the alcohol."

"I'll grab it," I grunt, stepping subtly between them. Tanner is spoiling for a fight and, with his girlfriend in the stands, Caden wouldn't say no to one either.

Tanner drags a hand down his face and lets out a pissed off grumble. "I need something way stronger than alcohol."

Caden decides to risk his life. "We all know what you need. It's five-foot-four and comes with pom-poms."

Tanner's eyes burn straight into Caden's, which only makes him smirk harder. "It's not that simple, asshole. She's got a fucking boyfriend."

Caden's smile drops instantly. "Then stop chasing her, *asshole*. If she's not available, she's not available."

"What if her boyfriend's a piece of shit, Caden?" Tanner bites back.

"Going after someone who's spoken for ain't exactly saintly either, *Mason*."

The first-name name-check has Tanner's body turning to stone.

"That's it," I decide, jerking the blunt tip of my thumb towards the other side of the rink. "Five laps each, both of you."

"Training's over, *Benson*," Tanner growls at me.

"We finished early, and you're still pent up. If y'all get blood on this rink I sure as shit ain't cleaning it. Do the damn laps."

Caden drops his helmet with a loud thud and doesn't say a word as he starts skating to the goal at the other side of the ice.

"He's such an asshole," Tanner mutters, a flash of real hurt in his eyes.

I don't have a clue what's going on between Tanner, Aisling O'Malley, and the boyfriend who I know nothing about, but it's obviously driving Tanner up the wall. I haven't seen him this stressed since we came second at last year's championship final.

"Five laps," I repeat, hoping that the distraction will calm him down.

"You have to get me a shit-tonne of alcohol, though," Tanner counters.

"Where do you think I'm heading after practice?" I ask.

He makes prayer hands and then turns to do his laps.

I head to the sin bin and heave myself down.

We've smashed two away games in the past two weeks

but I would feel a hell of a lot better about the wins if I'd had someone to celebrate with.

I texted Fallon to ask to see her again but she told me that her grant application deadline had been moved forward, so she's going hell-for-leather with the essay that she has to submit for it, not to mention the fact that we're smack-dab in the middle of essay season *and* her Sundays are unavailable because I got her a damn job. Basically, her schedule is so full that she barely has a second to text me back, let alone date me, and on the one occasion that she actually picked up one of my phone calls we were only talking for three minutes before her roommate grabbed her for cheer practice.

I'm itching to get back to the locker room so that I can text her about the party that we're doing at the hockey house this Friday. Knowing that Caden has his girlfriend staying over for the whole weekend he won't be leaving his bedroom for one single minute.

Tanner finally slumps down next to me and glowers up at Caden as he makes his way past us. Caden returns the stare, equally frosty.

"We might actually kill each other on Friday," Tanner tells me, head twisted over his shoulder so that he can hurt himself further by watching Caden slide to the edge of the rink where his girlfriend has gone to meet him. Caden dips down to press his face into her neck and then he tangles his hand in her hair, crushing his mouth over hers.

"What's the deal with you and Aisling O'Malley?" I ask.

Tanner shakes his head and then drops it between his shoulders. "Fuck if I know. I just have this feeling that something isn't right with the guy she's seeing."

"Know who he is?"

Tanner shrugs. "I know he's at college but he doesn't go here, thank fuck. I don't know his name and I don't know what he looks like. Ash has no social media."

I grimace for him. Fallon's Instagram photos are the

Pinkie Promise

only things keeping my blood pumping right now.

"Whoa," Tanner says suddenly, his head jerking up. He tips his chin at the door that the guys just went through and says, "Isn't that yours?"

I glance up, and then I immediately do a double-take. Fallon is standing in the doorway to the rink wearing a baby-blue two-piece. Her blonde hair is spilling over her chest and she has a cheer ribbon pinned at the back of it.

"Jesus Christ," I murmur as I heave myself up, my eyes running down to the apex of her thighs.

"Does she always wear that stuff?" Tanner asks, his eyebrows raised as he gives her a once-over. Fallon catches my eyes, smiles, and I start skating over to her as I grunt the affirmative. "You need to give her your jersey," Tanner continues, keeping pace beside me. "Stake a claim."

"I only have one fucking jersey," I mumble, quickly shoving a hand through my sweat-soaked fringe. "Where did this idea come from that college hockey players have a billion jerseys to give to their chicks? We play D1 ice hockey, we're not stocking merch on the NHL website."

But now that the idea is in my head, Tanner's right. She needs one.

"You know what, scratch that," I say. "I'd play shirtless if Fallon would let me put her in my jersey."

Tanner smirks. "That's the spirit."

We slide to a stop in front of Fallon and I subtly gesture at Tanner to fuck off. He gives me a wry look before brushing way too firmly past Fallon.

"Put your guards on, prick," I shout to him before he damages his blades any further.

He mouths *Benson* over his shoulder. I give him my middle finger.

Then I rake my hand through my hair and look down at the angel standing in front of me.

"I was just about to text you," I admit, my voice hoarse as her eyes meet mine.

"Sorry that I've been AWOL," she says, fidgeting with the gym bag that's hooked over her small shoulder. Seeing as the last time I saw her we were making out against the wall of her condo I'm having a hard time not closing the gap between us right this second. "There's just been a lot of stuff going on lately."

I shake my head and say, "It's fine, you're a busy chick. But I had something I've been meaning to ask you."

"Oh?" she asks, smiling a little, and it's that small hopeful smile that seals the deal.

I unhook the bag from her shoulder and place it down on the ground next to her soft white trainers. The shoulder she had hitched up drops with relief and, after a glance behind me to check that Caden is still occupied, I reach forward to grab Fallon's waist and I pull her to the threshold of the rink.

She gasps the second that I get my hands on her body and satisfaction overflows like lava in my abdomen. There's a centimetre of skin peeking between her crop top and her leggings and it's softer than sin under the rough grip of my palms. I pull her forwards so that her chest is flush against my jersey and she wiggles her hips as she feels my body pressing against her.

"There's a party at mine on Friday. Tanner's idea," I say. "I need you to come, otherwise I'm not going."

Fallon laughs and, without thinking, I accidentally buck my hips against her. Not gonna lie, seeing as I've already got her pinned in place with my palms, we're standing at the perfect angle for some solid friction.

She grips her hands into the front of my jersey and her eyes flash up to mine, desperate and sparkling.

"My essays—"

"Our door's open from seven, you can come over anytime. Ten p.m., eleven p.m. – hell, you could pull up in your pyjamas at three in the morning and I ain't about to kick you out."

Pinkie Promise

She smiles and shakes her head. "Hunter."

"I want you there, Fallon. I haven't seen you in weeks." I remove one hand from her waist so that it can get lost in those curls. "Unless you're avoiding me because you've got a boyfriend who I need to murder."

She gives me a naughty look and puts on a sexy voice as she says, "Hunter, I have *so* many boyfriends."

I bite down hard on my bottom lip to stifle the *challenge-accepted* grin that wants to break free. "You better be joking," I murmur as I hook my forearm around her ass.

"What are you–?"

Before she can finish her question I heave her up against my chest and push back on my skates so that we're the only people on the rink.

"You ever skated before?" I ask, as she squeals and grips her arms tightly around my neck.

"No, I haven't! Oh God, please don't drop me, please don't drop me."

I take one look at her face and realise that I have massively fucked up.

I stop still in the centre of the rink, thanking God that Benson isn't here or he would have my fucking balls for bringing her on the ice without skates.

"Fallon, I'm sorry – look at me. Are you scared of being on the ice? I'll take you back to the edge, just keep a tight hold, okay?"

"It's not that," she says, her voice a scared whisper. "It's just… you're carrying me… and… I don't want to be dropped again."

I remain completely still, looking at Fallon's eyes that are squeezed tightly shut. I move the hand that I had in her hair so that it's cupping her flushed pink cheek and she whimpers, the crease between her eyebrows knotting deeper.

"What do you mean 'dropped again'?" I ask her slowly. She drops her forehead to my neck and doesn't respond for a full minute. I feel guilty as shit.

I slide my hand around to the back of her neck and murmur, "Fallon, I'm not gonna drop you. Do you want me to take you to the edge? Can I skate us over there?"

I caress her pulse-point and hold her more firmly against my abs.

After another thirty seconds pass she finally whispers against my skin, "Are you sure that you're not gonna drop me?"

It's been a long time since I've even slipped on the ice but accidents can happen at any time. I brace my legs and tilt her head back with my palm, looking down at her beautiful face.

"Fallon, I would never let you fall. If there's even the slightest chance that we're going down, I promise you that you'll be the one on top."

"You promise?" she asks me, and I grip one of her wrists, pulling it away from my shoulders so that it's nestled right between my pecs. I unleash my own hand from the back of her neck and then lock my pinkie tight around hers, savouring the way that her body relaxes further into mine.

"I promise."

She nods her head but I can tell that she's still nervous. I carefully push off from my position and drag her hips higher up my front.

"Wrap your legs around my waist," I instruct her, and she does what she's told, her arm still compressed securely against my chest. She flattens her palm against one of my pecs and then looks over her shoulder so that she can watch as we glide.

"I should've asked before I got you up on here," I murmur, pissed at myself.

"I'm being a little baby," she whispers back, cute and teasing, but there's a tremor in her voice that has my heart clenching painfully.

"Why'd you think that I was gonna drop you? You're a

cheerleader. Surely you–"

And then this time I pause on the ice for another reason entirely. The memory of her down on her ass as she scowled up at me in the sports building over a month ago.

If I end up getting another concussion I am seriously going to lose my shit.

"Did someone drop you?" I suddenly ask her, leaning back so that I can look deep into her eyes. "Did one of your teammates drop you?"

She tries to hide her face but I get a hold of her chin so that she has no choice but to give me that stubborn pout. "I don't want to talk about it right now," she whispers sulkily.

Someone fucking *dropped* her? That's how she got a concussion?

Wait. That's how she got *multiple* concussions?

"Fallon–"

She presses her lips to mine and the whole world instantly stops. She's warm and tiny and soft, and tasting so sweet that I groan against her mouth. I moan her name as I take us to the edge of the rink, trailing kisses down her cheek and inhaling her deeply.

"Good fuckin' distraction," I murmur against her neck and a light laugh shakes her body, a small smile in her voice.

"I'll tell you everything at your party," she whispers, and relief settles low in my body.

She's coming to my place. I'm going to see her again.

"Thank you," I murmur, both of my palms roaming upwards until I'm holding the soft mounds of her ass. I pull back with hazy eyes, looking down at her lips for another taste.

"Text me your address?" she asks as I press my mouth against hers.

"I'll pick you up," I grunt. No way am I having her bail on me.

She shakes her head. "Don't be silly, you can't ditch your own party. I'll have Ash come with me."

Damn it. I can't say no when this might help Tanner's O'Malley situation. I pull away from Fallon's lips and press a firm kiss against her temple.

"Fine, I'll text you," I rumble. "As soon as you're at the hockey house I want you to text me so that I can come find you." I think for a moment and add on, "And don't bring any of your other boyfriends."

She laughs and then does a mock-sigh. "*Fine.*"

I skate us to the opening near the exit door and settle her carefully back on regular ground. Watching her slide those long legs from their vice-grip around my abs is going to be playing on repeat while I beat one out in the shower tonight.

Not ready to stop touching her yet I grab her waist again and lean down for another kiss.

"Sorry for freaking out on the ice," she whispers.

I shake my head. "I was an asshole for bringing you on it without asking."

"No, that was cute, I swear. I would… like to learn how to skate. With you."

I shove one of my hands through my hair, loving that idea so damn much.

I also mentally add the visual of one-on-one skating lessons with Fallon to my shower playlist.

"I'll teach you," I rasp.

Fallon beams, wiggles out of my grip, and then leaves me staring after her perfect ass.

"I'll text you," I call out to her, wishing that her beautiful thighs were still wrapped around my middle.

She flashes me one more smile and then disappears through the exit.

CHAPTER 13

Fallon

Carter U's D1 'hockey house' meets every expectation that I had about it and then some. It's laid out like a traditional multiple story home, only there are multiple bedrooms on each floor, and each floor is a different 'apartment', meaning that although the team are all technically housemates, only some of them will be each other's floormates.

When we get up to the top floor, which is Hunter's level, every soon-to-be-professional athlete that I've ever seen in the college paper is either sitting, standing, or leaning in his living area. There are two dark brown sofas in the centre of the room forming an L shape around a small coffee table, plus one deep navy armchair that is currently being occupied by Tanner.

Tanner's thighs are spread wide and he's running one palm through his thick mass of hair, although the sides are trimmed so short that they look borderline military. He's as tan skinned as Hunter and the intensity of his eyes makes him look downright dangerous.

I don't know Tanner too well but his reputation precedes him and, from what I've heard, he's a bad boy through and through.

Connell kindly offered to be the designated driver for Ash and me tonight, and when I peek over to the left into Hunter's open-plan kitchen I see that the entirety of Connell's football team is already here too.

"Your boyfriend is a hotshot," Aisling whispers to me, worming her way between Connell and one of his friends so that she can grab a bottle opener from the kitchen counter. Being the It Girl that she is, Ash brought two bottles of champagne with her as a kind of *thanks for the invite* party favour.

"He's not technically my boyfriend," I say to her, laughing when she gives me an over-exaggerated *yeah yeah* kind of wink. Connell is watching us with sharp eyes but his expression softens into a smile when he sees me looking.

"Here, let me," he says, offering his hand out to Aisling so that he can pop the top off the bottle for her. His entire team cheers when the cork goes flying and he flashes them a handsome smile before handing the champagne back to his sister.

Ignoring the hungry stares from Connell's teammates, Ash takes a pull straight from the bottle and we walk back into the living area.

Instinctively her eyes find Tanner in his splayed position on the armchair and she pauses for a second before rolling her eyes. Although this time I think that it's more to do with the fact that Whitney, my replacement top-of-the-pyramid cheer flyer, is sat squished up beside him with her legs draped over his lap. She's talking animatedly and waving a red Solo cup around but Tanner's eyes are on us, his expression one of shock and horror.

I get a look at Aisling's expression and immediately begin pushing her in the direction of the balcony to get her as far away from Tanner as possible, but Tanner has already shoved himself out of the armchair and is storming our way.

Tanner jumps over a small living room cabinet and I squeak in fear as he broaches the distance towards us before I can lock us both outside. His fingers grip the handle on the other side of the balcony door and I stare at him wide-eyed, not sure what to do next.

Ash is busy sipping champagne and ignoring Tanner, and Tanner's eyes are flicking wildly between the two of us.

"I wanna talk to her," he calls to me from the other side of the glass.

Aisling lets out a tiny huff.

A new song starts up on the speakers inside of the apartment and it sounds soft and muffled through the planes of the door.

"Move out of the way, Fallon. I'm opening this door and I don't wanna hurt you."

I've had enough door related injuries for one year so I release my fingers from the handle and Tanner immediately eases it open. As soon as he's outside he stares down at me for one heavy moment. Aisling is sizzling with energy and I can feel it heating up my shoulders.

"I'll take it from here," Tanner says, eyes sliding over my head so that he can look at my roommate.

Aisling rolls her eyes. "Leave me alone, Viking, or I'll pour champagne all over you."

A tender look touches his eyes, as if he'd love to be drenched in champagne at the hand of Aisling, and he steps around me.

The balcony door is still open and I take a tentative step backwards, closer to the interior of the house. I'm not one hundred percent sure what's going on between Ash and Tanner, but whatever it is feels too private for me to witness. Since Aisling isn't asking me to stay I feel like it's my cue to leave. I'm about to take another quiet step back into the living area when I suddenly feel a solid mass behind me and two big forearms envelop my exposed clavicle.

"You came," Hunter murmurs, a smile in his voice as he kisses my cheek.

His large chest is pressing heavily into my back and his pumped muscles feel swollen and warm. Actually, he's *too* warm – warmer than someone would typically feel through their clothing.

I spin around in his arms and find myself face to face with his naked torso.

"Oh," I squeak, my strength immediately draining from my body. His skin is richly tanned, as if he's spent the past seven summers working shirtless outside, and he's glistening with water droplets as if he's been sweating it up all night. His large hockey-player pecs are heaving right in front of me, and there's a sexy trail of hair leading down his muscled naval. It disappears tauntingly beneath the band of his grey joggers.

"Just got out of the shower," he says, running a hand through his hair. "Hope I didn't keep you waiting."

I shake my head, speechless, and he whips the towel from around his neck so that he can leash it around my lower back, yanking me towards him so that my chest is flush against his. He smirks as he walks us backwards, pulling me away from the darkness of the tiny balcony and into the warm glow of the loud apartment.

I can't help but notice Whitney staring intently through the balcony door.

"You want a drink?" Hunter asks, pulling my focus back up to his beautiful face. His eyes are slowly raking down my outfit as he murmurs, "You look so beautiful."

I feel my neck flush and Hunter swipes his tongue over his lower lip.

"Let's go to my room," he murmurs, dropping the towel from behind my back and tossing it into a deserted corner. His hands take my waist and he gives me a firm squeeze.

"You didn't bring any of your other boyfriends did you?" he asks teasingly.

"Oh, I forgot that I wasn't supposed to, sorry," I say, biting back a smile of my own.

He grunts and squeezes me harder. "Damn baby. I'll forgive you, but only because I know you wore this outfit for me."

In the next second my behind hits off something hard. I twist slightly and realise that Hunter has walked us to his bedroom door, one hand leaving my waist so that he can click the handle open. He presses into me with his bare chest and I stumble backwards, his palm keeping me steady.

"Wasn't sure that you would come," he murmurs as he closes the door behind us, before sliding both hands gently around the sides of my throat. "Thought you might be busy."

"With my boyfriends," I say, and he gives me that smug masculine grin of his.

"Yeah," he grunts, hunching down so that he can press his face into the warm hollow at the base of my throat. He takes a deep inhale and groans, "Fallon, you smell so good."

Feeling a little faint, I press one of my wrists against my forehead. "That's what all of my boyfriends say to me," I whisper, and his deep chuckle reverberates into my chest. I cautiously weave the fingers of my other hand through his thick dark hair and a low sound leaves his throat, encouraging me to tug at him even harder.

"I love your smart mouth," he murmurs, kissing up the side of my throat and over the rosy surface of my cheek.

"Thank you," I whisper back to him.

He smiles down at me and then kisses the tip of my nose.

I wait for him to kiss my mouth but he just continues looking down at me like he's waiting for something.

Suddenly I remember that when I last saw him at the rink I had told him that I would explain my extremely inconvenient long string of trauma to him, and the thought of that makes me groan loudly. I press my head into his chest and give him a little thump on the bicep.

He's going to make me earn this kiss, I think to myself. *He's trying to build trust between us.*

He strokes tenderly at the back of my hair, as if he can tell that I've come to this realisation.

I kick off my shoes, catching Hunter's attention, and he leans down for a moment so that he can stand them neatly beside his door.

Such a cutie, I think to myself as he stands upright again.

"You're going to want to sit down for this shit-show," I mumble against him, and two seconds later I'm flat on my back on top of his dark comforter. He eases his hips between my thighs and holds his body over mine. His forearms are pinned on either side of my head and his pupils have dialled out into total blackness.

"Or we could just lie down like this," I choke out. "Th-this also works."

He presses his solid chest down against my breasts and my eyes roll into the back of my head.

"Start talkin'," he demands, his gaze still burning into mine.

"The reason why I was freaking out on the ice," I whisper, as the heat from his chest begins burning its way down to my core. "The reason why I'm a little on edge these days... For the past three years at Carter U I've been the star flyer for the cheer team," I tell him, closing my eyes so that I can actually focus on what I'm saying, instead of his giant sexy shoulders. "I've been the cheerleader who's at the top of the centre pyramid. You get thrown around a lot because you're flexible and lightweight, but the girls underneath you are supposed to be able to catch you."

I shake my head slightly and press my thumb firmly between my eyebrows.

"Some of the girls who used to be on the comp team

graduated last summer so we needed some new girls to take on their positions and… one of the girls that got picked kind of *has* to be on the team because… it doesn't even matter. Long story short? She's a freshman who couldn't hold me up, and she ended up dropping me so many times that I ended up getting a concussion. Twice."

I open my eyes and see that Hunter's body has stilled entirely.

"Obviously, concussions aren't amazing for your health because they can have potentially lasting negative effects. Carter U doesn't want a legal nightmare or, you know, a dead cheerleader, so I was benched from the team to prevent 'further incidents'."

Hunter's eyebrows crease in the middle and he pulls a slightly pained expression as he moves one hand to caress over my hip.

"Baby," he murmurs, before pressing a kiss to my cheek. I wrap my arms around the back of his neck and clutch him tight, having never felt this kind of unconditional sympathy before. "Baby, that isn't fair. You shouldn't be the one getting benched. Why the hell would they keep that other chick on your squad?"

I swallow thickly and whisper, "If I tell you, you can't tell anyone."

He lifts his body and nods, his palm roaming up to massage my ribcage.

"She's the daughter of Carter U's president," I whisper, and he closes his eyes as if he instantly understands the predicament. "But because I'm no longer on the team it means that the sport scholarship I thought I'd get for my Master's is obviously no longer on the cards for me, which is why I'm busting my ass off for a grant from my department. Only the deadline moved up and my referee isn't getting back in touch with me, so who the hell knows if I'm actually going to be able to get it."

I try to just laugh it off but Hunter's serious expression

shows me that he isn't buying my faux amusement for one second.

He clears his throat and rumbles, "I have some ideas that could help."

I quickly look away from him, pretending to ignore that statement completely.

"It's my responsibility," I say in as strong a voice as I can manage. "I can't… ask for help. It's not how I was raised."

He frowns deeply and then wraps both of his forearms behind my neck. My head lolls backwards and his eyes drop to my throat.

"Where's all of this 'responsibility' stuff coming from?" he asks me quietly, before pressing his warm mouth against my neck. An unplanned whimper escapes my throat and he grunts so hard that I have to clench my thighs.

"This isn't the time," I whisper.

"Good a time as any," he replies, lifting himself up onto one elbow so that his bicep is brushing against my cheek.

"I hate talking about bad stuff," I admit. "I want to only talk about nice stuff when I'm with you."

He smiles warmly and his eyes crinkle at the corners. "Jesus, you're cute. But I can handle it, Fallon."

"Another time," I insist. "I do have some kind of good news too though."

He grins. "Hit me."

I smack his left pec and he smirks down at me.

"You know what I meant, bad girl," he murmurs, stroking one of his hands firmly down my back until he's tightly gripping a handful of my ass. Something hard suddenly flexes against my belly.

"So I'm not allowed to do the actual competitions with the cheer team anymore, and I can't get a sports grant for next year either," I reiterate, "but I can still do… like, the stuff that isn't legit. The stuff that's just for fun, I mean. There's a whole separate squad for, uh, college events and things? And Aisling told me about one that I might be the perfect flyer for… if I can get over the whole *I'm scared because I had two concussions* thing by the time that it rolls around."

I'm being vague deliberately but Hunter seems to be following well enough.

"So I'm gonna get to see you perform?" he asks. His eyes move down over my belly and the hand on my behind grips harder.

I swallow hard, not knowing the answer to that question just yet. "I haven't done any lifts since concussion number two, and I've been too nervous to do any practice that wasn't just a one-on-one with Ash. Plus I need to convince myself that I'm not going to fall again. I think… I think that I'm going to stay at the condo over Christmas break to train, although I'm not sure if it'll be any use seeing as I'll be doing it all on my own anyway."

"I'll train with you."

His words come instantaneously.

"I'm sorry, what?" I ask him, completely disbelieving what I just heard.

"I'll train with you," he repeats. "I'll stay over during the winter break so that you're ready for the next semester."

I blink up at him, confused. "But you don't know the routines."

He laughs out loud and rolls off my body, onto his back. I immediately want him back on top of me, the weight and the heat of him a comforting shield that I previously didn't realise I couldn't live without.

"I ain't doing the routines," he says, grinning down at me. "I'll just be on hand so that when you have to do your lifts and jumps there'll be someone there to practice the positions with. The cheer positions," he adds on quickly, his cheeks suddenly flushing. "You know what I mean."

I roll onto my side so that I can look up at his face. His profile is unbelievably handsome, his jaw strong and his skin tanned. I think that the perfect way to describe him would be 'rough-around-the-edges hot'. He has long black eyelashes and a masculine shadow of stubble, as if he's recently shaved but it's already growing back.

I let my eyes wander over the huge swells of his pecs and I have the most curious urge to tease his nipple with the tip of my tongue.

I've never been this close, physically or emotionally, with a man before, and, ironically, we haven't even done anything yet. I test the waters by snuggling my face against his bicep. He instantly lifts his arm up over my head and slides it around me, crushing me against his chest.

I can't resist. I give his nipple the tiniest flick with my tongue and he throws his free hand over his eyes, laughing and groaning at the same time.

"Are we going back outside to party with all of your tall attractive friends, or can we kiss properly now?" I mumble against his pec.

"Tall attractive friends?" he repeats, dropping the hand from his face so that he can stare down at me. "Which one do you like? Who do I have to kill?"

He rolls onto his side so that now I'm staring directly into the cavern between his pecs, and they're large and firm and smell divine. He tangles his fingers up in my hair and rubs his other hand over my hip.

"I need to tell you something," he says to me, tilting my head backwards so that he can stare down into my eyes. "After you, you know, say yes to me helping you out with your cheer stuff."

I give him one of my rare small smiles and it makes him pull me tighter against him.

"No way are you going to follow through on that," I say to him, "but it's the thought that counts so, theoretically, I say yes."

His frown is so deep that it makes my smile waver. "Fallon, of course I'll follow through. I'm not making you promises with the intentions of breaking them." He presses a kiss to my forehead and then another to my cheek. "You can trust me, I'm gonna prove it to you. I'm gonna help you all winter long."

I don't want to let myself believe him but the hurt in his eyes looks painfully sincere.

"Okay," I whisper. "I'm sorry, yes, okay."

"No apologising," he murmurs, pulling my body higher against his chest. "I'm glad you said yes, but no apologising anymore, okay?"

My palms slide up his pecs and his breathing turns shallow, his chest rising and falling in quickening pumps.

"I need… I need to tell you…" he says again, but then we're closing the space between us and he crushes his mouth on mine.

His touch is warm and firm, and I moan with relief as soon as he kisses me. The large hand in my hair travels down to grip my jaw and the palm on my hip skirts dangerously around the hem of my dress.

"I think about this every night," he murmurs, pulling back slightly so that he can watch me stroke at his chest.

"Your body's so big," I whisper, as my fingertips rub up the length of his happy trail.

"Fuck," he grunts, and suddenly he's rolling me onto my back. He grabs my hand with one of his and leashes it around to the back of his neck. "Don't do that, baby. We're just making out tonight. Touching me there makes me wanna do stuff with you."

He dips his mouth back to mine and presses my body harder into the mattress. I stroke my fingers into his hair and he moves one of his hands to my inner thigh. I gasp in shock, and the parting of my lips is all that Hunter needs. He eases me wide open and slides his tongue inside my mouth.

My hips squirm wildly beneath the soft cotton of his joggers and he grunts hard as he shoves my dress up to my belly. He rolls his groin against mine, making my brain blackout completely, and he rubs his tongue in long hot strokes against my own.

"Fuck, that's good, baby," he grunts, pulling away and cupping my cheek. "Can I keep doing that?" he asks. "Can I keep kissing you like this?"

"Please," I whisper, pulling him back down to me with weak arms. He releases a gruff satisfied sound as soon as he's kissing me again and my body splays bonelessly against his soft dark comforter. He slides his tongue back inside my mouth and lets out a long low groan, before he begins rubbing me so fast that I feel the pressure in my belly. His hips grind slow and hard between my legs, his bare chest occasionally brushing painfully over my aching nipples.

The long muscle in his joggers jerks hard against my heat and he groans into my neck, his breathing erratic. "Didn't mean to do that. Not wearing boxers."

I squeeze my eyes shut and whisper, "I can tell."

"Sorry," he murmurs before pressing a series of slower kisses against my lips. He licks at my tongue gently, his back muscles rolling in time with his hips.

"Hunter," I gasp, as his fingers suddenly grip at the curves of my chest.

"Yeah," he says hoarsely, eyes on his hand as it rubs a careful circle over me. He squeezes slightly and I stifle a sob.

"We need to stop," I whisper. "Someone could come in here."

He glances in a daze over to his door and then shoves his hand through his hair, panting hard. "Sorry," he says again, dropping his entire bodyweight on top of me. He presses a hard kiss against my temple as he tries to calm down his breathing.

"I don't think I'm ready to... I want to, but I'm not ready yet," I admit, feeling a little embarrassed.

His breathing is heavy as he holds me firmly against his

chest. "Didn't mean to make you think that I was tryin' to fuck you," he says quietly, groaning in anguish when his length jerks against me again. "I know we ain't there yet." He thinks for a moment and then adds, "Fuck, I don't even have condoms."

He rolls over onto his back and brings me along for the ride. I end up straddling his groin while my breasts remain compressed against his abdomen. He strokes one palm down to my ass and gives my cheek a rough slap.

"It's hard to take it slow when I've got you on my sheets is all."

He pulls me up his body and then cups his hands around my face.

The action is so sweet that I let out a happy laugh and Hunter does a half sit-up so that he can kiss me.

"You ever had a boyfriend?" he asks, stroking at my jaw. When I shake my head he grins and says, "You want one?"

I laugh as if he's teasing me, before gripping my fingers into his pecs for push-up leverage. He groans when my nails dig into him and it's such a beautiful sound that I decide to dig them in even harder.

"*Ugh*, yeah, keep doing that," he grunts, closing his eyes briefly as he shoves my hips down onto his lap, pressing me forcefully against his rigid cock. His mouth is set into a sexual sneer, his chest pumping hard. "Don't know if you can tell," he murmurs, "but I swear to God I could… I could finish just from this."

My thighs squeeze and Hunter sits up so that he can look down at me. He gives me a slow but firm kiss and warmth spreads deep in my belly.

"What were you going to tell me?" I ask him when he finally pulls away.

He tucks a curl behind my ear and drops his eyes to my waist. He encircles it with one of his hands and gives it a gentle squeeze as he shakes his head.

"Doesn't matter, I'll tell you another time." He leans

into my neck and presses a kiss to my skin. "Don't know if I already said it but you're the prettiest thing that I've ever seen."

I hide my smile against his soft dishevelled hair. "It's just the dress."

"It's the girl in the dress," he grunts. Then he says, "It's a short dress though. Aren't these thighs gonna get cold?"

I shudder as he slides his large warm palms up my arms. "We had the heating on in the car," I whisper, as he tangles his fingers in the flimsy straps of my lilac dress.

"You came in the car?" he asks quietly, as he kisses along my collarbone. "But I thought you didn't…" He pauses for a moment before lifting his head. Looking down at me he says, "Who drove you here tonight?"

It's at that moment that there's a loud knock on Hunter's door.

Immediately my eyes flash over to it and I whisper, "Did you lock that?"

Hunter looks down at me, conflicting emotions burning in his irises, and then his bedroom door swings open, Connell standing with his arms crossed in the doorway.

"Oh," Connell says casually, the music from the living area blasting loudly. He scratches at the back of his head and looks awkwardly away from the way that Hunter is holding me against his body. "Sorry. I just didn't know where else to find you. Uh, Ash is pissed and wants to go to a different party so… unless you were gonna, uh, stay here tonight…"

We remain speechless for a few long moments until, eventually, Hunter turns his head away from Connell.

"I'm sorry," I say quietly, although I'm not sure who I'm saying it to. "I'll just–"

I slowly lift up so that I can leave Hunter's lap, but the second that I begin to move he cups my cheeks in his large hands. In a strained voice he murmurs, "You brought Connell?"

"Connell brought Fallon," Connell says dryly from the doorway. I don't think that he means to sound as glib as he does, but I still shoot him a frosty look that makes him breathe a laugh and shake his head.

"Connell," I say, my voice shaking a little. "I'll meet you in a minute. Can you please close the door for a sec?"

He inhales and nods, his eyes locked in with Hunter's. Hunter gives him an emotionless glance, his eyes dark and blank.

When the door clicks shut I wring my hands in my lap. "Okay, this looks bad, but I promise it isn't what it looks like."

Hunter watches my hands, his cheeks burning crimson. "It's okay, Fallon, I get it. You're a beautiful girl."

Oh God, he actually thinks that I'm two-timing him.

"No no no," I say quickly, "Connell is my best friend's brother. He's DDing for us." I press my fingers into my temples and then mumble, "I should never have teased you with the '*all my hot boyfriends*' thing. You're going to think that I was being serious but I was just trying to be funny."

Humour, I have learned, is a very subjective thing.

Hunter's eyes briefly catch mine before he looks down again.

"Are you saying…" His voice is rough and he pauses to try and clear it. If anything, it just gets rougher. "Are you saying that you… aren't dating Connell? That I'm the only guy you're seeing?"

I nod adamantly.

He looks back at his comforter, to where I was lying beneath him only five minutes ago.

"Hunter," I say, closing my eyes. "I know that you think that I'm some sort of minxy cheerleader who has five billion guys blowing up her phone but…"

I open my eyes and he's watching me longingly.

I put my hand on my heart and whisper, "It really pains me to admit this but… I am a huge freaking nerd."

His expression changes completely. There's a new sparkle in his eyes, an almost-smile on his mouth. Then he shakes his head like I'm joking and says, "Sure. Right."

"Hunter."

I cup his stubble-coated jaw and he grunts involuntarily.

"I'm being serious, Hunter. Believe me when I say that I wouldn't lie to you about this. When you next come over to the condo I…" I shake my head and sigh. "I'll show you my Baby Yoda coffee mug collection."

Hunter laughs and shoves a hand through his hair, his heated eyes raking over me wildly.

"A cheerleader nerd?" he rasps, like I've just enunciated his deepest fantasy. "Tell me that you're not kidding," he says as he meets my eyes again.

"I don't lie when it comes to Baby Yoda," I whisper to him honestly.

He grins in relief and kisses me hard, a low sound vibrating through his chest as if his whole body is aching.

"Sometimes I wear glasses," I admit when he pulls away, and he drops his forehead to my shoulder, groaning like I'm torturing him.

"I really like you, Fallon," he says quietly, when we finally stand from his bed, holding me steady as I slide my feet back into my high heels.

Then I rise up onto my tip-toes and Hunter instantly leans down, meeting me in the middle for a small chaste kiss.

I'm too shy to say the words but it doesn't matter because he feels them anyway as he touches my lips with his.

I really like you too, Hunter.

CHAPTER 14

Hunter

"You coming to my away game at the end of the month?" I ask my brother Colton as he slides out from under the body of the car. He wipes the sweat from under his fringe with the back of his forearm, leaving a big black grease stain there in its wake.

I smirk and throw a hand cloth down at him.

He tosses it back as I shut the hood of the truck that we're working on.

"Got my own," he says, heaving himself into a sitting position before pulling a cloth out of the back pocket of his jeans. He swipes it roughly over his sullen face, then he picks up his phone, resting horizontally on the stool, and he selects a different song from his playlist.

I tap a finger against the spacebar on my dad's work computer, making it whir back to life, and then I open a spreadsheet to mark down which fixtures we just used.

"Mom and Dad ain't letting me," Colt finally grumbles, sitting in a hunched position while straddling the crawler board. He picks up his water bottle and drains the last few drops.

"Why ain't they letting you? Is it a money thing?" I ask as I finish my type-up.

"It's a me-being-in-high-school thing, and they're too busy to chaperone," he replies, reddening a little before tossing the bottle across the room into the trash.

"Good throw," I grunt.

He drops his head to hide his smile. "Thanks."

This is another reason why I've decided to go pro. If I'm playing NHL games that are aired on the regular then maybe my family will be able to finally watch one of them.

"Sorry," he says, his eyes on his beat-up sneakers.

"It's fine. When I get the date for our next home game, I'll save you a ticket."

"You don't have to do that."

"Why not? Hey, I could get you a plus one," I add with a grin, and his eyes fly up to mine.

He chokes before he can get the words out. "Why would you do that?" he croaks.

I smirk at him and he hides his face in his hands.

"What? Am I not supposed to know about the fact that you climb through the window of the chick next door's bedroom at night?"

His jaw drops as he stares up at me. "How the hell d'you know about that?" he rasps.

"Because mom has fucking ears, Colt," I say, laughing at his expression.

"Mom *knows*?" he asks despairingly. "We ain't doing anything in her room, I *swear*. We just, you know..." He trails off his sentence, looking away from me and swiping his tongue over his lower lip.

I could confidently bet my last five pay cheques on what Colt's been doing, or at least what he wants to be doing, but it's good to hear that he isn't doing the type of 'anything' that I know he would definitely tell me about.

"You being nice to her?" I ask him, folding my arms over my chest.

"What kinda question's that?" he says, looking up at me with a horrified expression. "Of course I'm being nice to her. Why wouldn't I be nice to her?" He thinks for a moment and then shoots up to his feet. "Did someone say I wasn't being nice? Tell me who said it."

Such a good kid. "No one's said anything," I reassure him. "Just wanted to make sure."

He gives me a cautious prolonged frown before letting out a deep breath and nodding to himself. "What about you?" he asks, kicking at a rogue piece of gravel from one of the tires. "You got anyone?"

Colton hardly ever asks me stuff like this and it makes me want to rough up his hair like he's seven years old. It's also the first time in my life that I can finally answer him with a, "Maybe."

He glances up at me with big bright eyes. "For real?" he asks. "You've got a chick?"

I snicker at his phrasing and then drop the eye contact, because now it's my turn to feel a little nervous. I haul one of the car's replacement tires off the far work bench and bring it over to the vehicle, just for something to do with my hands.

"There's, uh… there's someone I like," I say gruffly, keeping it vague. As if she didn't come over to our party last night and end up in my bedroom on her back. The memory of her opening up for me like she did, trusting me with what she's been going through, makes the tire in my hands feel fucking weightless.

"What's she look like?" he asks.

I smile, then try to scrub the happiness off of my cheeks. "Uh, blonde hair, big eyes." I rake a hand through my fringe and say, "She's kinda small."

Colton mulls that over and then asks, "How small are we talking here?"

Now I'm really laughing. I shove him in a headlock to diffuse the growing fuzzy feelings.

"Show me a picture," he grunts, his voice muffled against my forearms.

"Hell no," I reply as he rams his elbows into the meat of my abs. "I ain't sharing."

"You aren't sharing what?" A girlish voice sounds from behind us and we both whip around.

"Who the—"

I shove my hand over Colt's mouth as Fallon gives me a shy smile from the doorway.

"Sorry," she says, shaking her head and making her curls bounce. "It was weird of me to stop by without texting. I, uh, I brought you a coffee though?" She raises a paper to-go cup and I feel a painful constriction in my chest.

I give Colton a warning glance before I remove my hand from his face.

I walk over to Fallon while simultaneously jerking my chin, telling her to get her ass in here instead of waiting out there in the doorway. She takes a couple of tentative steps into the shop, eyeing Colton curiously around the swell of my bicep.

I hook my thumb over my shoulder towards him and say, "My brother, Colton. Want me to introduce you?"

She looks up at me with surprised wide eyes, shaking her head. "Oh no, I wouldn't ask you to do that, I'm not your girlfr—"

"Colton, this is Fallon. Fallon, that's Colton," I growl.

I hear Colton mumble a deep *hello* behind me.

"What aren't you sharing?" Fallon repeats, an amused sparkle in her eyes. I set down the coffee that she brought and then begin furiously wiping the grease off of my fingers.

"Uh, Colt wanted to see a photo of you," I admit when I hear the backdoor quietly click shut. I twist my head over my shoulder to see that Colton has given us some privacy.

Fucking angel child. I turn back to Fallon and scrub at my brow as I say, "My hands are too dirty to touch you right now, baby."

She blushes and says, "Why'd you think I wore dark colours today, Hunter?"

I drop my hand and look down at her, awestruck by her foresight. She's wearing dark jeans and a deep purple knit sweater, her hands retreating up the sleeves so that I can't watch her fingers twiddle.

"You serious?" I ask her, damn near twitching with need.

She nods and tentatively reaches one hand towards my belt buckle. My jaw turns slack as I watch her trace the ridge, my chest rising in quick pumps as her fingers slide up my dirty white vest.

"This looks really good on you," she whispers, smiling as her fingers explore my abdomen. "So this is what you do when you aren't playing hockey."

I swallow thickly. "This is actually a first," I rasp as she strokes her fingertips up over my pecs. Colton's music is still blasting from his cell and I take a deep breath to try and subdue my sudden testosterone overload.

"I came to apologise for last night – for unloading on you like that, and for the whole Connell thing. I feel like I come across as hot and cold sometimes and it's probably because I, uh… I don't have a lot of experience mixing with other people." She drops her hand and laughs nervously. "Which is probably obvious, seeing as I'm basically molesting you right now."

I grab her hips and pull her flush against me. She looks up at me with an anxious expression, gnawing on her sexy bottom lip.

"You hear me complaining?" I ask her.

She shakes her head at me.

"Then don't stop."

I find her hand and press it firmly back on my chest,

loving the way that her body relaxes as soon as she's touching me.

"You don't need to apologise for last night. My only complaint is that I couldn't keep you for longer."

Fallon scrunches up her nose and tries to hide her pretty smile.

"How'd you know where to find me today?" I ask her. "Did Tanner tell you?"

She gives me a guilty little look and I breathe out a laugh.

"Baby, why're you always looking so guilty for? I'm grateful that you're here."

The giant muscle that I've got pressing up against her belly is making that pretty fucking obvious.

"If you'd told me last night that you wanted to come by, I'd have picked you up this morning and given you a ride." I rub my thumb over her hand on my chest and say, "I like having you around."

I know that Fallon being here doesn't count as a date, but having her in front of me right now is making me wanna do things that I have no control over.

I walk her backwards a few steps until we reach the office desk, and then I press my groin into her slightly, encouraging her to sit back up on the counter. The song on Colton's phone finishes playing so our heavy breathing is now the only sound in the room.

I hear rustling from outside and squint briefly out of the window, taking stock of the thick grey clouds that haven't yet began their winter unloading.

"It's gonna storm soon," I murmur, swiping my tongue over my bottom lip. I turn to look down at her and I press my palms into the tops of her thighs. "You used to that kinda thing?"

She nods vehemently. "I'm from Colorado," she says, her voice light and breathless. "Did I never mention that? I'm not too far from here really."

Pinkie Promise

I raise my eyebrows because I didn't know that. "I fucking love Colorado," I tell her. "You know the winters here are just as heavy right?"

"Yeah, the past few that I spent here have been pretty solid. I haven't been snowed-in here yet though," she laughs.

Growing up we got snowed-in plenty, and I don't know how to feel about Fallon being in that situation over in Colorado. Winter at Carter Ridge technically should have started by now and, if the past years are anything to go by, the delay is only going to make it come harder.

"What'd you do during the other winters that you spent here?" I ask, gently easing her thighs open and pressing myself against her lap.

She looks a little embarrassed when she says, "I stayed in the condo with Ash when the weather got really bad. Or, if she was over at her boyfriend's, I'd just wait it out alone." She shrugs. "Some of our classes were online for like a month."

I make a low sound in the back of my throat, not exactly loving the idea of her trapped in the condo on her own for weeks on end. Before I can hone in on that too heavy she suddenly asks, "What did you do after I left last night?"

After Fallon left the apartment last night I locked myself in my bedroom and beat my meat while I could still feel her on my sheets. But I decide to bypass that part and just tell her, "Ended up watching a couple of games with the guys. Then some of the team hit up a club."

"You didn't go with them?"

"No," I say, tangling my fingers into her hair.

"Why not?" she asks.

"Because I knew that you weren't going to be there."

She looks deep into my eyes. She's so pretty that I look away.

"Did you mean what you said last night?" she asks, her voice nervous. "About training with me so that I can get back into cheer?"

"Baby, of course I meant it. I'd do anything you wanted me to."

She lets out a shaky breath and my eyes drop hungrily to her lips.

"Have you ever seen any of my performances before?" she asks.

"No," I say gruffly. Guessing that my dreams don't count.

"Okay," she says, nodding to herself. "We can still make it work. The solo bits before you pick me up might be a bit boring for you to watch, so thank you for agreeing to it," she adds.

I scrub roughly at my forehead. "It's, uh, definitely not going to be boring for me," I assure her.

She lets out a cute laugh and says, "When I train I have to do the same positions so many times, you might honestly want to bring your coursework with you."

"Fallon, I'm not going to be able to focus on coursework, rest fucking assured."

She suddenly realises that I'm practically panting and she leans slightly farther backwards on the desk, biting at her smile because she can sense how hot I am for her. I lean right over her and pull her chest up to meet mine.

"You got some essays that you're gonna leave me for in about three minutes?" I ask her, knowing that, with her schedule being so tight, there's no way that I'll be able to keep her here with me for the rest of my shift.

I can physically feel her stressing about the grant that she's been telling me about, so I dip my face to her jaw to try and kiss the tension away.

"I can give you five minutes," she says breathlessly, and when I lean up to look down at her I see that she's smiling. I stroke my hand through her hair and she wraps her arms tighter around my neck.

I need to get her on another date so that I can have her

for a longer period of time, but I choose to stow that agenda away for the moment, grateful that I'm seeing her at all in the first place.

"Can I kiss you?" I ask, moving the coffee cup out of the spill zone.

"The way you did last night?" she replies, gripping her fingers into my hair.

My hands slide right up the hem of her sweater and I'm immediately met with two soft handfuls of naked flesh. I roam my palms a little higher, until I'm massaging my fingers into her waist, confused as hell over whether or not she's actually got anything on underneath her jumper. I'm dying to shove my hands just a little higher, to confirm whether or not she's totally bare.

"Yeah. You liked that?" I ask, thinking about how last night was the first time that I'd slid my tongue inside her mouth.

She squeezes her thighs around my hips and murmurs a little, "Yeah."

She doesn't need to tell me twice. I pull her body to the edge of the counter and hunch down so that I can take her mouth with mine, this time slanting her open immediately and slipping my tongue deep inside. She lets out a quiet moan and I stroke her harder, grunting. I roam my palms up her ribcage, drinking in her shallow whimpers, and when I get my hands on those soft full breasts I growl like a motherfucker.

Bare. She's fucking bare.

"Knew it," I say gruffly, pushing my tongue back inside her mouth and rubbing her nice and hard. She whimpers, loving it, making me smirk as I palm her tits.

I give her a couple more strokes of tongue before pulling back to look at her on the counter. Her jumper is covering my hands, so I can't see myself as I work her, and I press my face into her neck when I realise that she's going to have car grease all over her breasts.

"I wanted you to touch me like this last night," she whispers shyly, making my damn temples throb. I lick a thick hot stripe up the sweet curve of her throat.

"Wanted me to touch your tits, like this, in my bed?" I laugh in disbelief, shaking my head. "Wouldn't have been able to stop."

"Maybe I wouldn't have wanted you to."

"Don't have any condoms," I remind her.

"Maybe I wouldn't have w–"

I crash my mouth back down on hers, claiming her lips on a possessive grunt. I give her breasts a domineering squeeze before rasping, "You on the pill?"

The red-cheeked look that she gives me tells me *no* without any damn words.

"Fuck." I drop my hands from under her jumper so that I can cup her delicate jaw and start giving her some kisses that aren't fucking unhinged.

I kiss her gentle and sweet, groaning when she rubs her chest up against mine.

"That's real nice," I murmur, shifting my belt buckle a good few inches to the side. Then I inhale a chest-swelling breath and tear my eyes away from her, steadying her by the hips so that we can cool off before she leaves.

I look unseeingly out at the front of the shop, grateful for the miserable weather because it means that no-one's on the streets. Although we're obscured in the office nook I feel guilty as shit that anyone could have walked in here right now and seen Fallon in this position.

I swallow hard and say, "Sorry, I lose my mind when I'm with you. I… I've never been like this before."

Fallon's fingertip traces a pattern over the swell of my pecs and I look down to watch her. "Me neither," she says on a frown. She doesn't seem too pleased by her emotions and the thought that she might want to fight this scares the hell out of me.

We both hear the door at the back click quietly open

and I turn around to see Colton enter the shop. His eyes are boring holes into the ground because he can sense that there's still a pretty chick in the room.

He glances up for half a second, just to make sure, and when he sees Fallon's knees hitched tight around my hips his tan face turns bright red, and he pretends to do something over on the far bench.

"He looks like you," Fallon whispers, making me smile as I look down at her. "Is that why he's your favourite?"

Now I'm really grinning. "You think I'm that shallow?"

In a moment of playful confidence Fallon fluffs up her hair and says, "Well, you are seeing me aren't you?"

I smirk and press a hard kiss to her lips. Having her acknowledge that what we're doing here is *actually* happening is the confirmation that I've been needing. I might actually be able to get some sleep tonight.

"Damn right I am," I murmur as I help her down from the desk, and then I turn her around so that her back is to my front. She leads the way to the front of the garage and tugs my arms tightly around her waist.

It's not quite blowing a gale but the weather isn't pretty so I grab my jacket from the wall and shove it over her shoulders when we reach the entrance.

She laughs and tries to shrug it off. I end up zipping her into it without even getting her arms into the sleeves. I pull the hood up over her head and the wind knocks it straight off.

She manages to wiggle her arms into place and I bite my lip as I take in the sight of her. If Colton wasn't already scarred for life on the other side of the garage I would have tugged her into me again so that I could give her a couple more kisses.

"Looks good," I grunt. "Can I give you a lift back to the condo?"

"You're busy, it's fine."

"Colton can hold the fort," I tell her but she's already

back-stepping so quickly that I have to grab her and pull her back to me. I give her hips a squeeze and she shudders lightly. "Text me when you're home?"

She pauses briefly on the word 'home' but then she relaxes and finally nods. I grip her jaw in one of my hands and press a kiss against her lips.

"I'll call you tonight and we can work out a training schedule, okay?"

She does a cute shrug. "Sure. Maybe I should send you a video of one of my past training sessions so that you'll have some idea of what I'll want you to be doing with me."

I shove my tongue in my cheek and nod.

She's going to send me videos of her cheer training sessions? Sweet baby Jesus.

"I should head now," she says, blinking quickly as she glances behind herself. I don't know what's going on in her brain but that tiny crease on her brow is making me really not want to let her go.

I hate watching her leave me.

After a lot of squirming on her part I finally release her waist, and she flashes me a soul-warming smile, as if I've actually put her in a good mood.

"Bye Hunter," she says. I press another hard kiss to her cheek, making her squeal happily before she turns to go.

"Bye Fallon."

CHAPTER 15

Fallon

I hold my palms face-down on the mat underneath me, slowly sliding them further and further forwards until my forehead touches the floor. I ease my shoulders backwards and begin widening the stretch of my thighs, until my body makes a full T shape, my legs in a horizontal split. I hold the position for a good thirty seconds, feeling the sharp burn in my loins, before I place my hands shoulder-width apart and suddenly push my body upwards.

A small gasp whooshes out of my lungs as I propel my upper body from the ground, my legs in a perfect one-eighty degree split and my arms unwavering. I smile secretively as my cheer playlist blasts out of my phone, and the sharp chords in the music give me the motivation to raise my legs from horizontal to vertical. I hold my body in an extreme handstand before slicing my legs in opposite directions so that I'm now doing a front split, as opposed to my previous straddle split. I keep my toes in an elegant point and then I slash my legs back through the air, holding the stand before dropping into another split.

The ping on my phone makes me tip my head to the side. I drop the position, letting my chest thump hard against the mat as I reach out with my extended leg and kick my cell into grabbing distance. I settle into a ground-based side split as I click open my Messages.

The text is from Hunter.

HUNTER: *Traffic's being a motherfucker, I'm sorry. Only one minute away.*

I look at myself in the wall-to-ceiling mirror in front of me, tempted to send him a photo of my current position. In the end I just switch back to my Music app and face-plant the mat in front of me, moaning as I move my hips and take the stretch as wide as it will go.

A warm tingle spreads through my waist and I hide my smile as I think about the other recent messages that we've been sending to each other.

After I finished my shift at the diner on Sunday, I showered and got into bed to send Hunter two videos that I had stored from my previous cheer sessions. They were instantly marked as 'read' and I clicked the top button on my cell, waiting for my home-screen to light up again with Hunter's response.

After a good few minutes I finally got a swathe of short breathless messages.

HUNTER: *Fuck.*
HUNTER: *Fallon.*
HUNTER: *Watched them both.*
HUNTER: *Multiple times.*
HUNTER: *Can we start tomorrow?*
HUNTER: *Need to see you.*

Smiling, I ignored his messages and went to bed in a

mood so good that I felt as if I would physically burst.

When I woke up I'd received four more messages at various points in the night, all of which simply read: *Fuck*.

So that's why Hunter and I are starting my pre-events team training now, instead of over Christmas. I'm glad that he won't have to stay on campus over the break for me because that would've made me feel guilty as sin, but, on the flip side, I'm also really happy that I get to start having more one-on-one time with him this term.

I push myself back into a handstand and hold the pose until I hear the jiggle of the lock on the door at the back of the room, followed by a series of heavy knocks on the wooden pane.

"Fallon? You in there?"

I cartwheel out of the pose and brush my clothes back into place.

I'm wearing my lilac two-piece because, although I would rather wear my cheer gear for total unrestrained mobility, I need Hunter to be focused on the lifts – not my butt in a cheer skirt – so that he's not at risk of dropping me.

I reaffix my ponytail and pad over the mats to unlock the door.

I pull it open to see Hunter with his hands on his knees, panting hard even before he looks up at me. When he meets my eyes he lets out a pained groan and then stands to his full height, leaning his body heavily against the doorframe.

"Hey," I say, opening the door fully so that he can get himself inside. "Thanks for coming."

He gives me a long hard look as he shoves his large shoulders through the narrow doorway. "Yeah," he says hoarsely. "Don't mention it."

"What did you think of the tapes?" I ask as I relock the door and make my way past him to the mat that has the imprint of my straddle split embedded into the surface.

Hunter tugs at his hair and follows right behind me, until we're both facing the full-length mirror. His eyes are on the sliver of exposed skin at my waist as he pulls his jumper off from over his head, leaving him in a short-sleeved compression tee and a pair of grey joggers, sitting low on his hips. He tosses the jumper in the general direction of my gym bag and then he settles his hands on my waist, his fingers sliding purposefully against the exposed sliver.

He meets my eyes in the mirror and dips down to press an unexpected kiss against my cheek. My heart flutters wildly in my chest.

"They were unbelievable. You're unbelievable. Didn't realise you were so..." Hunter swipes at his bottom lip and then squeezes my waist, firm enough to make me shiver. "So flexible. And strong. The way that you can flip from one position to another, while you're airborne?" He shakes his head, pressing his chest against my shoulders behind me. "I saved both of those videos to my damn camera roll."

I try to tamper down my smile. "Thank you. I thought that maybe we could start with basic lifts and throws today and, once you've grasped that, we can move onto you holding me while I do the flips."

His eyes are on mine as he nods but his hands are massaging their way up my ribcage.

"Hunter," I laugh warningly and he immediately pauses his hands. "If I'm training with you instead of the squad in preparation for me joining the events team then I need to know that you'll be focused while we do this. The whole reason why I'm not on the comp team anymore is because Blair wasn't strong enough to not drop me. The whole reason why I'm practicing with *you* is because I need to re-familiarise myself with being tossed around without psyching myself into thinking that I'm going to fall. I don't want the same thing to happen to me again, please."

He narrows his eyes on me and tightens his grip around

my waist. "You think that I'd drop you?" he asks, his tone low. "I'll admit it, I love looking at you, but you think that I'd let that get in the way of your safety? Are you serious?"

I feel my heckles rise on my shoulder blades. "Drop the tone," I tell him coldly.

He presses his face into my hair and mumbles out a "sorry".

I close my eyes for a moment and then open them with a little more clarity. "I'm sorry too," I murmur. "I'm nervous is all."

He leashes his forearms around my belly and presses his face against the side of mine, so that we're cheek to cheek. "We'll start small," he assures me. "You already know that I can lift you like a bag of candy."

"Cheer lifts are really precise," I warn him. "You have to get the angle just right and have your hands in place in seconds."

"I ain't dropping you," he replies, reading my mind. "Get that shit out of your head."

I nod and swallow faintly. "Did you warm up before you came here?" I ask.

He smirks. "Looking at you is getting my blood pumping just fine."

I roll my eyes and he nips playfully at my jaw.

"Okay, so we're going to start with you holding my waist and then you throw me vertical until you're holding me by my feet. Typically there would be two people to help with that throw but, you know, you're huge, so…"

Hunter grins to himself as he settles his hands on my hips. I'd sent him footage of this particular lift, so he should have a rough idea of what it looks like.

"'Kay," he says. "And then when I've got you by your feet?"

"I want you to hold the pose for as long as you can and then you'll release the position so that I can jump back down onto the mat, into a stand. We'll do it on the gymnastics mats," I say, gesturing to the trampoline-style mats over to our right. "You can stay standing on these ones," I say, digging my toes into the mat that we're currently on, "and then you can toss me over there."

He catches my eyes in the mirror, a concerned frown on his brow. "I ain't tossing you over anywhere. I'm gonna have you held real secure and then, when you give me the signal, I'm going to launch you safely, so that you don't hurt yourself. Your safety is important, Fallon. If those girls can't catch you, then they don't deserve to have the opportunity to drop you."

"I won't be doing it with those girls again. The events team is a different squad to the comp team, only they don't have as much training time because the events aren't crucial to Carter U's rankings, unlike the comps."

"What event is so special that you wanna pick this up again anyway?" he asks, still refusing to launch me up into the air.

I immediately lock my lips shut because this is a secret that I don't want to tell him about yet.

He can tell, and it makes him narrow his eyes further.

"Fallon," he says, his tone deep and even.

I decide to fight dirty. I spin under his palms, his thick fingers skimming my waist, and I lean up onto my toes so that I can reach his mouth and kiss him. He grunts in surprise but then quickly recovers, lowering one hand to caress my behind and lifting the other to cup my face. I run my palms up over his pecs and he makes a low satisfied sound.

"Hi," he murmurs, before kissing me from a different angle.

I try not to smile against his mouth, amazed that my decoy worked.

"Hi," I whisper back, pressing my chest against his for good measure.

"Jesus," he murmurs, flattening his palms against my

shoulder blades and pushing me up against him as he rubs his pecs over me. "You sure you wanna practice right now?"

"Would you rather just watch me train solo?"

He swallows hard, flushing crimson. "I, uh... I mean, if you'd let me..."

I lower myself to the soles of my feet and press my smile into his warm neck. "We'll try the lifts. If you can't do it, we'll stop. If you can—"

"Then you'll let me take you out again?" he asks, gently tugging at my hair so that I lean back and look up at him.

"You've got to be one of the only guys at Carter U who actually asks girls out on dates," I tell him, laughing.

He shakes his head and says, "Not 'girls', Fallon. One girl, singular. You're the only chick that I've asked to date me, ever. So yeah, maybe, I guess I'm pretty old fashioned."

"How old fashioned?" I ask, smiling as I prod the juicy swell of his bicep.

He hunches down so that he can look right into my eyes before saying, "Fallon, trust me. I'm *very* old fashioned."

I'm not exactly sure what that means but if he said it to pique my interest while simultaneously turning me the hell on, he has definitely succeeded with getting his desired effect.

Unable to maintain his sharp eye contact for a second longer I spin around, my ponytail whipping audibly against his chest, and I say, "I'm gonna jump in three. Grab my waist, throw me up, and then ease me back down – we're not gonna do the higher jumps just yet. Okay, one, two—"

Hunter's fingers grip around my waist, his thumbs digging securely into the small of my back, and then he thrusts me up at the same time as I coil and spring into the air. His propulsion is so strong that my posture stays vertical and I watch in the mirror as his hands hover just underneath my poised feet until I'm falling back down. Then he snatches at my waist again, immediately slowing my plummet and gently lowering me to my feet on the mat.

I turn to look up at him from over my shoulder and his body is locked rigid, his jaw ticking like crazy.

His fingers are one-hundred percent refusing to budge from my middle.

"Holy fuck," he pants, pulling me hard against his abdomen. He presses a rough kiss to the top of my head, his expression tortured as he searches my eyes. "This is... so dangerous, Fallon. You used to do this competitively?"

I flip a curl over my shoulder.

"Yeah," I say casually. "And I won all of my competitions, too."

He grunts and clutches me tighter. "Don't like the idea of other people throwing you around like this," he admits.

I shake my head. "It's fine as long as they catch me. Do it again."

"Again?" he rasps.

"Yes, and I want you to do it higher."

I take stock of the horrified look on his face and against my better judgement I decide to lower my guard. I turn around and wrap my arms around his neck. The thick bulk in his joggers drags roughly over my belly.

"You did that throw really amazingly. You're so strong that it comes naturally to you, and having you do this with me is going to put me back at the level that I really want to be at. Even if I'm not able to compete at American Elite this year, I'd really like the option to go out with a bang by doing a performance with the events squad. So please," I say, moving one hand to brush the stubble on his jaw, "do it again."

He looks down at me for one long moment, his chest rising and falling heavily as if he's contemplating a lot of different things. Then he presses a stubble-coated kiss against my cheek and grabs my waist again, spinning me around so that my back is up against his front. He nods at me in the mirror, and jerks his chin, giving me the go-ahead.

I smile and prepare my body for the jump. "On one, two—"

CHAPTER 16

Hunter

I click the *submit* button for my final graded essay of the fall semester and let out a deep exhale, closing the browser and then shutting the lid of my laptop. Caden, sat to my left, does the same, followed by Tanner to my right, who then rears back to grab a beer from the counter. He smacks the top of the bottle against the side of the table, popping the lid, and then takes a long pull. Caden and Tanner both have one more assignment to turn in before the end of term but the fact that we just destroyed our opposing team at our penultimate fall away game, added on top of almost finishing this term's workload, is enough cause for a weekend of letting go.

Caden scrapes back his chair from the kitchen table and casts a disgruntled glance out of the balcony window. His jaw ticks hard as he scopes out the weather.

"Fuck it," he grunts. "I'm goin' now."

I follow his eye-line and shove my hand through my hair. Caden's been jack-hammering his leg up and down for the past twenty minutes knowing that his girlfriend from home is meant to be flying into the Carter Ridge airport in the next half-hour. One look at the hail hitting hard against the window and the cords in his neck are about to bust, anxious to make sure that she'll be arriving safely. He heaves up off his chair and grabs a set of car keys from the wall hook.

"When's her plane arriving?" I ask as he pockets the keys and pulls on a hoodie.

"Fifteen minutes. Add on the check-in shit and maybe it'll be twenty-five." He re-ties the string at the front of his gym shorts as he shakes his head. "I ain't having her travel in this weather ever again. She's just gonna have to stay here during term time."

Tanner rolls his eyes. "I'm so glad that we had this thorough discussion about our new roommate before any decisions were finalised," he says dryly.

Caden smirks and grabs a travel mug. "Don't act like you wouldn't be doing the same if that Irish chick would let you anywhere near her."

"Her family has been in the States for three generations. She's more American than you."

Even I smirk at that one because Caden's family runs half of Kentucky.

"Dude, no-one's more American than him," I tell Tanner, and I catch a pleased look on Caden's face as he pours his drink.

Tanner narrows his eyes on the travel mug. "For a guy with a thigh tattoo, I wouldn't have expected you to be so crazy about hot cocoa."

Caden screws on the lid and begins kicking on his sneakers. "It's not for me, asshole. Some guys do more for their chicks than just layin' pipe."

Tanner's chair scrapes hard against the floor but I shove my foot against the leg of it so that he doesn't actually murder our roommate.

"Cade," I say warningly, shooting him a look as Tanner's eyes begin to flare.

He looks at me for a moment and then begrudgingly flashes his eyes over to Tanner. He's only a sophomore so I don't want Tanner pulverising him but he still has to learn when to shut his damn mouth.

"Sorry," Caden mutters. "I'm just stressin'. I gotta head."

Tanner watches him carefully and then finally nods and exhales. "Yeah, it's fine. Get your chick."

When the front door to our floor of the house shuts behind Caden, Tanner shakes his head and grumbles, "Lucky prick."

I pull my phone from the pocket in my joggers and decide that it's time to do some stressin' of my own. I'm supposed to be meeting Fallon to continue her balance training – no word of a lie, one-fucking-thousand percent my favourite part of my week – but after looking out of the window I'm hoping that this time she actually bails on me. No way do I want her heading to the sports building in this weather – not when the ground is already getting blanketed in snow, a thin icy layer that will only get worse as the afternoon progresses.

I pull up our texts and send her a quick one: *tell me that you're staying at the condo today.*

I shove my elbows on the table in front of me and stare at the rectangular screen, silently begging for her to tell me that she's gonna do the sensible thing and stay at home, even though my awareness of her dedication is warning me how unlikely that possibility is. The message changes from 'delivered' to 'read' and now my knee is bouncing up and down, waiting for her to land the blow to my abs.

Tanner kicks my foot and I shoot him a glare across the table.

"The fuck's up with all the bouncing? Y'all are making me anxious as hell."

I turn the screen so that he can read it and he lets out a grunt of understanding. "She wouldn't go out in this," Tanner says confidently, shrugging.

We both hear the notification sound and his eyes drop down to read her message.

"Uh, well, actually," he begins, scratching nervously at the back of his head.

My stomach drops like a tonne of bricks as I spin the phone back around and take in her text.

It reads: *you shouldn't come, the roads are dangerous*. I let my phone fall to the table so that I can drop my head into my hands and groan.

Tanner snickers and takes another pull on his beer as we both get to our feet. Obviously I'm fucking going, if only to drive her safely home.

"Where are you heading?" I ask as Tanner drains his drink and shoves on his trainers.

He shrugs. "Austin's coming back to the house and we'll drive over to some girl that he knows' party. See who's there. Might stay the night."

"Don't even know if driving back here will be an option," I say as we both grab our stuff and leave the apartment.

"And yet, you're still goin'," he says, sliding his eyes over to mine.

We stare it out, neither of us wavering. "And?" I ask finally as we reach the bottom floor.

He jerks his chin at Austin, who's waiting in his car just outside the now-open front door. "So you like her. Like, you'd happily get tornadoed in a snow storm level of liking her."

I roll my shoulders and grunt. "Okay, I like her, now shut up."

He grins and I give him a rough shove as we leave the building. Before it can turn into a full-blown hockey brawl Austin throws open the passenger-side door and says to

Tanner, "Hey man." He tips his chin at me and asks, "You coming?"

Tanner ducks down into his seat and throws a smirk at me. "He's busy. He's tryna wife up that cheerleader."

Austin raises his eyebrows, his expression impressed. I shake some hail from my hair, well aware that it's starting to stick like snow. "She's still seeing you?" Austin asks. "Y'all have been going at it for weeks."

Tanner's smirk gets even bigger at Austin's phrasing but he doesn't say anything to correct Austin's assumption. I give him an appreciative jerk of my chin before saying laters to Austin and trudging over to my truck.

I'm surprised that I don't end up skidding during the drive because the roads are almost slick enough to play a decent game of hockey on. By the time that I reach the sports building my abdomen is in knots wondering how the hell Fallon will have got herself here. I park up and make my way to the room that Fallon has been training in, rapping on the door when I see that it's locked as usual. I can hear muffled talking coming from the other side and it pauses momentarily when she hears the knock.

I shove my hands in the front pockets of my joggers and wait for her to open up.

The lock twists and the door opens a millimetre. Fallon's big eyes look up at me from the crack.

Hey, she mouths. She pulls the door open so that I can get inside and I see that she has her phone held up to her ear. I can also see that she's wearing her cheer skirt today and I'm instantly hard as fuck. I lock the door after myself and Fallon turns back around to the mirrors, padding to her usual mat and saying quietly into her cell, "I know, he's right, I know. Look, I have to go now. Text me if you decide you're staying there, okay? Okay, bye."

Her hair is damp. My jaw clenches.

When she disconnects the call and settles her phone on top of her gym bag I notice that her hands are slightly trembling. I close the distance between us and take one of her wrists so that I can hold still her frozen hand.

"Fallon, you're shaking." I look down into her eyes and she stares stubbornly back at me. "You walked here?" I ask.

I get a defiant chin-lift in response.

"You know how dangerous that was?" I ask her. "Why the hell didn't you stay at home?"

"Why didn't *you* stay at home?" she retorts, lightning flashing in her eyes. Damn if I'm answering that one. "This day has been bad enough. I told you that you didn't have to come here."

My body is immediately rigid. "Why has your day been bad?"

"You don't want to know."

"I do want to know. Who was on the phone?"

She throws her head back and lets out a dramatic sigh. She's wearing one of her sparkly cheer tops and the little crystals all over her breasts are making it hard for me to concentrate.

She swallows hard and turns around, allowing me to hold her back against my front, and she watches me cautiously in the mirror.

"It's December, right? Well, my grant's due for submission and the professor – Dr. Ward – who I asked to be my referee hasn't responded to my emails since November. I need her to give me my reference before the Christmas break so that I can submit it in time, and I'm starting to think that she's bailing without telling me. It shouldn't have been a big deal to her – I mean, it's just a random reference – but I guess that sometimes the staff get weird about giving recommendations when they know that their peers will be reading them or something, so…"

She's twiddling anxiously with her fingers. I try to keep my breathing steady.

"Connell told me that Dr. Ward was a bad choice, and I should have listened to him. But I'm just so not used to getting good help, good advice, that I got defensive with him when he brought it up at the condo yesterday. We had an argument – well, *I* had an argument, he listened and then told me that he'd talk to me again when I'd cooled off. Obviously, I then got even *more* angry. So when he left the condo post-argument, Ash sat me down and talked it all through with me.

"I feel horrible for snapping at him, but also lucky, and then feeling lucky makes me feel even worse. Because I can't believe that I have someone in my life who is actually good enough to be let down." She presses her fingers into the centre of her brow and says, "And now I'm talking to you about another guy, and now you're going to be pissed off with me too, even though I only see Connell like he's my brother. I'm literally just the worst person in the world right now."

Her trembling shoulders are the final straw.

"Hey," I say, my voice a command for her to look up at me. I wrap my forearms firmly around her belly and try not to enjoy how goddamn sexy she looks in her outfit while pressed up against my abdomen.

Not the time. Definitely not the right time.

She meets my eyes in the mirror and I press a kiss to her soft cheek. Her beautiful eyes grow shimmery with tears.

"What're you crying for?" I ask quietly, even though she hasn't let her tears overspill yet. "If some piece of work is bailing out on all of your hard sloggin' then we'll find you a different referee–"

She shakes her head. "The deadline is January, it's way too close."

"You have time, Fallon. I'll help you get all the staff's email addresses and then we'll send a request to each of them."

"But what if Dr. Ward finds out?" she says, panic seeping into her voice.

"To hell with Ward," I growl. "She missed her chance.

You're gonna get a reference that's a fucking billion times better than hers would ever have been."

Fallon gnaws anxiously on her bottom lip, looking away from me with an unsure expression. "I have… *everything* riding on this."

I rub my jaw gently over her cheek and her lashes flutter closed as I scrape her up with my stubble. She's been hinting at the significance of getting this grant since the first time that she told me about it, and I can't hold back any longer to find out why she needs it so bad.

"Fallon." She peeks up at me like a scolded schoolgirl and it makes me feel guilty as hell for using my hockey captain voice on her. To balance it out, I nuzzle warmly against her temple and murmur, "Why's the grant so important to you, baby? You don't have to tell me if you don't wanna, but if you do…"

She watches me without blinking for a good ten seconds before dropping her eyes and muttering to her toes, "I wanna."

It's the first time that I've caught a hint of her accent sounding remotely country and it's so cute that I huff out a laugh against her cheek. But then she slowly lifts her hands to cover her eyes and they're shaking so badly that I immediately spin her around in my arms.

"Fallon," I say frantically, frowning as I hunch down so that we're at a more even level. I keep one arm around the back of her shoulders and I use my other hand to hold onto one of her wrists. I want to ease her hands away from her face so that we can look at each other but, as soon as I see two big silent tears streaking down her pink cheeks, I release my hold on her wrist and stroke my fingers through her ponytail instead.

The fact that she's crying soundlessly, as if she doesn't want me to notice, makes my heart hurt even harder.

She nods, her fingers still pressed into the space between her eyebrows. "Sorry," she whispers. "Give me a moment, and then I'll explain."

"Fallon, *I'm* sorry, you don't have to–"

She removes her fingers from her face and lowers her trembling hands to hold her belly.

"Um, okay," she says quietly. "So, I'll understand if you don't get it when I explain this, because I think that a lot of people might not be exposed to, uh, certain types of… parenting when they're growing up, so they might not realise that some… *styles* actually exist. Which is fine, I won't be offended if you think that I'm being dramatic, or if you think that it couldn't have really been as bad as I'm making it out to be, but…"

She takes a deep breath, avoiding my eyes by looking at my chest instead.

"I didn't exactly have the happiest start growing up. I feel like it's pretty obvious but, in case my total fear over communication didn't make it clear enough, my parents weren't exactly the nicest people. They're ex-Olympians with three daughters and their sole goal with all of us was to make us follow in their footsteps. And that would have been fine, except for the fact that they were really… *brutal* with forcing us into it. There was a lot of over-exerting us, a lot of unfair diet regimens. We had to stay on top of our homework or they'd make us skip meals – that kind of thing. I mean, I actually didn't mind the schoolwork side of things because getting praise from my teachers was the only positive enforcement that I was exposed to, but having to physically train that hard, as a kid? It wasn't the easiest thing. It was alright for a while, up until around the age of thirteen. They wanted to keep my sisters and I competitive so they didn't let us sit together, and we were pretty non-verbal growing up because we were all ostracised from one another. We just kept our heads down, got good grades, and basically tried not to piss our parents off.

"Then I started high school and I thought that maybe things would be different now. When I was in the middle of

Pinkie Promise

my junior year there was this guy – literally no-one important, just a guy in my class who was nice to me – and I remember him asking me out and I felt so... *wanted*, for the first time ever. So I was like, 'hell yeah'," she says, laughing wetly before her expression crumbles and she shields her eyes with her hands again. "I told my parents that I was maybe gonna go out with this guy and they... they lost their shit. Like, my dad chased me up the stairs and broke the door down when I tried to lock myself in the bathroom. I hadn't even gone out with the guy, and they were acting like I'd... I don't even know what. I'm pretty sure that very little in the world would have merited the reaction that they gave me but, long story short, it was a really long, really terrifying night, and then they ended up grounding me for, uh" – she swallows hard – "a really long time."

My voice is nothing but gravel when I ask her, "How long did they ground you for, Fallon?"

"Until I graduated from my class," she says, her voice light and strained as she lowers her hands from where they're swiping at her cheeks. She waits a moment before finally meeting my eyes. "Until I graduated from, uh, my senior class."

It takes a few seconds for the words to register, but as soon as they do I feel anger begin to course and spread through my veins.

"You're telling me," I grit out quietly, "that your parents grounded you... for your entire senior year?"

She's searching my eyes, trying to understand my emotions. Worse still, I think that she's trying to work out if what happened to her is normal or not. Safe to say, being grounded from the age of seventeen to eighteen is not fucking normal.

"Well, yeah," she says quietly, crossing her arms over her chest and her brow pinching in the middle. Then she lets out a small humourless laugh and says, "Obviously it made having friends a little impossible but being in my room gave me the time to study, to teach myself things. I was still on the cheer squad for the national high school comps, but that was the only extracurricular that they would let me out of the house for. On the plus side, I used to borrow books from the school library and it was an escapism that I couldn't believe even existed. Books were a lifeline for me and they kind of still are. I've honest to God cried at every happily ever after that I've ever read."

She gives herself a moment before she continues.

"I knew that college would be the time that I could start my life over, so I swatted up like crazy, aced my way to my sport scholarship, said adieu to my parents and" – she shrugs – "here I am."

She lets out a small laugh, as if the severity of her self-sufficiency hasn't even registered in her mind yet.

It's clear as day to me that this is why she doesn't like getting close to people or letting people get close to her. No wonder she doesn't want to risk leaning on anyone for a little help here and there. If she wasn't even safe to trust her parents then how the hell can she be expected to trust anyone else?

"So that's why I can't go back home – it was never my home to begin with, really," she finishes. "That's why I want the grant: so that I can have one more year at Carter U, the only haven that I've ever known. Maybe I can work on this manuscript that I've been writing – not that I'll do anything with it but, you know, it's kind of my happy place. And then once I work out what the hell kind of job someone like me can do once they graduate, maybe I'll get my own happily ever after."

The shy smile on her face makes my heart crack in two.

Suddenly she presses her face into my neck and whispers, "Sorry for unloading. I should've just kept my mouth shut, shouldn't I?"

I can't take it anymore. I tug her head backwards until

she's tilted up for me and I crush her mouth with mine, groaning when she sighs happily.

"Stop saying sorry," I murmur, as she lays her palms over my pecs. I press a few more kisses to her lips and say, "It was real strong of you to tell me all of that and I promise we don't ever have to talk about it again, unless you want to. I'm so fucking angry for you."

She makes a small whimper as she stands on her tip-toes, helping me get the angle to slide my tongue inside of her. I compress her entire body against my front and make a gruff sound as I feel my way around the backs of her bare thighs.

"We're gonna get you that money," I tell her as her head falls backwards, letting me scrub the bristle on my jaw down the curve of her throat.

I try not to think about the fact that I've already deceived her when it comes to cash, facilitating the job for her at the diner while knowing damn well that she's got this whole independence complex. Now that I know the reason behind it I feel even goddamn worse about it.

"You're always so confident," she whispers when I tower over her again. "And determined. You must always get what you want."

My stomach muscles contract. I wipe my palms over her cheeks, getting rid of all traces of her tears.

"The weather's getting worse," I tell her, changing the subject. "I wanna give you a ride. A ride home, I mean," I say quickly.

She makes a humming sound and maintains our eye contact, giving me a playful head tilt that tells me exactly what she's thinking about. That she's thinking about what I'm thinking about. That she knows how badly I wanna ride that tight little–

"We're doing the handstand lift today," she announces, back-stepping out of my arms only for me to grab her waist and pull her against me again.

"No way. I'm taking you home, like right now."

"But we're already here. How much worse could the weather really get?"

I hoist her around my middle and then cart her over to the window so that she can see the fucking blizzard that's going on out there.

"Hm," she says.

I keep her dangling above the floor as I walk over to grab her phone and her little lilac gym bag, handing her the cell and throwing her bag over my shoulder.

"Tell me that you didn't walk here in your cheer outfit," I say to her as I walk us down the stairs of the sports building, her thighs rubbing me up and down with every step that I take.

She grins up at me. I lean down to kiss at one of her cheek dimples.

"No," she admits. "The bikini that I came here in is right there in the bag."

I breathe out a laugh and grip her thighs a little tighter.

"Kidding," she says quietly. "I've got pants and a jumper in there."

I grunt. "Good."

"Do you like it though?" she asks quietly. I look down at her face and see those big eyes twinkling up at me.

"Your cheer outfit?" I ask, giving myself a couple of seconds to glance down at the crystals shimmering over her tits.

"Yeah," she says, leaning back a little, helping me get a better view of her.

I tear my eyes away from her as my temples begin to throb. "You don't wanna know how much I like it, Fallon."

When we get to the entrance of the building, I shove her a little higher up my body and then jog the distance to my truck, not liking the rising intensity of this snowfall one bit. Once I've got Fallon in my passenger seat, tucking herself into the belt, I close her door and round the front of the truck.

I toss her stuff into the back and get the engine going, shoving a spare jacket onto her lap before I crank up the heating. As I carefully manoeuvre out of the lot I tuck my tongue into my cheek, tapping the window wipers into action as the flakes begin falling thicker and faster. When we reach a red light I let myself glance down at Fallon, who's just made my fucking week by snuggling up inside my jacket.

"Looks good on you," I say as the light turns green, but in the next second I'm stomping hard on the brake as a car from the other lane swerves onto our side of the road. It brakes just in time to prevent itself from colliding with the vehicle right in front of us, but it's close enough that everyone around us starts laying on their horns.

"Jesus," I mutter, as the driver slowly makes their way back into their lane and the traffic flow resumes. My right hand is gripping into Fallon's soft thigh, and she places hers hesitantly on top of it, stroking my knuckles to calm me down. "We need to pick a place and wait it out there until the snow stops," I tell her. "We've gotta be equidistant from the hockey house and your condo right now so, uh, if you wanna choose where we stop off at…"

She slides her fingers over mine and I choke back a gruff sound. "We're closer to your house," she murmurs. Her eyes are on her lap, giving me a whole host of ideas.

Very, very bad ideas.

I grip her thigh more firmly as I see the turn that I'll need to take if we're heading to my place.

"You sure?" I ask. "You wouldn't rather me take you to yours and I'll just wait it out in the foyer?"

I feel her eyes on my face. Then she crosses her bare thigh over my hand.

"Right," I grunt, before hitting the indicator, knowing damn well where this is about to go.

CHAPTER 17

Fallon

I grab my gym bag from the backseat as Hunter opens up my door, taking my hand as I step down into the rising blanket of snow. He hoists me up his body as soon as he realises that I'm already ankle-deep, he shoves the door closed, and then jogs us to the entrance of the hockey house, slipping my bag from my fingers so that he can take the weight of it on his right shoulder.

I wriggle to dismount as he takes the first steps inside but his fingers tighten on my body, silently telling me *no*. I wrap my arms around his neck, silently replying *okay*.

"Tanner's out," he says as he reaches his right hand into the front pocket of his joggers for the key to his floor. "Don't know if Caden will be back yet. He was picking up his girl from the airport."

"Girlfriend from home?" I ask, surprised.

Hunter wedges the metal o-ring halfway down one of his fingers, before raking a hand through his hair, melting the rogue snowflakes down the side of his tan face.

"High school sweetheart – that's why he's living on our floor. Tanner and I have less through traffic than some of the other guys on the team." His cheekbones flush a deep ruddy colour and he rumbles, "Sorry. Maybe that was a bad way to word it."

It might have been a bad way to word it but, for some reason, my belly begins to pound.

"Through traffic," I repeat, secretly intrigued.

He drags his hand down his stubble, taking the stairs two at a time. "You know what I'm talking about, right?" he asks, his tone low. "Like, the kind of stuff that goes on at the frat houses. That's why Caden lives with us, because Tanner does his stuff elsewhere and… and, uh, and I…"

He rolls his lips into his mouth, shutting himself up before he can say anything else. He glances briefly down at me and I feel my pupils dial out at his towering angle.

Suddenly he drops me to the floor and, when he moves me so that I'm in front of him, I realise that we've reached the door to his floor.

Now that I'm not facing him I have the courage to ask, "And you?"

His large palms ease his jacket from my shoulders and, holding them firmly, he gives them one rough knead.

"Sure you wanna know?" he murmurs.

I nod, still looking blankly at the unopened door.

His chest swells against my back and he presses his mouth against my ear. "Then I'll tell you later."

He rams his key into the lock and then kicks the door open.

We're instantly met with a loud squeal followed by a muffled chuckle, and I watch as Hunter's burly roommate shoves himself over the back of their living room sofa to grab a hold of the waist of a petite pink-haired girl who's belly-down on the couch. He pulls her up hard against his abdomen, one arm keeping her in place as his other hand rubs and tickles at her ribcage.

He's wearing a pair of pyjama pants and she's wearing the matching top.

"Cade! Oh my God, stop!" she yelps. A thrilled giggle leaves her throat as she lifts her head up, shooting me an apologetic look from over the arm of the sofa.

He smirks against her flushed cheek and rumbles, "Whatcha squealing for, piglet?"

She bursts into another fit of laughter and hides her face under her cotton-candy cloud of soft pink hair. She rolls onto her back and then kicks at her boyfriend, making him grunt as he tries to wrestle her back down.

"The door," she laughs breathlessly. "You gotta stop, there are people at the *door*."

Hunter's roommate immediately lifts his head up before compressing himself down on top of his girlfriend, a shocked look on his face. "S-sorry man," he blinks. "Didn't hear you."

Feeling like this whole situation is too precious and intimate to be intruded on I take a small half-step backwards, but Hunter's palm spans on my lower back and he gives me a gentle but firm shove over the threshold. Then he kicks the door shut behind us, winds his arms around my front, and yanks up the zipper on my jacket, hiding my sparkly cheer outfit. He wraps his forearms over my chest and gives me a hard belly-flipping squeeze.

"You didn't hear him?" the pink-haired girl laughs, shoving hard at her boyfriend's chest so that he sits upright between her legs. His eyes are trained on her as she gets to her feet and, as if compelled, he immediately does the same. "He almost broke down the damn door."

Her boyfriend settles his hands on her shirt-covered hips, giving me an eyeful of his darkly tattooed forearms.

Lord almighty.

"I was otherwise engaged," he says huskily, his southern accent low and rough. Then he casts his eyes back up to Hunter and he says, "We'll go to my room."

His girlfriend flashes me a grin and I can't help but smile back at her.

"Oh, will we now?" she says in her light honey drawl. Her boyfriend starts pushing her forward, walking them out of the living room, but she reaches a slender arm out to me, making him pause in confusion. His eyes trail down to her fingers as if he doesn't want anyone else touching her.

"Winter," she says, her eyes sparkly and a little nervous. Her boyfriend shoots his eyes directly into mine and I feel Hunter's arms lock harder around my body.

I take her hand and we do a little shake. Another laugh tinkles out of her.

"Fallon," I squeak in reply.

Hunter's chest is moving hard against my back. "Winter, Fallon. Fallon, Winter. And that's Caden, but y'all aren't shaking hands."

Caden lets out an exasperated exhale, his gaze still burning into his girlfriend's hand.

"Y'all can have the living room if you want," Winter says when we let go of each other, gesturing to the sofa that she was just being mauled on. "We really will stay in Cade's room."

I shake my head. "Oh, no, I probably won't be staying! I'm just… because of the roads… but the weather will probably be fine in a minute."

I glance out of the balcony doors behind them and notice that, if anything, the blizzard is getting worse. Hunter lets out a quiet snicker.

I glance up at him over my shoulder and he gently wraps one fist around my ponytail. "We might put a movie on or something. So thanks," he says, calm and authoritative.

I look back at Winter and see that her eyes are on my skirt, poking out from beneath Hunter's jacket. She tucks her hair behind both of her ears and gives me an excited look as she says, "You a cheerleader or somethin'?"

"Alright, that's it." Caden grabs her by the biceps and

begins steering her towards his bedroom. She shoots me a mischievous grin from over his shoulder and then howls in delight as her boyfriend bites into the curve of her neck.

Hunter's hand slides around the front of my throat, stroking me gently as he presses a kiss to my jaw.

"We're gonna watch a film?" I ask him curiously as he walks us over to the sofa and settles me down onto the padded cushion.

He stays standing upright and he pulls his jumper off from over his head, tossing it beside me before raking his fingers through his fringe. His shirt lifts up as he tugs at his hair and I stare entranced at the happy trail rupturing its way down the centre of his thick abs.

"Yeah," he grunts. "Seeing as you won't let me take you to the movies again."

I look at him coyly from under my lashes. He maintains my eye-contact while untying the knot at the top of his joggers.

"I've been busy," I tell him. "*We've* been busy."

He gives me a half-smile, dropping his cell onto the coffee table behind him. "Your schedule's so damn tight. Thank fuck I get to spend some time with you over Christmas break."

I purse my lips and he pauses his fingers.

"What?" he asks, his jaw ticking.

"It was really sweet that you said you'd stay here over Christmas but… you don't have to do that. You should spend it with your family."

"My family lives here, Fallon, in Carter Ridge. I don't need to spend the whole break with them to see them."

"But you have siblings, little cute ones. You should go."

"Fallon, it drives me fucking insane how hard it is to get a hold of you."

His chest is pumping in fast swollen drives. When I pull down the zipper on his jacket it starts pumping even faster.

"You got any work you wanna do while you're here?" he

asks as I shrug the sleeves down my arms. His eyes land on my cheer outfit and he rolls both of his shoulders.

"Nope," I tell him, dangling the jacket out for him to take. "I don't have my laptop. I'll have to wait until I'm back at the condo."

"D'you, uh…" He scratches at the back of his neck and glances towards his bedroom. "D'you wanna change into something more comfortable?"

I kick off my little shoes and prop my feet up on the coffee table. He rakes his eyes up my legs, swiping his tongue over his bottom lip when he reaches the top of my thighs.

"I thought you liked what I was wearing," I say quietly, cocking my head and lacing my fingers over my waist.

He grips both of his hands behind his head, exposing his large tan biceps. They're thicker than my thighs and I'm completely in love with them.

"Okay," he rasps out. "I'm gonna go to the kitchen – make some drinks, grab some food. You can pick a movie and, uh… if the weather stays like this, you can take my bed. I'll sleep on the couch."

"I'll sleep on the couch," I counter.

"Fallon, no."

"Hunter, yes."

He stares down at me with a dangerously calm expression. I tilt my head again and he gives me one of those self-assured jerks of his chin. "Then it looks like we're both sleeping on the couch."

He kicks off his shoes and gestures over to the TV.

"There's a stack of DVDs if you wanna pick one. Or I can grab my laptop and download something. Literally anything. Whatever you want."

"What snacks are you getting for me?" I ask, a smile in my voice as I watch him walk to the kitchen and begin pulling bowls and packets from the cupboards.

He turns to flash me a boyish grin. "All the sugary

stuff."

I smile back at him before clambering upright and padding over to their DVD stack.

"You were really good at our previous training sessions, by the way," I tell him as I settle cross-legged on the floor and set the pile of DVDs between my knees. "When you had me standing balanced on your hands and held me steady so that I could do the split kicks? I didn't actually know that you'd be able to handle it."

I hear him still in the kitchen, his eyes burning into my cheeks. "I promised," he says simply.

My cheeks turn a little pink as I fight back a smile. Yeah, he *did* promise. He made a promise and he kept it.

"It sucks that we didn't get to do any of the positions today though," I continue, my fingers stilling when I land on a DVD that I definitely was not expecting to see in this stack. I re-read the title three times before confirming what I already know by turning it over to look at the back.

Oh my.

The gentle thud of bowls and mugs hitting the coffee table sounds to my left and I glance up at Hunter whose eyes are on mine.

"We had to hit the road before the weather got worse. You know I've been lovin' helping you train so I'm sorry that we couldn't do it today." He swallows and adds, "I don't think that it's safe to do any positions in the apartment."

I hold up the DVD in my hand and ask him, "Not even these kinds of positions?"

As soon as he sees what I'm holding his eyes go wide and he stumbles over the side of the table, trying to get to me. I shoot to my feet and run to the back of the armchair, a surprised yelp leaving my throat when he storms after me, rounding the chair, and making me scamper back over to the sofa.

I jump up onto the arm and then run across the

Pinkie Promise

cushions, screaming excitedly as he leashes his forearms around my thighs, incapacitating me from running further, and then pulling me down onto my knees. I try to hold the DVD out of his reach but he kneels behind me and thrusts forward so that he can grab it.

I moan in defeat as I watch him toss the DVD back over to the armchair, but then his hands settle on my hips and he makes a rough sound against my ear.

"You don't wanna watch that," he murmurs, fingers sliding under my skirt and rubbing over my panty-covering cheer shorts.

"Oh, but I think I do," I reply, a hot and frenzied feeling throbbing in my belly.

He slides his fingers down my thighs until his palms are fully encasing the backs of my knees. "It ain't mine, if that's what you're thinking."

"It's in the communal pile," I whisper. "I bet you all use it."

He presses his jaw against my cheek, the feeling of his stubble making me shiver. "I don't watch that stuff. I have a different source for what I need."

"You're telling me that you've never watched it?" I whisper, turning my head so that I can look up at him. The hard expression on his face makes my breathing hitch.

He shoves his tongue into the side of his cheek and then he eases himself upright behind me, pulling me along with him by gripping his hands into my waist. I turn on my knees as he stands from the sofa, and he cups my jaw before leaning down to kiss me.

"That DVD? It was a Secret Santa thing from last year. One of the guys gave it to Tanner." He huffs out a humourless laugh and says, "Okay, yeah, I watched it. It's pretty niche. There's probably not a lot of ice hockey themed pornos out there. Not that I've ever checked. Fuck, it's getting real warm in here."

He yanks the neckline of his shirt away from his chest

and pulls a pained expression as he looks briefly away from me.

"That video's like… the guy's coming back from an away game and, uh, she's his wife I guess and they just, you know… they just end up fuckin' in every room of the house." He winces hard and scratches at his stubble. "I'm gonna shut the hell up now."

My eyes slide over to the cover of the DVD on the armchair. "She looks small," I acknowledge.

Hunter struggles down a swallow. "Yeah," he chokes out. "Hockey guys are pretty big so…"

"Is that your thing?" I ask him in a whisper.

His eyes scrape down my front as he rasps, "Isn't it obvious?"

I lean forward so that I can press my chest against his abs and I say quietly, "I wanna watch it."

He groans loudly and bites hard into his forearm.

"Is that a no?" I ask, teasing him a little.

"You can have it," he says hoarsely. "But we can't… not together."

"Why not?"

"Because I won't have any control over… I'll need to…" He wraps his fingers around the sides of my throat and looks desperately into my eyes. "That's not why I brought you here."

I frown up at his beautiful tan face. "Don't you want us to?"

"Yes," he growls. "I want that so much. But you're literally trapped in my apartment because of a damn blizzard, Fallon. Doing anything while you're vulnerable like that would be taking advantage of you."

"But what if I want it?"

He scrubs his palm against his forehead and angles his hips away from my belly. "Maybe don't say things like that," he pleads quietly.

I stare up at him, unsure about his hesitance when I

thought that it was quite clear that he liked me. I couldn't have been more open with him today, and a dull ache begins to spread in my chest as I wonder if I was *too* open.

I've been closed off to romance since I was a junior being scared out of my mind in my parents' house, and I thought that I'd waited long enough. I thought that, now that I'd distanced myself from them, I would be able to move past those fears. From the moment that I saw Hunter I knew that he was perfect on the outside. The only problem was that he ended up being perfect on the inside too.

Or maybe he's not. Maybe I'm too damaged, even for someone with a heart of gold.

I drop my arms from around the warm expanse of his shoulders and I scoot away from him, slipping off the sofa.

"What are you doing?" he asks, his voice still gravelly as I pick up my gym bag.

"I'm going to get changed," I tell him. "Which one's the bathroom?"

"Fallon, you don't have to…" I position myself on the other side of the sofa and we watch each other with cautious expressions. Hunter's chest is rising and falling so violently that I'm surprised he hasn't actually tackled me back down onto the couch.

He flexes his hands, thrumming with testosterone.

"You can get changed in my room if you want," he says in a voice that makes me think that that's what *he* wants. He sounds sad and sorry, as if he thinks that he's done something wrong.

Maybe he can't see that having had no romantic interactions in my past means that every wrong move I take with him is simply me dipping my toes into the water because I don't know what the right moves are yet.

"The bathroom's through that door, but you really don't… I didn't mean to…" He stops himself and then stabs a thick digit towards the sofa. "I'm gonna be here. If you'd rather have some time to yourself, that's fine. Take my bedroom. But after you get changed if you still wanna hang out here..." He looks at me with those beautiful sparkling eyes. "I'll just be waiting."

The sincerity in his tone makes my heart ache.

Unsure about what I want to do versus what I should do, I nod and then I quietly close myself into Hunter's bedroom.

CHAPTER 18

Hunter

I'm a damn idiot, that's what I am.

I sit with my elbows on my knees, hands raking through my hair as I stare blankly at the hockey game that's quietly playing on the screen. Fallon has been in my bedroom for what feels like hours and I'm so strung out for her that I can barely sit still. I'm dying for her to come out here so that I can give her an apology. If not for the fact that there was a fucking porno lying around our living room, then at least for the fact that I just mounted her from the back while she was wearing a damn cheer skirt.

I glance at the beer on the coffee table that I grabbed from the fridge, wanting to take a damn long pull on it but knowing that adding alcohol to this already fragile situation will only make things worse. Only make me want her more. Then I look over at the one *Star Wars* movie that we had in our stack, that I've positioned in the centre of the table just in case Fallon does come back out here, and I get a sharp stab in my gut over my lack of self-control.

I try to refocus on the game and not think about the beautiful girl alone in my room.

A door opens quietly behind me and my shoulders immediately swell. I drop my head down and stretch out my hands, waiting for her to come over here instead of rushing her like I want to. When the room remains quiet, the only sound the muffled noise coming from the game on the box, my breathing starts to get a little heavier, coming in faster deeper pumps. I wait her out for another ten seconds but then I can't take it anymore and I finally turn around to look at her.

My blood throbs faster.

She's wearing a Carter U cheer team jumper that's slipping down one of her shoulders and a pair of joggers, but really the one thing that I can't stop staring at is the *get over here and undress me* bra strap that's holstering her tits up and peeking out from her top.

My knee starts jerking up and down as my cock thickens in my boxers.

"Hey," I rasp, trying not to swipe my tongue over my lower lip as I give her a once-over for the fifteenth fucking time.

"Hi," she says quietly, glancing briefly at what's on the screen.

I want to stand up and go over to her but I also don't want to freak her out any further, so instead I grip my right fist in my left hand and say, "I'm not watching the game. You can change it if you want. I, uh…"

I breathe out an embarrassed laugh as I lean forward and pick up the *Star Wars* DVD that I'd left out for her. I don't even know if it's the one that she likes but I face it towards her anyway, just in case.

"I found this in the pile… I don't know if the little Yoda's in it but…"

A small smile appears on her face and my heart skips a beat.

Pinkie Promise

"Little Yoda," she repeats, one of her dimples popping.

"Uh, yeah," I say, throwing the DVD back down and moving over to one side of the couch so that I'm not positioned right in the middle.

She sees my silent invitation and starts padding over to me, so light on her feet that I can't help but stare.

I spread my knees a little wider.

Fallon lowers herself to the cushion on my right and tucks a curl behind her ear before glancing up at me. My pupils expand like crazy and her beautiful eyes get even wider.

"I'm sorry," I say hoarsely, "for being such a dog. I think about you all the time, so when I finally get you alone I just…"

Fallon laughs and shakes her head, her soft curls bouncing around her perfect face.

"Hunter, I should be the one apologising. I'm the one who was pushing you. I don't have much experience with other people and sometimes I guess I take things too far."

I stare at her intently, disbelieving what I'm hearing. "Fallon, trust me, it wasn't you who took that too far. If things were different I would… I would be encouraging things to go even further."

She takes a little swallow, her chest pumping almost as fast as mine. My mind is racing. I can't tell exactly what she wants and I need solid confirmation before I take this to the next level.

"I hate communicating my feelings," she confesses, watching as I splay my thighs even wider, wanting her to straddle up on me like a little cheerleader cowgirl.

I take one of her hands and lace our fingers together, tugging her gently so that she scooches closer. "You're good at communicating," I tell her, loving the way that it feels to have her knees pressed up against my quad. "You don't need to be hard on yourself."

A small crease appears on her brow. "I find it really hard

to be open with people, to be normal with people. I've never wanted to let anyone in before and I'm worried that I'm doing it all wrong."

I look deep into her eyes, heat spreading through my chest.

"You haven't done a damn thing wrong," I tell her, but suddenly her hands are on my stomach and my mind is going blank. I inhale fast and sharp as she delicately presses her fingers against my abs, and I swipe my free palm over my forehead as she roams them up to my pecs. I groan and add, "Everything you do is perfect."

"I thought maybe you didn't want to do anything with me anymore 'cause of what I said today," she winces.

I tug hard at my hair as I watch her palm my chest. "Hell no," I say breathlessly. "I want you *too* fucking much. And I want you to love it, that's why I'm pacing it. That's why I need you to be sure. And, uh… I need us to go slow with it so that I don't… so that I can…"

She blinks up at me with those big sparkly eyes and I drop my hand to her collarbone, tucking my digits beneath her bra strap. I wrap my other arm behind her and shove her up onto my lap, my jaw turning rigid when she settles down exactly where I need her to.

"Fallon," I say, my voice way too deep. She nods up at me with a nervous expression and hell if that doesn't make me grip her tighter, press her down harder. "Remember when you came over here a while back, when we were throwing a house party? I had you in my room and I told you that there was something that I needed to tell you?"

"Yeah," she says, her hands resting on my shoulders.

I splay both of my palms against the small of her back, pressing her warm body up against mine.

Then I bite the bullet.

"I haven't done this before," I murmur. "Not just the dating thing, or the girlfriend-boyfriend thing. I'm talking about…" I take a hold of her hips and gently force her down into my lap, rubbing her up and back over the thick length of my dick. She swallows quietly and her lashes flutter closed.

My cheeks have turned ruddy, nervous about how she's gonna respond to what I'm silently telling her, but she wraps her arms tighter around my neck and buries her face into the side of it. I roam my hands down from her hips so that I can grip into her soft behind, taking a deep inhale of her hair as I begin palming her more firmly.

"Are you being serious?" she whispers, her fingers leashing into my hair. "You've never been… physically intimate before?"

I nod against her before pressing a kiss to her temple. "Yeah, baby," I murmur back. "I told you. I'm traditional."

She nuzzles into me harder, her full breasts squishing against my rigid pecs. "That's why you've been wanting to go slow?" she asks. "Not because, like, you don't want me?"

I huff out a laugh and then shove her down harder against my cock, rubbing us together at a quicker pace than before.

"I don't wanna go slow," I pant quietly. "I want you in my bed, right now. But I want our first time to be real special, and I don't wanna ruin it by needing to spurt my load after the first three thrusts."

Fallon whimpers and drops limply against my pecs.

"Jesus," I mutter, swiping my wrist over my forehead. "If I find out that you like it when I say stuff like that, I'm fucking done for."

She releases a tiny pained laugh against my throat. I stroke my palm over her jaw and she leans into the warmth of my touch.

"I also, uh… I want you to be mine before we do it. I don't want this 'no labels' shit. I wanna put labels all over you."

She peeks up at me with the cutest smile that I've ever seen.

"What kind of labels?" she asks.

"Girlfriend, fiancée, wife – you know the sort."

She laughs in delight and I flip her down onto the cushion beside us, pinning her on her back as I push my groin against her lap.

I jerk my chin at her as she struggles playfully. "You gonna be my chick or what?"

She throws her head back and laughs uncontrollably, her eyes squeezed shut, and her cheer jumper rides up right beneath the cups of her bra. I get one look at her smooth belly, her tiny waist, and I sit up between her thighs, pressing my palms into her naval.

"You want kids?" I ask her, and something excited flashes through her eyes. She bites into her smile as she looks up at me towering over her.

"I've never thought about it before," she admits in a happy breathless whisper.

I rub my thumbs into her harder. "I think about it all the time."

I smirk when I see her pulse fluttering like crazy in her neck and, unable to stop myself, I lean down to kiss it.

She wraps her arms around the breadth of my shoulders and whispers, "How many babies do you want?"

A silent laugh rumbles through my chest as I start slowly kissing my way across her collarbone. "You don't wanna know."

She shivers hard and this time I laugh out loud.

"I'm one of six, Fallon," I remind her quietly, leaning up on one of my forearms so that I can look at her pretty face. She looks like she's on the brink of passing out. "I've grown up with baby after baby after baby. I'm real good with kids."

She swallows and asks, "So you want... six kids?"

I grin down at her. "Why limit ourselves?"

Her eyes widen and I press my face against her neck, laughing quietly.

Pinkie Promise

"I'm only kidding, baby," I murmur, even though I literally want as many babies as she'll let me pump inside of her. I kiss at her cheeks and then, when I reach her mouth, she leans slightly up for me, wanting it as much as I do.

I kiss her gentle and chaste until she starts rubbing her lap against mine, making my swollen cock even harder than before. I slide my tongue slowly into her mouth, groaning when her fingers slip their way up my shirt. I pull back, gratified as fuck to hear her panting, and then I rip my shirt clean off over my head. I stuff it down the back of the couch before pressing my full bodyweight on top of her.

"I can't have you on the road when the weather's like this," I tell her as she grips at my pecs, her cheeks all pink.

"I already said I don't mind staying on the couch," she whispers, pulling me back down so that I can fill her up with my tongue again.

"Not happening," I murmur back to her. "You know you're taking my bed."

She clutches me tighter and her jumper slides up over her tits again. Without looking, I yank the hem back into place, my neck burning red.

"Your bed is big enough for the both of us," she points out, before whispering tauntingly, "and I am very small."

I tuck my tongue in the side of my cheek, knowing damn well what she's doing.

I snicker and shake my head, running my palms along the waistband at the back of her joggers. "Yeah, I bet you're real small everywhere."

Then she lets out a shriek of laughter as I shove my hands down her pants, giving myself two big handfuls of her sexy cheerleader ass. Her thighs fall wider around my hips as I knead her soft little mounds and my eyes drop to her chest, knowing exactly what I wanna get my hands on next.

"You wanna share the bed?" I ask her, palming my way up to her waist.

"We don't have to do anything," she whispers. "Just this. Just kissing." She brushes the backs of her fingers down my abs, all the way to the drawstring on my joggers.

I stifle a low groan.

"It's been a long day, we probably both need time to think through what we've told each other. And" – she shrugs – "I kind of like that you want to go steady with me."

I stare down at her, my breathing uneven, before finally nodding.

It's hard to want to go steady with Fallon when her little pussy has been warming my cock for the past ten minutes, but I nod anyway because I want to make our first time together special. Binding. Not on the spur of the moment on the couch while I've got a game on in the background.

Although, being honest, fucking her on the couch is definitely on my to-do list.

"Okay," I rasp. "We'll both sleep in my bed, but we'll take it steady." I press a firm kiss against her cheek and a shiver runs through her body. "Should I get my laptop so we can download a movie?"

She shakes her head and glances at the hockey game still playing on the box.

"I don't mind watching this. I mean, I obviously have no clue what's going on," she laughs, "but that's okay. I'll need to, uh… I'll need to get my glasses though."

Every drop of blood in my body rushes south.

"Get them," I say hoarsely.

CHAPTER 19

Fallon

We started off on opposite sides of the bed.

At first we were lying side by side, Hunter's chest rising heavily as he stared unblinkingly up at the ceiling. But after five minutes of being more awake than we'd felt all day Hunter had reached his hand out to mine and gently locked our pinkies together. We turned to look at each other and in a matter of seconds he'd encircled me in his arms, pulling my front up against his chest and wrapping my thighs around his abs. He crushed my mouth with his, sounds of pain and relief vibrating through his chest.

"Is this okay?" he'd murmured, shifting me higher up his body.

I'd nodded eagerly and he rolled me onto my back, kissing me impatiently, as if he hadn't had me in his arms all evening. He gave me a warning growl when my hands started skirting his deeply cut V and then suddenly my back was to his front, my wrists locked down under his forearms. He leaned forward so that he could kiss me from behind and then, when I started to bonelessly submit to his touch, he'd pulled away with a grunt and buried his face in my hair.

I didn't think that I'd be able to fall asleep, my body so painfully aware of the man pressed up behind me, but when I open up my eyes I realise that I've just had the most amazing sleep of my life.

Hunter's arms are still wrapped tightly around me, his bare forearms pressed against my belly under my shirt and his chest heaving steadily against my shoulders. I move the tiniest inch and his grip immediately intensifies, loosening only when I go back to laying still. The thick muscle between his thighs is digging halfway up my back, a long hot brand that makes my thighs press together.

Hunter's hips suddenly thrust against my ass and he grunts himself awake. His breathing is immediately laboured and his hold on my belly becomes firmer, his stubbled jaw pressed against my temple as he takes a deep, chest-swelling inhale.

"Fallon," he murmurs in his rough morning voice. His arms shift from around my middle and his palms settle on both sides of my waist, squeezing me indulgently as he rubs his erection between my cheeks. "Fallon, you awake?"

"Yes," I squeak, as he flattens his hands over my stomach and pushes me against him. He rubs one of his palms all the way up my body, between my cleavage and up my throat until he's gripping at my jaw, and then he gently turns my face to look up at his.

I squirm without meaning to, his eyes so much darker and more dangerous looking when he's pressed up against me at God-knows-what in the morning. His stubble has grown in the night and his skin looks even more tan against his sheets.

"Hey," he says quietly, leaning down to kiss my lips. My eyes flutter closed and I reach back with one arm to stroke at his jaw. He releases a contended groan at my nervous petting and a warm feeling sparkles wildly through my

Pinkie Promise

chest.

And the sensation only gets warmer as Hunter slides his digits beneath the hem of my top, making me whimper quietly when I feel just how hot he is. He rubs his big warm palm firmly up my belly until he's growling into my mouth as he roughly massages my breasts. The sensation is so intimate, so unfamiliar, that I become slack in his hold, enabling him to roll me quickly onto my belly and start grinding hard against my ass. The hand on my jaw slips loosely around my throat and the palm rubbing my breast begins squeezing frantically.

"First time waking up like this," he grunts, knocking my knees apart with his so that he can position his thick quads between my thighs.

"You feel like a seasoned professional," I whisper breathlessly, and he huffs a laugh against my cheek.

"I wanna have you so bad," he murmurs, gripping his hands around my hips so that he can pull my behind up against his straining length.

"Really?" I tease. "I never would have guessed."

He grins and bites his perfect teeth into the side of my neck, making my whole body drop limply into the soft sheets of his bed. He groans into my throat and shoves my thighs further apart.

"Move in with me," he rasps, making me smother another giggle into his pillow. His gravelly morning voice is making my stomach pound dangerously. I try to push myself up from the bed but he keeps me firmly in place without needing to flex one damn muscle.

"I need to go, I have things to do," I tell him, wriggling.

He grips his fingers into my ass and murmurs, "Squirming like that ain't helping me wanna let you leave." I fall still against the mattress and he mumbles, "Actually, that ain't helping either."

I try to roll onto my back and he lifts his torso so that I can. Then he settles his bodyweight back down on top of me and strokes gently at my cheek.

"I don't want you to go," he tells me simply, looking straight into my eyes.

"I need my laptop so that I can stress-email every other member of the English department, and you literally have work to go to, Mechanic," I remind him, although, really, I don't want to go either.

The real problem here? I'm terrified that I'm about to fall in love with him.

I've only known him for two months but he's treating me so good that it feels like I've known him for two years. Because of that, I need to put as much distance between us as possible right now.

But first I give myself a little treat, by roaming my palms over his beautiful chest.

"The shop'll be closed if the roads haven't been cleared. And I won't drive you back to the condo if they haven't been, either."

I grin, loving the way that his deep voice reverberates through my body. "You can carry me piggy-back style," I say teasingly.

He laughs down at me and shakes his head. "Fine. You got more essays left to submit this semester or something?"

"Yeah, although technically they're all done. I just need to proof-read them. And then I have thesis revisions but I'm so ahead on that I literally don't have to look at it until January. I meant what I said yesterday by the way, about you going to your parents' for Christmas. Like, no way am I going to be the thing that prevents that from happening. I don't want you to think I'm depending on you for company. Dependency..." I trail off, shaking my head. I'm pretty sure that I've mentioned it to him before, about how I hate being at the mercy of other people. Everything that I told him yesterday explains why I'd rather not be in that kind of situation again.

When I look up at him he's frowning slightly, his jaw

ticking and his eyes aflame. Then he looks quickly away from me, as if he was going to say something but thought better of it.

He settles himself heavily onto his back and I can't decipher the hard look on his face. Without glancing down at me he wraps his arms around my waist and drags me up so that I'm lying on top of him.

I prod at the stubble on his tan jaw and he gives me a lazy smirk.

God darn it. Why are country boys so damn cute?

"I'm going out tonight by the way," I tell him, flipping my hair subtly over my shoulder.

His smirk instantly drops and he sits us bolt upright.

"I'm sorry, what?" he asks, his voice deadly calm.

"It's a cheer thing, end of term and all," I say absently, moving to get off of him and being secretly thrilled when he shoves me right back down. His arousal practically impales me as he forces my lap on top of his.

"Where are you going?" he demands.

"One of the sorority houses, seeing as half of the team can't get into the bars."

He watches me long and hard before gently easing me off his lap and getting up to rip open his curtains. Whatever he sees makes the large muscles in his back tense up. He curses roughly as he shoves them closed again.

"Have the roads been cleared?" I ask, overflowing with this golden sunshine feeling at the knowledge that Hunter wanted to keep me here for the rest of the day. That Hunter wants to keep me, period.

He climbs on top of me, his jaw working hard. "Yeah," he grunts. "Still don't want you goin' over there in any neck-breaker heels or anything," he mumbles against my throat.

I stroke my fingers into his hair and he releases a rumbling exhale.

"When I pick my outfit maybe I'll send you a photo," I

whisper.

"*Baby*," he murmurs into my neck, before leaning up and kissing me gently. When he pulls back he says, "Over Christmas I might take my siblings to the rink, get them comfortable on their blades for the first time. If you want…" He shoves one of his hands through his hair and then drops it to my waist. "If you want, I could bring you with us. I only take one sibling at a time, it's not like I'll have the whole bunch," he laughs, although his cheeks start flushing red and he glances down as if he's getting nervous.

"Okay," I agree, loving the idea of seeing Hunter teaching his baby siblings how to skate. I also secretly want him to teach *me* how to skate, but I save that thought for another time.

"Yeah?" he asks, tilting my chin so that I can look up at him. He's wearing a sleepy half-smile that has my heart doing crazy things.

"Yeah," I whisper back, before pulling him down for one more kiss.

*

A champagne cork shoots across the living room and I let out a tipsy yip as I duck out of its way. Aisling throws a pillow from our sofa over to the girls in the kitchen, and they scream and scamper, laughing profusely. I look back into Ash's little compact mirror and finish my coating of mascara as she switches up the song on the playlist, blasting it out of the speaker on the countertop.

"How was last night?" I ask her as she tosses her cell and stands up on the couch to catch the rogue cushion being thrown back at us. She's wearing a strapless baby blue mini dress, silver stilettos, and the biggest pair of diamond earrings that I have ever seen in my life. She sinks back down next to me and we share an amused look.

Aisling was at her boyfriend's last night and, from the

aggressively hot outfit that she's wearing for our cheer Christmas party, I can tell that she isn't pining too hard for him right now.

"I mean, I kind of want to kill him," she laughs, rolling her eyes and downplaying her emotions. "Like, at first I didn't mind that he's such a dog because he's also really good at spoiling me, but now that we're 'exclusive' and his phone is still pinging off every five seconds... I don't care if he's already been drafted – he has a girlfriend, so his past hook-ups shouldn't be pursuing him anymore. He let me scroll through his DMs, and he isn't even responding to them, but it's getting to the point where his popularity is downright annoying. I knew what I was signing up for with him but I think that we're reaching the end of the rope."

She runs her fingers through her hair, laughing humourlessly as she shakes her head.

"I knew that I should never have said yes to being exclusive with him. Honestly, I think that the most important lesson that I've learned from this is that it isn't just the guys that you need to keep your guard up around – it's the girls too. If I hadn't met you at cheer when we were freshmen, Lord knows what I would do."

I give her a little "aw", genuinely touched.

She waves her wrist quickly, wafting away the sentimentality. "I know, I'm sappy, I'll shut the hell up now."

"No no no–"

Ash picks up a shot-glass from the coffee table and stares at the sparkly red liquid, the crushed candy canes around the rim giving it an extra festive feel. She tentatively sticks the tip of her tongue into the glass and then pulls a face that sends us both into hysterics.

She passes me a shot of my own and we tip them back in unison.

"Can I just... say one more thing?" she asks hesitantly, poking at the candy rim so that she doesn't have to meet my eyes.

I nod vigorously, the red liquor warming my veins.

She glances over her shoulder, her fingers running over her diamonds, and then I watch her eyes pool with tears, making me scooch forward and wrap my arms around her.

"I can't trust anyone Fallon," she whispers. "Not even the girls on the damn team."

I know the problem before she even says it. "Who was messaging him?"

She frowns at her lap before mouthing *Whitney*.

My jaw drops open and she scrunches up her nose.

"Whitney? As in, the girl who replaced me as the head flyer?" I hiss, pressing my fingers hard into my temples, unable to comprehend a betrayal by someone on your own *team*. Especially when, as the captain of Carter U's comp team, Ash is close with all of the girls on the squad.

Seeing as Ash just assigned Whitney the position of the comp team's star flyer my brain is fizzing like crazy over the idea of her betraying her.

I feel like I'm forgetting something but the sparkly liquor is making my thoughts hazy.

"I know," she whispers, smoothing out her dress as we walk to get one last drink from the kitchen. In my light state of tipsiness it takes me a second to realise that Blair, the girl who dropped me so good that I ended up getting multiple concussions, is standing right next to us at the counter.

My cheeks heat up, feeling a little betrayal of my own.

Our eyes meet and neither one of us knows what to do. She offers me a small unsure smile, her brow creasing with guilt, and I give her a tiny smile of my own, not exactly sure where we stand with each other. After a few seconds of nervous eye contact she takes a glass from the tray and takes her leave.

"Speaking of betrayal," Ash murmurs, and I give her a *let's not even get into it* look as we prop ourselves against the dark counter.

Pinkie Promise

With her connections, Blair's position on the team was a guarantee, and there's nothing I can do about what has already happened. Plus, I can join the events team seeing as I was only barred from doing comps and, with my aim to now get a grant from the literature department instead of from my sport, I technically don't have anything to complain about.

Aisling hasn't reached that kind of enlightenment yet though.

"I want to kick Whitney's ass off the team," she says casually, giving me a naughty little smile as we take a sip on her extremely expensive champagne. "Obviously I can't, because we need her for Elite, but seeing all of the messages really stressed me the hell out, and then *he* started stressing out because *I* was stressing out…" She rolls her eyes. "I just set myself up for disappointment after disappointment. Like, going into it with him, I literally knew that we wouldn't last. And it's not even fair to him because he isn't encouraging it – being hot can be such a curse sometimes."

She laughs wetly and then covers her eyes with her hands. I wrap my arms around her shoulders and give her a comforting squish.

"I don't know what to do anymore," she murmurs, and in the very next second a big warm presence presses up behind me.

I turn my head and Connell is bearing down on me, a frown on his face as his eyes flick between his sister's face and mine. The cheer squad and the football team are getting a fleet of Ubers to take us to the sorority house, so Connell's teammates are filing into our living room as they wait for the girls to finish getting ready.

I haven't spoken to Connell since I argued with him about my grant and, now that he's looking down at me like an all-knowing big brother, I have guilty eyes and a sad pout on my lips.

"What's she crying for?" he asks me gruffly, flicking his chin over to his sister.

"Nothing," Aisling says immediately, her head snapping up. "Everything's fine. I was being stupid."

I purse my lips, not wanting to explain a secret that isn't mine to tell.

Connell narrows his eyes on us and Aisling subtly shakes her head at him, telling him not to press it.

"Nice earrings," he comments. "When did they happen?"

She scowls up at him. "Just an early Christmas present."

He scowls back down at her. "You sure it wasn't an apology present?"

Aisling's eyes widen and I feel my cheeks getting very hot.

"He better not be buying your loyalty, Ash," Connell says quietly, his words making me wince even though he doesn't mean them maliciously.

Seeing the look in her eyes, Connell presses himself up behind me, reaching his arms around the both of us and squeezing us into a bruising football-player hug. Aisling fervently swipes under her eyes.

After a minute she pulls back and says, "I'm gonna check my make-up and then I wanna get extra tipsy. Make me something strong," she orders him as she slips around us and jogs over to our bathroom, looking flawless in those shimmering heels.

I wriggle to get out of Connell's grip but he simply turns me around, his expression hard and sure.

"I'm sorry," we both say at the same time. His mouth ticks up into a half-grin.

"No, *I'm* sorry," he says. "I have no fucking right to try and give you advice about money."

"You were right though," I argue back. "I should've listened to you from the get-go. Literally all I've done today is mass-email my ex-professors so that I still have a shot in the dark at maybe getting this grant."

He hands me our bottle of champagne and I take a little willing sip. I pass it back to him and he drains half the bottle.

I roll my eyes and laugh.

"I'm still sorry, Fallon. What you're doing takes guts. When I knocked on your door a million times last night and you didn't answer, I thought that you were never going to forgive me."

I stare up at him, confused, and then my cheeks get a little pinker.

"Oh," I whisper. "I didn't know that you came by last night. I... I wasn't at the condo."

He watches my face carefully before his chest suddenly swells. In a deep voice he says, "Hunter?"

I nod.

"Right," he says, before glancing down at my body. "Are you okay?"

I blink up at him. "What do you mean?"

He looks over his shoulder before giving me a secretive *isn't it obvious?* look. "Like... Hunter Wilde is a big guy, Fallon," he says, laughing nervously as he takes stock of my body. "You know what I'm saying."

"Oh my God," I groan, before laughing with embarrassment. "Connell, for one, you're huge too, and you've tried to get with me before."

He gives me a cocky grin. "Don't try to butter me up, Fallon. I know that Hunter's got twenty pounds on me."

We both laugh as I try to fan away the heat from my cheeks.

"We, um... we didn't actually do anything like what you're thinking. I was only staying over because the weather got crazy and he didn't want me on the roads during the blizzard. I know the whole 'hockey captain' thing gives him that player vibe but he's, uh... traditional. Respectful. You wouldn't even believe how gentlemanly he's being with me."

Connell nods, his expression more serious now. "Good," he says, his voice confident and sincere. "You look hot as hell by the way."

I glance down at my outfit – a pretty lilac mini dress, matching with Aisling's blue one – and I prop my hands on my hips, cocking him a happy cheerleader pose. "Thanks," I say, and he crushes me into another laughing bear hug.

"Let's not argue again," he says, as we all begin filing out of the condo. He gives me a grin and adds on, "Second baby sis."

Aisling locks her arm with mine as half of the cheer team and the football squad squishes into the dark elevator.

"Well, this is safe," I say dryly and Connell snickers as the door tries to close again.

Ash still has music blasting from her cell and, tipsy on champagne, we scour her playlist for our next target. By the time that we're in the back of the Uber I'm so excited for my night out that I *really* wish I'd invited Hunter. I slide my phone from the side of my panties and tap on the screen so that it lights up.

I ignore everything on the home screen except the six texts from Hunter, smiling secretly to myself as my eyes scan over his messages.

Instead of texting him a response, I pull up the camera app and hold my phone an arm's length away from me. Connell is sitting directly across from me and he smirks, shaking his head, already knowing what I'm doing.

"You're gonna drive him crazy," he says to me.

Then he elbows one of his teammates in the ribs when he catches him staring at my legs.

I squeeze my chest up with my free arm and look up at the camera as the flash goes off, before zooming into my own cleavage as I check the pic. I bite at my thumb, giggling because I'm nervous and excited.

Then I attach it to the Messages app and shoot it off to

Pinkie Promise

Hunter.

Three seconds later Hunter is calling me, making me bite back a laugh and arch my neck against the headrest.

I click the answer button.

"Baby," Hunter grunts, his breathing hard and laboured down the line.

"Hey," I whisper back to him, smiling at the sound of his voice. "How'd your shift go?"

He inhales deeply and I hear the sound of metal unzipping in the background. "I only just got back to my parents' house. Needed to finish up this car 'cause the owner's picking it up on Monday."

"My strong hardworking man," I whisper teasingly.

He groans through the speaker and I hear a door lock click shut. "You drunk, baby?" he asks, his voice painfully deep.

"No," I lie, smiling when he laughs down the line.

"Wish I could be with you right now," he murmurs, sounding exhausted. "Text me when you get home?"

"You'll be asleep," I say, bouncing slightly as the Uber brakes to a stop.

"Baby, the thought of you going out looking like that, without me by your side? I'm not gonna be sleeping for a damn month."

I step carefully down onto the snow-scraped driveway and then I hold Aisling's hand as we begin walking on our heels up the sorority steps.

"I gotta go," I tell him as we enter the house, before whispering teasingly, "Have a nice long shower."

He lets out a sexy pained laugh that has my heart thumping wildly. "Baby, I swear to God. 'Bouta be the longest shower of my life."

CHAPTER 20

Hunter

Fallon wanted space over the winter break – to finish up her grant application and to have some alone-time with her secret manuscript – and, feeling like a damn saint, I respected her wishes.

Didn't mean that I had to like it though.

The thought of Fallon lying on her belly as she worked the keys on her laptop had me very fucking tempted to ignore her do-not-disturb rule. There was nothing that I wanted to do more than to pull up unannounced, Carter Ridge's snowfall be damned. But maybe it was a good thing that she set up some winter boundaries because, if we'd done it my way, we would have stayed in Fallon's bedroom for the entire winter break.

But she knew that. She knew that if we continued hanging out while everyone had gone home, there was no way that we could've waited it out this long. I'm not so arrogant as to think that once we start having sex I'm going to be able to focus on anything else, which is why I used our time apart to finish up as much college work as possible. Because this semester I only want to be doing two things.

Hockey.

And Fallon.

I spent every night of the winter break looking at that beautiful photo she sent to me from the back of a crowded Uber. Sending it to me because she knew that I'd need something to keep me going while I gave her space. I've had my hands on Fallon's body a good number of times, but that photo is a reminder of everything that we haven't done yet, and a promise of what's to come.

I scrub my towel over my hair while zooming into the photo, the steam in the bathroom fogging up my reflection in the mirror.

Damn, she's perfect. Satisfaction swells in my abs, my cock instantly hard and heavy. I give myself a minute to look at the photo, my fist gripping beneath the head of my dick and then suddenly tugging towards the thick base, my hips pistoning forwards as I give myself a few rough pumps.

The sight of Fallon squeezing her breasts together is driving me damn feral. I don't know how the hell a chick her size managed to grow tits like that, and I am not for one second fucking complaining.

Warm moisture spurts out of the tip and I grunt back to the present. I let go of my shaft and gently settle my phone on the sink, cleaning up the mess before I finish off my towel-drying.

Term starts in two days which means that my ban on disturbing Fallon's study-time is finally up. I got a little *finally finished, come get me* text an hour ago so, now that she's submitted her grant application, I'm finally going to take her out as promised. I finished up in the garage earlier than I should have but Colton's going to handle it while I'm not in the shop.

I toss the towel into the laundry basket and pull up a pair of boxers and jeans. I slip my cell into my pocket as I unlock the bathroom door and then I roll my shoulders back as I step out into the hallway.

Or I would be stepping out into the hallway if Archer, my youngest brother, wasn't right outside the door, looking up at me with a terrified expression and his hands covering the front of his baby cargos.

"Ah shit," I say quietly, quickly swooping him off the ground and into the bathroom, knowing from his face that he's about to pee his pants. I hold him over the toilet so that he can do his business while asking him in as nurturing a tone as I can manage, "Why didn't you knock, buddy? When you need to use the bathroom all you've gotta do is knock."

After doing what he came to do his spirits are immediately lifted, and he tries to hug at my leg as I get his trousers back over his tiny feet. We're both equally impressed that he didn't actually pee himself.

I toss him over my shoulder like a kitchen towel and he squeals and kicks his legs happily as I walk us down the stairs.

My mom is in the living area with Wren and Ryder so I settle Archer on the couch beside her and explain the *no-knocking almost-peed-himself-again* situation.

Wren, my baby sister, is resting in my mom's arms and she's smiling up at me with her adorable sparkly-eyed smile. She's not one-and-a-half years old yet but she has a head of fluffy blonde curls and the longest black lashes that I've ever seen.

She drops the soft toy that she had loosely clutched under her arm and I give her a grin because I know that she did it just to make me play with her. I pick it up, wait for a second, and then I tickle it up her belly, making her giggle and squirm wildly in my mom's arms.

Once I finally stuff the toy back under her little hand, I

lean down to give her a kiss on her forehead. Archer is immediately back on his feet, hugging at my leg again because he can tell that I'm about to go.

They see me at the weekends during term but spending the whole winter break at home has meant that they've grown used to having me around. I look down into Arch's eyes and see that they've gone dangerously big and glossy.

I try to defuse the tear-bomb by roughing up his messy hair and then picking him up by his ribcage and tickling him into distraction.

While he laughs and kicks at me I say to my mom, "I've got all my stuff in the truck. I'll see you Saturday."

She catches Wren's toy before it makes another 'accidental' fall to the floor and she says, "Have fun. Maybe I'll see you stop by the diner on Sunday."

That last part is said with a smug smile and zero eye contact. My neck burns red as I release Archer and I grab my jumper from the arm of the couch.

"Hey now," I mumble, embarrassed as hell. Because yeah, during a couple of Fallon's shifts last term I stopped by the diner just so that I could flirt with her. But, in my defence, I did time my visits with when I knew my mom wasn't going to be *in* the diner.

I pull the jumper over my head and tug at my hair.

"Please, uh, remember not to mention anything to her," I say gruffly.

My mom looks up at me like I'm a fucking idiot.

When I asked her to take Fallon on I'd told her the situation: Fallon needed cash but I didn't want her knowing that I'd pulled strings with my parents to get her the job because, if she knew, she never would have accepted it. At that point she low-key hated my ass, but now that she kind of likes me it's actually even worse.

Something that my mom is evidently very aware of.

"You really like her?" she asks.

"Yeah."

"She your girlfriend now?"

I roll my shoulders and try to will away the heat in my cheekbones. I swallow hard and rumble, "Uh, kinda."

"Is it serious?"

I shove my tongue in my cheek and look down at the wooden flooring.

My mom rolls her eyes. "So how exactly are you going to get her to 'meet the parents' at some point when she's already technically *met your mom*?"

I rub my hand down over my jaw. Yeah, as soon as I'd made the plan I'd realised how terrible it was, but in the moment it had seemed like the right thing to do. A way to help Fallon with her financial predicament and also, you know, maybe get a little closer to her.

"I'll think of something," I mutter quietly. Knowing that I'm lying to Fallon every moment that I don't tell her that she's working at my family's business is making my temples throb like hell. I honest to God can't think of a way out of this fuck-up.

Maybe we'll just never do the meet the parents thing. I mean, given her parental situation I don't know if she'd ever want me meeting hers, so maybe I could just do the same–?

"If you're thinking about never getting her to meet your parents right now, so help me Lord," my mom says, and I press my palm into my forehead, letting out a pained laugh.

"Get outta my head," I mumble, but we share a smile anyway. I know that she's looking out for me, and she knows that I'll try my damn hardest to make this right. "I'm meeting up with her now," I admit as I trudge to the doorway to pull my boots on. My mom follows me with Wren, who's watching me curiously from her arms. "Taking her to the rink."

Originally I was going to bring one of my siblings with me but I've had them skating hard over Christmas and, if it's just the two of us, I'll get to have one-hundred percent of Fallon's attention.

"Have a lovely time," my mom says. Then she pointedly adds, "Be safe."

My eyes flash to hers and a silent conversation passes between us. I mean, she's one to fucking talk. I'm almost twenty-two and my parents are barely forty. Do the math.

"We haven't got there yet," I grunt reluctantly, because apparently I don't have a filter when it comes to my mom. My skin is on fire I'm so damn embarrassed.

She nods at me anyway, her expression composed and kind. "It isn't my business, but I want what's best for you is all. Be seein' you."

I let the kids hug at my legs again before tipping my chin at her and heading out to my truck.

"Be seein' you."

*

I text Fallon's phone as soon as I pull up outside of the condo, stepping down from my truck and rounding the hood to head towards her building. The weather still isn't great but it's not as hostile as it was a few weeks ago, so with the roads being constantly managed we'll get to the rink hassle-free.

I'm about to start crossing the lot towards the entrance of the building when Fallon suddenly appears, her petite form bundled up under a big white puffer jacket. I stop dead in the road, feeling like a huge weight has just lifted from my chest.

She has a soft lilac scarf wrapped around her neck and she's wearing a pair of skin-tight leggings. The second that she spots me I swear she almost trips over her little snow boots, her cheeks flushing pink and her hands moving to her earmuffs, stroking over the fur as if she needs something to do with her hands.

Once she's only about ten feet away from me I can't

keep still any longer. I rush her and grab her by her waist, loving the way that she squeals excitedly when I lift her up and compress her against my chest. Then I grab the back of her head and hold her in place so that I can crash my mouth down to hers.

She makes a sweet surprised sound that melts into a moan as I walk us carefully to my truck, my mouth never leaving hers.

We've had over three weeks of keeping our distance, and I have every intention of making up for lost time.

When her back hits the passenger door and she lets out a little gasp I slip my tongue inside her mouth and start stroking her deep and slow.

She wriggles against my lap, making me pull away and smirk down at her. She hastily reaches up to reaffix her earmuffs and I press into her slightly harder.

Her eyes widen and black out.

"Fallon," I rumble, setting her down onto her feet.

"Hi," she breathes back to me. "Happy New Year."

I grin and click the handle on the door behind her, helping her clamber up the step so that she can get herself onto the seat. I also get a real nice view of her bent-over ass in those leggings, the kind of view that has me readjusting my dick through my jeans as I head over to the driver's side, ready to take her on our date.

Once I'm inside the car and both of our doors are locked shut I immediately get my hands on her hips and drag her over the stick-shift onto my lap.

"Happy New Year, baby," I murmur, before leaning down to kiss her again.

She moans into my mouth as she begins pulling at her scarf and the zipper on her jacket. I lean back so that I can see what she's got underneath it and she shows me her fitted thermal shirt, her chest rising and falling quickly beneath it.

"I finished my application," she says, her eyes wide as

Pinkie Promise

she looks up at me. Something about her expression is so hesitant, so hopeful, that it makes me wonder if I'm the first person she's told this to out loud.

Which is why I squeeze my hands around her little waist and say, "I'm so proud of you, baby."

Her lashes flutter sleepily and she lets out a small sigh of relief, resting her forehead against my chest as if she can finally breathe.

I bite back a smirk.

My girl likes to be praised.
And I am more than willing to provide that service.

"Wanna know where we're going?" I ask her as I roam my palms down over her behind. I already told her last semester that I wanted to take her to the rink but I thought that I'd bring it up again in case she'd forgotten.

"'Kay," she says, pulling back so that she can look up at me.

I reach one arm behind me to where all my shit is in the back, and when I find what I'm looking for I get a grip around the box and hold it up next to her.

Her gaze immediately flashes to the gift-wrapped box in my hand and her beautiful eyes get even brighter.

"Is that... a Christmas present?" she asks, her fingertips twitching against my abs in hopeful anticipation.

"Yeah, seeing as you had me doin' time during the break and wouldn't let me see you, I had to save 'em until now," I say with a grin. Then I reach back and grab a second box, making her squeal before she kisses me.

I laugh and kiss her back, my day already made.

"I hope you like them," I murmur, massaging her ass a little harder. "The first gift is plain selfish, but the other one is so that we can start doing certain stuff together. Stuff that I can open up your world to, so that you can have a clearer understanding of mine."

"I love them already," she mumbles, making me chuckle as we break the kiss.

She peeks up at me, curious, and I jerk my chin at her. "Open 'em, baby."

She waits a grand total of three seconds before grabbing the first box from my hand and resting it between us on my lap. She rips straight through the paper and feels around for the lip of the lid. Once she gets her fingers underneath it she pushes the lid back and a small happy noise leaves her chest.

She presses her hands against her cheeks but I pull them away so that I can see her dimples.

"Did you… get me your jersey?" she asks, squealing when I lean forward and kiss at her neck. There are no words to describe how good it feels to know that your girl is excited to have your name on her back.

"Got in touch with the company that stocks Carter U and asked for them to do me a custom one," I murmur, sucking at her skin when she tightens her arms around my shoulders. "Didn't know if they'd be able to but turns out they could."

"Hunter, this is so…"

I lift up from her neck and she's shimmering with happiness.

I clear my throat, pleased. "Next one," I tell her.

She carefully places her new jersey to the side and gets to work on unwrapping the second box. When she rips it open she inhales a happy gasp.

"You bought me skates?" she whispers, beaming up at me with the most amazing look in her eyes. "You got me skates, so that we can skate together?"

I try to scrub away the heat from my neck. Fallon gives me a little smile as she strokes at the pretty lilac laces.

"You like 'em?" I ask gruffly.

"Yeah, I like them," she says with a grin, lifting one of them tentatively from the box so that she can get a better look at it.

They're a figure skating type of boot rather than the ice

hockey type, but I can tell from the way she's handling them that they're slightly heavier than she expected. You can get lightweight figure skating boots but I wanted to make sure that Fallon had the most secure and comfortable skate that I could find.

"Purple," she adds, giving me a prolonged look as she toys with the laces that I got custom done for her.

I grunt and nod. Yeah, okay, I've noticed her favourite colour.

"I'm hoping they're gonna fit," I say, even though I'm positive that they will. I saw her shoe size during the first time that she ever came into my bedroom, when she kicked off her high heels before we'd started fooling around on my sheets. The memory has my lids getting heavy and my palms massaging her harder.

She replaces the lid on the box and gives me a shy smile before she leans up to reward me with a kiss on the cheek. Like we're in damn middle school. Laughing, I use one hand to replace the box in the backseat while using my other hand to grip the back of her neck and pull her up for a real kiss. She loops her arms around my shoulders and lets me slant her open, stroking my tongue around hers as my thigh muscles begin to flex.

"What if I'm no good?" she whispers suddenly, pulling back a millimetre so that she can flash her eyes in the direction of the box. "I mean, skating for fun isn't as dangerous as ice hockey but I've seen the accidents that people can get themselves into."

I move a hand to her throat so that I can rub my thumb up her jaw.

"I'm not gonna let go of you," I tell her, meaning those words in every way that they can be interpreted. I want her to experience the thrill of gliding seamlessly over the ice, but I also want to be right behind her, holding her steady. Holding her, period.

To be honest I'm betting that she's going to be a natural

on the ice, although I can't deny that I'm going to enjoy her clutching onto me as she first gets a feel for it.

"Thanks," she says quietly, smiling when I dip down to kiss her neck.

"I missed you," I murmur gruffly. "So freakin' much."

I heard that forced proximity was the thing that made a guy fall for a girl, but it turns out that forced distancing makes things a million times worse.

"Oh," she breathes, blushing as she smiles. She pats at one of her earmuffs and teases, "How ever did you cope?"

I breathe out a laugh and scrape her pussy straight up my lap, wiping that smug little expression right off her face.

"Take a wild guess, baby."

She lets out a shaky breath and I press a kiss against her temple.

"Are you gonna let this – us – happen this semester?" I ask her quietly as the air in the truck grows warmer, more intimate. "Gonna be my girlfriend?"

Last term she was so busy stressing about her future, constantly putting measures in place so that she could achieve her goals. But I'm hoping that now her grant application is submitted and her role with her new cheer team will be starting up, she'll have the freedom to make time for herself. To make time for her needs.

Needs that I'm hungry to fulfil.

It's a conversation that doesn't usually happen, this laying down of the fine print so that we're both on the same page, but it's one that I need us to have before I take this to the next level. I already know that I want her. I just need to know that she wants me too.

I try to ease the pressure of communicating her innermost thoughts by gently stroking at her throat and kissing her. She purrs lightly, making my cock flex and throb.

"I know you don't like talking about your feelings," I murmur, "and I promise we won't have to talk about them often. I just need an answer for this one, baby. Can I start

Pinkie Promise

treating you the way that I've been wanting to?"

Her hands fist my shirt, gripping me closer.

"You want me to be your boyfriend, you just say the words. Because I sure as hell want you to be my girlfriend. I sure as hell want to make you mine."

Before she meets my eyes she strokes tenderly up my stubble, the bristles scraping loud and rough against her fingers.

"And we never have to talk about feelings again?" she asks, trying to tamper down her smile as she looks up at me from under her pretty lashes.

I half-laugh, half-groan. "How is it that I've found the one chick who doesn't wanna talk about emotions? You read romance books, baby – I thought that they'd be full of this stuff."

She ponders that for a moment, a thoughtful expression on her face. "There's... usually very little time for emotional development. It's more like, they meet and then after a couple of chapters they're in bed together. Well, maybe not in a bed, specifically. It's sometimes so urgent that there isn't enough time for them to find a bed."

I tug at my hair. "Jesus."

"But, um, in answer to your question... yeah. I wanna... I'd like us to..." She presses her fingers against her forehead, drops them, and then lets the words out in a gust. "I wanna let this happen."

Warmth shoots through my chest. *This is finally happening.*

"Is that a yes?" I ask, my heart thundering in my ears. "You're gonna be my girl?"

She hides her face in my chest, giggling wildly as she nods her head.

"Baby," I rasp, grinning when she beams up at me. I instantly hunker down to kiss her, growling victoriously as she moans. "Mine," I say gruffly, and she laughs delightedly as I smother her in kisses.

CHAPTER 21

Hunter

Experiencing the ice for the first time with Fallon in her new boots is the cutest thing I've ever felt in my life.

It's winter and it's a Saturday so there are a decent amount of skaters at the rink, but I'm so focused on easing Fallon into this that I don't notice the families moving around us.

I step onto the ice and spin on my blade to face her, holding out both of my hands so that I can keep a hold of her as she takes her first steps.

As soon as the tip of her blade touches the ice she immediately pulls her leg back up, squealing nervously.

I laugh and give her a little tug. "Baby, I've got you. Get your little ass over here."

She lets out a shaky breath as she hesitantly slides one boot onto the rink, and when she's got both of her feet on the ice I pull her easily against my chest.

She slides the one-foot of distance between us and nibbles at her lip.

"I don't think that I'm going to be able to move my legs," she admits on a nervous whisper, her brow pinched in pain as she looks down at her new boots. "How the hell do you do this every week?"

I begin slowly skating backwards, still holding her up against my body, and her fingers dig hard into the sides of my throat, securing herself.

Jesus Christ. I love it when she's rough with me.

"It's your first time on the ice," I say hoarsely, my voice coming out lower than I was expecting it to.

From the look that Fallon flashes me it came out lower than she was expecting too.

"We're getting you used to the feel of it, baby. We don't need you to be doing triple-spins and split-kicks. You're riding with me today."

Unable to resist, I move my hands to her waist and turn her gently underneath my palms. She lets out a little gasp that has me wishing we were alone on the ice because, if that was the case, my hands would definitely be climbing higher.

I press her back up against my front and settle my chin onto her shoulder. I nudge her pretty boot with my big one and she breathes out a nervous laugh as she takes in the size difference.

"Bend your knees," I murmur.

Her body shivers at the command.

"I don't think that we're supposed to do this on the ice," she whispers back to me. "It's a family place."

I grin and tug at her earlobe with my teeth.

"You gonna be difficult?" I ask her, rubbing my thumbs into her back. The naughty smile on her lips tells me everything that I need to know. "Fine."

I slide my hands down to her hips and push firmly, making her breathing hitch as I settle her into a slight squat position. My dick is wedged right against her ass, making my chest heave like a motherfucker as her body presses against mine.

"Now lean to the side on your blades," I rasp. "I'll move with you."

"Which way?" she asks breathlessly.

"Either."

She hesitates for a moment before crouching a little lower, and tightening her body as she leans infinitesimally to her right.

My voice comes out in a gravel scrape, too damn aware of how taut her body is under my palms. "Good. Do the other side."

She slowly leans her bodyweight over to her left and I press myself up behind her, following her movements.

"Now we're gonna go back to the centre and you're gonna kick your blade off of the ice like you're trying to pedal. Just a soft kick that'll carry you a couple of feet forward. You're light as fuck so you don't need to do it too rough."

We can save all the rough stuff for when we're off the ice.

"Okay," she breathes, realigning her body so that she's almost standing fully upright. The only difference now is the slight bend in her knees. I keep my hands on her hips as she lifts her arms to balance herself and then she kicks slightly on her blade, scooching forward about half a centimetre.

I can't help but laugh, pressing a kiss against her cool cheek. "Harder, baby."

Her body shudders against my torso and my grip on her hips becomes a little less gentlemanly.

She kicks her foot slightly harder and this time she's really moving.

"Keep doing that, baby. Both sides," I tell her, even though she's doing it naturally, only wobbling when she glances back at me over her shoulder. I can tell that she's got this on lock, her core cheerleader strength meaning that her balance is unbelievable, but I keep my hands on her anyway for purely selfish reasons.

I don't need to hold a squat to skate so I stand to my full height and move my hands just beneath her arms. She has both of them slightly extended and she's kicking harder and faster, a pink blush nipping the tip of her nose. My digits are only a millimetre away from brushing over her breasts meaning that, out of the two of us, *I'm* the one who's breathing unevenly.

"Fallon," I murmur, gripping my fingers harder into her flesh.

She turns in a spin that I didn't even teach her and she beams up at me, glowing with adrenaline.

"This is wild," she says excitedly, somehow naturally skating backwards.

I roam my hands down over her ass and pull her flush up against my body. "You're real good, baby. You're a total natural."

Her eyes sparkle and she squirms a little, preening.

"No way," she says, lowering her lashes, even though I know she knows that she's killing it.

We skate the rink for a good half an hour, Fallon anxiously pushing back against me when I press my arousal into her behind. I scrape my stubble up and down the side of her throat and she tenderly places her hands over mine. Her icy cold fingers have me holding her tighter against my chest, wanting to warm her up from the outside in.

By the time that we get back to the truck I really can't get my hands off of her.

I wait until I've pulled up outside of her condo but, once we're parked up, I can't take it anymore. We can't even climb into the back because I have all of my shit back there – all of the stuff I took home over the winter break that I'm now taking back to the hockey house.

I need her on me, her heat teasing my cock as she straddles my lap, riding my body like she goddamn owns me.

I know that she's not about to let me have her for the first time in the front of my truck but I get her wrapped up in my arms anyway, leaning over the stick-shift and dipping down to take her lips with mine.

I kiss her slow and gentle, easing my tongue inside of her, and her little whimper is so sexy that I grunt straight into her mouth.

She's squirming on her seat, kneeling to get better access to me, and it's damned impossible to stop my hands from travelling past where I should be keeping them.

"Got an away game next week," I murmur as I kiss my way down her neck. She leashes her fingers through my hair, tugging harder than I expected. I smirk into her skin and palm roughly at her ass. "You're coming."

I look up at her from my position in front of her breasts and I smile as she blinks down at me with dialled-out pupils.

"For an away game?" she asks, surprised and breathless. "Are you sure? How would I even get there?"

"There's a bus."

"For the *team*," she says, glancing around like she's about to be arrested.

I huff out a laugh and lean back up over her. "Sometimes we hire one for Carter U supporters. This is one of those games." I decide not to add why this particular game warrants more significance.

"How much is it?" she asks quietly, looking sideways with a pink expression.

Something fractures in my chest.

I open up the glove compartment and pull out the slip for the coach. She chews on her lip as I tell her, "It's on the house, baby."

"How much *was* it?" she rephrases, looking up at me with those big eyes, staring nervously like she thinks she owes me something.

"Nothing, Fallon. Don't even think about it." It was

Pinkie Promise

forty-five dollars and it doesn't merit a conversation.

She narrows her eyes on me, like she thinks she's going to get me to confess. I decide to give her something else to help her understand where I'm coming from, as vaguely as I can.

"It's not a significant game for the new players on the team, but I'd like you to be there," I rasp.

My voice turns rough when her breasts brush against my chest. I swipe my tongue over my lower lip and let my gaze drop.

Those curves are so pretty my mind momentarily stills, the need to get my hands on her making my whole body turn rigid.

Just one touch, one handful. I've felt them before, but it was too damn long ago. I need a reminder of that fullness so that I have something to focus on tonight, when I brace my arm against the wall and fuck my fist in the shower.

"Will I have to stay over?" she asks, bringing me back to the present.

I make a gruff sound and quickly rub my palm over the swell in my jeans. "Don't have to if you don't want. The team's got a whole motel booked but…" I glance away from her for a second, not wanting to tell her what I had in mind.

I'll sort out the accommodations that I want us to stay in, but whether or not it ends up happening isn't up to me. It's up to Fallon. And I don't want to freak her out by coming across as way too forward.

"Do you want me to?" she presses, settling down on her knees.

"Yeah," I grunt, meeting her eyes. I want her beside me in every bed that I sleep in.

She nods up at me and then bites back a smile as she leashes her forearms around my neck, dragging me down so that we can kiss again. It sets off a fucking red diesel engine in my abdomen.

"That a yes?" I ask, squeezing her ass like she's my damn property.

"Yeah," she pants, laughing breathily when I groan.

I know exactly what she's thinking. I can tell from the way that she's letting me make out with her so damn dirty. She's moaning into every tangle of my tongue, rubbing herself up against my hard and heaving pecs.

She's telling me that she hasn't forgotten our deal from December.

She's telling me that, whereas the last semester was spent focusing on school, we're going to spend the rest of the winter getting triple-figure Fahrenheit hot.

CHAPTER 22

Fallon

The coach for the Carter U supporters set off five minutes before the coach for the Carter U players, a fact which has had Hunter blowing up my phone every thirty seconds with photos of our bus's rear end.

> HUNTER: *your driver is going way too fast*
> FALLON: *we are literally on the highway. what's he supposed to do? go slow?*
> HUNTER: *you're riding with us on the way back*
> FALLON: *wait. please tell me that the supporter coach leaves tomorrow, same time as the team coach?*

A deafening silence has me checking the bus slip that Hunter gave me last week.

The supporter coach leaves tonight, whereas the team's coach leaves tomorrow morning.

Oh my God. How did I not think to check this?

FALLON: *I can't ride with your team Hunter! wtf!*

Hunter sends me a photo of the inside of the team's bus with the caption: *which seat do you want? you're with the captain so you get first dibs.*

Then he sends me a smiley face that makes me groan out a laugh.

"Oh my God," I mumble, pressing my fingers into my forehead. I can tell from his texts that he's got that hot smug grin on his face.

Suddenly nervous about the warm fuzzy feeling in my belly, I click the button at the top of my cell and turn my phone off for the rest of the ride.

I wriggle my hands up the sleeves of my cardigan and smooth out the pleats of my skirt with my new sleeve-paws.

I'm sat beside Winter, Caden's girlfriend who doesn't even attend Carter U, but seeing as Caden bought her ticket the college is none the wiser about her being here. She's spent the past twenty minutes trying to share candy-floss flavoured grapes with me, peeking at me sideways as my face probably turns more and more green.

I've never been great with long distances.

She glances at me after my little outburst with my cell and she laughs as she watches me shove my phone into the bottom of my bag. I didn't actually see Hunter before the bus left the Carter U lot but I watched from the window as Caden kissed goodbye to his girlfriend. They're such a visual contradiction that I found it hard to look away.

Winter twizzles a soft pink curl around her fingers, curiosity shimmering in her eyes as she watches me.

"Wanna use mine instead?" she asks, holding her phone out to me with her earphone cord dangling over my arm. "If you wanna listen to music or something."

The gesture is so trusting and thoughtful that I feel a small bloom of warmth in my chest.

"I'm okay, honestly," I rasp, stifling a dry-heave.

She smiles at me as she slips her phone inside her bag, nestling it beside a literal full-sized Holy Bible. She crosses her legs towards me, and nudges at my shoe with the pointy toe of her cowgirl boot.

"We'll only be on the road for, like, another fifteen minutes. You get car sick or something?" she asks.

Wow, my face must be *really* green.

"Mm-hm," I admit, breathing shakily. "I've been doing long distances since I was a kid but my body never got used to it. When I was on the cheer comp team and we used to go cross-country? I'd be the girl lying in the aisle, trying not to pass out." I laugh at the memory, fanning my embarrassed cheeks with my hand. "The driver actually had to pull over one time so that I could recalibrate my body. It felt like I couldn't breathe which, obviously, is not ideal."

Winter laughs and gives my shoulder a little nudge. The action almost makes me retch, and she gives me an apologetic laugh while handing me her bottle of water.

"You need a good distraction, is all," she says as I sip the water like my life depends on it. Right now, it feels like it does. "I used to get it too, but when I started travelling with Cade it honestly went away. When I'm not riding with him I just listen to music. Long songs that I know all of the lyrics to. I'll listen to the ten minute version of 'All Too Well' twelve times and suddenly I don't want the two hour road-trip to end."

I glance over to her, hearts in my eyes. "You're a genius," I tell her.

She pats delicately at her soft pink blow-out. "It has been said."

Fifteen minutes later the coach is pulling up at Larch Peak University's D1 hockey rink and the second that my feet hit the ground the players' coach is pulling up right next to ours.

The door slides open and the guys begin to slowly dismount, eyeing us casually as they saunter to grab their gear from the side compartment. As soon as Hunter muscles his shoulders out of the doorway his eyes find mine and a smile tugs at his lips.

My jaw drops to the floor when I see what he's wearing.

He quickly grabs his gear from the pile-up and then he's leading me around to the side of the bus so that he can kiss me without his teammates watching.

"You're wearing a suit," I whimper, as he tugs my body up against his. His pecs are so big that the buttons of his shirt are literally straining.

"Yeah," he grunts, kissing at my mouth. "Protocol."

Before I can tell him that he's the hottest man I have ever seen, he grips one hand at the back of my neck and leashes his fingers through my hair, angling me so that he can kiss me deeper. I moan quietly as he slips his tongue around mine, and he uses his other hand to stuff something into my palm.

I pull away panting so that I can look down at it.

It's a bag of Jelly Babies.

Hunter's molten eyes meet mine and I instantly know what he's thinking about – us at the movies, Jelly Babies spilling all over my lap.

Suddenly my face is on fire.

"There's a couple of hours before the game starts," Hunter states, his voice gravel rough as his eyes rake me up and down. "Get those down your neck."

My eyes go wide, my skin aflame, and I realise that this is a side of Hunter that I haven't seen before. He's in full-on game-day mode.

It's so intimidating that I can barely breathe.

"Okay," I say breathlessly, tucking them into my bag for safe-keeping.

I feel his large palm stroke at my ponytail, making my cheeks burn even hotter.

"Nice bow," he grunts, eyes on the cheer bow in my hair.

"I wanted to support," I say back to him, feeling a little self-conscious. It's in Carter U's colours to match the team's hockey gear.

He flashes me a satisfied smirk, which makes my belly pound and flip.

"Good," he murmurs. "I want these Larch Peak fuckers to know exactly who you're supporting."

His hand tightens around my ponytail before he smoothes his palm down the length of it. Our gazes lock together, and heat licks in my abdomen.

Seeing Hunter in his suit for the first time – a tradition for Division I athletes at Carter U when they're doing tournaments like this – reminds me that, while I'm no longer doing sport competitively, Hunter is, and this game could be a really big deal for him.

I know that he's intending to go pro when he graduates and I'm guessing that the higher Carter U ranks in the college league the better his potential NHL team will be. He's already the captain at a Division I college which clearly proves how powerful he is, but the sight of him and his team looking like they're going into battle is enough motivation for me to give him as much support as possible.

And right now he looks every bit the bad boy hockey player that girls love to assume he is.

But I've spent three years being the good girl cheerleader, and now is the perfect time to put it to use.

Hunter spent our entire last semester supporting me, and it's time to return the favour.

I stand up on my tip-toes, wrap my arms around his neck, and his expression immediately softens into a contented boyish smirk. I press a little kiss to his sharp tan cheekbone before leaning further up so that I can whisper in his ear.

"Is now a good time to tell you that I brought my pom-poms?" I ask teasingly.

Hunter chuckles and scrubs at the back of his neck, his

cheeks turning ruddy. He looks around to check that no-one is within hearing distance and then he towers over me and murmurs, "Really?"

I give him a tiny nod and he drops his eyes, smiling shyly.

"Jesus, baby," he rasps, rubbing his thumbs into my belly.

"After you win, I'll show you how I use them."

His eyes burn into mine, his throat muscles rolling, and after a beat he smirks, pressing a firm kiss against my lips. "Baby, I've been needin' you for so long that you won't be able to hold onto those pom-poms when I finally get my hands on you."

I let out a whoosh of air, way out of my depth, but then I'm biting back a smile as Hunter gently kisses my cheek.

Hunter Wilde is the most beautiful contradiction I have ever met.

"Carter U?" a voice suddenly calls from the entrance doors to the Larch Peak U rink. "Your team is free to head into the changing rooms now."

I tense up a little as I glance at the guy in the doorway. He's kitted out in the home team's gear, evidently a player on their roster, and he looks kind of pissed off at having been assigned door duty.

The Carter U team eye him with varying levels of unfriendliness as they trudge past him. Some jerk their chin at him but, if anything, that just seems to piss him off more.

Hunter looks completely disinterested.

I try to pull out of his arms and Hunter's attention snaps back down to me. He realises that we're going to be separated until his game is over and his hands on my waist immediately tighten.

"I'll find you straight after the game," he murmurs, low and husky. I lean up so that he can kiss me and he grunts hard as he rubs our tongues together. He must feel my slight tremor of nerves about watching him play his crazy brutal sport again because when I pull away he says quietly,

"Don't worry, it's gonna be fine. We're gonna win, no problem."

I nod up at him, trying to hide my little wave of anxiousness. "I know," I whisper. "You're amazing, you're going to win."

He watches me intensely for a moment and then in the next second he presses his forehead against mine, a move so gentle that I gasp at the contact. Hunter sighs and something painful blooms in my chest. It's so intimate that it hurts.

"Yo, didn't you hear me?"

I feel Hunter's back muscles swell underneath my fingertips, before he turns his head over his shoulder to where the guy on the opposing team is still standing at the door. His arms are folded across his chest and his face is bright red.

He looks like the kind of guy who shotguns a lot of energy drinks.

Hunter lifts up, releasing me from the cage of his chest, and stands to his full height, showing the guy at the door exactly what he's dealing with. A guy who's built like a damn monster truck.

Hunter stares at him wordlessly until the other guy scoffs and looks away. Then he turns around to me, his boyish sweetness replaced by the competitiveness of a Division I athlete.

He pulls open his bag, grabs his jumper, and he stuffs it into my arms, a heated look darkening his features. He tips his chin at it and says hoarsely, "Wear that for me during the game."

I can't help but think back to the first time that he gave me his jumper, and the fact that he told me that he would find a reason to give it to me again.

Hunter Wilde is a man of his word.

I bite back a smile as I clutch his soft jumper against my chest and then I lean up for one more kiss, showing Hunter exactly who I'm going to be supporting tonight. He grunts and licks his tongue against mine, once, twice, until my arms are locked tight around his neck and I wish that I never had to let go.

"Okay," I whisper, nodding as he kisses my cheeks. "I promise."

CHAPTER 23

Hunter

It was all going perfect until the last three minutes.

As soon as we got on the ice I clocked Fallon in the box of Carter U supporters, pulling the sleeves of my jumper down over her hands and smiling at something that Caden's girlfriend was whispering in her ear. I'd also managed to avoid brawling with any of the Larch Peak guys during the first two periods which, considering their play, was fucking altruistic.

Being the home state to one of the best teams in the NHL should mean that they pride themselves on smart strategy and quality players, but whenever we've come to face off here that's never the case. They're so desperate for a high ranking that their game is dirty, but it had never been *personal* up until now.

Having already scored three of the six goals that are about to make our win against Larch Peak U undeniable, I skate to the other side of the rink, analysing our team's formation, checking to see if there's anything that we can work on for our next game.

I pass Coach Benson and he gives me a subtle nod, telling me with that one gesture that he's satisfied with our team's play. I nod back at him and skate to the Carter U box, wanting to get my eyes on Fallon one more time before this game is over. I pretend that I'm taking a moment to catch my breath but really I'm done with this game and I'm dying to finally have my girl in my arms.

And not in the motel with the rest of the guys.

Having her in Larch Peak is important to me, and I've put the necessary plans in place.

From the way that my body's feeling under my gear I can't deny that I'm probably going to have a few bruises. The guys at Larch Peak U have hard-ons for getting up in your personal space and, even though I haven't been brawling back, well aware that my chick's in the stands watching my every move, most of this game has been push-and-shove. No-one's more pissed off than Tanner, who took a bunch of deliberate hits before finally lashing out. It ended with Tanner snapping the other guy's stick and then taking up full-time residence in the already-packed sin bin.

I don't blame him. We shared a damn low-five before the ref escorted him off the rink.

Because at the end of the day, Tanner and I grew up in Carter Ridge. We were raised with a tight moral code but we'll only take so much before we put you back in your damn place.

As soon as I reach the Carter U box I'm biting back a smile, looking at Fallon snuggled down in my jumper and giving me a shy thumbs-up. I check the clock on the screen and then mouth *two minutes* at her, a promise that this is almost done and then I can finally give her the night that she deserves.

She nods at me and her ponytail swishes, the cheer bow in her hair sparkling when it catches the light. And damn if that symbol of her loyalty to Carter U doesn't make me the most satisfied guy on the ice right now. I drop my eyes briefly to her bare thighs, a gruff sound of approval rumbling in my chest, before I give her a jerk of my chin and finally turn around.

And that's when it starts to go downhill.

The player who ushered us in and looked like he had a big-ass chip on his shoulder skids up right in front of me and flashes his eyes to where Fallon is sitting. The name on the back of his jersey reads O'Neill, and even that kind of pisses me off because it gets me thinking about Connell O'Malley.

I know that my slow-simmering irritation with O'Malley is unwarranted because I know that Fallon only sees him as a friend, but no-one ever said that love makes a man rational.

O'Neill's eyes lock on Fallon and I immediately move my body, blocking her from his view. When his eyes slide over to mine I give him an emotionless look of my own.

The sly smile on his face starts a warning throb in my temples.

"That yours?" he asks, gesturing with his stick towards the box behind me.

I watch him blankly for a couple of seconds before turning my head to glance over at Fallon. Her eyes have gone wide and she's no longer smiling, as if she can sense the impending shit-storm that's about to go down.

When O'Neill called over to us while we were making out earlier I could tell that Fallon sensed that he was bad news. I could tell from the way that she tensed up under my palms and subconsciously pushed her little body up against me. She didn't know yet that this is what all of the Larch Peak U players are like. Hell, a whole load of hockey players in general can be good-for-nothing motherfuckers, but it's the same for every sport, and with experience my team has learned to take the good with the bad.

I tip my chin at her, letting her know that I'll handle this, and then I turn back to O'Neill, pushing forward on my skates so that he has no choice but to back up. I want him as far away from Fallon as is physically fucking possible.

I also don't want her to hear hockey smack-talk, especially when this guy's team is about to lose. Guys like this one will do anything to get under your skin.

"Yeah," I grunt, shoving his stick out of my path when he tries to catch my boot.

"Way out of your league," he comments, and I momentarily pause, grinning at that one.

"Hell yeah she is. She's way out of everyone's league. Tell me something I don't know."

The puck is nowhere near our goal and I'm scanning the rink to see if our team is about to slide in one last finisher when his next words suddenly get my muscles tensing.

"Cute bow," he says. "She a cheerleader or something? Gotta wonder why the hell she's with you – cheer chicks only bang footballers."

My shoulders swell under my jersey and my quads start throbbing like they've got energy to expend. As if I haven't been going hell for leather on the ice and secured my team another win.

I look down at O'Neill and suddenly I'm itching for a fight.

"*Oh*," he says, drawing out the word with a shit-eating grin. "She *does* know some footballers. That's eating you alive, huh?"

There's nothing in this for him except hoping to rile me enough to fight and then getting me a bollocking from my coach. Right now that's a consequence that I'm open to taking.

Because Fallon *does* know some footballers, Connell O'Malley being one of her closest damn friends. And although I trust that she would never cheat on me, I also wouldn't blame O'Malley for shooting his shot if he wanted to.

And from the way that I've seen him looking at her? I bet he's fucking wanted to.

O'Neill laughs and I take a steady inhale, twisting my stick slow and hard into the ice. Anything to occupy my hands from what they really want to do, which mainly involves dislocating O'Neill's jaw.

He can tell. Which is why in the next second O'Neill pushes his chest straight into mine, trying to get me to shove him back, but I just grunt and strengthen my position as I keep my balance strong.

Benson's words from October come to the forefront of my mind.

You think you're all noble dishing out justice? That's the ref's job, not yours, Wilde.

There's got to be no more than thirty seconds left of this game and I'm not trying to get into a fight when the whistle's about to blow, especially when we're coming out victorious.

I roll my neck and look down at O'Neill. "I really don't recommend doing that again, man," I tell him quietly.

He flashes me a grin before ramming his shoulder straight into my gut.

A guttural sound rips from my chest, and I keep my stance wide as I shove the punk off of me. "The hell's your goddamn problem?" I growl, trying to keep my cool.

Don't let Fallon see you lose your shit. Don't let her see the kind of fighting that you're capable of.

And that would have been the goddamn end of it if he hadn't spat the next words out of his mouth.

"She friends with your Carter U quarterback or something? Hell man, that's gotta suck. Knowing that she wants to deep-throat that raw NFL pipe—"

My stick hits the ice at the same second that my quad connects with his groin, and I tear the strap on my gloves open with my teeth as O'Neill stumbles on his blades. The malicious look in his eyes turns to something more aggressive and he throws down his helmet, the clank of it drowned out by the sounding buzzer calling time.

He might be angry that I've just bruised his balls, but I'm fucking furious.

If he wants to fight dirty, I'm game.

He swipes his helmet off the ice and swings it hard at mine, red hot pain immediately exploding in the side of my face. I'm so pissed off that I revel in the bite of it before chucking my own helmet down and roughly rolling back my shoulders. O'Neill uses the second of distraction to ram his torso into mine and this time we hit the ground with a loud resounding thud, O'Neill cursing explicitly as he lands at a stupid angle on his side.

I shove up from my position and grip him into a headlock, leaning closer so that he can hear me over all of the arena noise.

"Y'all fuckers weren't taught any manners at this college, huh?" I ask him, swiping my shoulder over my cheek when I feel something warm and wet on my skin. I grunt at the sting and then rub my hand over the area. When I pull it back I see that my digits are coated red.

"You're too bulky for this game," he grits out, probably because, now that I've got a forearm around his throat, he's realising how stupid it was to bait a guy who weighs two hundred and twenty pounds. "Quality players are lean."

I snicker, because that has got to be the dumbest shit that I've ever heard, and I shove his hands away from me as he tries to land a backwards hit. "I'm too bulky? We're in the same division, asshole."

I push O'Neill off of me and exhale gruffly as I slowly get to my feet, disorientated by the scuffle and feeling a pounding in my head. Not sure if it's because O'Neill got me with his helmet pretty good or because his words have fucked me off pretty bad. Either way, I shove a hand through my hair and try to regain some sense of balance because the past ten seconds have thrown me the hell off.

O'Neill is still shouting smack and I suddenly realise that Fallon might be able to hear him. Still a little unbalanced I turn to skate over to the Carter U box before realising that my teammates are grouped around me. They're holding off O'Neill as he tries to shove his way in my direction and I almost huff out a laugh at how stupid that is.

If we brawl you'll end up on a gurney, lightweight. Take a fucking hint, man.

The audience must have finally caught on to the fight because there's a thunderous rise in the crowd's volume, making me unsteady. Tanner grips a hand around the back of my neck in a rough gesture of support, and we trudge on our skates over to our exit gate, my breathing erratic as O'Neill's words course through my mind.

It's not *what* he said, because Fallon's sex life before I came into the picture is none of my business, unless she chooses for it to be. It's the fact that he dared even think about it, to talk about it like that when she was only ten feet away from him. Potentially within hearing distance. For the sole purpose of ruining her night.

Hurting me? Fine.

But hurting her? Not a chance.

I try to get my eyes over to where Fallon is sat with Winter but there are too many people in the way obscuring the view. I turn on my boots and jerk my chin over at Caden. He skates up next to me and I nod my head towards the Carter U seats.

"Can you get the girls?" I ask him, my voice low and hoarse. I need to get my hands on Fallon as soon as possible so that I can apologise about the shit-show that I accidentally just put on for her.

You want her to trust you but you just showed her that you're a damn brute.

What the hell is wrong with me?

Caden grunts and I give him a *thank you* shove with my shoulder as he leaves the exodus so that he can slide through the gate to the girls.

"What the *hell* was that?" Benson is practically shaking when we reach him at the edge of the rink.

Now I'm pissed off all over again because he's flipped the switch on me after a damn ten second hockey brawl. Big fucking deal. Guys in the NHL fight in every damn game.

The look that I level him with has him narrowing his eyes and shaking his head at me.

"The game was over, idiot. What were you thinking?" His eyes move to my cheekbone and he rubs his hand over his mouth. "Jesus Christ. Someone get this fucking moron a towel."

Tanner's hand tightens, warning me to keep my cool.

"He got a knee to the balls. You can't even get arrested for that shit."

"Uh, actually you fucking *can* depending on the situation," Benson argues back, "and there was no need for brawling when y'all won the damn game."

My jaw muscle rolls, adrenaline still pumping hard and fast in my veins. "It had nothing to do with the game."

"Then you should have kept it *off the ice*. When y'all get back to the motel before I head off to Carter Ridge I'll decide whether or not you're fit for the next game, Wilde."

"I'm not going to the motel," I tell him, and his eyes suddenly flash. Tanner subtly steps between us as Benson takes a big step forward.

"What'd that fucker say to you?" Coach Benson asks, giving me a surprised once-over. "What the hell happened out there to make you lose your shit? You fucked up at the start of the year but you recouped your game. What's gotten into you to make you change that now?"

The whole team can sense it – the fact that Benson is about to realise that I broke his one goddamn rule.

We stare at each other long and hard, my expression emotionless as I try not to think about what O'Neill said.

My eyes flick over to the Carter U box and my chest swells as Fallon finally comes into my line of sight.

I look away quickly, knowing that – if I keep looking at her beautiful face – my defences are about to crumble.

Benson follows my line of sight and arches his neck back, finally coming to his realisation.

"You have got to be kidding me," he mutters, scraping a hand over his head. "You've got a girl with you? Is that what this was?"

Benson meets my eyes again, disbelief etched on his face, and suddenly I'm done with all of the chaos that has happened tonight. The shitty opponents, the overbearing coach, the one stupid rule that should never have been made in the first place.

So I keep my distance as I trudge past him and I mutter, "It ain't your damn business, man."

It's only when I reach the door at the start of the narrow corridor that Benson calls out, "It will be when I bench your ass."

The whole team stills and the air around us immediately tenses, but after the longest ten seconds of my life I decide to keep walking. By the time that I reach the changing rooms I'm slamming my locker open and ripping off as much of the kit as I can. I'm not about to put my suit back on because it's a fucker to get into so I pull my jeans and a shirt out of my bag instead.

I rip the protective gear off and shove that shit into my gym bag, needing to get the hell out of here before I can reconsider the premature end to my brawl with O'Neill.

The low-road is sounding damn satisfying right now.

As I pull a hoodie over my head Caden trudges in and I immediately ask him, "You get Fallon? Is she alright?"

I hide the tremble in my hands by gripping my gear bag nice and tight.

Caden nods and tips his head towards the door. "They're on their way." Then he gives me a brief appraisal and murmurs, "Maybe clean your face up first."

Instinctively I swipe my palm up my cheekbone and I curse quietly.

That shit stings.

But before I can pull the gauze from my bag to staunch the flow I hear the sound of two soft voices nearing the door, at that sweet feminine pitch that you don't find in the guy's changing room. In the next second I'm grabbing all of my shit and shoving my way past my teammates.

I see Fallon as soon as I shoulder my way out of the door and all of the emotions that I'd been grinding down flood to the surface as I get my eyes on her.

I was worried that she was going to be apprehensive and freaked out because she's never seen me lose control like that before, but instead she's rosy cheeked and her chest is pumping heavily, and she launches herself straight into my arms the second that our gazes meet.

I grunt as I grip her behind, helping her wrap her thighs around my body, and I slide my other hand under her hair, seizing her by the back of her neck and pressing my face into the warm curve of her throat. She's making small, quiet noises that almost sound like she's crying and I squeeze my eyes shut in anger, pissed beyond measure over what the hell I just did.

Her arms wrap tightly around my shoulders and she presses her rapidly heaving chest up against my pecs.

I almost stumble at the sensation – her breasts feeling so soft, her breathing coming so fast – but I steel my jaw and continue walking us down the corridor. The hallway is loud after another win, the guys smacking high fives and slapping their hands against each other's backs.

"I'm sorry," I murmur to Fallon, pressing a kiss against her hair. She mumbles a quiet *it's okay* and I shake my head as I kiss her again.

"It's not okay," I tell her, and she pulls back to look at me. I splay my palm against the exit door, shove it open and breathe in the calming scent of Larch Peak's fresh mountainous air.

"You're hurt," she says, her brows pinched taut in the middle.

"I'm an idiot," I reply, quickly scanning the lot to see where our Ubers are idling.

The guys are going to be taking them to the motel this evening, and tomorrow morning they'll get them back here in time for the coach transfer to Carter Ridge. What I had in mind for Fallon means that we aren't going to the motel, but our stop is on the way so we'll ride part of the distance with the guys.

"Hunter, I need to clean your wound," she says, quiet but serious, and a moment later I feel something soft pressing firmly against my cheekbone.

I wince slightly and gently tug at Fallon's wrist. When I see what she's using to compress the cut, pain spreads through my chest and I shake my head at her.

She's rolled up that little cardigan that she had on earlier and she's holding it against me to stem the blood loss.

"No, baby," I murmur, feeling more guilty by the second. "Don't ruin your top, not for me. It's my fault. I'm sorry."

I ruined our fucking night. I don't deserve her to be all sweet right now.

"You didn't do anything wrong. Hunter, look at me."

I can't look at her because I've got too much shit pounding through my head.

O'Neill. O'Malley. Brawling in front of my chick. Potentially getting benched by Benson.

Ruining a night that was supposed to be special because we're *here*, in Larch Peak, and I wanted Fallon to love everything about it.

I scrub roughly at my forehead and rap my knuckle against the window of one of the Ubers. The driver rolls down the window and I give her our name, so that she knows she's picking up the right group.

The guys pile in once I've got Fallon inside and when the driver eases onto the road I subtly slip Fallon onto my lap. We're riding with Tanner, Austin, and some other guys, and they're quietly playing music from one of their phones.

Fallon turns her head to look up at me and I slip my large hand around the front of her throat, dipping down to meet her so that I can kiss her lips.

"Where are we going?" she whispers.

I press my forehead against her temple. *It was supposed to be special.*

I sigh as I gently caress her throat. "The guys are going to the motel," I murmur, although the guys who are legal are going to hit up the town bars after they've dropped their kits off because there's a fucking hurricane of testosterone in the back of this car right now. "We're going somewhere else."

My eyes lock in with Tanner's and he gives me a nod. He knows exactly where we're going.

"If you don't like it, we can join the guys," I add, because I want to make sure that she's okay with it.

Hell, if she decided that she wanted to head back to Carter Ridge right now I'd get her a First Class flight without a damn second of delay.

All I want is what's best for her.

I just secretly hope that what's best for her is me.

"We're almost there," I promise her, wrapping my forearms around her middle. I sink my teeth into my bottom lip when I feel her press her cardigan against my cut again.

"Baby," I murmur, trying to get her to stop sacrificing her shirt for me, but she keeps it firmly in place and then leans up so that she can kiss me.

It's small and gentle but we're in an Uber full of guys so the testosterone in this cab has just ascended to a dangerous level.

Tanner clears his throat beside me but I just ram my elbow in his ribs.

The guys are definitely going out tonight.

And Fallon and I are staying in.

CHAPTER 24

Fallon

Hunter gives Tanner fifteen bucks to pay him back for our portion of the ride and when the Uber pulls up to our destination Hunter clicks open the door and helps me out by my hips.

Gravel kicks up off the road as the Uber drives away, and then it's just the two of us.

Hunter has his gym bag and my tote over one shoulder, and my body tucked safely underneath his bicep, and he uses the hand that isn't gently stroking at the front of my throat to pull an o-ring of keys from his front pocket. He twists the key in the lock until we hear the *click* and then he pushes the door open, his eyes tentatively dropping to meet mine.

The second that our gazes meet heat begins to spread its way up his throat, all the way to the top of his cheekbones, bringing my attention back to the cut that's now drying there. Realising that I'm looking at his injury Hunter's cheeks burn even brighter and he turns his head ever so slightly so that I can't see as much of the blood.

He leans into the doorframe so that he can flick on one of the inside sconces and then his eyes are back on mine as he jerks his chin in the direction of the house in front of us, soundlessly asking me to look at where we are.

I watch him for a few beats before reluctantly tearing my eyes away from him.

My eyebrows rise as I take in the view in front of me.

It looks like a summer house with exposed walls and beams, and the wooden panelling is stained a warm golden brown. The front door opens pretty much straight into the living room, with the kitchen off to the side and a stairwell at the back, leading presumably up to a bedroom and a bathroom. It's small and intimate, the furnishings rustic and cosy, and when I look at the untreated wooden floor I see worn away patches which tell me that this house has been very much lived in and very much loved.

I raise my eyes back to Hunter and he's watching me with a nervous, slightly hopeful look in his eyes.

"What is this place?" I ask him.

I don't mean for it to come out as a whisper, but in the silence that has fallen around us I don't want to disturb the peace. The only other sound in the area is a gentle lapping, like water rippling in a creek.

Hunter pushes the key back into his pocket and he looks into the house.

"It's, uh... I used to come here a lot. I'll explain but–" His eyes flash back down to mine as he tilts his head towards the interior of the cabin. I breathe slowly, attempting to calm the tingle in my belly at how deep his voice has gone. "You like it? 'Cause if not we can go to the motel or I can book us a–"

I push up onto my tip-toes, cupping Hunter's jaw in my hands, and I press a kiss against his mouth that immediately has him gripping my waist, making us stumble into the entrance as he shoves the door closed behind us.

He reaches out to turn the lock, showing me that this isn't his first time in the cosy house, and then he replaces both of his hands on my body, cupping my ribcage in his large palms. His thumbs begin pushing upwards, telling me exactly where he wants them to be touching.

"I need to disinfect the cut," I murmur as he pulls me up against his chest, making my feet dangle above the floor while he grabs a bottle of something from the small kitchen.

He makes a rough sound in his throat before crashing his mouth back down to mine, his dark hair tickling my forehead as he begins carrying me up the narrow stairs.

"Are you going to let me?" I ask breathlessly as he shucks our bags onto the floor of the landing.

I pull away so that I can look at him and he has an anguished grimace on his face. His eyes stay laser-focused on my lips for a good five seconds before he forces himself to look away and he runs a hand down his stubble.

"I don't deserve you nurse-maiding me, Fallon."

There's something so raw and humble in the way that he says it, making my limbs feel heavy as I press myself against him, that solidifies my need to do just that. To look after him. To be there for him in the way that he seems to have forgotten he was there for me.

I look around the small upper-story corridor, scanning the open doorways for the bathroom, and when I spot it I begin pushing him towards it with one hand, reaching down to pick up his gym bag with the other.

The bag is so damn heavy that I literally topple over.

"Baby, fuck," Hunter curses quickly, swooping his arm behind me so that I don't hit the floor. He takes the bag from my white-knuckled fist and hefts it easily over his shoulder.

Hunter punches on the light switch, tosses the bag onto the bathroom counter, deposits the bottle from his other hand, and then releases me completely. He steps back with his arms folded cautiously over his broad chest and his

Pinkie Promise

expression is patient, albeit a little pained.

"Did you bring the whole rink back with you in that bag?" I tease, tipping my head towards the carry-on on the counter and trying to lighten the mood.

His mouth ticks up slightly at one side and he breathes out a laugh, running a hand through his hair.

"It's just my gear, Fallon," he murmurs quietly, although the small smile on his mouth makes me silently exhale with relief.

"Do you have salve and stuff in there?" I ask him. "So that I can try and heal up the wound—"

"Baby," he says, his tone deep and intimate. "I don't deserve you nursing me like that. It's just a scrape."

He moves his body up against mine and reaches one arm behind my back, pulling up the bottle that he brought from the kitchen. I glance at it as he uncaps it, his eyes still burning into mine, and my brow raises a little as I realise that it's straight-up whiskey.

He flicks the cap onto the counter, presses his thumb over the opening, and then he lifts it to his face and pours it straight down his cheekbone.

My eyes go crazy wide. He curses as the spirit burns his cut.

"Hunter," I say, reaching up to take away the bottle. My fingers are shaking slightly as I set the bottle onto the counter and as he rubs his palm over his forehead I realise that Hunter's fingers are shaking too.

He tentatively lifts his large hand so that he can brush his knuckles over his name on my chest. *Hunter Wilde. Hockey Team Captain.*

I shudder involuntarily and he lets out a low sound from deep in his chest.

"Lean back on the counter," I instruct him, and his stroking instantly stills.

He meets my eyes and then glances at the counter behind me. I grip my hands around his biceps and steer him so that we turn one-eighty, swapping positions.

He raises his eyebrows but doesn't protest, and I begin unzipping his gym bag in search for something to wipe the blood away with. Hunter leans back and spreads out his thighs, and I settle in closer as I inspect the small bottle of saline. I arch around him for the bag of cotton pads that I spotted on the counter and I hope that whoever owns this house doesn't mind my using one of them.

"Who owns this place?" I ask him, disguising what I really want to say.

Why did you bring me here, Hunter? I can tell that this place is special to you.

I tip some of the solution onto the pad and then look up at Hunter's face, so close to my own that my breathing pauses in my chest. Hunter's pupils dial out and I feel my cheeks burn pink.

Throwing a nice big bucket of ice on the situation I press the cotton pad to the tip of Hunter's cheekbone and his jaw suddenly tenses, his muscles flexing.

"Does that hurt?" I ask, my eyes flashing to his with concern.

He studies me for a moment before slowly placing his hands on my hips and pulling me right up against his groin. I choke on a little swallow and his large chest swells and expands.

"Not anymore," he rasps quietly, his thick sex flexing against my belly. He keeps his eyes on my waist so that he doesn't have to look at me while he winces.

I lift my free hand to his jaw and gently stroke over the dark bristles. He closes his eyes and leans into my touch.

It doesn't take long for me to clean the injury. When I finish, I wrap my arms around Hunter's shoulders and tuck his face into the warm curve of my neck.

"*Mm*," he murmurs, as I stroke my fingers through his hair. His hands slide slowly under the hem of the jumper that I'm wearing, his restraint palpable as he forces himself

Pinkie Promise

not to roam any higher.

"Tell me about today," I whisper to him and he groans into my throat. I tug harder at his hair and he nods against my shoulder.

He repositions himself slightly so that he's leaning back against the counter, towering over me as I hug my arms around his middle.

"I'm embarrassed," he murmurs, the creases in his brow making my heart ache. "It was a good game and I fucked up right at the end. You came all this way with me and I blew it to shit."

I shake my head fervently, my fists tugging at the soft fabric of his hoodie. "You didn't mess it up, Hunter. Something bad happened but it was still a good game. I watched you hit the puck right over the goalie's shoulder," I add with a playful nudge. "Your scores are always crazy good."

He drops his head, trying to hide his smile from me. "You saw it?" he asks, his voice low but hopeful.

"Yeah," I nod.

His smile gets a little wider. "Did you see me look for you in the crowd straight after? We were at the other side of the rink but I pointed at you."

My cheeks ache because I'm smiling so hard. "I saw," I whisper, pushing into him more intimately as I try to get him to meet my eyes.

When he does, he looks excruciatingly shy. "Never wanted you to see me like that, Fallon. A little brawling on the rink is fine but, as much as I hate to admit it, Benson was right. We were just plain fighting."

"Why were you fighting?"

A muscle rolls in his jaw and he clutches me tighter.

"He was talking about you," he murmurs, and my lips pop open.

"I'm sorry, what?" I ask, disbelieving what I'm hearing right now.

He doesn't even know me. Why would he be talking to Hunter about me?

"He could tell that you were a cheerleader," he continues, lifting a hand so that he can stroke at my hair. "He was smack-talking and, uh, he started to talk about the whole cheerleader-football player kinda stereotype and…"

I thud my forehead against Hunter's chest, immediately understanding what the other player must have been insinuating without Hunter having to tell me anything else. He kisses the top of my head and squeezes his arms around me tighter.

"I'm sorry," he murmurs. "I shouldn't have gotten all… possessive."

That word makes me grind my forehead against him harder.

I like it, Hunter. I know I shouldn't, but I do.

"I… don't mind," I whisper, and he turns his head away from me, hissing through his teeth. His heart begins pumping harder against me.

"Don't say that," he murmurs quickly. "It isn't okay for a guy to lose his composure when his girl is around."

"You were defending me," I reply, nuzzling further into his chest. He smells intoxicating, and his hoodie is soft and warm. I want to pull it over his head and rub my palms over his heaving chest.

"Yeah," he says hoarsely, his jaw flexing hard as he lowers his hands to grip my behind. He lets out a rough exhalation and curses as he palms me.

"Why did you bring me here?" I ask him, my own voice becoming husky too.

I don't specify whether I mean why did he bring me to this beautiful rustic house or why did he bring me to watch his away game in Larch Peak in general because, deep down, I think I know that there's an invisible string tying all of these pieces together.

"I, uh… I used to come here every summer with

Tanner," Hunter explains. "This was his family's summer house."

"Was?" I ask, and Hunter finally looks down at me.

"All of the kids are grown up now so Tanner's parents were gonna sell it. I knew that once I signed to a team – got an NHL contract – I'd be able to afford it, so I asked them to hang onto it, just for another two years. And as soon as I've got that paycheque I told them I'll pay them the same damn day. Larch Peak's college team might be crazy, but the Larch Peak pro team? Their NHL team? That's where Tanner and I want to sign. Since we started coming here as kids we knew that Larch Peak was where we wanted to be. Larch Peak's pro team is killing it in the league and, on top of that, this place is kinda special to us."

He breathes out a laugh and shakes his head.

"It's stupid and sentimental, I know. But Tanner's parents are holding onto this place for me and pretty soon I'm gonna take it off their hands. Have it as my home base for a while, while I'm pro at least. Maybe when my hockey years are over I'll head back to Carter Ridge, but right now this – here – is where I wanna be." He squeezes me until I'm nuzzling against him again and then he murmurs, "Right here."

I stifle a gasp as his fingers suddenly slip beneath my skirt, fingers massaging me over my underwear as his eyes burn darkly into mine.

"That's why I brought you here," he finishes, dipping his head so that he can press our foreheads together. "That's why this place is important to me. This is where I'm going to have my hockey career. That's why I needed you to come."

"To see if I like it?" I pant as he begins kissing his way down my cheek.

"To see if you'd be happy to move here," he clarifies in a murmur. My belly suddenly overflows.

"What?" I gasp.

My eyes drop to his abdomen as he rips his hoodie off over his head. He pulls me flush against his chest and he's so damn warm from his game that my brain goes blank, my hands mindlessly gripping at the cotton over his swollen pecs.

"If you let me keep you as my girlfriend after we graduate I'm gonna want you living with me, Fallon. I'm gonna need you in my house."

I blink rapidly, my lashes fluttering like crazy.

"After we graduate you'd want me… to move in with you? Here?" I ask, staring at the cosy wooden bathroom as if I'm seeing it for the first time.

"Yeah," he grunts. "Even if you do that extra year of study. As soon as that's up, I want you to pack your stuff and get the hell over here."

"Oh my God," I whisper, feeling so overwhelmed that I'm dizzy.

"That's why I got so pissed with myself tonight. I wanted everything to be perfect for you." He gives me a small smile and murmurs, "I wanted it to be an easy decision."

I blink up at him in sheer disbelief, the handsome smile on his face making my belly tingle. I never imagined that one person could be so good, that even when they did inevitably make mistakes they could immediately call themselves out on it. I can't believe that he can be so hard on himself while managing to stay so gentle with me.

I press my body as firmly as I can against his abdomen and he groans out a laugh, one hand raking through his hair.

"Hunter," I murmur, the tone of my voice making his laughter fade.

His eyes darken with desire as he lowers his hand to stroke my cheek. "Yeah?"

I take a nervous inhale as my heart begins pumping faster and then, with my temples pounding, I lift my face up to his.

"Choosing to be with you is the easiest decision I've ever had to make."

Hunter heaves my body against his abdomen and takes my lips with his, a deep rumble in his chest as I whimper gratefully into his mouth.

"You promise?" he murmurs, groaning as we kiss.

I nod my head and moan as he slips his tongue inside my mouth. "Yes, I promise," I whisper breathlessly.

"And I won't mess up again," he pants, pinning me to the wooden wall beside the counter as he rolls his body purposefully against mine. "I promise."

I move my hand to where he's kneading my thigh and, smiling slightly, I brush over his pinkie finger with mine.

"Pinkie promise?" I ask.

He breathes out a laugh and immediately hooks his finger around mine.

"Hell yeah," he grunts. "Yeah, I pinkie promise. I'm gonna be so good to you, Fallon. I promise I'll give you everything you need."

I drop my head back against the wall as he kisses his way hungrily down my throat, pulling away when he reaches the neckline of the jumper so that he can look at his name written over one of my breasts. His eyelids are half-mast and his chest swells as he watches me.

He gently sets me down, placing one of his palms above my head, and he leans in closer, towering over me. I swish my ponytail and turn one-eighty, my back to his front as I flatten my palms against the wall.

I look over my shoulder to watch his expression and I feel dizzy with satisfaction as his breathing gets heavy. His eyes stay trained on the big number 9 on my back and he moves his large hands to take a hold of my hips. He pulls my behind up against his body and grunts when I'm in the position that he wants me in.

"Seein' you wear this…" he murmurs, and I arch into

him more deliberately. He squeezes roughly at my hips and then one of his palms moves to the centre of my back, rubbing upwards until he's gripping over one of my shoulders.

I tilt my head backwards and his hand roams to the front of my throat, gently pulling me against him so that he can kiss me from behind. His mouth is warm and firm, but still gentle like he's teasing me.

Feeling his need pressing hard against my behind, I whisper breathlessly, "I saw something else in your bag when I was looking for the saline, Hunter."

He pulls himself back with a gruff sound in his chest, before glancing down at his opened gym bag to see the box that I found.

"We don't have to do that tonight," he rasps, choking slightly, and he turns me around so that we're flush chest to chest. He crushes a hard kiss to my mouth and then a tiny one to the tip of my nose. "I wanna keep you forever. I'm not in a rush."

I press my face into his chest and smile.

Hunter Wilde? I think I'm in love with you.

I grip my fists into the front of his shirt, twisting the dark fabric away from his abs.

"Forever sounds like a really long time," I whisper teasingly, looking up at him from under my lashes as his mouth lifts into a cocky grin. "To make sure that we get good at it, we should probably start practicing."

Realising that I want this as badly as he does, Hunter presses me up against the wall.

"That so?" he asks, tangling his thick digits in my ponytail. "'Cause I really wanna put those condoms to use, baby, but I need you to know that I'm being serious about waiting for you. You'd still make me the happiest man alive if we did nothing but sleep in that bedroom tonight."

I press a small kiss against his stubble-covered jaw and he rolls his shoulders, twitching with need. "You brought the box with you, Hunter," I purr. "You clearly had something in mind for me."

He clears his throat hard and I run my fingers over his heaving pecs. "Got 'em just in case," he rasps. "In case you wanted to. So I could, you know, keep you protected."

I play dumb, making my eyes go wide and fluttering my lashes. "Protected from what?"

Hunter understands my game and he grins down at me, grazing his teeth over his lower lip.

But in the next second he's ducking down, shoving his shoulder into my belly, and throwing me over his broad back, making me squeal with delight as he gives me a rough spank on the ass. He grabs the condoms and punches off the light switch as he carries me into the master bedroom.

When he breaches the doorway he switches on a lamp, making the room look even cosier.

"Don't you know what can happen when a man takes a woman to bed, baby?" he asks as he tosses me onto my back in the centre of the mattress, his voice a low growl, and a playful glint in his sparkling eyes.

I giggle and squirm as he wraps his palms around my thighs, heaving them to the bottom of the bed and settling his large stance right between them. He smirks down at me as he rips his shirt off over his head.

My breathing turns shallow as I take in the sight of his bared body, his muscles pumped swollen after the night's rough game. His abdomen is thick and tan, his pecs are large and heaving, and he yanks me up by one of my wrists so that he can press my palm over his heart.

"You never do Sex Ed, baby?" he rasps, giving me an indulgent grin when I smile up at him, delighted by our game. I fumble a hand out behind me to stop my body from falling into the mattress. "This is what I need to protect you from," he murmurs, slow-trailing my hand down the cavern between his pecs, over his ripped abdomen, and then coming to a stop as we reach the top of his jeans.

He must have left the changing room in a hurry because he doesn't even have his belt on, but that just enables easier access as he flips open the top button with his thumb.

"Gotta protect you from what I'm packing, baby," he murmurs, and his cheeks turn ruddy as we both laugh breathlessly.

Hunter squeezes my hand in his, capturing my full attention, and then he drops his hand to his side, fingers flexing as he waits patiently, seeing what I'll do.

My hand is still pressed against the top of his jeans so, going slow, I brush slowly and gently through his happy trail.

Hunter arches his neck back and releases a long groan.

"What you're... packing," I repeat quietly, keeping our gazes locked as I press a kiss to his belly button. He flexes his jaw but doesn't move from his regimented stance. "Do you, uh, want me to feel you?" I ask him, stroking my thumb beneath his waistband so that he understands what I mean. Then I whisper, "I don't need to be protected if I just use my hand."

Hunter rips open his fly, his pupils blacking out his dazzling irises.

"Please," he rasps back to me. "Whatever you want. It's all yours."

I sit up on my knees and slide my fingers inside his warm boxers. He drops his forehead to my shoulder and releases an anguished groan.

"Baby," he moans, gripping his palms tightly around my waist. I sink my teeth into my bottom lip, stifling my gasp at how big he is. His muscle is so protracted that he makes a low tortured sound as I caress him, silently telling me that he's agonizingly sensitive. "Never had – never had someone do this to me before," he pants, sliding his hand beneath his underwear so that he can help me get my fingers around the thick base of his cock.

I give him a small preliminary tug and he grunts so hard that my legs turn weak.

"Hurts, baby," he rasps and I immediately slip my hand out of his boxers, pulling my whole body away from him as I whisper, "Sorry, I'm sorry."

"No, no," he says quickly, as I scoot backwards on the bed. He kicks off his clothes until he's left in nothing but his underwear and then he grips my ankles for leverage and he heaves himself onto the mattress. He spreads out on his haunches, his thick quads knocking my knees apart, and then he lowers his weight slowly on top of me.

It's been a long time since we lay on a bed together and feeling his heaviness holding me down makes me feel like I'm finally home again. I lift an arm back to ease the cheer ribbon from my hair and I gently tug my waves out of the ponytail. Hunter looks down at me with a flexing jaw as my hair spills behind me on the pillow.

"I don't want to hurt you," I whisper, setting the ribbon on the nightstand.

He glances over at the ribbon and then absently slides one of his palms through my hair. His fingers feel so good that I arch into his touch and make a quiet moan.

"I didn't mean it in a bad way, baby. It hurts, but it's good. So good." He moves one of my hands back to his boxers and he murmurs, "Do it again."

I bite my lip, my breathing shallow.

"Guide me?" I ask, my eyes imploring.

He swallows hard and drops his gaze as he nods. Slowly, he pushes our hands beneath the cotton waistband and I nuzzle my face into the tan curve of his neck as he presses a kiss against my temple.

As soon as he has my hand wrapped around him his chest expands, his hips thrusting on instinct. The power in his movement makes my eyes widen and heat spreads wildly through my aching breasts.

"S-sorry," he murmurs, kissing his way down my cheek.

I tilt my head back to meet his eyes and he looks down at me with pained adoration. I grip and stroke firmly around his base, although his arousal is so large I haven't even felt the tip yet.

Hunter ducks down to press his lips against mine and his free hand slips under the bottom of my jumper. When he feels my bare skin beneath the thick material he lets his palm roam higher, his strong hips meeting the tentative movements of my hand.

His fingers meet the back of my bra and he thrusts faster, slipping his tongue inside my mouth and growling in pleasure.

"You're not wearing a top," he murmurs against me, and his voice is so deep that my thighs fall open.

He grunts, sliding his tongue back inside, and he pulls our hands from his underwear. He shoves my arm around his shoulders before he pushes his hand up my skirt.

"Under my hockey sweater," he rasps, his fingers tracing the lace of my panties. "You ain't wearing anything under there other than your bra."

"Is that so?" I whisper, teasing him with his words from earlier.

I may or may not have taken my top off before Winter and I went to watch the game.

Hunter smiles and heaves up onto his haunches, his hands moving from beneath my skirt to the hem of the jumper. "Feels that way to me, baby," he murmurs.

I stretch my arms up over my head and rub my heat against the large bulge in his boxers. "See for yourself."

Hunter keeps his eyes on mine as he rolls the jumper up my body, pulling it up my arms and then tossing it to the floor. His cheeks are ruddy and his breathing is fast, his gaze still locked on mine as if he won't allow himself to look down.

I sit up on my elbows, wearing nothing but my bra, my skirt, and my panties, and I tilt my head to one side, biting

Pinkie Promise

back my smile as I wait for him to look at me.

His eyes drop down to my chest and he scrapes a hand down his jaw.

"Christ."

He slips his fist back into his boxers, cursing quietly as he begins frantically stroking his cock.

"They're uh…" He swipes his tongue over his bottom lip. "They're beautiful. You're beautiful."

"*You're* beautiful," I whisper, and he immediately shakes his head, laughing. I reach up as he lowers himself down, and we laugh breathlessly as we kiss.

"You gonna let me touch them?" he asks, his hands moving up to grip tight around my waist.

"With or without the bra?" I ask, giggling when he groans against my neck.

"Uh… I uh…" He pulls back and scratches at his jaw, unable to tear his eyes away from my chest. "Any way you want it, baby."

I arch up, rubbing myself against his pecs, and Hunter drops his face into the pillow behind me with a desolate groan in his throat.

I use his moment of distraction to roll over onto my belly and Hunter is instantly positioning himself behind me, pushing my skirt over my ass and palming eagerly at my soft cheeks.

"The clasp is at the back," I explain innocently as I watch him from over my shoulder. He pins me with a heated stare because he knows that I'm being a little tease.

He shoves his tongue into his cheek and smirks down at me knowingly. I wiggle my ass against his thick cock and he grips the waistband at the back of my skirt, yanking me up against his arousal and grunting hard.

"Hunter," I gasp, and two of his digits are suddenly at the back of my bra, his arm tugging roughly backwards and making the whole thing snap open.

I fall forwards onto the soft red quilt and Hunter presses

his chest domineeringly into my back. He eases my bra straps down my arms, humming appreciatively as he kisses my cheek.

"You sure you haven't done any of this stuff before?" I ask him in a little whimper, and he chuckles against my ear. He releases my wrists from the straps and then places the bra carefully on the side of the bed. His cheek ticks up as he looks at the pretty lilac cups.

"I've had a lot of time to fantasise," he replies, pressing his face into my hair and taking a big shoulder-swelling inhale. His arousal jerks against my ass and I roll my lips together, preventing my moan.

"What do you fantasise about?" I ask quietly, wishing that I was brave enough to say: *am I the star of your fantasies?*

But Hunter Wilde can read me like a book.

He smirks against my cheek and I slap playfully at his shoulder.

"I fantasise about you, Fallon," he rumbles, deep and placating. "I'm down so bad for you, baby."

I squirm my behind again and ask, "Do you ever think about us doing it like this?"

His chest heaves against my back and he lowers his mouth to my neck so that he can lick possessively up the warm curve. I fall limply into the quilt and he drops right down on top of me, continuing his warm lapping while slow-thrusting against my behind.

"Yeah," he grunts. "I wanna have this pussy from the back and play with those tits at the same time."

"*Hunter*," I whimper, twisting so that I can reach his mouth with mine. Despite the dirty things that he's been murmuring he kisses me gently, his tongue warm and adoring.

"Can I put you on your back?" he murmurs, his palms around my ribcage making my shallow breaths even more constricted. "I gotta see you."

I peck a series of tiny kisses over his stubble and nod my

head.

He eases me onto my back, his body towering over mine, and then he looks down between us, gently cupping my naked breasts.

"I've been needing this so bad," he murmurs, as he swipes his thumbs over my nipples.

I wrap my forearms over his shoulders and whisper, "I want to give you everything that you need."

In seconds he's grinning, and then we're nothing but kisses and laughter until he's pulling himself upright again, ripping his boxers down his quads and showing me just how big he is.

"Oh my God," I whisper, my body growing weak beneath his.

He spreads his knees wide, grabbing the waist of my skirt with one hand and gripping his length with the other, and then he begins slowly pumping his fist up and down. When he's right beneath the head he suddenly pistons his hips forwards.

"*Hunter*," I moan, lost for words at the sight of him.

He yanks my skirt more roughly until I'm pressed right against him, the soft backs of my thighs knocking against the muscles of his quads. My eyebrows pinch higher as he rubs himself against my panties.

"Yeah?" he grunts, tossing himself against me now.

Warm moisture touches my thigh. I bite back a mewl.

"H-Hunter, is that… are you…" *Oh my God, am I really going to say these words out loud?* "Are you… coming? I felt… moisture, on your… on the…"

Hunter shakes his head and breathes out a laugh, a lazy smirk on his face as he slowly works his fist. "Pre-come," he murmurs.

His eyes drop to my belly, making him thrust faster.

"If I was coming, you'd know about it, baby."

"W-what?" I breathe, arching against him.

Hunter lets go of his shaft and presses a kiss to my lips.

His fingers search my skirt for the zipper before easing it down my thighs.

His eyes drop to my purple panties and his breathing becomes heavier.

"You never seen a guy come before?" he asks me gruffly. "It isn't just a drop, baby. Takes a lot of pumps to unload."

"How many?" I ask, as he presses a kiss to my jaw.

"Enough to give my girl another orgasm before I finish."

His hands grip the sides of my panties and he slowly tugs them down my thighs.

As soon as he frees me of my underwear his mouth meets the centre of my chest, and he makes a delicious groaning sound as he squeezes my breasts together.

I stroke my fingers into his hair as he drags his bristled jaw over my breasts, looking up at me for confirmation before sucking a nipple into his mouth. I arch up off the bed and he grunts roughly, lapping at me relentlessly and making me lose my breath.

"*Hunter, Hunter, Hunter–*"

He smirks and murmurs, "I love it when you say my name, baby." Then he sucks me even harder as two digits press against my clit.

"Hunter, I need you," I whimper as he moves his mouth back to mine, his arm pumping roughly between us as he works my little nub.

"You're gonna have me," he assures me, his pecs rubbing hard against my breasts. "I promise, baby, I'm gonna give you every damn inch."

He licks his tongue against mine and rubs my clit even faster, using his other hand to reach out and grab the condom box beside us.

His breathing becomes more laboured, his cock leaking against my thigh, and when I look over to the box I notice that Hunter's hand is trembling. I reach slowly over to it, taking the box from his fist, and his cheeks stain red as our eyes lock together.

Despite all of Hunter's sexy swaggering hockey captain charm, he's still as new to all of this as I am.

I slowly tease open the box and then peek inside.

The curiosity on my face makes Hunter breathe out a laugh, and he presses an amused kiss to my pink cheeks as I shake out a couple of vacuum-sealed squares.

He releases a rough sound when he sees the three foil packets in my hand.

"Oh wait, what's your favourite number again?" I ask him innocently.

He waits a beat and then rasps out, "Nine."

On the inside I'm shimmering. *Nine, like his jersey number.*

I shake out six more condoms before placing the box beside my cheer bow, and I flash him my best girl-next-door smile as I lean my arms up above my head.

"Then we better get started, Captain," I whisper, laughing as soon as he does.

"You're perfect," he murmurs, kissing me possessively. Then he brushes eight of the condoms to the side of the bed, picking up number nine and tearing into it.

He uses both of his fists to ease the rubber down his thick cock, his chest heaving and his shoulder muscles bulging. When he's got it in place he presses his torso back down on top of mine and kisses me tenderly, groaning when he licks at my tongue.

"You sure?" he asks, tangling one of his hands in my hair.

I press a kiss to the small cut on his cheekbone, and then I lock our pinkies together. "All yours."

"Baby," he murmurs, lifting our hands above my head, holding me in place as he begins pushing at my entrance.

A deep rumble sounds in his chest as he looks down at me and slides inside.

I moan loudly and he drops every ounce of his weight

on top of me.

"*Fallon*," he pants, his voice hoarse with lust, and my body squirms instinctively, a whimper leaving my throat. "Oh *fuck*, baby, yes," he rasps, pumping his hips the second that the sound leaves my lips. He eases his length slowly backwards and murmurs, "Is this okay, baby?"

"Mm-hm," I whisper, locking my legs around his middle. He brushes his forehead over mine and kisses gently at my lips.

He frees my pinkie so that he can squeeze his hand around my ass and I clutch at the muscles in his back as he rolls his body firmly into mine.

"That's it," he murmurs, his shoulder muscles bunching. "Hold onto me, baby, just like that."

He momentarily removes his hand from my behind so that he can pull the red quilt cover over the top of us. It shields us from the gentle glow of the bedside lamp and once it's in place we're both laughing again. Hunter hisses with pleasure and presses his mouth over mine, groaning as he slides his warm tongue inside of me.

"You're l-literally huge," I whisper, whimpering when he squeezes my breasts.

"Yeah," he grunts, smirking down at me. "And you're so tight it hurts."

"Hunter," I moan, as he thrusts into me even harder.

"I'm not gonna last long in here, baby," he murmurs gruffly against my cheek. "Can't pace myself in my girl's wet little pussy."

"But you're a star athlete," I pant, making his smirk grow more cocky. "You're s-supposed to have control."

He laughs and thrusts languidly, making both of us groan. "I think tonight made it pretty clear that I have zero control when it comes to you, baby."

I lick over the swell of his pec and he grunts as he watches me. "Then m-maybe," I whisper, "you should hand over the reins."

His movements become faster, pumping frantically as he looks into my eyes.

"You mean" – he clears his throat, his voice gravel-deep – "you mean, you gettin' on top?" he asks, his eyes dropping to my chest. "Having you ride me?"

"I mean, you are a country boy," I murmur, smiling up at him, and trailing my fingertips down his shoulders until I can squeeze at his pecs. "Are you telling me that you never wanted to wrangle yourself a cowgirl?"

With a growl, he wraps his arms beneath me and rolls heavily onto his back, keeping my hips slightly raised so that he isn't filling me to the hilt. He keeps his eyes on mine as he pulls the quilt up over my head and then he settles his large palms on my hips, jerking his chin at me.

"Have at it, baby," he grunts.

I lower my palms to his thick abdomen and shift down the tiniest bit.

My eyes go wide and Hunter chokes, his chest heaving violently.

"Oh God, y-you don't have to go all the way down on it, baby," he pants, rubbing his palms over the small of my back and pushing me closer to his chest.

But then my nipples brush softly over his abs and his hips shoot up involuntarily, making Hunter exhale roughly as he fills me with those last four inches.

"Fuck, sorry, sorry," he says quickly, trying to withdraw, but I shake my head, wanting to give this to him. His expression is heated as he leans up on one elbow, gripping my jaw with one hand so that he can pull me down and kiss me.

He growls hungrily as he slides his tongue inside of my mouth and I sigh, submitting to him, as I pump him tenderly inside of me. When the warm strokes of his tongue become too much to bear I pull back, moaning breathlessly, and Hunter settles his palm back down to my hip.

He reclines back, his expression so cocky that it makes

me giggle, and as soon as he sees the dimples in my cheeks he grins back at me, meeting my little grinds with eager thrusts.

I grip harder into his pecs and he kicks his legs out wider, clutching firmly at my hips so that I can't escape the force of his movements.

"Doin' so good, baby," he grunts, thrusting his hips fervently between my thighs.

His rough palms stroke down my legs until he's cupping behind my knees and he eases them outwards until I'm spread into the splits.

He groans in satisfaction, pumping faster.

"Fallon, I ain't gonna… I ain't gonna last much longer," he pants, his eyes burning into mine. "I gotta put you on your back, right now."

I immediately nod my head and I feel his forearm on my back as he rolls us over, pinning me down with his hips.

"I can't believe this is h-happening," he groans, pushing his forehead into mine.

I cross my ankles tightly over the rolling muscles in his back and he buries his face in my neck, the jerks of his hips becoming rougher and sloppier.

He traces his thumb down my naval until he reaches my sensitised nub and my breasts rise and fall, out of control.

"Please," I whimper, wriggling beneath him and begging him to push me over the line.

He exhales harshly against my skin, his cock slipping in and out at a maddening pace.

"Gonna let me finish you?" he asks gruffly, his thumb a millimetre away from where I need it.

I push my breasts up against his pecs and whisper, "Make me yours."

His thumb presses down against my clit and my back arches off the mattress, a loud whimper catching in my throat as he pumps himself inside of me.

"How'd it get even tighter?" he groans, his voice pained

as he caresses at my nub.

My body tenses and explodes, and I grip my fingers into his thick hair, gasping in pleasure as he starts thrusting even faster.

He grunts hard against my cheek as I moan and fall limp, and then he sits up on his splayed knees, his palms gripping either side of my belly.

"Gonna stay on your back for me?" he asks, his voice so low that my core clenches.

I nod my head and he smirks, pleased.

He smacks his palm hard against one of his shoulders and orders, "Legs up here, baby."

We lift my trembling legs up to his shoulders and he slowly slides his length back inside.

"Oh yeah, atta girl," he grunts, sliding quickly in and out. "Almost there, baby, I promise."

We both moan desperately, his movements turning frantic, and the second that he leans down to kiss me his hips jolt ruthlessly and he begins to come undone.

Fast, rough strokes, with his abs smacking firmly against the backs of my thighs, his palms squeezing at my breasts as he licks his tongue furiously against mine.

"I'm there, baby, I'm there," he grunts, thrusting with an anguished expression on his face. He pumps himself a few more times and then he drops his weight on top of me, a low rumbling sound in his throat before he slowly pulls himself out.

I make a small whimper at the loss and he pulls me against him, kissing me hard. One hand cups at my cheek as the other rolls off the condom.

"My girl," he whispers, kissing at my blushing cheeks. "This is how it's gonna be, Fallon, just the two of us. You being all mine, and me being all yours."

I'm sleepy and overwhelmed but there's just enough wherewithal left inside to make me tenderly rub his pinkie with mine as I cuddle up to him.

"You promise?" I whisper, laughing as he kisses the tip of my nose.

A satisfied smile pulls at his lips and he wraps our pinkies together. "Yeah, baby. I promise."

CHAPTER 25

Hunter

I reach up with a groan, tucking one of my hands behind my head and tangling the other up in Fallon's soft hair. Her flushed pink cheek is squished against one of my pecs and her arms are draped loosely over my shoulders.

I stroke firmly at the back of her neck and she releases a tiny moan, making the muscle between my thighs thicken and throb.

Easing my hand from its position between me and the pillow, I take a quick peek under the covers and bite back a smirk.

Fallon's legs are wrapped around one of my thighs and her little ass is out, looking all round and tempting.

She's soft, spent, and totally fucking naked.

I drop the quilt cover back down so that it's covering her up to her chin and I fumble quietly on the dresser beside us so that I can grab my cell. I need to order her breakfast from the local Door Dash service before we get an Uber back to the coach.

I remember what she liked when we were snowed in at the hockey house so I order two coffees, both for Fallon, and then I browse the food options, searching for something that looks good enough for her. The delivery time is fifteen minutes so once I've sent the payment I toss my phone back onto the cabinet, and this time I slip my hand under the sheets, getting a handful of Fallon's behind, and then scooping her up my body until she's close enough for me to kiss.

I press a long kiss against her forehead and she's immediately stirring, her nipples rubbing up against my chest and making my cock flex against her thigh. I palm firmly at her cheeks while stroking my other hand up and down her throat, pressing a series of kisses down her face as her arms begin tightening around my shoulders.

"Hey, beautiful," I murmur, breathing out a laugh when she starts rubbing herself against my abdomen. My testosterone levels are suddenly off the damn charts.

She peeps up at me with her big sparkly eyes and I cup my hands around her jaw so that I can kiss the life out of her. A deeply satisfied sound rumbles in my chest as she palms at my pecs, getting me even hotter for her than I already was.

I roll her onto her back and her hair fluffs up around her face.

"Best night of my life," I grunt, as I give her a savouring once-over. I give her waist a little squeeze before rubbing at her jaw again. "Tell me how it was for you. I gotta know, Fallon."

She does a belly-quivering half sit-up to reach my mouth making me smirk a little as I let her kiss me.

"So so so good," she whispers, her lashes fluttering like crazy and one of her hands moving between us to try and get me back inside of her.

I drop my face to her neck and take a big shoulder-swelling inhale.

"Condom," I remind her, reaching blindly to the dresser for the only condom out of the nine that we didn't use last night.

Yeah, it's been a *long* night.

I grab it between two digits and then slap it down onto the bed beside us, trying not to get even more excited as I think about all of the stuff that we did in the last twelve hours.

One of Fallon's hands cups my jaw and suddenly she's kissing around the cut on my cheekbone, making me groan at how damn sweet she is.

"Baby," I murmur, pulling away to stop her. I press my knuckles against the cut and flinch slightly, although the pain is barely there and it'll fade in a day or two.

I go to shift off of her so that she doesn't have to look at it but she pulls me down hard, making me huff out a laugh. I feel like the luckiest guy in the world.

"Is it bruised to shit?" I mumble as she goes back to kissing around the area.

She pauses for a beat before she answers. "It's a little bruised," she admits quietly, "but the cut has pretty much healed. And, you know, it looks kinda…" She shrugs her shoulders coyly and then starts squirming when I raise my eyebrows at her.

She's into how I look when I'm roughed up?

"You like that?" I ask her, smirking when she starts laughing, covering her blushing face with her hands. "You like your man a little rough around the edges, huh?"

I bite my teeth into her neck and she squeals with laughter, kicking playfully at my back as I rub my big palms around her tits. I squeeze her roughly, the way she's wanting it right now, and she moans in delight, making me thrust up against her thigh.

I release her throat and tower over her. I jerk my chin and ask, "One more round until we go get the coach?"

But before she can answer there's a sharp rap at the

door, and her eyes fly up to mine, another giggle slipping past her lips.

Biting back her smile she gives me a mock-scared wide-eyed look and gasps, "Oh no, do you think that it's the pyjama police?!"

I grin down at her naked body and roll her onto her belly, yanking her hands behind her back as she howls with laughter.

"Better not be," I growl, "otherwise you'd be under arrest."

"You wouldn't allow it!" she squeals. "I have the right to remain panty-less!"

I bury my face in her hair, addicted to how cute she is, but suddenly I'm groaning because my cock has slipped right between her thighs, and now the head of my shaft is getting a good taste of just how wet she is.

"Damn right I wouldn't allow it," I murmur, pressing a hard kiss against her cheek before heaving myself off of her. I need to pull back before we actually *do* start getting hot and heavy without a condom.

She peeks up at me from over her shoulder, all sparkly eyed, and I give her ass an affectionate spank before I climb off the bed and toss the sheets back on top of her.

"Ordered you breakfast for before we head back to Carter Ridge," I explain, pulling on my boxers and jeans and then yanking one of my white vests from my gym bag.

"What'd you order?" she calls out as I pull the vest down my chest, taking the stairs to the bottom floor two at a time. I jog to the front door, probably looking like I've just been doing exactly what I *have* just been doing, and I thank the guy as he passes me a cardboard cup-holder and a rolled-top brown paper bag with Fallon's breakfast in it.

I jog back up the stairs and hold them up to Fallon once I'm back in the entrance to the bedroom.

Our future bedroom.

That realisation hits me like a damn truck.

Pinkie Promise

I clear my throat as I take in the sight of Fallon half-sitting in the plush red blanket fort, her hair messy from getting fucked all night, and completely unaware that I'm over here borderline planning the rest of our lives together. With my neck turning crimson, I look quickly away from her, and place the cups and the take-out bag on the dresser by the jamb.

Then I close the door behind me and flick open the top button on my jeans.

"Coffee," I tell her, pulling down my zipper as I make my way back over to her, "and I got you a stack of pancakes. That sound okay?"

She nods her head as I slightly lift up the quilt cover, hunching down beneath it and then settling myself between her thighs.

"That's really sweet of you, thank you," she says quietly as I begin kissing my way up her throat.

"No problem," I murmur, my hands squeezing eagerly at her sexy hips.

"It's a big bag though," she whispers. "That's got to be a lot of pancakes."

I smirk against her skin and say, "Yeah, probably."

"I, uh... if I can't finish them all please don't think that I'm being rude."

I pull back so that I can look down at her and she genuinely has a nervous expression on her face. As if it would bother me if she didn't finish the whole damn box of pancakes.

It's the strict parents thing, I can tell. I don't even want to know how overbearing they were when she was living at home if she's worried that her *boyfriend* will be angry at her if she doesn't finish a meal.

"Fallon, have as much or as little as you want, okay?"

I brush a thumb over her cheek, wanting to ease the concern in her big eyes, so I try to take a more teasing approach to lighten up her mood.

271

"And, hey, I'm not gonna complain about you leaving me your leftovers."

She twists up her lips, trying to hide her small smile, and she scrunches her nose as she prods at one of my biceps.

"Really?" she asks.

I give her the cockiest grin that I can and lean down so that my mouth is against her cheek.

"I'll lick your plate clean, baby."

She laughs and grabs my face so that I can crush my lips down on hers.

I shove my jeans and boxers down my thighs as I fumble for the condom. I grab it, spread out my knees and sit back on my haunches, towering over Fallon as I rip open the foil and begin rolling the rubber down my length.

She makes a hot little *fuck me* moan as I slide one hand beneath her hair, my other fist gripped tight around the base of my cock.

"You want it?" I ask her, loving the way that she can't stop staring at my pecs, pumped and swollen beneath the vest.

"Please," she whispers. "Please, I want it, yes."

"Yeah?" I ask. "Eyes up here."

Her eyes fly straight up to mine as I nudge the head of my shaft against her heat and then I'm slowly pushing my cock inside of her, making her back bow off the bed.

I drop my forehead against hers, breathing heavily as I slide it in.

Before we reach the last few inches I pull back again, teasing her with long languid strokes so that she can get used to the size before I start actually giving it to her.

She reaches up to press a small kiss to my cheekbone and I'm instantly fighting a smile, ducking down to take her lips with mine as I run my fingers through her hair.

"Was last night really the best night of your life?" she whispers, pink cheeked and panting, and I breathe out a laugh, nodding my head at her.

"Yeah," I murmur. "It was the best night of my next life, too."

She laughs happily and I encase my palms around both of her hips, starting to thrust it a little faster, a little deeper.

"Is this the vest that you wore w-when... when I saw you working at your daddy's garage?" she pants, clinging onto me tighter as I pump her harder against the bed.

"Yeah," I grunt, my eyes dropping to her bouncing tits. *Holy fuckin' shit.* "M-maybe don't use that word right now though," I add, well aware that she knows which word I'm talking about.

"You like that?" she whispers, the smile evident in her sexy voice.

I laugh and then groan, my hands gripping harder to hold her in place. "I definitely fucking like it," I murmur. "That's why I'm beggin' you not to say it right now."

I pull up onto my haunches so that I can watch my girl take my pumps.

"Did you like that thing that we did last night?" I ask, jerking my chin at her.

She looks up at me with wide eyes, her cheeks turning red when she realises what I'm talking about. I'm saying it without saying it, because I want to make sure that she liked it just as much as I did before I do it to her again.

She grips her fists into the front of my vest, twisting it in her hands to make the dirt-stained cotton lift higher up my abs. Her lips pop open as she looks at the dark hair running down from my naval to my shaft and I thrust into her faster, my cock growing heavier by the second.

"Yes," she whispers finally and I groan in relief, dropping down so that I can pin her to the bed with my chest. I capture her lips with mine before filling her up with warm strokes of my tongue.

She whimpers into my mouth and her body is instantly clenching, her thighs tightening around my middle as she ascends into her orgasm.

"Gonna let me do it again?" I ask, pumping her faster as she moans against my neck. I push one of her knees up against the pillow and she cries out my name, making me grunt and thrust messily, my sac smacking loud against her ass.

"Yes," she pants. "Please, yes."

I slip my tongue back inside of her mouth, rubbing her up as I finish her off, only pulling back to look at her when she falls limply against the sheets.

I pull my vest over my head and toss it beside us, knowing that we're gonna need it on hand in less than a minute. Fallon's lashes flutter sleepily as she lets herself stare at my chest, her hands reaching out tentatively as if she wants to touch me.

I grab her wrists in my fists and shove her hands right against my pecs, letting her grip and massage at me, my cock still wedged deep inside.

She moves her hips slightly and I smirk, rubbing my hands up and down her forearms.

"You sure?" I ask her, slow-pumping it in and out, keeping myself right on the precipice.

"Yeah," she whispers, one of her hands stroking up towards my stubble.

I ease my cock out of her and Fallon immediately moans, struggling beneath me because she hates being empty.

"I know, baby," I murmur as I roll off the condom, and then I sit back so that she can get a look at me bare.

I wrap my fist around myself and grimace as I look down, my shaft thick and heavy, the head already leaking.

I take one of Fallon's hands and pull it down to my cock, wrapping her around it and gripping my fists over hers. Then I pump my dick against her belly and she bites her lip, whimpering loud.

"Keep making those sounds, baby," I tell her, my voice deep and demanding. I shove our fists down to the base and piston my hips forward, my jaw turning rigid as I find a rhythm and start thrusting.

Fallon wraps her naked legs over the backs of my calves, spread wide in my jeans, and my eyes drop to her big breasts, those soft peaks driving me crazy. I immediately hunch down and take one of them in my mouth, tossing harder and faster as I suck at her sensitive pink nipples.

I move over to the other side, sucking at that one too, and I release one hand from my length so that I can palm her at the same time.

"Almost there," I grunt, squeezing her tits while I toss myself. "You took it so well last night, all over these beautiful tits."

"Hunter, p-please," she moans, tugging at my hair and clawing at my back.

And I can't take it anymore.

I groan hard, my thrusts pause, and then I'm jerking onto her belly in warm thick spurts.

She gasps and moans and writhes like I'm still inside of her.

My vision blurs as I start shooting it over her breasts, one hand pinning her down by her shoulder and the other frantically tossing my shaft.

"Baby," I grunt, and she instantly pulls my face down to hers, letting me slip my tongue inside while I splatter the rest of my load against her pussy. "So good to me, baby," I groan. "You're so damn good."

With one last tug, I drop heavily against her side. I wrap one arm under Fallon's head and use the other to hold up the thick quilt cover, a satisfied sound rumbling up my throat as I look down at her beautiful body.

She looks up at me with those big eyes and I start pressing kisses against her forehead, wanting to reward her for being so good to me.

'Cause she's covered in me. My girl is downright covered in me.

I lower my hand to her belly and rub my fingers through the mess. She tucks her face into the side of my neck and I roll heavily on top of her.

I'm aware that the coach leaves in just over an hour but that's plenty of time for me to clean Fallon off and get her fed. I bury my face into her hair and feel my shoulders relax as I wrap my arms behind her back.

"Been wanting to ask you something," I murmur, laughing as pushes my jeans all the way down my calves with her toes.

"Yeah?" she asks, her voice small and breathless.

"Yeah," I say, kissing at her cheek.

This year is really important to me, and not only because it's my final year at Carter U. It's the year that I've been assigned as my team's captain, it's the year that I'm gonna get signed, and, to top it all off, it's the year that the Carter Ridge Rangers are finally the favourites to win the NCAA Division I championship.

And I want Fallon to be there to watch it happen.

"Last night's game was an important one for us. Not only because Larch Peak's NHL team is where I want to get signed to, but because, uh…"

Shit, I'm nervous. I lean up on one of my elbows so that I can look down at Fallon's face, scraping a hand down my jaw and willing my neck to not flush red.

I don't exactly love the idea of telling Fallon about our team's previous fuck ups, but in this instance it's kind of intrinsic for what I want to ask her.

"Last year, Carter U got to the NCAA Frozen Four finals," I tell her, brushing a curl away from her face. "And it was fucking amazing, baby. Our whole team was in shape, on point, and ready to go. The only problem was the team that we were playing against."

I breathe out a laugh, shaking my head at the memory.

"Larch Peak U was the team that we were up against and they put on the dirtiest game that we've ever played.

Pinkie Promise

Tanner was our captain last year, and the only reason why he didn't keep the post this year is because during the final game he ended up getting sent off. The Larch Peak U guys were fucking filthy and they fouled their way to a last second victory.

"We were pissed the hell off but shit happens, so we took the loss and decided to focus on next year – *this* year – which is why beating Larch Peak U's ass last night was damn significant. With the Conference tournament games done and now that we've got those Larch Peak U fuckers out of the way, we're the favourites to win the championship. The final is in March, which means that we've got just over a month to hold onto our position, but there isn't a doubt in our minds that this year is *our* damn year. Which brings me to what I wanted to ask you.

"Last year the tournament's Frozen Four – the semi-finals and the finals – were held here in Larch Peak. The rink that we lost the tournament on last year is the same one that we won the game in last night. But this year, we're hosting. On our home turf, in Carter Ridge. You know how good that'll be for us, baby?"

Fallon drops her eyes, looking shy and a little flustered. "Um, yeah… I mean, wow. I, uh… I actually kinda… I actually already knew about all of that."

My eyebrows fly up and I blink down at her.

"Huh?" I ask, unable to stop myself from smiling. "You been researching us or something? How'd you know all of that?"

She meets my eyes, blushing, and warmth rips through my chest.

"N-no, not exactly," she stammers, looking nervously to the side, but I swoop down and crush a kiss to her lips anyway, loving the idea of her keeping tabs on us. I'm not sure how Fallon will have gotten her hands on all of that inside information but I decide to push that thought to one side so that I can just relish in the idea of her being as into me as I'm into her.

I pull back panting and Fallon looks up at me with dazed eyes. I smirk down at her and then readjust my position between her thighs.

My shaft is ready for another pumping but with no condoms in arm's reach I need to not press myself against her.

"Do you know where I was going with this?" I ask, stroking tenderly over the side of her belly. "Do you know what I was going to ask you?"

She shakes her head, still with that slightly nervous look on her face.

"I'm asking you to make sure that you're free that night so that you can watch your man win the hockey championship, at home in Carter Ridge."

I smile down at Fallon but she just stares up at me, unblinking.

After ten full seconds of her not giving me the confirmation that I wanted, I feel my cheeks beginning to burn, feeling like the world's biggest idiot.

Have I read too deeply into this relationship? Am I coming off way too strong right now?

Fallon starts nibbling on one of her fingers, evidently a nervous tick.

The fact that she's doing that now, when I've just asked her to come support me at the biggest game of my college career? Not a good sign.

She must realise from the way that I've turned rigid on top of her that I'm embarrassed as hell and feeling like a total idiot because she quickly stops biting on her finger and cups my jaw in her hands.

"Sorry, that was a weird reaction," she says quickly, pulling my face down to hers so that she can press a few little kisses to my mouth. I close my eyes briefly, savouring the sweetness of her affection. "I would love to come to watch your game but I just... it might not be in the way

Pinkie Promise

that you think."

I have literally no idea what that means.

Failing epically at not frowning I pull back from her and ask gruffly, "You think we won't make it to the final or something?"

Her eyes go huge and she shakes her head. "No, of course not! I definitely, definitely, *definitely* think that you'll make it to the final. That's not it at all, I…" She suddenly smacks her palm down hard on her forehead, the sound so loud that my eyes go wide.

I pull at her wrist, forcing her hand away so that she can't hit herself again.

"This isn't coming out right," she mutters, more to herself than to me. Then she looks deep into my eyes and says, "I will definitely come to your game, but I don't want to say anything about it yet. Just… trust me, okay?"

She's smiling up at me now, which makes me think that whatever is going on in her head is a good secret, not a bad secret, and I'm dying to know what it is, not wanting anything kept between us.

I stare down at her for a few long beats and then drop my head to the pillow, breathing out a nervous laugh.

"Okay," I say, holding her tighter, even though I'm still a little unsure by her hesitant response. I trust Fallon completely and if she says that she'll try to make it to the final, should we get there, then I'm going to choose to believe her, even if there's obviously something that she's thinking about that I'm not currently in on.

And from the way that she's pushing my hand up her body, over the soft curve of her waist and up to her beautiful breasts, I know that she's trying to reassure me. Trying to tell me that she's mine, even if she's got some kind of secret that she doesn't want to tell me about right now.

"I trust you," I murmur, before hefting my body off the bed, pulling Fallon right up with me, and then grabbing the box of condoms that we knocked off the dresser last night.

She lets out a happy squeak as I haul her lap up my abs and I suck hard at one of her nipples as I stride down the corridor and into the bathroom.

I kick the door shut and ease Fallon down my body, so that I can get the shower spray running and the foil packet torn open.

Then I smirk down at her and jerk my chin as she wraps her arms back around my shoulders.

"Get up here, baby."

CHAPTER 26

Fallon

Hunter is sitting on the edge of the bed with his legs spread wide, elbows on his knees, chin on his fists, and he's watching me intently as I work my hair into a half-up half-down ponytail, secured in place with my cheer ribbon.

When I start slowly combing my fingers through the fluffed up ends he scrapes a hand down his stubble and finally glances away from the mirror, his cheeks staining red and one of his hands moving to grip at the bulge in his jeans.

As soon as he realises that I'm now just messing with him because I love seeing him entranced when I do girly things, he grabs both of our bags and then borderline shoves me into a headlock, making me howl with giggles as he muscles his way out of the bedroom.

"How'd you learn to do all that stuff with your hair?" he grunts, and I peek up at him from under his bicep, shimmering with mischief as I see the grumpy aroused look on his face.

"You mean, how'd I learn to tie a ponytail?" I ask, unable to stop myself from grinning because only a guy as masculine as Hunter could be *that* clueless when it comes to girls.

"Yeah," he says, genuinely serious.

I bury my face into the side of his chest, shaking with laughter as he lets out a frustrated huff, as if he thinks that I'm keeping inside information from him.

He's so cute, I can barely cope.

"I thought you had a sister," I remind him. "Surely you've seen her do her hair before."

He pushes open the front door and lets me step out before he follows, turning around for a second so that he can lock up before we walk to the Uber.

"Wren's fresh. She's barely got hair."

I can't contain myself. I burst into a round of truly baffled laughter, so confused by Hunter's country talk that I literally have no idea what he's talking about. He shoots me a sullen scowl before opening the Uber door for me.

"Hunter, I swear, I'm not laughing *at* you," I giggle, pawing at his abs as he heaves himself down onto the seat beside me. He jerks his chin at the driver, asking her to set off. "I just have no idea what any of that sentence means."

He yanks my seatbelt over my belly before clicking in his own, and then he lays his arm heavily over my shoulders, dragging me into his side as he settles against the upholstery.

"I mean that she's, like, fresh out the womb. She's a baby. Her hair isn't like this," he says, glancing down at my head as he tangles his fingers up in my ponytail. "She just has those little baby curls right now – tiny ringlets, like the ones you've got around your forehead."

He works his fingers through the lengths of my hair for another minute and then he settles his hand around the side of my neck, squeezing me gently.

"Do you wanna learn how to do it or something?" I ask

him, feeling a little guilty about teasing him when he's such a sweetie.

He stares out of the window for a moment, most likely trying to hide that red blush on his cheeks, but after a few beats he looks down at me and rasps, "Yeah, I'd like that."

When we pull up at the Larch Peak U rink, where the bus is still parked up from yesterday's journey, I see that a bunch of other larger Ubers are just driving off, presumably having brought the guys back from the motel, and Hunter's teammates are all filtering towards the team transport bus.

I bite anxiously at the tip of my thumbnail, knowing that I should *not* be joining them on that coach.

I feel stupid knowing that I'm about to be an unwanted intruder.

"Hey." Hunter squeezes me with his forearm and snaps me out of my internal tumult. He tips his chin at me and says quietly, "No stressing. I want you here, with me, and none of the guys are gonna have a problem with it."

Hunter helps me out of the Uber and then he's hauling me to the bus, our bags thrown over one of his large shoulders.

I'm snuggled securely under the other.

Tanner steps out of one of the Ubers and as soon as he sees Hunter a huge grin spreads across his face.

Hunter mumbles a resigned "*ah Jesus*" as Tanner swaggers his way over to us, his sharp eyes flicking keenly from Hunter's face to mine.

"Nice face," Tanner says, smirking at Hunter's cut cheekbone and bruised eye.

I prevented myself from telling Hunter how hot he looks with his game injuries because I don't want to encourage him to engage in more fights.

But truth be told, he looks crazy sexy right now.

Hunter smirks, brushing off the taunt.

"Busy night?" Tanner asks.

It takes me a moment to realise that he's talking to me.

"Oh, um… you know…" I lift my eyes up to Hunter but he's looking dead ahead, his tongue poking roughly in the side of his jaw. He flashes a look across to Tanner but Tanner just grins back at him.

"So what'd y'all do?" Tanner continues. "Polish the cap's helmet?"

I try to work out what the hell that means while Hunter socks him in the gut.

When they finish their little brawl Hunter clutches me back under his bicep, exchanging a loaded glance with his roommate. I can tell that their fight is totally non-malicious but Hunter still jerks his chin at him and says quietly, "Watch your mouth."

Tanner looks far too pleased with himself.

I narrow my eyes on him and make a mental note to Google locker-room language.

I step up onto the coach and Hunter braces his arms on either side of the frame. He gives me a subtle nudge with his chest as he says, "Go sit at the back, baby."

I turn around to face him, my cheeks burning red when I realise that I'm the first person boarding.

"Hunter," I hiss quietly, absolutely mortified by the fact that his whole team is stood behind him, watching me and waiting to get their seat on the coach.

"I need to have a word with the guys."

"But–"

"Fallon." He gives me a heated look, his deep hockey captain tone making something twist in my belly.

I nod my head, spellbound, and then I scamper to the back of the bus, hoping that his teammates really will be as cool with my being here as Hunter is saying that they are.

Knowing that the windows are tinted I peer out so that I can watch Hunter give some sort of pep-talk to his team. They all look pretty laidback about whatever he's saying, nodding and occasionally glancing my way, as if they can sense me back here.

Pinkie Promise

I pull away from the window and quickly settle in the corner at the far left, folding my knees up under my chin as I wait for Hunter to come join me.

Part of me wonders if I should be embarrassed by my feelings towards Hunter. I told him from the get-go that I didn't like depending on people – that I needed to be strong, stable, and stand on my own two feet. But right now I love the sense of wholeness that being around Hunter gives me, a sensation that I've never felt before and now wouldn't want to live without.

I wonder if it's the same for him.

Hunter's teammates begin filing onto the coach and in less than a minute Hunter is right beside me.

He drops down next to me and then he hauls me up onto his lap, kissing fervently at my cheeks as he wraps one of his arms around my upper body.

"You smell so good," he murmurs quietly, his other palm squeezing my thighs.

I can't help but notice that all of his teammates have left the rest of our row empty.

Hunter notices me looking at the three free seats to his left and he smirks indulgently.

"Captain's orders," he says simply, his voice gruff and satisfied.

"You're gonna make all of your friends hate me," I tell him, peeking over the headrest in front of us to make sure that no-one is literally sat in the aisle.

He snickers and says, "Fallon, are you kidding? The only thing that my teammates wanna do to you is have you for themselves."

"Hence the hiding you just gave them out there?" I ask, hitching up an eyebrow and crossing my arms over my chest.

"They're my friends, baby, I didn't give them a hiding. I just, you know… gave them a warning."

Can I be a feminist and find a guy's possessiveness attractive at the same time?

I add that to my mental list of things to Google and then snuggle down into Hunter's chest, deciding to stop pestering him about his protective streak when I'm secretly enamoured by it. Honestly, I wouldn't want him to behave in any other way.

"Thank you for letting me stay in your future home last night," I whisper up to him, smiling when he looks down at me, a sexy crease dimpling in the middle of his cheek.

"It's never felt more like home than when I got you through the front door," he replies, the hand on my thigh giving me another firm squeeze. "Besides, it's gonna be *our* home as soon as you finish up at Carter U."

I roll my eyes playfully although my heart feels like it's about to burst.

"Do you know when you're gonna hear back about your grant?" he asks, burying his face in my hair and groaning quietly after he takes a deep inhale.

"Just before summer break," I admit, wincing inwardly. "I know it's crazy far away and it means that I'll have no time to give myself a Plan B if I don't get the outcome that I want, hence why I took the job at that cute diner. You know, so that I won't have to take out any loans that are too crazy, if needs be."

Hunter chokes briefly and then rasps, "Uh, yeah. The diner."

"Yeah," I continue. "I mean, it's just really good to be able to do something for myself, you know? Not owing anyone anything, standing on my own two feet. That kind of thing is really important to me."

Hunter takes a long pull on his water bottle, his cheeks bright red. His eyes are looking at anywhere but mine.

"Uh…" I laugh nervously as he tosses the water bottle next to him and tugs a hand roughly through his hair. "Are you okay?" I ask, raising an eyebrow.

He grunts and nods. "Just dehydrated, sorry." He

Pinkie Promise

glances down at me and pulls me tighter against his chest. "You liked your pancakes?" he asks.

I nod up at him and he smiles, his chest swelling contentedly.

"Good," he says. "Now tell me that you can stay over at the hockey house tonight."

"Hunter," I say, unable to stop myself from smiling.

Who knew that being so wanted would feel so good?

"Say it," he whispers, tickling at my ribs to make me squeal and squirm. He grins against my neck and suddenly sinks his teeth into my skin.

Before I gasp and capture the attention of every man in this vehicle Hunter presses one of his palms over my mouth and then he bites down even harder.

My eyes practically roll into the back of my head. I shift on his lap and his arousal digs into the softest part of my thigh.

"Fallon," he rasps, keeping his hand over my mouth. "I want to have you in my bed tonight, tomorrow, and every day after. Then I want you over the kitchen table and up against the shower wall. So I'm gonna need you to stay over, okay?"

My pupils have blacked out, showing Hunter exactly how much I want that too, but I shake my head anyway, determined to keep at least a small semblance of self-control.

"Cheer," I mumble against his hand. "My thesis. And m-my shift at the diner."

He drops his head forward and groans, removing his hand from my mouth but nodding anyway as he closes his eyes.

I lean up to kiss at his jaw and his cut cheekbone twitches slightly with pleasure.

"And you have that secret manuscript that you're writing," he reminds me, opening one eye to gauge my reaction.

I try not to look too shocked that he remembered about my secret little dream, but whatever he sees in my face makes him laugh out loud.

"You really don't know what you'd do if you didn't get that grant?" he asks me quietly, his palms roaming down so that he can hold me by my waist.

I frown and shake my head, unsure at what he's getting at.

"Interesting," he says dryly. Then he compresses me against his pecs with a hard squish from his pumped forearms.

Just before I close my eyes he asks in a low rasp, "Do you wanna come by the rink next week so we can skate together again? I, uh… I kinda loved it, having you on the ice with me."

Hunter Wilde, you are so darn cute.

"Yeah," I tell him. "I'll let you take me for another spin."

He lets out a low laugh and then tucks my head under his chin.

I close my eyes and nestle further into his chest.

For the first time in my life I don't feel car sick.

CHAPTER 27

Hunter

Coach Benson's punishment for my fight with O'Neill consisted of making me sit five consecutive practice sessions in the stands and disallowing me from playing this week's game. He looks as pissed off about the arrangement as I am, but neither one of us is saying anything about it because we were both in the wrong.

I shouldn't have brawled with a sore loser who couldn't keep his mouth shut, but Benson shouldn't have had restrictions on his players' personal lives when it's none of his damn business in the first place. So we're letting our frustrations simmer down before we finally broach the subject with one another.

The free time that I gained from missing this week's game meant that I could finalise this semester's essays, along with finishing up my thesis and getting it sent off to my supervisor.

Knowing that I'll end up sharing what grades I get with Fallon has been the shove that I needed to actually put some effort into finishing my assignments.

Fallon only stayed at the hockey house one night this week because she has a crazy amount of essays to finish, on top of this secret cheer training that she's refusing to tell me any details about. I could tell that she was barely conscious from how hard she's been working so we took the evening easy. We watched a hockey replay on my bed and then made out a little before we went to sleep.

Obviously, after a night of no action I woke up harder than fucking steel, but I wasn't about to try anything on with her when Fallon still seemed so exhausted.

But my week of hockey punishments is now over, as are a bunch of Fallon's essays, so after my first practice back this afternoon she's going to come to the rink and let me skate with her for a while.

Before I head to the ice I drive my truck to my mom's diner. I made the mistake a couple of days ago of answering her FaceTime call while forgetting that I had a whole black eye, meaning that she lost her shit and has insisted to inspect my face.

I pull up into a parking space and flick my keys around my finger as I walk my way toward the diner doors. Fallon only works Sundays so she definitely shouldn't be here but I'm still nervous as hell about the idea of bumping into her, and then her somehow realising that the woman she's working for is her boyfriend's mom.

I've been meaning to tell her everything – to explain my fucked-up logic of getting her this job without telling her about it – but it's so damn backwards that I can't bring myself to do it.

How the hell do I tell a girl who explicitly told me that she hates involving other people in her personal business that I went behind her back and orchestrated this whole thing?

There's no justifying something that stupid, not when I could have been upfront from the start. My only option so that I don't seem insane is to keep on lying to her, even though I'm essentially just digging myself a bigger hole.

I grip a hand through my hair and shoulder-shove the door open, my brain in overdrive.

Fuck it. She needed a source of income and I was able to help her get it. I didn't want her working somewhere shady, so I did what I had to do. I know she'd hate that I pulled some strings, but I can't bring myself to regret the decision.

I just hope that when I finally do tell her what I did, she won't think that I crossed a serious line.

I jerk my chin at the regulars who have been coming here since I was a kid and then I open the counter-door, ducking through the back to find my mom.

She's leaning over her desk in the small back office, inputting data into a spreadsheet as I rap my knuckles on the open door.

Wren peeks up over our mom's shoulder and starts kicking her feet excitedly.

"Sup Tiny," I grunt, walking into the room so that I can steal her from my mom's arms.

My mom shoots me a look as I heave up the baby, narrowing her eyes on my healing cheekbone and giving me a scolding triple-tut. Then she turns her attention back to the keyboard.

I smush a kiss to Wren's cheek and then pull the hood of her baby-grow over her head. It's small and furry and has teddy bear ears at the top.

"Can I bring her to practice?" I ask, only half-joking.

My mom shuts her laptop and turns to me with her arms folded over her chest.

"If your face is any indication of your ability to skate, then absolutely not." She points a finger up at my eye and asks, "What the hell happened?"

"Some jackass talking smack–"

"*Language,*" she says in a frantic hush, her eyes wide as

she gestures towards the baby in my arms.

"Shit, sorry." I cover one of Wren's ears and repeat quietly, "There was a jackass talking smack."

"Oh my God." My mom presses her palm between her eyes. "You do realise that you actually just said more curse words, and then repeated the ones that you said before, right?"

She tries to take Wren from my arms but I hold the baby higher so that my mom can't reach her.

Wren giggles loudly, making me smirk down at my mom.

"See? She likes it when I hold her."

"Why did you get into a fight that was so bad it gave you a black eye? Don't you see how irresponsible that is?" My mom squints up at my cut and adds, "How'd you clean it?"

My cheeks instantly flame because technically *I* didn't clean it.

Fallon did.

I tuck Wren back against my chest, rocking her so that she doesn't do her little attention-seeking scream thing, and then I grumble quietly, "That's a lot of questions, woman."

My mom stares at me for a beat before rolling her eyes. "Oh Lord, you really are your father's son, aren't you? Did you get into a fight over that cute girl you've got working here?"

My beet red cheeks answer her question for me.

"Aw, honey," she coos, breathing out a sigh. "Why are boys so silly?"

She brushes past me out of the office and I follow her into the main room of the diner.

I can't really justify acting like a brute, but I give it a shot anyway.

"You know I've stopped brawling like I used to. The fight was one-sided for a good two minutes before I finally got involved. The guy on the opposing team was talking shi–"

My mom shoots me that *you're holding a baby* look so I quickly rephrase.

"I mean, the guy on the opposing team started saying some... real crude stuff, about her. About Fallon. And she was in the crowd too so I was worried that she'd hear him. Then he started pushing on me and when he said this one final thing I just..."

I shake my head at the memory. Wren bats my face with her baby-grow paw.

My mom collects the empty mugs from her patrons and when we get back to the counter she asks, "What did Fallon have to say? Is she the one who disinfected the cut?"

I look down and clear my throat. "Yeah, she cleaned the cut."

She also kinda told me that she didn't mind watching me fight, but I decide to leave that part out because I'm trying to *not* feel good about being a bruiser.

"That's very sweet," my mom says, reaching up to take the baby back.

My mom is pretty young for a mother of six. Somehow she always looks even younger when she's holding Wren in her arms.

I give my mom a peck on the cheek and then jerk my thumb over towards my truck. "I have to get going. I've got practice and then..."

My mom raises an eyebrow at me with a knowing smile on her face. "And then...?" she teases.

I scratch roughly at the back of my head, avoiding her eyes.

"Uh, yeah," I mumble, laughing nervously to avoid her question. "See y'all later."

"Mm-hm," my mom smirks, and I hide my smile as I duck out of the front door.

*

Benson blows the whistle, calling time on today's practice session.

I tear open the fastenings on my gloves as I work my way over to the other side of the rink with my teammates.

"Wilde. A word."

I pause and turn my head to glance over at Coach. He's staring out at the rink with his arms folded across his chest, radiating almost as much displeasure at the idea of having to talk out our differences as I am.

Fallon is about to be here in less than three minutes, so I want this conversation wrapped up as soon as damn possible.

"Yeah, Coach," I say, tucking my gloves and my stick under one of my biceps and then pulling off my helmet so that I can quickly shake out my fringe.

He stays stoically silent for a few long beats and then he releases a sigh, stepping down from the substitution box so that we can talk face to face.

"You understand why I had to freeze your play for a week, don't you?" he asks.

I nod my head. "Yeah. 'Cause I did some dumb shit at the Larch Peak U game."

"Even after I warned you at the start of last term to keep your game clean," he reminds me, narrowing his eyes slightly.

I shove my tongue in my cheek, irritated, but I nod again anyway. "Yeah, you did. I lost my head for a second and it won't happen again."

Benson watches me carefully before nodding in agreement. Then he clears his throat and begins, "So about the girl–"

"Coach," I warn him, because this is one thing that I *won't* be changing my stance on.

He holds up a palm, asking me to hear him out.

"I only ever give my players the advice that I wish I'd been given, and telling y'all to not get too invested with anyone was a precaution so that you would never hinder your game. For this exact reason. For the type of thing that happened over at Larch Peak. *But…*"

He glances away from me briefly and rubs his hand down his jaw.

"I can see now that what I was really doing was hindering my players. I should have been coaching you about how to handle the heat, rather than preventing it from happening completely. I mean, that's my damn job – to coach you about every aspect of the game, not just the physical play. And there's more smack talk in hockey than trucks on the damn highway.

"Having some good-for-nothing chip-on-his-shoulder yuppie prick get under your skin when you beat his ass on his home turf is inevitable, and I take full responsibility for going the wrong way around this situation. Jesus, Hunter – you're one of the best players I've ever coached. I know that I've always had the 'tough love' approach but in this instance I'm gonna give it to you straight. I'm in the wrong. My players' relationships off the ice are just as important as their relationships *on* the ice. Don't think I didn't notice the fact that when you came to practice after the Larch Peak U shit-show your cheek had been freakin' tended to."

My face grows hot, remembering how Fallon took care of me that night, in every way that I needed.

"That's a good thing, Wilde, to have someone behind the scenes who has your back like that. Not to mention, it's damn well *rare*. So," he says, clasping his hands together like he's about to wrap this up. "You apologised, and now I apologise. And as long as you can work through the fact that some guys are gonna try and push the nastiest buttons that they can get their hands on, and as long as you *don't* try to murder them when they do, I want us to put this shit behind us and get back to winning the damn championship."

He said exactly what I needed him to, so I don't hesitate

for a second.

"Yes, Coach."

He nods once before heading down the corridor to his office.

I watch him go until he shuts himself behind the door and when I turn back to the rink I feel like I've had a weight lifted from my shoulders.

I set my gloves, helmet, and stick down by the audience seats and then I step back out onto the rink just as the doors push open.

Fallon peeks around the door and I'm immediately skating my way over to her. She pads delicately towards me, a small smile on her lips.

She's wearing that baby blue two-piece and she has the box with her skates in tucked under one of her arms.

I skid to a stop at the edge of the rink and step out so that I can join her in the stands.

"Hey – *ah!*" she squeals as I pick her up by her ass and bury my face in the warm curve of her neck.

"How'd you always smell so damn good, baby?" I murmur, walking slowly over to the nearest seat so that I can set her down and help her put her skates on.

Before I get her sat down her hands fly to my face, her fingers moving delicately as she inspects my cut.

Over the days that we've been apart this week she's been texting me for daily updates. I wanted to play it up at first because her petting me is damn addictive, but after around three days the cut was basically completely healed.

But Fallon's still looking at me like I'm a wounded soldier and – I have to admit it – I'm loving her affection.

"The bruising has almost faded," she says quietly, stroking a knuckle over the slight mark.

I smirk as I free her skates from the box and lower myself down onto one knee, asking her teasingly, "You gonna miss my black eye?"

She squirms a little on the seat, her cheeks growing pink,

Pinkie Promise

because I know damn well that she loved me looking like a bruiser.

I wink at her and she swallows a little gulp.

Then I pull her trainers off and begin sliding her feet into her skates.

"You looked like you were in a good mood when you came in here," I tell her, wrenching her laces taut so that I can tie the boots as securely as possible.

"I had a lot of closure this morning," she admits with a smile.

My eyes fly straight up to hers and my fingers pause their pulling, because the word 'closure' doesn't exactly sound great to her new boyfriend.

"Oh my God, no, I didn't mean with us!" she says quickly, and I drop my head straight down to her thighs, letting out a groan of relief.

She leashes her fingers through my hair and my shoulder muscles immediately relax.

I grind my forehead against the heat of her lap for a few more seconds, calming my breathing, before pulling away and getting back to work on her laces.

"I mean with school stuff and cheer stuff," she continues, her hands moving down to massage the back of my neck.

I arch into her touch, grunting, and she works her fingers into me harder.

"I got an email from Parker Ward, the professor who I originally wanted to be my referee, and she was all apologetic about not being able to help me with the grant submission. I mean, she could be totally lying but it sounds like she's had an insane few months, and you never know what someone's going through, so it felt good to get some closure on that because it also all worked out anyway. My new referee did an amazing job."

I nod my head and get to work on her other skate.

"And then on top of that I ran into Blair. You know, the

girl who kind of gave me two concussions?"

This time, I stop completely, stilling my hands so that I can look up at Fallon's face. I've never met the chick who got Fallon benched from her comp squad and I don't exactly have great feelings about her.

"What'd she say?" I ask, my jaw ticking slightly.

Fallon giggles at my murderous expression and leans forward to press a kiss to my mouth.

I'm immediately kissing her back full force, wrapping one hand up in her hair as I slide my tongue inside of her.

"Hunter," she laughs, scrunching her nose like I'm embarrassing her. Maybe she thinks that there are cameras in the rink or something and we'll get caught on tape.

Seeing as there actually *are* cameras in the rink I ease up on mauling her.

"Basically," she says, flipping her hair over her shoulder, and exposing the swells of her fucking beautiful breasts. "Basically, she was all embarrassed about what happened. She told me that she ended up dropping Whitney a bunch of times too – not that that makes things any better. I mean, that actually makes things worse – but she told me that, even though she'd always wanted to do competitive college cheer, she realised that she was severely messing things up for the squad, so she's stepped down off the team and she's going to take over the managing side of things next year instead. I mean, it doesn't take away from the fact that I literally couldn't compete this year and therefore I became ineligible for the Master's sport scholarship but…" Fallon shrugs and gives me a cute smile. "I guess everything happens for a reason right? If I hadn't been kicked off the team then I wouldn't… I wouldn't have met…"

I feel my heart stop momentarily in my chest.

If Fallon hadn't been kicked off the team, then she wouldn't have met me.

It's not an option. The thought of us not being together is something I won't even let her comprehend.

"Fallon, I promise you, I would find you in every lifetime."

I caress both of her calves so that she knows I've finished lacing her up and Fallon's eyes finally drop down to my position in front of her. Her irises turn sparkly as she takes in my stance for the first time since she sat down.

I've got one knee pressed into the ground and the other cocked up next to hers.

I breathe out a laugh as I realise what's going on in her head.

"Get used to it," I grin. "This ain't the last time you'll see me down on one knee."

A little gasp leaves her throat as I drag her up to her feet, feeling way too pleased with myself as her body wobbles in my arms.

"Don't be silly," she says breathlessly as I walk us out onto the ice, her soft peachy behind pressed up against my front.

"You think I'm kidding?" I ask her, settling my chin against her shoulder. I wrap my arms around her middle and kick off gently on the ice. "I'm man enough to tell you that you're wife material, Fallon."

She stays quiet but snuggles further into my chest, silently letting me know that she likes what I'm saying.

This is the cool down that I needed, in more ways than one. Reinstating my professional relationship with my coach after the fight at Larch Peak, and then reclaiming my romantic relationship with Fallon after almost a week away from each other. Plus, I love that she's also had a bunch of her academic relationships fixed, so that she has two less things to stress over from here on out.

While I let myself physically unwind on the ice, Fallon gently pushes at my hands that are currently encased around her ribs, and she kicks off away from me, gliding fast to the centre of the rink.

I follow her lead and start circling around her, keeping a

slight distance as she wraps one hand around her ankle.

My eyebrows fly upwards and I halt to a stop as she suddenly kicks up her leg into the air and begins spinning like a ballerina.

"*Fallon*," I rasp, quickly swooping towards her. It takes about ten seconds before she finally loses her balance so I grip my arms tight around her back and she laughs into my chest, her cheeks flushed with excitement.

"The hell was that?" I pant, clutching her desperately to my pecs. Something catches my eyes in the periphery of my vision, and when I lift my head to the sidelines I realise that half of my team is watching us.

They're standing there with their jaws on the floor because they just watched Fallon spin more beautifully than a trained figure skater.

Tanner shoots me a smirk because he's just realised how flexible my girlfriend is.

I give him a long look at my middle finger as I press a possessive kiss to Fallon's forehead.

When I pull back she grins up at me, looking incredibly pleased with herself.

"I thought I'd watch some skating videos and maybe try it out on you," she laughs. Then she pats at her blown-out curls and says happily, "I guess I'm a natural."

"Damn straight," I tell her gruffly, hauling her roughly against my body.

She senses the eyes on her as I spin her on the ice and when she glances over to my teammates she's immediately shy.

"How long are y'all staying up on here?" Tanner asks, his eyes straying briefly to Fallon's cute skates.

"Why?" I shoot back. "You wanna watch?"

Tanner laughs and shakes his head, and I smirk right back at him.

I begin skating over to them with Fallon tucked up under my arm, and she paws at my chest as I rub my free hand around her waist.

"That spin was beautiful," I tell her quietly before we reach the guys. "Almost gave me a heart attack though," I murmur, and she laughs prettily into my neck.

When we reach my teammates at the edge of the ice I say, "We're chilling here for a bit. I'm not heading to the bars tonight."

Tanner shrugs. "No sweat. Gives us time to plan how we're gonna fuck you up for your birthday, anyway."

"Your birthday?" Fallon asks in surprise, and hell if the whole room doesn't go sub-zero silent.

What is it about a group of guys hearing a girls' gentle voice, and suddenly the whole pack is pumping testosterone like a bunch of damn cavemen?

I shoot them a hard glare because I can *feel* their pheromones God damn it, and then I turn all of my attention down to Fallon, stroking at her hair. "My birthday's next week but it isn't a big deal, baby. We don't go crazy for birthdays," I tell her calmly.

Austin snorts. "Uh, *yeah* we do – you just can't remember last year because you blacked the hell out."

Fallon gasps and looks up at me with wide eyes.

I shove my tongue in my cheek and make a mental note to sucker-punch Austin later.

"That was for my twenty-first," I say, caressing her waist as she stares up at me. "It won't be like that this year."

"Well, I ain't sure about *that*…" Tanner says, squinting over at me as he tries to smother his laughter.

Fallon glances at him, horrified, and I give him an *I'm gonna murder you later* smile.

"What are you doing this year?" she asks him, one of her fists gripping fearfully into my jersey.

"We haven't decided yet," he admits. "Usually we just hit up the bars… or the frats."

"I'll plan something!" Fallon interjects immediately, her brows arched high.

"Fallon," I say soothingly, even though I want to kill Tanner right now for stressing her out. "He's just being an ass. You don't have to plan anything."

"But I could," she says quickly, spinning around to face me.

Way too many sets of eyes drop down to her ass, so I splay my palms over her behind, blocking the view.

"I mean, if you would like, I could host something for you guys. I'd make it good, I promise."

That little promise strikes me right through the chest.

"Fallon, I'm being serious. You don't need to do anything."

"I want to," she says, shooting a nervous glance to the guys behind her. Each one of those fuckers is getting a right hook straight in the jaw later. "It can be, like, a surprise thing."

I'm frowning because I don't want to put her out of her way, but there's also no way that I'm saying no to Fallon when she's *asking* to spend time with me. We don't hang out half as much as I'd want to so any opportunity to see her is one that I'm grasping with both hands.

"You sure?" I ask her, even though it looks like *I'm* the person who is unsure right now.

She nods excitedly. "Yes, I'm definitely sure."

I glance up at the guys and jerk my chin at them because I don't want them to hear the rest of this conversation. "See y'all in a bit," I say gruffly before hauling Fallon back onto the ice with me.

When I'm sure that we're out of earshot I tell her quietly, "I don't want you spending any money on me, Fallon. If you wanna put something on for my birthday, I don't want it to cost you a single cent."

She shakes her head, smiling up at me. "Ash and I will host it at the condo. I'll text one of your friends the details so that they know what to bring."

The thought of giving any of my teammates her number

Pinkie Promise

makes me hold her even tighter.

"We'll bring the alcohol," I tell her, because drinks aren't cheap, and I refuse to let Fallon spend her hard-earned cash on any of these fuckers.

"Fine," she says, rolling her eyes playfully. "What day is your birthday?"

"Next Friday. We've got a game on Thursday and we're travelling back that night."

"Would something in the early afternoon work? I don't have classes next Friday."

I do have classes next Friday but for Fallon I'll bunk every single one of them.

"That's perfect," I tell her, and I dip down to gently kiss her lips. When I look back at the stands I see that my teammates are still watching her, getting themselves nice and comfortable in the seats with no intentions of leaving.

I can't blame them.

Fallon Ford is the most beautiful girl that I've ever seen.

We skate together until she's sleepy and then she howls with laughter as I flip her over my shoulder, hauling her off the ice like a proud caveman.

My teammates can't take their eyes off her for one single second.

CHAPTER 28

Fallon

Ash pads around the side of the pool, half of our cheer squad already submerged in the hot lapping water, and she sets down another small cardboard crate of bottles. I'm laying back on a padded recliner, my large towel draped across my body covering me from the top of my chest to the apex of my thighs, adding songs to Aisling's playlist. She sits cross-legged on the recliner next to mine, unfastening about ten thousand dollars' worth of jewellery from her wrists.

"I needed this," she sighs, dropping another diamond-encrusted bangle to her little pile. "Like, an excuse to hang out with some hot guys."

As soon as Tanner mentioned that Hunter's birthday was coming up I knew exactly what we could all do to chill out and celebrate, and luckily – seeing as my idea consisted of taking over the top floor pool at Aisling's parents' condo for the day – the timing had been perfect for Ash too.

After weeks of to-ing and fro-ing, she finally had

Pinkie Promise

enough and decided to end things with her boyfriend, so now she's back to being sophomore-year-Ash, who was officially the hottest heartbreaker on campus.

She's wearing a pale pink bikini that makes her golden tan pop, and her hair is scraped back into a high ponytail that ends somewhere halfway down her back. She looks like a Hollister model on summer break.

My phone blips beside Aisling's and I smile when I see the name on the screen.

"The guys are here," I tell her, a magical shimmer in my belly. "I should go buzz them up."

Aisling, the hostess with the mostest, gives her ponytail a dazzling flip.

"Nu-uh," she counters. "Today's all about you and him, and he should be sweating about seeing you for as long as possible. I'll buzz them in."

She swipes a beer bottle from the crate and quickly tip-toes her way around the pool, so that she can head back to our room for a minute and let Hunter and his teammates up here.

I set a new song on the playlist and wiggle my freshly polished toes as I wait for Hunter to get himself up here.

The top floor pool is light yet somehow still cosy, like a hot-tub deck at a mountain resort. The music on our playlist mingles in with the laughter from the pool, making me feel every bit the college student that I never used to allow myself to be.

When the doors straight across from me are pushed open I shoot to my feet, clutching my towel around my body, and I begin running carefully around the side of the pool.

As soon as Hunter comes into view he shoves a hand through his hair, his eyebrows raised in surprise as he takes in his surroundings. He catches sight of me and immediately grins, striding my way before I can reach him at the door.

He scoops me into his arms, towel and all, and tucks his face into my neck, shaking his head as if he thinks that he's dreaming.

"Happy birthday," I whisper, clutching him tighter, while the girls in the pool behind me scream their *happy birthdays* at him too.

"This is way too much," he murmurs back to me, but I can hear the smile in his voice so I know that he likes it. He pulls back so that he can look down at me and he says, "How'd I get so fuckin' lucky?"

I preen like a spoiled kitten and then practically purr as he starts kissing my neck.

"Didn't know y'all had a pool up here," he admits, before placing me back on my feet and scratching roughly at the back of his hair. "Shit, I don't have any swimwear with me, baby."

"Why'd you think she was texting me?" Tanner interrupts, shoving his shoulder straight into Hunter's, before reaching into the gym bag over his shoulder and slapping a pair of swim shorts into Hunter's chest.

Hunter breathes out a startled laugh as he catches the garment. "What are these?" he asks Tanner.

"Your present. Happy birthday."

Hunter shakes his head dazedly and then grins back at his friend, his teammates already heading to the guys' shower area to get changed.

"How are you feeling after yesterday's game?" I ask, as I borderline drag him towards the showers where his teammates are located.

Hunter is fully preoccupied.

Now that he's realised that I have a towel wrapped around my body – and for a good reason too – he's staring at the fabric like he's trying to burn a hole through it with his eyes.

"Earth to Hunter," I laugh. "How was your game?"

He presses himself up behind me as his eyes follow the

shapes beneath the towel. "We won," he says simply, his hands cupping around my hips.

I already knew that they'd won seeing as he'd texted me about it last night.

I also knew that he felt *extremely* good about the celebratory selfie I sent to him, seeing as he'd followed up his texts with a photo of his post-game body before he hit the showers.

He was *not* wearing a towel.

"I meant are you sore or anything," I explain, but then suddenly I'm yelping as he hauls me up, stashing me into one of the small enclosed saunas and closing the door quickly behind us.

I burst into a fit of laughter as he grazes his teeth up my neck and then he pulls away with heated eyes as he trails his gaze hungrily down my front.

"What you got under there?" he asks, jerking his chin at my towel.

I cock a hip and taunt, "Wouldn't you like to know."

He scrapes a hand down his jaw before resettling it on my waist.

"You wearing something that's gonna get you in trouble?" he asks me quietly.

I swallow a little and then whisper, "I hope so."

His eyes burn into mine. "Show me, baby."

I peek out of the steamed-up window to check that no-one will be able to see in, his guys already changed into their swimwear and joining the cheer girls on the other side of the pool, and then I look up at Hunter as I finally open up my towel.

"Happy birthday."

Hunter arches his neck backwards, taut muscles rolling dangerously in the thick column of his throat. His eyes roam across my breasts spilling out over my lilac bikini top.

Then he lifts a hand to the back of his neck and rips his shirt clean off.

"What're you doing?" I squeak, going wide-eyed as he flicks open his jeans with one stroke of his thumb.

"Getting changed," he explains, making a little clothes heap on the floor.

I let out a shaky breath as he strips off his pants and boxers, his stance unabashedly confident as he bares himself to me.

He gives me a good ten seconds of staring time before he finally swipes the shorts off the floor and pulls them up his quads. When he finally drags me into his arms I fall limply against his chest.

"Gonna keep you pressed up against me just like this, baby," he tells me. "No-one else is gonna see what you had on for me under that towel."

I giggle as he collects the rest of his clothes using his free hand and then he shoves open the sauna room door, my front still up against his torso as he walks us from the room. He tosses his clothes roughly in the vicinity of the guy's shower area before heaving me up by my ass and carrying me over to the edge of the pool.

Hunter sets himself down and I extrapolate my legs from their straddle on his waist, slipping quickly into the pool and grinning when the water sloshes warm and wet around my chin.

He steps in after me and I burst out laughing at the fact that the water doesn't even cover his pecs.

The size difference between us makes my heart feel warm and fuzzy.

"So damn tiny," he murmurs, his smile-creases giving me butterflies.

Wanting to play, I decide to tease him a little.

"Oh no, you're too big for me!" I exclaim in dramatic mock-horror, holding the back of my hand to my forehead like a damsel about to faint. "Whatever will I do?"

He laughs and grabs my waist beneath the loudly splattering water, making me scream in delight as he restrains me from swimming away from him.

He presses a hard kiss to my cheek as I squirm against his hold and then he bites into my neck as he murmurs, "You'll take it."

My body grows slack under his forearms and I feel him smirk against my skin. He gives my breasts a rough squeeze under the water before taking my hand like a gentleman, and leading me over to where our friends are lounging.

I hear the loud slapping sound of feet hitting the wet tiles behind us and I turn my head slightly to catch Tanner finally leaving the shower room. His eyes are locked in on Aisling and there's a hard set to his bristled jaw.

She flicks her ponytail antagonistically and calls out over the blasting music, "Took a while to find a pair of shorts that are small enough for you, huh?"

He gives her a humourless smirk before smoothly heaving his body down into the water.

Even Ash, who has made a point of publically hating on Tanner since our freshman year, can't help but stare at his gigantic body.

Like Hunter, Tanner is pure home-grown Carter Ridge brawn.

Tan skin, swollen pecs, and abdominal muscles that are thick with brute force. He notices me looking, rolls his shoulders, and winks.

Good Lord.

I quickly turn back to Hunter who looks ready for murder, and he kisses me hard on the forehead before mouthing some choice words at his roommate.

Ash stares at Tanner's chest until he raises his eyebrows at her. Then she lifts her chin in defiance and turns her back to him completely.

He reaches around her to grab her beer and then he moves in behind her so that he can murmur against her cheek.

"If you're tryin' to insult me by giving me your back, I'll

have you know that it's my favourite position."

Ash snaps her head around to face him and he doesn't back away an inch.

"Actually, I *remember*," she hisses, snatching back her bottle before moving quickly to the other side of our circle.

Uh, *what?*

I stare open-mouthed at Ash and she gives me an *I'll explain later* eye roll.

WHAT? No! I need those details now!

How the hell can I have lived with her for these past few years and have *not* known that she previously got with the guy that she hates?

I go to make a beeline for her but Hunter wraps his forearm over my belly, tugging me back against his hardened groin. I release a small yelp that has him grunting against my ear.

"Y'all can talk tomorrow," he murmurs. "Today you're all mine."

I turn my head so that I can look back at him and he strokes his other hand up my throat.

"Not just today," I whisper back to him, smiling when his eyes go black and sparkly.

Not wanting to get too sentimental in front of his teammates I change the subject and ask, "Where's your other friend?" The water sloshes around me as I twist in the pool looking for Winter's boyfriend, twining my arms protectively around the back of Hunter's neck. "Caden, right? The guy from the South?"

Hunter tentatively touches the bun wobbling on top of my head.

"Caden doesn't come to stuff like this when his girlfriend isn't in town. He's real traditional."

"Kinda thinking that he might not be the only one who's real traditional," I say quietly, pursing my lips to hide my smile when Hunter meets my eyes.

"You got that right," he grins, and he hauls me up

Pinkie Promise

against his middle. I wrap myself around him tighter, laughing when he presses a kiss over my breast. "You know, I went to see my baby siblings this morning. Got me thinking about some *real* traditional stuff that I wanna do with you." He smirks to himself and then adds, "Well, *to* you."

I gasp as he teases my nipple, hard beneath my bikini, with his teeth.

He jerks his chin at me and murmurs, "Let's make a baby."

I lose all control of my limbs and he slides his hand down the back of my bikini bottoms.

But just as he's about to dip down and kiss me I feel something large press right up against my back.

I jerk at the feeling and twist my head to find Tanner towering over me, his eyes boring straight into mine.

Hunter's hand grips into me harder and I press my front up against his pecs, eliciting a satisfied sound from deep in his chest.

"What the hell's she doin'?" Tanner asks me, unfazed by the fact that I'm now the jam in a hockey player sandwich.

I blink up at him in confusion. "W-what are you talking about?" I ask.

He jerks his head to his left, and I try not to go cross-eyed as Hunter presses hungry kisses over my cleavage.

I glance over in the direction that Tanner is gesturing towards and I breathe out a light "*hmmm*" as I watch a two-hundred-pound hockey player wrap Aisling up in his arms.

"Care to explain?" he asks quietly, the vulnerability in his voice recapturing my attention.

We share a long look that has my heart aching for him.

"I thought Ash had a boyfriend," he says. "Why the hell's she lettin' Tristan grind on her from the back?"

I wince and swallow. "Ash broke up with her boyfriend."

Tanner's eyebrows skyrocket.

"Come again?"

"Please don't make it a big deal," I whisper desperately, slapping my palm over his mouth before he can say anything else.

He narrows his eyes on me and folds his arms over his chest.

"I guess she's just hard-launching the fact that she is now very much single. She's been so low up until today, she deserves a little relief."

Tanner removes my hand from his mouth and says, "Trust me, Fallon, I can give her relief."

I choke on thin air because I have no idea how to respond to that.

But to my surprise, Tanner doesn't spend the rest of the afternoon trying to one-up Ash by flirting with our friends. Instead, he fully turns his back to the group and starts a detailed conversation with Hunter about the NCAA Tournament games, ahead of the coveted Frozen Four final that they've been working towards.

Hunter holds me gently by my belly, his front against my back, and he rests his chin over my shoulder, slowly scraping his stubble back and forth over my skin.

By the time that Hunter is on his second bottle of beer my skin is so affectionately sensitised that I'm thinking, *maybe I could make a baby.*

He takes a pull on the beer and then holds the bottle in front of my lips, giving me a small baby sip and then smiling at me like I did a good job.

"I missed you this week," I tell him, scrunching up my nose at how insecure that sounds.

He places his bottle beside the pool and then cups my cheeks with both of his hands. "Yeah?" he asks.

I nod my head and his chest swells with satisfaction.

"I missed you too," he says, his voice low and deep. "Thought you were needing space or something."

My cheeks turn crimson as I mutter, "I thought that *you*

would have needed space."

He stares at me for a long moment before shoving a hand through his fringe. Water droplets trickle down his pecs and my brain goes a little fuzzy.

"Baby," he murmurs, massaging his thumbs up my jaw, "are you tellin' me that you thought I needed space, so you decided to *give* me space, even though, in reality, neither one of us wanted space?"

A dimple pops in my cheek as I scrunch my nose up even harder.

"Baby," he laughs, before leaning down so that he can kiss me. I whimper quietly at his affection but it's so loud in here that only Hunter hears it. "It's okay, baby, we'll make up for all of the time apart. And we're going to keep on doing that until you know that this is a forever thing." He presses a small kiss to the tip of my nose, his rigid dick digging roughly into my belly.

"Is that a promise?" I ask breathlessly, enchanted by the words that he's just spoken.

Something about hearing him say the word *forever* makes my soul shimmer and sparkle, like it's finally kindling to its twin flame.

Handsome creases appear in his tan cheeks at the exact second that Aisling puts on one of our favourite songs.

I squeal and spin around to face her and she flashes me a sinful grin, knowing that we're about to sing the whole condo down.

Hunter lifts me higher in his arms so that I can wrap my legs around his waist, and he gives me an adoring smile as I squish my body against his.

"Yeah baby, I promise," he murmurs, before leaning back so that he can watch me sing.

His grin grows even wider and I feel my whole heart burst.

CHAPTER 29

Hunter

Damn if I didn't wait it out as long as I could.

But after two hours of having Fallon's perfect tits pressed up against my pecs, and slow-drinking my way through three bottles of beer, I have well and truly reached the end of my rope.

My dick is in physical pain and this whole cute girl-next-door thing that Fallon has going on really is not helping my situation.

"Baby," I murmur, re-hoisting her up around my middle.

Her cleavage breaches the surface of the water and her breasts are so full and wet that I momentarily go fucking blind.

"Yeah?" she asks, smiling excitedly up at me.

She's been so sweet today – doing this for me, being here with me – and I can't believe how damn lucky I've become. Her eyes are all sparkly and her cheeks are flushed. I guess it won't be from the alcohol because Fallon has had a grand total of four sips of beer, so I'm hoping that it's more a sign that she's as ready for some alone time as I am.

Seeing the heavy pump of my chest Fallon drops her chin to her clavicle and, looking up at me from under her lashes, she whispers, "Is there something that you need?"

I jerk my chin at her, my biceps flexing. I didn't expect myself to still be kind of shy when broaching the subject of needing Fallon physically but here I am, my throat so damn tight that I can barely choke any words out.

"Yeah," I rasp.

"And what exactly is it that you need?" she asks, trailing her fingertips teasingly over my shoulders.

Hell, there's no point denying it. I lower my mouth to her cheek and murmur, "My girl, on her back."

Fallon blinks quickly, her legs fumbling on my waist.

"Can I take you away now?" I ask, wincing slightly when my dick slaps against her inner thigh. I let out a pained laugh and admit, "I'm dying here, baby."

Fallon glances quickly to our group and I follow her gaze.

Originally it was a game of water volley but, with Aisling and Tanner taking on the positions of team captains, it has since descended into a game of goddamn murder ball.

Fallon's roommate fires the ball straight at Tanner's skull, and he curses and dodges it before shooting her a burning glare.

Then he starts striding towards her.

"Oh Lordy," Fallon says, immediately trying to swim over to Aisling. I grip my hands around her hips and heave her back against my abdomen.

Tanner is not about to hurt Aisling O'Malley. If anything, he's probably about to tell her that he wants to kiss her. But seeing as Fallon is clearly concerned I shove her up the side of my body and intercept Tanner's steps, pushing my palm against his shoulder so that he backs up.

His eyes snap straight to mine before they lower down

to Fallon's.

"What?" he asks her, before glancing briefly back over to Aisling.

"We're about to go," she explains, "but I can't do that if I think that you're about to… I don't know, commit homicide? I can't tell if you want to murder Ash or marry her and, honestly, both of those options are a little disturbing given the circumstances."

Tanner levels her with a look. "Fallon, I want to fuck her brains out. Can't put it any more simply than that."

Fallon looks up at him open-mouthed, before flushing red and twiddling nervously with her blonde bun.

"Well, I… I'm not sure that this is the time or the place to… well, to f-word her brains out."

Tanner glances around at the pool filled with all of our friends.

"You think?" he asks dryly. "I'm not gonna do anything dumb, Fallon. Just… when it comes to meeting someone… sometimes it's instant. And for Ash and me…" He glances in her direction and takes a deep calming inhale.

Fallon's breathing pauses, taken aback. I rub my palm over her hip and give her a reassuring squeeze.

"Just ease up on it," I tell him finally, because I can't afford one more detour away from Fallon's bedroom.

Tanner gives me a nod, mainly to placate Fallon. Really we both know that he'll be tailing Aisling all night, trying to understand why she won't give him another shot.

Tanner and I smack our shoulders together, and then I'm carrying Fallon out of the pool, grabbing her towel from the pile of my clothes and holding it around her as she walks to the chicks' shower room.

I lean my bicep against the wall without breaching the entryway, my eyes raking up and down her beautiful body.

"I'll be two minutes tops, and I'll wait for you by the exit doors. Take as long as you need, baby."

Fallon looks behind her, checking that we're alone, and

then she pushes up on her tip-toes to kiss me, gasping as soon as I slide my tongue inside of her.

I walk her backwards against the inside wall, my hands cupping her cheeks as I fill her up with my tongue. I lick her in a frenzy, groaning hard when she tries to meet my firm strokes with little sweet ones of her own.

"Not here," I grunt, as she tries to push my hand down her panties. "I need to see your bedroom. Need to have you in there, baby."

She huffs dramatically before she finally relents, shoving me roughly in the chest to try and get me to back up.

Awesome. I'm gonna die from this hard-on.

"Two minutes," I repeat, before heading to the guys' shower room.

I give myself the fastest hosing of my life, yank on the jeans that I came here in, and then I gather up my shit before standing at the doors like a bouncer, ready to toss Fallon over my shoulder and haul her ass to her bedroom.

To say that I'm excited to have her after our stint of no sex is the understatement of the damn century.

A minute later she leaves the girls' shower room with her big towel wrapped around her body and a secret smile on her lips.

It's only when I notice that her bikini is *dangling from her fingers* that I understand why she's smiling like that.

My eyes almost bulge out of my head.

She's wearing nothing beneath her towel right now? In front of my whole damn hockey team?

I close the distance between us, lift her up, and then thunder out of the room, my eyes sniper-focused on the silver lift in front of us.

She giggles quietly against my ear. I give her a nice firm spank over her towel.

"Technically, wearing a towel is more covered up than wearing a bikini," Fallon says in that sweet voice of hers, looking up at me with her sparkly eyes before squishing her cheek against my shoulder.

I swallow hard and try not to let my palms slide any higher up her thighs.

"I hear the logic in what you're saying, baby, but I'm finding it really fucking hard to think clearly right now."

Fallon smiles cutely before giving me a playful bite on my pec.

My chest puffs out like a damn animal.

The elevator dings at Fallon's floor and I punch the *open* button like my life depends on it.

"You're excited," she smiles.

"You're telling me," I grunt.

She hums contentedly as I walk us to her door.

"Key?" I ask her as soon as I remember that we aren't at my place.

Seeing as she doesn't have any clothes on I'm guessing that she's forgotten her key, but that's not a problem because I'm more than happy to bust her door down.

"On top of the sconce," she murmurs sleepily.

My breathing pauses in my throat.

"What's that now?" I ask, leaning back so that I can see if she's joking.

She meets my eyes and instantly realises that that was the wrong answer.

"Uh…" she breathes shyly, dropping her gaze down to my chest.

I don't want her to feel bad about it and no way am I going to lecture her on it, but I'm not exactly jumping for joy that she left a spare key outside of her front door.

I reach above the sconce, swipe the key, and let us in.

"Please don't do that again," I murmur, using the key to re-lock the entry from the inside. Then I toss the key on the kitchen counter and set Fallon down on her feet so that she can choose our next move.

"I won't," she mumbles, looking sulky.

Her expression makes me laugh, causing her to look up

Pinkie Promise

at me like a wounded kitten.

"Hey, I'm not mad at you, baby," I tell her, dropping my clothes on the side of her couch as she carefully walks backwards. I put my hands back over her waist as she takes us closer and closer to her bedroom door. "I want you safe. You're my priority."

She nods her head, one of her fists toying with the front of her towel.

"Have I pissed you off?" I ask her, as her back thuds against her doorframe. I want her so badly right now but her little flash of shyness has me thinking that I should ease up. We don't have to do anything if she doesn't want to. I'd be the happiest man on the planet if she'd just let me hold her.

"No," she says, quiet and slow. "I'm just… nervous… about showing you my room."

My eyebrows rise because that is not the response that I was expecting.

"What're you nervous for?" I ask, pressing our foreheads together. Her bedroom could be a moat-guarded vampire lair and I'd still be stoked as fuck for her to let me inside.

She must be able to sense my thoughts because she gives me one of her dimply smiles.

"You feelin' shy about showing me your Baby Yoda shrine or something?" I ask her teasingly, and she laughs out loud, turning in my arms so that she can push her door open.

Her room is beautiful. It's a perfect continuation of the living area, with mauve walls and warm sconce lights, a plush little bed in the centre of the small space, making it look cosy and full.

There just isn't much of *Fallon* in here. There's a tidy stack of school work on her desk, next to a small pile of paperbacks, but she doesn't have an excess of clothes spilling out of the dark cherry-wood dresser or pictures from home taking up her windowsill.

She wasn't kidding when she said that school is her life. One look at her room and it's as clear as day.

"What size bed is that?" I ask, looking for something neutral to talk about as she tentatively steps inside.

Fallon turns around and tugs me in by my hand, making my chest swell victoriously with the knowledge that she needs this as much as I do. She gently pushes the door shut behind us and I feel practically high.

"It's princess size," she admits, brushing a little curl away from her temple. She wraps her free arm around my neck so that she can drag me down to start kissing her.

"Fitting," I murmur. Then I growl out, "Show me the shrine."

Fallon practically falls over laughing and then, to my absolute fucking delight, she actually pulls me over to her wardrobe, opens the door, and there at the back is a small collection of Baby Yoda pictures, grainy as hell because she obviously printed them on a college printer.

"Can't deny it. Knowing that you're a secret nerd gets me fucking going, baby."

I slip my hands beneath her towel so that I can start rubbing my palms over her belly.

"D-do you have… you know… protection?" she asks shakily as she closes her wardrobe door.

I smile smugly against her cheek, one of my palms still underneath her towel, and I dip my other hand into my front pocket as we move over to her bed. I pull out a handful of rubbers and toss them down onto her sheets.

"Told you I'd keep you protected," I remind her as I pull back her quilt cover so that she can climb up underneath it.

My eyes suddenly land on the jersey that I gave her for Christmas, stashed half-hidden beneath her pillow. My dick immediately grows heavier, the muscles in my legs becoming tense.

"Do, uh..." I clear my throat hard, my voice so deep that it makes Fallon squeeze her thighs together. "Do you sleep in my jersey?" I ask her, my irises now completely swallowed up by my inked-out pupils.

"Maybe," she whispers.

Hot fucking damn. I think I just grew another five inches. "Tell me that you wear it every night," I demand.

She gives me a sweet little smile and then she whispers, "Make me."

I groan long and low as I shove Fallon's towel from her body. My dick swells painfully as I stare down at her breasts and she lifts her arms in the air as she unties her little bun.

Her hair cascades over her golden shoulders and she almost ends my fucking life when her curls bounce against her nipples.

"Fallon," I rasp, my fingers instinctively unzipping my jeans. I kick my pants off my legs and fumble blindly for one of the condoms. Fallon sits daintily down in the centre of her bed, her feet tucked under her ass and her arms braced in front of her, squeezing her breasts together.

I quickly blink away from them, dropping my eyes down to my dick as I roll up the rubber, trying not to pre-come before I'm even inside of her.

I drop the foil packet to the floor and heave up onto Fallon's bed, the springs groaning loudly beneath my knees.

Looks like this soft princess mattress isn't used to taking the weight of a six-foot-four hockey captain.

Pink-cheeked and giggling nervously Fallon clambers over to me, wrapping her arms around my shoulders and her thighs around my groin.

Holy fucking shit. I push her onto her back and fall heavily on top of her, and my brain damn near explodes as my cock slaps against her belly.

"You're not tipsy, right?" I ask her breathlessly, scanning her eyes to make sure that she isn't inebriated. "Like, you can still consent? If you can't, just say so and I'll stop right now."

She pulls me down for a kiss, moaning when I slip my tongue inside of her.

"I'm not tipsy," she whispers. "I barely had a sip."

I grunt, pleased, and after a moment she asks nervously, "Do you?"

"Do I what?" I rasp.

"Do you consent? Are you… tipsy?"

I pull back for a second, surprised by her question. I'm a little buzzed but, at my size, three beers barely scratches the surface.

"Baby," I pant, "I consent so fucking hard." To emphasise my point I wrap her fist around my definitely-sober rock-hard dick. "The only thing that I'm drunk on is you. Let me have you," I say gruffly, hunching low so that I can kiss my way down to her tits. I push them together with my palms and suck roughly at her nipples.

Her back arches off the mattress and I look up to see her nod.

I release her with a *pop* and push her all the way to the top of the bed, getting her nice and comfortable on the pillows as I align myself up with her heat. Leaning on my left forearm I look down at her body, her hair spilling all around her face and her pulse fluttering wildly in her neck.

Keeping her in place, I start to slowly push inside.

"You don't have to admit it, Fallon," I murmur as she moans beneath me, "but it's satisfying as hell to think about you wearing my jersey while you're in bed. Knowing that my name's on your back during the nights that I'm not."

I breathe out a laugh and thrust roughly inside of her, ripping a grunt from my chest as she gasps and writhes beneath me.

"Your future name," I rasp out as I drop my forehead to her temple.

"You c-can't say things like that," she whimpers, digging her nails into the thick muscles of my back.

I reach behind me to grab the quilt cover and I shove it up over the top of us, blocking the rest of the world out. It's just her and me, one-hundred percent focused on each other.

I hear the condoms that I'd tossed onto the quilt splatter down to the floor and I shove my tongue in my cheek, trying not to think about what my brain is conjuring up. Namely, the idea of forgetting all about those condoms after we finish this round, and then spending the rest of the night going at it bare.

I lean down so that I can kiss her, exhaling roughly as I slide back inside.

"I've missed you so much, baby," I groan, one of my hands tangled up in her hair. Her thighs fall slack from around my middle and my abdomen swells. I'm always going to be hungry for the feeling of her body going soft beneath me.

I withdraw slightly and then thrust it in a little deeper, keeping a few inches back so that I can tease her pussy.

"This is all for me, isn't it baby?" I ask, squeezing at her waist and building up a little tempo. "Every inch of you, Fallon. This beautiful body is all mine. And now you're going to take every inch of me."

Fallon digs her nails hard into the back of my neck, moaning for me as she pulls me down and communicating to me in kisses. Soft gentle ones that tell me she *is* all mine, followed by her pained little sounds telling me to give her what she wants, this damn second.

With shaking fingers she pushes up my hand to her breast and before I can think about it I'm shoving myself inside to the hilt.

"*Hunter!*" she whimpers, and a growl leaves my chest.

Hearing her gasp out my name is the best sound in the goddamn world.

"Can't believe I'm having you in your bed," I rasp, rolling my hips into her again. I knock her knees wider apart so that she can make more room for me and I thrust harder between her thighs. "Can't believe you're letting me pump this perfect pussy."

Fallon makes an anguished sound, barely able to keep her thighs around my hips as she moans, "I've m-missed you s-so much, Hunter."

"God, I love hearing that." I try not to grunt as I slant my mouth over hers, licking our tongues firmly together. "Might be the last day I let you spend in this condo, baby. After tonight, we're moving you into my place."

"Hunter," she laughs, but then she's moaning again as I shove her thigh backwards and begin pumping her faster. Her heat makes wet little sounds that have me groaning into her hair.

"This is everything that I think about, Fallon," I rasp, massaging firmly at the back of her knee. "You taking me. You being mine. I'm gonna look after you, Fallon. You know that, right?"

I'm not the biggest talker in the world and Fallon hates communication even more than I do, but sometimes some things are too important to not be said.

I look deep into Fallon's beautiful eyes, a resounding sense of responsibility spreading through my chest as she lets me take the lead with her, trusting me to be the kind of man in her life that she's never had before.

The kind who will put her first and lift her up, instead of holding her back and pushing her down.

"I'd never ask that of you," she whispers, her voice so light and sweet that I can't help but kiss hungrily at her lips.

"Don't have to," I tell her. "You need cash or another place to stay, you come to me for that. Grant or no grant, once I get that NHL cheque *I'll* be the one who can put you through school. And when you've accomplished that goal you'll get your ass back to Larch Peak and start warming our bed. *Ours*, Fallon. You and me."

I tower over her, working her pussy, and I allow myself

to savour the fact that she already *is* being taken care of by my family's money. She doesn't even know it yet but it's *our* money that's keeping her financed, keeping her fed. I know that I should have told her about it weeks ago but I don't want to risk her refusing the help when I want to give it to her so fucking much.

"H-Hunter," she says breathlessly, her breasts bouncing like crazy beneath my pecs.

I jerk my chin at her, my eyes zoned in on those plush tits.

"Oh God, oh *God*, d-did you just... did you just get bigger?"

My cock jerks, making me slap it in extra sloppy, and I clear my throat hard, not expecting that question. Our gazes lock for a moment before I drop my eyes from hers. My whole face is on goddamn fire.

"...No," I lie, fucking mortified, because I did not think that she was gonna notice that.

Seeing right through me she pleas, "H-how is that even possible?"

I make a gruff sound, shaking slightly as I reposition myself so that I can take her from a steadier angle.

"You, uh... you sure you wanna know?" I ask, trying to pace my thrusts when really I just want to pound her.

I mean, I'll happily tell Fallon why she just made my dick get even bigger but I'm not exactly a pro at dirty talk yet, plus I only wanna do it if I know that she likes to hear it.

"Mm-hm," she nods, squirming when I drive back inside her again.

"Okay," I say, sitting up and back on my haunches. I look down at where we're joining and shove a hand through my fringe. "Uh, I get, uh... I get harder when I fully, you know... take in the sight of you. When I lift up and see you panting beneath me, letting me stroke you up with" – I swallow hard, disbelieving that I'm telling her this right now

– "with a thick, dirty cock... and you're so hot and tight and—"

Fallon releases a high-pitched moan, making my eyes flash down to hers like a bolt of damn lightning.

"This okay?" I ask her. "Me, talkin' like this?"

It's been weeks since our first... ten times, and I want to re-solidify the fact that she likes me talking like this before I let out any more Carter Ridge country filth on her.

She bites into her lower lip, laughing nervously.

"Yeah," she says, and now I'm smiling too. Smushing kisses into her cheeks to make her wriggle and laugh wildly. Then she makes a cute little sound, humming prettily for my full attention, and she gives me a shy look before saying, "More, please."

I grunt and cock up one of my quads so that I can quickly squeeze my balls, my sac heavy as hell after that sexy little request.

"More, huh?" I ask, flashing her a smirk as she giggles beneath me.

Damn, she's cute.

"Okay, baby," I tell her. "Gonna flip you over. Sort you out from the back."

She gasps as I slip it out of her and in the next second she's pinned down on her belly.

My quads tense and flex as I peruse her bent over position, feeling every bit the two-hundred-and-twenty pound man that I am.

I grip my palms around her hips, rubbing them firmly up to her waist as my eyes rake over her perfectly rounded behind. My pecs swell and heave as I align myself with her pussy, my chest shoving down on her back as she whimpers in anticipation.

"This is all mine, isn't it baby?" I murmur, driving my hips forward and grunting when my groin slaps against her cheeks.

My whole world splinters.

Pinkie Promise

I withdraw and hit it again.

"*Hunter*," Fallon whimpers breathlessly, and I groan and lick the curve of her neck.

I grab a fistful of her soft hair, tugging her head back, and I almost smirk as she moans for more.

"Our first time fucking like this," I pant, feeling like a goddamn beast as I jerk her roughly into her pillow. "First time taking my girl on her hands and knees. You like it or what?"

I pull her head back harder so that I can gauge her response and she lets out a whimper so pretty that I shoot out a whole damn spurt of pre-come.

"*Yes*," I rasp, dropping my body on top of her, and wrenching her hips back into my lap as I pump her faster. "Not gonna last," I grunt, my temples pounding. "N-next time, I'll last longer. I'll get better, baby, I promise I'll get better."

Fallon wriggles her soft tush, silently asking me to lift and let her move, and when I give her an inch of space she turns her face to meet mine. She's sparkly eyed and moaning, but it's her beautiful blush that sends me over.

I swoop forward, kissing her, and then I'm grunting down her throat, the pressure in my balls finally snapping and releasing a flood of pleasure-pain.

"Sorry – fuck – sorry," I groan, burying my face in her neck as my hips pound her fast and furious.

I roam my palms up her front so that I can massage her tits, and her pussy tightens around my shaft, making me curse and rub her faster.

"Told you I was gonna hit it from the back and play with these tits at the same time," I say hoarsely, stroking gruffly over her nipples, breathing hard against her neck.

I jerk my hips harder, addicted to the feeling of finishing inside my girl, and Fallon's hands fumble up to meet mine, making me grope her breasts more roughly.

I suck in a sharp breath and finish like a motherfucker,

releasing long warm surges as I greedily caress her breasts.

"These *tits*," I groan, not letting up my strokes until Fallon is crying out my name and shuddering violently on my cock. "I love everything about you so much, baby," I tell her, still pinning her body hard against her bed. "I love these tits, and this belly, and these soft spreadable thighs. And – goddamn – your tight little pussy?"

I squeeze her breasts and she whimpers into her pillow.

"I love every fucking inch of you Fallon," I tell her, kissing relentlessly at her cheeks. "I love you, Fallon. I fucking love you."

"*Hunter–*"

Oh fuck. Oh *fuck*. I should have said it weeks ago, but now that she knows I can't stop fucking saying it.

"I'm so in love with you," I tell her, pressing my forehead against her temple. "Didn't know what it'd feel like but I know now. You're the one, Fallon. You're my girl, you're the one."

When I pull back I see that her eyes are shining, wide and sparkling, with surprised tears that are about to overflow.

"Hey, hey," I murmur quickly, immediately pressing kisses to her lips. "I didn't mean to overwhelm you. Don't cry, baby. I love you, please don't cry."

She looks stunned. A round tear falls down her cheek as she blinks up at me, her lips parted.

"Hey, what is it?" I ask her, kissing gently at her jaw. "It's okay, baby. Tell me."

Finally she whispers, "No one's ever said that to me before, Hunter."

It's instantaneous. As soon as the words leave her lips I'm immediately kissing her, slow and sweet, hoping that she can feel how deeply I love her.

"I'm going to tell you how much I love you every day," I say to her, "every morning, and every night, baby."

I lace both of our hands together, hers so small in mine,

Pinkie Promise

and I kiss the tips of each of her fingers.

"The second that I saw you in that hallway in October I knew that, really, I was the one who was gonna fall for you. I could feel it in my chest, Fallon, and since that day it's only grown stronger. It hurts so fucking much, and I wouldn't change it for the world. You're the love of my life, and my love is unconditional."

I feel her fingers twitch between mine and suddenly I'm smiling, lifting her whole hand up to my mouth and pressing an extra hard kiss to her pinkie.

She lets out a gentle laugh, already knowing what I'm going to say, but I say it anyway, because it's the truest thing I've ever said.

"I love you, Fallon, and that's never going to change." I squeeze her pinkie in mine and murmur, "I promise."

CHAPTER 30

Fallon

I've had three official weeks of being loved by Hunter Wilde.

On the school side of things, I have completed my thesis with time to spare meaning that, once I finally click that *submit* button, I'll only have two more essays to finish before legitimately being done with my senior year. That gives me a good few months to take more shifts at the diner so that, if I don't get the grant that I've been hyperventilating about all year, at least I'll have saved some cash that can go towards it.

Hunter's words come back to my mind, making me smile secretly to myself as I slide back behind the counter at the diner.

When I told Hunter that I'm basically only two essays away from being done and dusted with all of my classes he gave me that heavy look that he sometimes has and he said, *"Proud of you, baby. Now you got lots of time to finish up your manuscript."*

Pinkie Promise

I press the back of my hand to my flaming cheek, my insides sparkling at how much hope Hunter has for me. How much trust he has in my abilities, how much belief he has in my shattering through the glass ceiling.

I know how rare it is for a writer to get published so I've never allowed myself to dream beyond writing for fun. I'm not a nepo-baby with a ghost-writer or a movie star with an instant one-million readership following. I don't even mind the nepo-babies and the movie stars – I mean, having a book with their name on it is cool as hell, so good for them – but I know that it makes it harder for the little people to have their voices heard.

And after telling Hunter about my upbringing of getting good grades and keeping quiet, I'm pretty sure that he's even more adamant than I am for me to have my voice heard.

So maybe, after I finish my final senior year essays, I *will* work on finishing my labour-of-love manuscript...

Just for fun, I think to myself, although there's a golden warmth spreading in my chest telling me that maybe – just maybe – my life has more potential than I ever previously dared to dream about.

I feel the vibration of my phone in my pocket and that golden feeling glitters even brighter, because I know without checking that the text is going to be from Hunter.

I turn my back to the patrons and quickly slip my cell out of the side-pocket of my fifties-style diner dress.

HUNTER: *What time do you finish work tonight?*
HUNTER: *Picking you up and keeping you with me at the hockey house.*
HUNTER: *Need my mascot in my bed before the big game.*

I sink my teeth into my lower lip, feeling so happy my whole heart could burst.

Because, aside from my academic assignments almost

being wrapped up, Hunter's past three weeks have been the most epic that I've ever seen.

The Rangers have had hockey game after hockey game and they've won every single one, meaning that, in one day's time, they're officially fighting for the title of NCAA Frozen Four Champions, right here in Carter Ridge. And, on top of that, Hunter is only two goals away from being the Carter Ridge Rangers' top goal scorer of *all time*, so as long as he scores one more goal, he's going to receive the joined title of 'Most Goals Scored' in the team's history.

After their win at their penultimate championship game, Hunter showered at his place and then showed up at the condo, with wet hair, grey sweats, and a brown paper bag of movie theatre candy that ended up long forgotten on the kitchen island.

The second that he saw me wearing nothing but his Carter Ridge Rangers jersey, he slung me over his shoulder and walked us straight towards my bedroom.

As soon as we got inside he had me up against the door, his big palms cupping my cheeks, as he gave me the kind of self-satisfied kisses that made me know that he was smiling.

That gave me a pretty good indication of how his latest game had gone.

"How did it go?" I had asked anyway, dizzy and breathless but determined to make sure that the Rangers had come out on top. Mainly because I want as much success for Hunter in his college hockey career as possible but also, secretly, because there's something that I've been working on, and the Rangers making that final game is completely at the heart of it.

He pulled back, one arm braced on the door above my head, and gave me a lazy smirk that had butterflies fluttering wildly in my belly.

When Hunter is cocky I get so flustered I can barely breathe.

"Annihilation, baby," he grinned, rubbing his thumb

firmly up my jaw. "Final's in the bag, and you're gonna be in those stands to watch us win it."

I must have turned beet red, my own secret wanting to burst out of me, because he just chuckled quietly before ducking down to kiss me again. Soft, gentle kisses that had me pawing up his vest, moaning at the feel of his swollen post-game pecs.

After he stayed over, we spent the next day snuggled up in my bed, but in the evening he left so that he could go home and prep for a weekend at the garage with his dad.

I'm more than a little curious about Hunter's family, due to the fact that they've raised a freaking angel, but I'm not about to push him for me to meet them. When he wants that to happen, he'll do it in his own time.

Another text bubble appears on the screen and I wait patiently for his next message to pop up.

HUNTER: *Please do NOT get the local paper this week.*
HUNTER: *I love you :)*

A giggle tickles in my chest as I text him back, *why? lol.*

His text bubble pops up and disappears a dozen times before his message comes through.

HUNTER: *This is physically fucking painful for me to type, baby.*
HUNTER: *My photo's in there.*

I suppress a squeal and then send him a downpour of sparkling heart emojis.

I have never wanted to own a copy of the local paper so much in my whole time at Carter U.

HUNTER: *They want to hype up a local crowd for the final game.*
HUNTER: *Had to let them shoot a pic because I'm the captain*

and I didn't want Benson hounding my ass.

Knowing Hunter, the most effortlessly masculine man that I've ever met, having his photo in the local paper is probably the most mortifying thing that he's experienced all semester. I can sense his ruddy cheeks from his gruff texts alone.

FALLON: *I wanna see.*
HUNTER: *No, baby.*

I think about it for a moment and then smile to myself.

FALLON: *A pic for a pic?*
HUNTER: *Please God yes.*

Giggling excitedly, I slip into the back office and pull my glasses out of my apron. Then I raise my phone up in front of me so that I can send Hunter a photo to drive him wild.

Two loose curls are swept on either side of my forehead and my hair is pulled back into a tight little bun. With the glasses on my face and the diner uniform on my body I'm pretty sure that I'm the epitome of Hunter's sexy nerd fantasy.

I can see his texts popping non-stop at the top of my screen, and I picture him finishing up in his dad's workshop, sat on a stool by one of the trucks, knee bouncing in a frenzy as he waits for a naughty-but-nice picture of his girlfriend.

I pop open two buttons, tilt my head, and snap the picture.

But just before I return to our text thread the screen of my phone goes completely black. An almost-empty battery sporting one red bar of juice flashes in the centre of my cell before disappearing again, making me know that it's out of charge.

Pinkie Promise

I blink at my own reflection in the black screen, a little taken aback by the sudden shutdown, until my eyes flick over to my manager's desk, thinking that potentially *she'll* have a charger in one of her sockets, and that maybe I can slip it into my phone for a couple of minutes.

But before I can even begin to scour the wall for a plug, something else entirely catches my attention.

My breathing falters as I do a double-take.

I tuck my phone back inside my pocket and I move tentatively over to the desk.

Excluding the first ever shift that I had when she was familiarising me with the place, Willa, the owner of the diner, is a rare sight for me to behold. Still, I don't exactly want to get caught snooping in her office, so I quickly chance a glance behind me to ensure that I'm alone and then I pad the rest of the distance to the desk, cheeks warming the second that I see it.

It's the paper that Hunter was talking about, and right there on the front page is the headline *CAN THE CARTER RIDGE RANGERS SCORE THEIR FIRST CHAMPIONSHIP VICTORY?*

My heart pounds wildly in my chest as my eyes drop to the photo, a perfect black and white capture of Hunter beside the hockey bus. He's flushed with embarrassment and the most handsome man that I've ever seen. The thick column of his neck is arched slightly backward so that he's looking down at the lens, his sparkling eyes almost amused, but too gracious to start smirking.

He's the most beautiful person in the entire world.

How on earth is he in love with me?

With shaking fingers I pick up the paper, dizzy with the fact that fate itself left it right here for me to find, and I begin reading through the article, my patrons long forgotten. I'm so enraptured with everything that the journalist has written about Hunter's undisputable NHL future that when a small knock sounds out behind me I yelp and gasp, dropping the paper before spinning around, totally startled.

The owner of the diner looks at me with an equally surprised expression as she drops her fist from the doorframe, sending me a small nervous smile as if *she* was the one caught doing something wrong.

"Oh my God, I'm so sorry," I say quickly, brushing my loose curls out of my face and stuffing my glasses back into my apron. "I literally… I don't even know what I was doing back here… I just got distracted and I–"

She shakes her head, glancing briefly at the paper that is now lying face-up on the floor.

Her eyes shoot back to mine, her smile becoming a little strained. "It's no worries," she says, before gesturing behind her toward the main room. "We just filled another table so I was wondering if you could run me their orders is all?"

I'm borderline palpitating. I can't believe that I just risked my job like this – sniffing around in my boss's office while she is literally in the back kitchen. What the hell is wrong with me?

"I'm so sorry," I say again, my temples aching. My behaviour just now was downright stupid. "I just saw the paper and I–"

She releases a nervous laugh and says lightly, "The paper? Oh right. Yeah. Well, we just had it delivered so I thought I'd toss it in here for now." She swipes quickly at her forehead before saying in a gently urging tone, "If you wouldn't mind taking the orders at that new table, honey…"

I nod immediately because I like my boss. We don't have much reason to talk during my shifts but the pay is good and she has the kind of sweet maternal energy that I've never experienced before.

"Yes, ma'am," I say, swallowing thickly. "And, again, I'm totally sorry–"

She waves me off, her eyes straying back to the paper.

Pinkie Promise

"No worries, honey. I'll be out front in a minute."

I scamper out of the room, scooting quickly beneath the counter, before pulling up at the new table and jotting down their orders.

No more falls or failings, I remind myself. *You secured this job and you will* not *mess it up.*

I'm unbelievably grateful to *have* a college job, so the idea that I could have put it at risk just there makes my stomach hollow out a little, my brain feeling fuzzy.

Just as I slip back behind the counter to pour up a batch of coffees the door chimes open and a young-looking delivery guy walks in.

I set the cafetière down and smile, the universal gesture for *what can I do for you?*

"Hey," he says, his breathing laboured like he just ran to get here. "Sorry I'm late."

I laugh in surprise and shake my head.

"Late?" I ask. "Did we order something?"

He drops a large cardboard box onto the counter, before whipping out his electronic receipt-of-delivery pad. "It's the papers that Willa ordered – kind of a special thing for her, you know?"

He hands me the pad and the digital pen so that I can mark the item as received, but I look up at him while I scribble in my signature, a little confused.

"I, uh…" I finish writing in my name and pass the machine back to him. "I was just talking to Willa… I thought that the papers had already been delivered?"

"Huh?" he asks, his eyes still focused on the device. "Oh, uh, maybe she meant that she'd already bought one in town. She ordered these Special Delivery on Friday so that she had a bunch of them ready – dunno what she's gonna do with them all but she's a proud mom, you know? It's what moms do when their kid's in the paper."

I blink at him, my head tilted to the side, not understanding why Willa would lie about a paper delivery.

An odd sense of foreboding settles in my gut, but I brush it off as generalised paranoia.

"…Right," I say, pulling the box over to my side of the counter.

And that would have been the end of it, if I hadn't seen the name at the top of the address.

My eyes fly up to the delivery guy just as he turns on his heel to leave.

"Hey, wait," I say quickly, my blood pounding in my ears.

That can't be right, I think to myself. *There's just no way.*

"You mentioned Willa's kid… what did you say that their name was again?" I ask slowly, willing away the alarm in my voice. Then I flick my eyes back to the surname on the label, printed in bold and clear as day.

The delivery guy raises his eyebrows and amusement dances across his features.

"You don't know?" he asks, smiling in disbelief. "Willa's kid is practically famous around here. He's on the college hockey team and they're about to smash up the NCAA championships. Name's Hunter."

My lips pop open and the whole world stops.

"You're telling me," I say slowly, "that Willa's son – my boss's son – is…" I swallow hard, pressing my fingers into my forehead. "Willa's son is Hunter Wilde?"

The delivery guy chuckles in relief, like he just *knew* that I'd get there in the end, but my heart stumbles in my chest, my world tilting on its axis.

I'm working for Hunter's mom… and Hunter never mentioned it to me?

"Yeah," the guy says, nodding his head in that way that men do when they're talking about another guy who they can't help but admire. "He used to work here, you know? Was kind of bummed when he handed in his resignation."

I drop my fingers from my forehead, my eyes widening.

"I'm sorry, what?" I ask him, my voice high-pitched in

Pinkie Promise

disbelief.

"He quit at the end of last year, just before you showed up I guess." He gives me a pitying laugh when he sees my expression. "Hey, don't feel bad – I'm sure you'll get to meet him. Just because he doesn't work for his mom anymore doesn't mean that he won't stop by here and there. He's a real good guy. Those are few and far between."

I press my fingers over my lips, realisation hitting me like a damn truck.

Of course I didn't just *find* the perfect job.

Hunter *gave* it to me.

Hunter quit his job so that I could have one.

And I have no idea what to do with that information.

My mind races backwards to when Hunter sauntered in here, finding me embarrassingly excited to have *finally* found a good job that I could keep.

"Knew you'd find one," he had told me, so confident and proud that I hadn't questioned it for a second. I'd just blindly trusted his calm authoritative demeanour, eagerly submitting to it, despite knowing that jobs around campus are rare as hell once term begins, because all of the organised people already secured them before the summer ended.

I take a small step backwards, knocking into the bench at my right, and making the coffee mugs clank together.

Hunter telling me that he loves me is one thing, but Hunter *showing* me that he loves me is another thing entirely.

Words, I can handle. I've spent my life lost in books, reading the words of others to navigate the world when I felt as though I didn't belong. And from my obsessive consumption of the English language I've also learned that things can get lost in translation. You can say one thing, and someone might perceive it in another way entirely. I mean, the weight of a word like 'love' to one person may not even come close to what it truly signifies for another.

But actions? Actions, generally speaking, are

undisputable.

And to give an action of love without even *asking for recognition* has got to be the purest form of love that I've ever seen.

I rub my hand against my chest, so overwhelmed by Hunter's generosity that I have no idea how to handle it.

I can't believe that he would have done this for me. After years of being treated like a burden to my parents, I don't know what to do when I'm being treated like a prize.

My mind begins whirring at a mile a minute.

If Hunter is behind getting me a job, behind making me smile, behind making my life liveable, *how the hell will I cope if I ever lose him?*

I almost laugh as I think about the fact that I *specifically* told him that I needed to be independent – and then he went behind my back and did the damn thing anyway. Being there to take care of me even when I didn't know about it is the most Hunter thing that I've ever heard in my whole life.

"Fallon, I would never let you fall."

When he said those words to me on the rink all of those months ago I took them literally. It turns out that he meant them in more ways than one.

Hunter has been picking me up from my lowest points since the first moment that he met me.

Am I mortified about the fact that Hunter most likely forced his mom to hire me and that, when I told him that I needed to do this thing alone, he didn't freaking listen? Yes. But most of all, the strongest feeling in my chest is an all-encompassing tide of gratitude, making my heart physically ache because I can't believe that he would be so considerate. Hunter barely even *knew* me back then, and he still went out of his way to get me the cash that he knew I was desperate for.

Hunter Wilde is the perfect man, and my long-neglected heart doesn't know how to handle all of his love.

I jump as I hear a door close behind me, and I whip around with my hand clutching my chest.

Willa – Hunter's *mom* – is standing right there, her eyes wide as they look into my own, and suddenly I know that she's been here the whole time.

"I…" I shake my head, unsure of what to say. *Thank you for hiring me? Sorry that you fired your son?*

There are only two things that I'm sure of.

One, I'm very overwhelmed.

And two? I love Hunter Wilde.

I untie my apron, give her an apologetic look, and in less than three seconds I'm out of the front door.

CHAPTER 31

Hunter

Can't deny it, I'm feeling pretty good.

The culmination of years of training and dedication means that our team is one game away from becoming the NCAA's Frozen Four champions, a win that will be even greater knowing that Fallon is going to be in the stands, on our home turf, watching us win it.

One bad thing that happened in the lead up to the final is the fact that Tanner is now sporting a less than ideal injury. During our last game one of the opposition players spent all three periods body-slamming him and, in the final round, he fully rammed him to the ice.

The ref paused the game and we pulled the guy off of him but not before it became clear that Tanner was going to have to be out for the rest of the game.

The attack was so unprovoked that even Tanner was in shock, but he still managed to give the guy a clean right hook before we pulled him over to the team box.

Pinkie Promise

I checked the back of the guy's jersey to see if we knew him, to see if he had some kind of personal motive, but the name Brennan didn't ring any bells.

Benson didn't give Tanner a second of shit for it, probably because it was the most unbelievable on-ice assault that any of us had ever seen, and after the final two minutes played out we took Tanner to the hospital to ensure that nothing was broken.

So now Tanner is in recovery on the couch, nursing his mild sprain, although I know for a fact that he's going to insist on at least one period's worth of play during the final.

I don't blame him for a second – not only has he worked his ass off on this team, he also previously captained it. It would be a slap in the face if he wasn't involved in us securing the biggest win we've ever gotten.

I duck my head as I lock up my truck, smiling as I think about how fucking lucky I am right now. On my way to collect my girl, ready to bring her back to my place. I breathe out a laugh as I think about how Tanner is probably going to try and crash our movie night and, because Fallon's such a sweetheart, she'll probably let him.

I check my phone again as I trudge towards the diner, the last message in our chat staring back at me.

Can't lie, after what she said, I kind of thought that she was going to send a cute picture of her smiling up at me in her adorable uniform during her break. Then again, she was literally on shift, so maybe her tables got real busy and she didn't have the time.

Doesn't matter. I get to see her now and that's the important thing.

I pull open the door to the diner and step inside, rolling my shoulders as I scan the room for her. When I don't see her at the tables or behind the counter I send her a quick text to say *I'm here, baby*. Then I slip my phone in my pocket, cross my arms, and wait.

My leg starts bouncing after three minutes pass.

Something just... doesn't feel right. In normal circumstances, she would have responded to my message if she was held back in the kitchen or something. She knows that I'll wait as long as she needs me to.

But all of this silence? It doesn't bode well for me.

I decide to breach customer etiquette and duck around the counter, even more alarmed than before when I realise that she isn't in the kitchen.

I rake a hand through my hair and then flick my eyes over to the back office, knowing that it's unlikely that I'll find her there but willing to give it a shot anyway.

I rap my fist on the door and call out, "Fallon? You in there?"

It takes five seconds for the door to open and, when it does, it's my mom who's standing on the other side.

I quickly glance around, checking that Fallon isn't in the vicinity.

Then I feel something slap hard against my bicep and I drop my eyes back to my mom.

She shoves the paper that she was wielding roughly against my chest and when I look down at the front page I see myself staring back at me.

Heat stains my cheeks and I hide the paper under my arm.

"Where's Fallon?" I ask gruffly, not liking the feeling of suspense in the air.

"Hunter, she knows."

The Band-Aid is off before I've even registered what she's talking about. My chest heaves in one fast pump, indignation coursing through me.

"She knows what?" I ask, just in case I'm not understanding her correctly.

"She knows that you gave up your job so that she could have one, and she knows that she already met your *mom* and you failed to mention it to her."

I scrub angrily at my hair. "I'm a fucking idiot," I

murmur.

My mom doesn't argue with me on that one.

"Did she already leave?" I ask, and my mom nods her head.

"*Shit*," I curse, looking around in a panic. "How the hell do I explain this to her?"

How do I tell her that I wanted to do what was best for her, because I hated seeing her struggling all on her own?

This is not good. This is really, *really* not good.

"I already messed up too many times," I say hoarsely, adrenaline coursing through my body and making my hands itch to do something. To *fix* something.

My mom narrows her eyes. "How do you mean?"

"I'm the reason why she got fired from that feminist Hooters-type joint in the first place, not to mention I'm the reason why she got another damn knock on the head."

She blinks up at me. "What are you talking about?"

"I slammed a door in her face."

"You did *what?!*"

"See?" I say, gesturing towards her jaw-on-the-floor reaction. "This is exactly what I mean. I was just trying to make amends, to atone for all of the dumb shit that I did when I first met her. I just went an unusual way about it."

My mom levels me with a look. "Hunter, I think that she's going to need some time to process this."

"To process what?" I bite out.

"The fact that you lied, Hunter. That you went behind her back when she specifically asked you to *butt out*. Maybe she wanted to be her *own* hero."

I squeeze my eyes shut and press my palms against them.

"I was trying to do the right thing," I rasp. "Fallon can be so remorseless with herself. I needed to help her out, and I couldn't handle her struggling anymore when the solution was right there. Right *here*. I wanted to be someone that she could count on, someone who would make her life that much better."

"You should have just told her, Hunter."

"I am very fucking aware of that, Mom."

She takes the newspaper from under my arm and gives me another little whip across my pecs.

I breathe out a laugh and drop my head.

Then she does something that I didn't see coming. She tosses the paper on the cabinet beside us and wraps her arms around my middle, pressing her cheek gently to my chest.

I circle her shoulders with my forearms, willing away the stinging behind my eyes as I rest my cheek against her head.

"You'll figure it out," she tells me quietly, before giving me a reassuring squeeze. "Don't hound her, though. She might need a little time to wrap her head around how illogical her silly boyfriend is."

I don't like the idea of giving Fallon time. Especially not when I'm supposed to be winning the Frozen Four final *tomorrow* and it's only worth winning if Fallon is there with me.

"I'm going to head to her place and try to talk to her," I decide, already making my way back around the counter.

My mom follows behind me. "What if she doesn't let you in?"

Damn, I hadn't thought of that.

"Think she'll hate me even more if I break her door down?" I ask.

"Hunter, you have a huge game tomorrow. It would probably be a good thing if you try not to get arrested before then."

Fuck, fine.

Then I'll try the condo and, if she doesn't let me in, I'll call her. And if she doesn't pick up, I'll text her.

And then I'll just hope and pray that I see her tomorrow in the stands.

Because if she isn't there, then I'll have my answer.

CHAPTER 32

Hunter

I pull the last stripe of tape over the toe of my stick, yank the roll taut, and then cut it clean with a violent rip of my teeth.

"Uh, okay," Tanner says, tentatively confiscating the roll from my hand.

I don't bother looking at him as I start tearing the tape off, but I can feel his worried eyes on my face as I sort out my stick. Irony is, *Tanner* should be the player that everyone is worried about due to the fact that he should still be on injury rest – although no way is anyone going to stop him from at least one period on the ice when he's worked as hard as any of us to get our team to the position that we're in right now.

Caden has been in charge of the pre-game playlist so we're buzzed to the point of fucking cardiac arrest. I finish up with my stick, toss it beside me on the changing room bench, and then I pull my phone into my lap one more time, my jaw rigid and ticking as I stare at the blank screen.

According to her roommate, Fallon wasn't at the condo when I pulled up yesterday evening, and she didn't seem to be lying which was almost as bad as if she was.

I mean, what's worse? Your girlfriend not wanting to see you because you acted like a lovesick idiot before you were even a couple, or your girlfriend not being *at home* for another reason entirely?

'Cause like… where the hell was she? She better *not* have been at fucking Connell's place because, if I find out that she was, I am punching that prick square in the jaw.

My next move was to call her but it went straight to the network, meaning that either she'd turned off her cell or the battery had died. Neither of those prospects made me any happier than her not being home.

I couldn't exactly wait outside of her condo all night because, one, I'm not a fucking stalker and if the girl needs space then I'll listen and give it to her. And two, yesterday evening the Rangers decided to pull a last-minute grind on the ice ahead of the big game. Being honest, I was damn grateful for it because it gave me a space to work off some of my pounding adrenaline.

I texted Fallon this morning hoping that, if her battery had died the day earlier, she would have charged it by now and she would be able to see my message telling her that I love her, and I'm sorry that I behaved like such an idiot.

I want more than anything for her to be in those stands for me, but I would understand if she wasn't because I know I crossed a line. I came off too strong and it finally caught up to me.

I roll my shoulders and pull up our text thread.

Because, hey, a guy can still hope.

HUNTER: *Baby, the game's gonna start in five. I'm sorry about last night. I'm gonna win this for you.*

Please be in the stands, I think as I press send, but I don't ask her if she's going to be there because I don't want to deal with that kind of rejection right now.

I tap my phone against my knee, willing her to give me some sign that we're okay. I hope to God that I didn't screw this up beyond repair.

Benson comes into the changing room and signals to Caden to turn the music down.

Caden cranks it higher.

Benson gives him the finger.

"Alright Rangers, this is what you've been training for," Benson shouts, making us all get to our feet, arms crossed and chests heaving.

We make a rough circle in the room. The music from the rink is blasting so loudly that it's mixing with Caden's playlist here in the changing room. My heart starts pumping hard, the phone in my hand crushed in a death grip.

Give me a sign, baby, I think to myself. *Just one little sign.*

"We're stronger, faster, and more agile than those fuckers. Three periods and" – Benson points his finger in my direction – "I want you scoring in *every damn one.*"

I give him a jerk of my chin, feeling some of the team clap me firmly on the back, and determination immediately shoots up my spine.

"Got it, Coach."

"Get your asses out there and win this damn thing, *now!*"

We're instantly moving, shoulders knocking into shoulders, but as I go to toss my phone down the screen suddenly lights up.

I borderline bulldoze into Tanner as I lunge forward to catch it from falling.

He bites back a gruff sound and then thumps me with his uninjured leg.

"Door's that way, genius," he grunts. Then he catches a look at what *I'm* looking at and his expression lightens, his eyebrows lifting up as his tongue swipes over his lower lip.

It's one sentence from Fallon and all it says is, *I'm here.*
It's exactly what I fucking needed.

"*Yes.*" I practically growl as I move my thumbs across the screen, ready to send her back a damn essay about how much I love her, how grateful I am that she's here, but then Benson is grabbing the phone from my hands and using it to point towards the exit.

"Now!" he barks, his face as serious as I've ever seen it. "You can text your girlfriend *after* you win, Wilde."

Tanner does a double-take. "Wait, what? You're telling me that we're allowed to have girlfriends now?"

"Jesus Christ." Benson muscles us through the doorway, his face beet red.

"How come you're only telling me that in the year that I graduate?" Tanner exclaims, genuinely in shock. "I could've been securing Ash this *whole fuckin' time?*"

"Watch your fuckin' mouth," Benson says, disregarding the fact that he just used the exact same language that Tanner did.

Benson gives us one last push until we're standing at the far end of the rink with our teammates, strobes of light whirring over the ice as the guy on the mic hypes the crowd into total chaos. I can see some of the Michigan guys near the away teams' player's box and I roll my shoulders as I get a good look at them, shoving my hands into my gloves.

"We still have four minutes 'til they let us on the ice," Austin says, so ready to go that his shoulders are bouncing. "Why'd they bring us out here if there's still four freakin' minutes?"

It's a good point but I don't care because I'm going to spend the next four minutes scanning the stands for my girlfriend.

Shit, can I still call her that? I mean, surely she wouldn't come to the championship finals if she was going to break up with me... right?

Or is she here as one final show of support before

Pinkie Promise

telling me that we need to go our separate ways?

I swallow thickly, shoving my mouth guard between my teeth like a chew toy. I gnaw on it for a few anxious seconds before shouldering Caden and saying, "Hey, hypothetically speaking, if a chick was going to break up with you–"

"Why are you asking Caden about break ups? The dude's borderline married. Ask Tanner," Austin says, smirking wickedly.

Tanner uses his stick to smack Austin's to the ground.

"Good one, asshole, but you can't experience a break up if you've never been in a relationship."

Then he turns to me like he's about to say something but, just before he does, his eyes flit to the other side of the ice.

He throws his own stick to the floor and presses his gloves up against the glass.

"What the hell is that?" he says hoarsely, as he stares over to the other end of the arena.

The music changes overhead and we all follow his line of sight.

And the second that I see her, my jaw hits the floor.

"Oh my God," I say, my heart thundering in my chest.

Because directly in front of us on the other side of the rink, on those long unused mats beneath the huge Carter Ridge Rangers curtain, is Carter U's cheer squad dressed in their home team colours, cart-wheeling into position, their red bows twinkling.

"What in the ever-loving fuck is happening right now?" I rasp.

But as soon as the words leave my mouth, I know.

That secret event that Fallon has been preparing for ever since she left the comp team?

This *whole time* she's been training for this – to perform for the home team at the championship finals.

A surge of gratitude spears through my chest as I watch

her flip on the mats, psyching herself up for her imminent performance.

I shove my glove against my helmet, my head spinning.

So this is why Fallon didn't quit cheer completely after leaving the comp team, why she was so secretive with me about what she was practising for, and why she already knew so much about the Rangers' championship game plan.

And even though I won't allow myself to believe it, deep down I want to think that she's doing this for me.

"She looks so fucking good," I murmur, my eyes unblinking as we all stare out across the ice.

"I can't believe that this is the first time we've had our home fucking girls cheering for us pre-game," Tanner says incredulously, his gloved-fist resting hard against the clear board. "Can you believe that *this* is what we could have been walking out to for four damn years, for every home game we played? Jesus Christ. I'm gonna murder those football guys for stealing them from us this whole time."

"Which one's yours?" Austin asks me.

I elbow him in the gut and he ducks away, smirking.

Fallon is dead centre and already posed for action, spinning in sync with two other gymnasts that are flanking her sides. The three of them tuck in their pom-poms and back-flip straight into the arms of their teammates' cheer baskets, landing steady in their awaiting arms before ditching the pom-poms, jumping, and then landing in handstands that are so incredible my entire team is saying *"ohhhh shit!"*

"How long do you think it'll take before our boners die down?" Tanner asks, giving me a look of legitimate concern. "Never played while hard before."

"Good to fuckin' know," I say, shoving him as far away from me as possible.

"I'm serious, man!" he exclaims. Then he adds, "This song slaps."

I've been so focused on Fallon's little waist in that red

Pinkie Promise

and blue costume that I can't recount a single lyric.

"What's the song?" I ask, not taking my eyes off of Fallon as her teammates spring her upwards, making my heart jump to my throat. She swings into the next cheer basket, this time landing on one leg, her other one perfectly straight at a one-hundred-and-eighty degree angle. I get an eyeful of the little cheer panty-shorts that she wears under her skirt and my dick goes from semi hard to fully erect.

Great.

"Something by Taylor Swift, I'll add it to the group Spotify," he mumbles, his tongue practically hanging out of his damn mouth.

The commentator on the speakers brings our attention back to the countdown, and my adrenaline thunders in time with the increasing tempo of the music as he announces that there's thirty seconds until the players will be on the ice.

Can't deny that the team has never been so pumped, every one of us agitated and itching to do some damage.

Just as the song pounds faster towards the imminent final chorus I see Fallon's teammates throw her up into the air. She does so many twists that I can't even count them, but I recognise the move because she had me try it with her one time.

Fallon lands in their hands on her feet, and then the girls holding her grip each of her ankles. They toss her again, a straight vertical throw this time, and instead of catching her on her feet again they move like a wave on either side of her, helping her drop into the cleanest horizontal split that I've ever seen in my life.

My jaw borderline dislocates.

But without waiting a single second, the chorus flares to life at the exact same moment that Fallon back-flips like an Olympic athlete straight into a second cheer pyramid stationed behind her, where she lands on her feet, kicks one leg in the air, and smiles the most enchanting smile that I've ever seen. She stretches her arms out at her sides, fully completing their pyramid.

The buzzer sounds overhead and suddenly both team gates are opened, players instantly swarming onto the ice to do one minute of protocol and warming up before the real game begins.

But I'm immediately skating to the other side of the rink where Fallon's teammates are already lowering her down. They collect their pom-poms and then they're getting ushered into the stands so that they can watch their guys win them the championship.

"Fallon!" I bellow, rapping my glove against the clear wall between us as her team steers her in an excited frenzy towards the seats.

The second that she turns around to look at me, her cheeks pink with exertion, I'm shouting, "I'm gonna explain everything, baby, I just have a game to win first, okay?"

I don't know what I expected but it definitely isn't what I get.

She wriggles her way out of the arms of the campus security and she runs right up to the board, pressing her hands against the glass, jumping up onto her tiptoes, and then giving the wall that separates us the biggest kiss that she can.

I align my gloves with her hands and drop my forehead down to hers.

"It's okay!" she shouts, but she's already being forced back to the rest of the audience, making my blood about boil as I see campus security put their hands on her. "Everything's okay, I promise!"

Then she whips her ponytail around to her front and turns her back to me before looking over her shoulder.

My eyes drop to the back of her cheer top and my heart misses a beat.

I rub my glove around the back of my neck as my cheeks grow red, but I manage to give her a grateful smile

Pinkie Promise

before she's fully out of sight.

Because there on the back of her top is a big number 9.

CHAPTER 33

Fallon

There are twenty cheerleaders crammed into the front row beside the Carter U player's box, screaming at the top of their lungs as the third and final period of the game begins, and pounding their palms against the boards as the Rangers burst their way back onto the rink. My heart thunders wildly as the puck flies across the ice, the Rangers weaving it fast and furiously around the Michigan players until all of the guys are crowding around the goal, trying to slap it under the goalie's shields. It takes a lot of braced thighs and shoulder shoving but, after Hunter's roommate Caden flicks it to Tanner, Tanner smashes it into the top corner.

The giant scoreboard dings as the number 5 turns into a 6, and the crowd goes crazy, knowing how hard it will be for Michigan to catch up when Carter U is four points ahead of them.

Tanner didn't play during the first and second periods and now that he's being smothered with love by his teammates I can see why. Even as he claps them back I can see the strain on his face, the way that he's holding his body at a slight angle as he limps back into position.

Tanner's obviously still recovering from an injury but with the prospect of winning the NCAA tournament within reach no way is he going to miss the chance to be a part of it.

"I think I'm gonna throw up," Aisling says, her face blanched of all colour and her eyebrows arched high. Ash is the only cheerleader who isn't wearing their cheer outfit, due to the fact that she's on the comp team, not the events team, so she didn't take part in our home-pride pre-game performance just now.

The fact that she decided to come anyway has me peeking over to her with curious eyes and a little knowing smile.

In the second period Hunter scored his second goal of the game and the crowd went crazy as he threw his stick down and raced across the ice.

All of the Carter U supporters knew what that meant.

It meant that Hunter Wilde had just become the highest goal scorer in Carter U ice hockey history, and we were here to watch him take that title.

I could barely contain myself as he skated right up to our section yelling, *"You see that, baby? Did you fucking see that?!"*

And now we're in the final minute of play, with the Rangers dominating possession of the puck, and my heart is about to burst as the last countdown begins on the screen. Hunter has already scored a third goal during this round but as I watch him whip across the ice I know that he's going to try and get one more point for Carter U.

Tristan hits the puck towards another Ranger and they all begin flying down to the opponents' goal, the big screen above the centre of the rink showing that there are thirty seconds left before the tournament is over.

Everyone is pounding on the boards as the Rangers begin passing the puck, before Tanner gets it, raises his stick, and tosses it at lightning speed towards Hunter, who slams it right into the centre of the net.

We're all screaming, the whole arena on their feet, and the Rangers can't help but celebrate as the clock moves into the final ten seconds. The audience begins a deafening countdown as the referee moves the players back into position, even though we already now know exactly who the championship winners are about to be.

"Three! Two! One!"

And as the crowd shouts *"one"* the final whistle blows, and every Ranger on the ice throws down their helmet, celebrating victoriously as they smash their bodies together. The Carter U substitutes in the booth beside us jump their gate and flood the ice, hurtling over to the rest of the Rangers as we scream our lungs out in the stands.

As the commentator announces the winners of this year's national championship Hunter's eyes find mine and I push my body up against the clear board, hands on my cheeks because they hurt so much from smiling.

His eyes are sparkling the brightest that I've ever seen them, and he hits me with his signature smirk, making my heart skip a beat.

I have a million things that I want to say to him but the ref rounds up the teams so that they can go through the protocols of handshakes and other formalities before they're allowed to fully revel in what just happened. So I wait my turn, bouncing up and down with the rest of my squad.

As soon as they've gone through all of the red tape and regulations, the Rangers are celebrating all over again, but Hunter tears straight over to the player's bench on our right, ripping off his gloves so that he can open up the gate beside us.

Once I realise that he's trying to get to me I squeeze my

Pinkie Promise

way through the crowd of squealing cheerleaders until I'm up at the miniature border that separates the stands from the ice, hovering on it like a precipice because I'm pretty sure it would be seen as illicit behaviour if someone from the audience got onto the rink with no blades.

But that doesn't stop Hunter. The second that I'm within touching distance he grabs me by my hips and hauls me up against him, albeit keeping me dangling over on the audience side of the border, and making me laugh as my feet wiggle above the floor.

"Baby," he rasps, his voice the most hoarse that I've ever heard it. "Baby, I'm sorry, I've got so much explaining to do–"

I cup my shaking hands around his stubbled jaw and lean up as high as I can so that I can kiss him.

He groans, long and low, and hunches around me, shielding me from the view of his teammates and those ever-looming ice hockey cameras.

"You don't have any explaining to do," I say breathlessly, letting out a little yelp as he yanks me higher up his chest.

This moment – Carter U winning the championship – is incredible and Hunter doesn't need to apologise for anything.

His eyes drop between us, to where my front is crushed up against his, and his mouth tilts up into a handsome smirk because our outfits completely match.

Then he shakes it off and looks down at me with a serious expression.

"I was really fucking stupid, Fallon. I wanted to help you but I didn't wanna come on too strong, so I withheld the truth like a goddamn idiot. You told me that you needed to be independent and I still couldn't stop myself. That's not okay, Fallon. I don't expect you to be okay with me doing that."

I kiss him again and this time he doesn't hold back, his

palms gripping roughly at the back of my thighs as he slides his tongue inside my mouth.

I can't help but laugh as I realise what he's doing, pulling back from his firm strokes because I'm about to have a full-on giggle fit.

"What?" he rasps, his expression unbelievably anguished.

I press a few more kisses against his mouth because I can't believe what's going on inside of his head right now.

"Hunter," I finally whisper when I pull back from his beautiful face.

"Yeah, baby?" he asks, burying his face in my neck.

I stroke my fingers through his hair as I whisper, "Did you think that I was about to break up with you or something?"

When he grinds his forehead more desolately against my skin I begin pressing kisses against his messy post-game hair.

"Hunter, I'm not mad at you, and I'm not breaking up with you," I admit, rubbing consolingly at his shoulders as I feel his breathing become unsteady. I can only imagine how overwhelmed he is right now. "Hunter, look at me. You just captained Carter U into winning the national championship. I am *so* proud of you. I'm not freaked out about what you did for me. If anything, I'm grateful."

That makes his head lift up, so tan and strikingly handsome that butterflies flutter wildly in my belly.

"You're not freaked out?" he asks quietly, looking behind him to check that no-one's listening.

Which is obviously not the case, because half of his team is standing behind him, arms across their chests like we're in a group therapy session.

"Jesus," he exclaims, clutching me tighter. "Give us a minute, okay guys?"

Most of them back away grinning, but Tanner doesn't. He locks his eyes in with mine and then spits out his mouth guard.

I give him a long intense glower as he gets comfortable on the seat beside us.

"I'm not freaked out," I murmur quietly, wiggling my feet nervously. "I was a little at first, but that's because I don't know how to handle affection. It's all so new to me. I left the diner last night because I was sort of in shock, and then I ended up having to go to a last minute cheer practice for our performance tonight... and I was just thinking about how lucky I am to know you, because you're willing to do what's best for me even when *I* don't know what's best for me. And as much as I've been afraid of letting people into my life, I realised that if I continue avoiding *good* people then I'm perpetuating my own vicious cycle. And I don't want that. I want... this. I want you. And I'm going to want you for, like, ever, so I hope that – even after a mild freak out – you're going to still want me, too."

Hunter's eyes are wide as he looks at me for a few seconds, but then his chest is heaving and he crashes his mouth down on mine, one hand firmly caressing the back of my neck and the other sliding even further up my thigh.

"Thought you were going to break up with me," he pants. "Thought you came here out of, you know, pity or somethin'."

I breathe out a laugh and wrap my arms tighter around the back of his neck. "Even with that big red number 9 on my back?" I ask him, grinning. "I came here to support my big, strong, sexy boyfriend, and to thank him for giving me all of the love that I've never had before."

"Oh Lord," he murmurs, hunching down to kiss me again. It's soft and sweet, the kind of kiss that *really* turns Hunter on, and he pulls away with a grunt before pressing his forehead against mine. His chest moves in quick pumps as he says, "Should probably stop doin' that before I get carried away."

I press a happy kiss against his jaw and he groans

quietly.

"Yeah, we probably should. Especially considering who's in the crowd," I tell him, unable to hide my smile.

He looks down at me for a beat, before following the direction that I'm pointing in with his eyes. His chest almost doubles in size, his hands becoming vice-like as he realises who else is here for him.

"Baby," he chokes out, his amazed gaze flying down to mine. "Did you do that for me?"

His eyes are shimmering dangerously, his beautiful cheekbones a ruddy red. He drops his head back into my neck and my heart tears a little as his shoulders gently shake.

"First time they've ever seen me play," he says hoarsely, and I squeeze him all the tighter.

I glance down at Tanner who has been impassively watching our entire exchange, and when he meets my eyes we have a little secret of our own.

It isn't exactly easy to get tickets to the national ice hockey championship final but Tanner has his ways, which is why Hunter's family is in the stands, for the first time ever.

I squish my cheek against Hunter's soft messy hair and then wiggle myself free, dropping gently to the floor as Hunter's hands slide up to cup my ribcage.

"I love you so much," he murmurs, after scrubbing his dampened cheeks against the shoulders of his jersey. "So fucking much, Fallon."

I grin up at him and ask, "Enough to secretly employ me at your family's business?"

He smirks down at me and gives my ass a rough squeeze. "Hell yeah, baby."

I jump up so that I can press a kiss to his cheek and he breathes out the world's most beautiful laugh.

"Well, that's good," I say, "because I love you so much too."

Hunter crushes me against his chest and covers me in kisses.

"First time that you've ever said that to me," he murmurs, not pulling back for air as he smothers me in his love.

"First time that I've ever said that to *anyone*," I whisper back, giggling happily when he claims my mouth with his.

I think this is the happiest that I've ever felt in my whole entire life.

Hunter's large palms hold me securely against his chest and he kisses me adoringly, my arms tight around his neck.

"Can't give you a proper introduction to my parents tonight," he says gruffly when he finally pulls back, easing himself over the barrier as someone hands him a pair of skate guards. He releases me only until he's finished slipping them on. "Gonna need a good week's worth of just you and me time before we make that happen."

Warmth spreads in my belly as I imagine what he's thinking about right now.

He gives me an appreciative once-over and then murmurs, "Actually, let's make that a month."

I hide my face in the nook between his biceps and his pecs, and Hunter smirks as he squeezes me against his body.

"You want some you and me time, baby?" he asks when I finally lift my face to peek up at him. He smiles smugly, palming me possessively over my skirt.

I move so that I'm in front of him, walking backwards as I rub my hands up over his chest and batting my eyelashes flirtatiously. His grin gets even cockier and he hauls me up by my ass, grunting quietly in satisfaction when I wrap my legs around his middle.

My feet waggle happily above the floor as we join the large crowd of Hunter's teammates who are all making their way back to the locker room. The corridor is lined with their closest friends and family members, although most of the supporters are still in the stands. The celebrations for their huge win are nowhere near even starting yet.

"Heading back to our place," Tanner announces loudly to the exodus, and he's met with cheers and knowing smirks, probably because, with Tanner being Tanner, every pretty girl at Carter U will already be at their place.

Tanner claps Hunter on the back and says, "That includes y'all, by the way. No sneaking off to her condo on win night."

"Doesn't matter where we are, as long as she's with me," Hunter says.

My heart thunders in my chest and I hold onto Hunter more tightly.

When we reach the entrance to the changing room Hunter helps me dismount from his body, jerking his chin at his guys to say *give us a minute*.

He walks us just past the doorframe and cages me protectively against the wall.

His back is to the locker room, shielding us from view, and he pulls me up against his body, smiling self-assuredly.

"This has been the best year of my life," he says, and my heart bursts in my chest. I duck my chin to hide my blush but he tips it back up with two warm fingers. "Wouldn't be where I am right now if I hadn't had you by my side. Making me want to do better. Making me want to be better. All of this right now, it's all because of you."

I shake my head although I'm still smiling. He grins down at me and rubs the apple of my cheek.

"You okay coming to our place tonight? 'Cause it don't matter what Tanner said – if you wanna go straight to your condo, I'm down as fuck for that."

I laugh at his countryism and nod my head excitedly. "I want you to celebrate with your team, Hunter, of course I'm okay with that. I am very, very happy to come to the hockey house with you. If you want me to."

He squeezes my waist, yanking me closer. His eyes are

so molten that they're making me dizzy.

"I *really* want you to. And I'm gonna give you a real thank you for how fucking beautiful your performance was tonight."

I'm so happy right now that I can feel my dimples puckering my cheeks. "You liked it?" I ask, toying with the front of his jersey.

"Liked it?" he asks, his eyes on fire. "Watching you up there on centre stage, showing everyone how talented you are with *my number* on your back?" He huffs out a laugh and borderline growls, "Yes, Fallon. It's safe to say that I liked it."

I kiss happily at his stubble and he cups the back of my head in his hand, a content rumble happening deep in his chest.

"We practiced some of those positions together," I remind him when I drop back down from my tip-toes.

"We'll be practicing a couple more tonight."

Oh Lord.

As I stumble and swoon dizzily up against his chest, one of his teammates clomps out of the changing room and says, "Uber's here in three. You gonna get changed before we head?"

Hunter turns his head and gives him a nod before refocusing on his limp girlfriend who has just lost control of her knees.

He smirks, pleased, and tries to help me steady my feet.

"You don't need to get changed," I say breathlessly. "You're just going to be taking your clothes off in ten minutes anyway."

He looks even more pleased now, his eyes dropping to my chest as he contemplates my very rational, not at all biased comment.

"I'm gonna have the world's fastest shower, so that I'm all clean for you," he says.

I howl in anguish and he laughs quietly.

"And then," he adds, "when we get home, we can work together to get all dirty again."

Oh, he's good. He's very good.

"Fine," I say, shoving him off of me, knowing that it's only going to make him grip me harder. He buries his face in my neck, scratching me up with his stubble, and I try not to go slack as he licks gently at my skin. "And, uh," I pant, now remembering that I should probably congratulate him on becoming Carter U's top scorer of all time. "Your goals," I gasp. "They were very good."

"Huh?" he murmurs gruffly, just as distracted as I am.

"You, uh, you… you're the t-top goal scorer in Carter U history. Your goals were s-so good out there tonight and I'm so proud of you, Hunter. So proud."

Hunter lifts his head up, his beautiful eyes dazzling me senseless. He smiles as he rasps, "It's because of you, baby. Those goals were all for you."

I blink up at him, still breathless, and I swallow as I ask, "What do you mean?"

He flashes me his perfect smile before pressing a kiss to my pink cheek. My heart sparkles warmly and I give him a little smile of my own.

"What I mean, Fallon, is that I couldn't have done any of that if you weren't out there watching me." He squeezes me tighter as I stare awe-struck in his arms. "Those goals, Fallon? They were all for you, because nothing feels better than making you happy. And that's what I'm going to keep on doing for as long as you'll let me. I love you, baby. You're the greatest score of my life."

EPILOGUE

Hunter

Two and a half months later

I wake up to the feeling of something warm and soft snuggling up to my pecs.

Breathing out a quiet laugh, I squeeze my arm more firmly around Fallon's shoulders, and then I slowly heave myself onto my side as she wraps her arms around the back of my neck.

My eyes fly open and I look down between us.

Hell, I didn't drink a drop last night but I had somehow forgotten the fact that Fallon had gone to sleep *topless*.

My shoulders swell as I stare down at her breasts, the touch of her soft pink nipples making my cock thicken and throb.

"Baby," I rasp quietly, the word coming out fifty octaves deeper than it should.

Fallon cuddles me tighter and I clear my throat. Hard.

If this were any other morning I wouldn't be fighting the need to give it to her right now, but this isn't any morning so I'm going to do the right thing and wait.

I keep one arm around her shoulders, holding her against me, and I cup my other palm around her cheek as I press a kiss to her forehead.

It's grant allocation week, which means that I've been distracting the hell out of Fallon to try and ease her nerves.

At the start of the week we drove just outside of town so that I could take her shopping for the first time, and she picked out what she wanted to wear for last night's Carter U Division I Sports Ceremony.

Can't deny it, spoiling Fallon gets me going. Having her looking up at me with those big beautiful eyes as she showed me the dress that she wanted to try on, and then getting in that changing room with her as she modelled it for me was something that I never knew that I needed. I told her that the price didn't matter because whatever she wanted I'd be able to cover and, if anything, it got me even more excited for when I start playing pro, because the second that I get that NHL cheque I know exactly what I'm going to be doing.

Namely, treating Fallon to everything she's ever wanted.

She picked out a small sparkly lilac dress and a pair of matching heels, with sexy ribbon straps that she tied in little bows at the backs of her calves. And now that dress is strewn on the floor next to my suit as the morning light tries to breach the curtains of our soon-to-be bedroom at Larch Peak.

Fallon suddenly lets out a little gasp and I immediately know that she's remembered what day today is. It's the day that she'll receive an email about whether or not her department has awarded her the Master's grant.

I hold her more firmly against my chest, much to the distress of my rock-hard dick, and I kiss my way down her cheek hoping that she doesn't start panicking too hard right

Pinkie Promise

now.

"Hunter," she whimpers, trying to hide her face in my neck. She says it in that pained voice that has me knowing she's stressing.

I'm aware that the only form of praise Fallon received until recently was the kind that she got through high grades and good report cards, so I know that whether or not she gets awarded with this grant is playing heavily on her sense of self worth right now.

It's my job to remind her that the opinion of a couple of tutors isn't worth jack shit in the scheme of things. There's no telling why one tutor can give a student a particular grade but another tutor could give them the complete opposite, and it's the same thing when it comes to grant allocation. With sports grants, it's pretty surface level because your performance shows your skills, plain and simple. But for a grant in the Literature department? It's subjective as all get out.

It's like the author thing. There's no end to the amount of stories you hear about authors being rejected from a hundred publishers, but then as soon as their book gets into the hands of the right readers they're a *New York Times* bestseller.

Whether or not they give her this grant, I'm going to make sure that I help her achieve her goals. She wants to stay at Carter U for another year? Then she's going to… even if I selfishly want her to get the grant and then tell me that she'd actually rather move straight to Larch Peak with me instead of doing a year of long distance.

I'll admit it: in reality, that's what I want. I want Fallon by my side for good.

I want to start my career at the NHL while Fallon gets to work on writing her book, even though she's still a little shy about doing it.

But I can do one more year of back-and-forthing to Carter U's campus, spending my weekends with Fallon before getting back to training or being on the road. I'll make it work, no problem.

"You've got this, baby," I murmur gruffly, grinding my forehead against hers. "Remember what I told you last night?"

Fallon bites into her lower lip and looks to the side with a contemplative expression, probably thinking less about what I said to her last night and more about what I *did* to her. Her eyes flash up to mine as the memories play behind her irises. Her cheeks get a little warmer as she smiles shyly against my chest.

I swallow hard, trying to stay focused.

"You deserve that grant and if the board has any sense, they'll give it to you. But it doesn't matter if they don't, because if those assholes withhold your funding then *I'll* finance you. You're doing the Master's regardless of the grant, so long as you still wanna do it, baby. I'll give you that cash."

Fallon squishes her body even harder against mine and my brain blanks out like a television in a thunderstorm. I immediately shove my body on top of hers and then we're kissing in a hot hungry frenzy.

"I would never, ever, ever, ever ask that of you," she pants breathlessly as I begin palming at her breasts. It's taking every ounce of my self-control to not push inside of her right now.

"I know you wouldn't," I murmur, "but as soon as my paperwork is signed, I'm gonna be able to afford it. Your studies. This house. A little closet full of sexy lilac underwear."

She breathes out a tinkling laugh and I fucking pre-come on her belly.

"Sorry, I'm sorry," I choke out, sitting up on one elbow, grabbing a Kleenex from the nightstand, and using it to gently rub it off of her.

She's still giggling as I toss the tissue to the floor so,

even though my face is crimson, I smile back at her, at least relieved that I'm managing to distract her a little.

"You'd really get me a little closet just for my lilac panties?" she asks me teasingly.

I roll onto my back, tucking my hands behind my head. "Fallon, I'll *build* you a closet just for your lilac panties."

I remove one of my arms from its position against the pillow and I use it to hug Fallon against my side, knowing that I'm probably going to need to give her a bit of space right now while she checks her emails for the results.

"Want me to stay here?" I ask, rubbing my thumb into her shoulder. "Or do you want me to go downstairs and make you some breakfast while you... you know."

I don't want to mention the g-word – *grant* – anymore so I just tip my chin in the direction of her phone.

She climbs on top of me and gives me a little kiss. I palm her breasts in my hands and try not to groan too loudly.

"I need... five minutes," she whispers, and I nod even though I'm barely breathing.

She slips off of me and I stay on my back, panting for a couple seconds, before pushing the sheets off and getting heavily to my feet. I can't help but give myself a few tight pumps before shoving my legs back inside my suit pants, kissing Fallon on her cheek, and then exhaling shakily as I make my way down to the kitchen.

Five seconds later there's a loud crash and pounding footsteps.

I'm immediately bounding up the stairs, meeting Fallon in the middle as she races her way down. There are tears running down her face so I scoop her up without hesitation, even though I don't know yet if these are good tears or bad tears.

"Tell me, baby," I say to her, rubbing at her waist while I manoeuvre us into the open plan living area. The curtains are still drawn from last night, and Fallon's pretty lace thong is dangling off the arm of the sofa.

We may have only gotten *naked* when we hit the hay in our bedroom last night, but that doesn't mean that we made it to the bedroom without going at it downstairs first.

I didn't drink at the Sports Gala last night knowing that I was going to be driving late with Fallon so I'm remembering last night clear as day.

I'm pacing blindly as I gently bounce her against my chest, hoping that she's been given the outcome that she wanted.

She managed to shrug on the shirt that I was wearing last night before tornadoing down the stairs just now so I slip my hand beneath the hem and caress her lower back.

"Hunter, I–I–" she begins, stuttering wildly as she tries to catch her breath. She fans one of her hands in front of her face and shakes her head, apologetic and embarrassed.

"Whatever happened, I've got you," I remind her, putting on my game-day face so that she knows that she's fully backed and supported.

She nods her head quickly and then, without further delay, she whispers, "I got it."

"*Baby*," I murmur happily, and she giggles as she bites her bottom lip, shaking her beautiful fluffy hair as if she almost feels guilty. "I'm so freaking proud of you, Fallon. My sexy little cheerleader."

Fallon throws her head back, giggling uncontrollably, and then my mouth is on hers as we stumble through the living area.

"So – fuckin' – proud," I growl, as her fingers tangle up in my hair and I rip my shirt clean off her body.

She's trying to shove my suit pants down my legs with her feet, and it makes me smirk against her mouth because she did the same thing last night.

And we both know what ended up happening there.

"You like it when I wear a suit, huh?" I murmur with a grin.

The reason why only Fallon's panties are dangling off the couch? Because when we came in last night and I flicked on a lamp, we ended up slow-kissing on the sofa until suddenly we weren't. Fallon's dress was around her waist, my suit pants were shoved halfway down my quads, and then Fallon was on her belly as I mounted her from behind, fully clothed.

Gripping Fallon's hips in my palms as I pumped her from the back in a suit wasn't something that either of us knew that we'd be into, but now that I know she likes it I can't wait to do it again. Even better if she's wearing another pair of thousand dollar heels that I couldn't stop myself buying for her.

Maybe having her do another year at college won't be so bad if we can at least have our weekends spent like this.

Then, once she finally graduates, I'll convince her to be my hot cheerleader live-in.

Is now the wrong time to talk to her about putting a rock on her finger?

Just as I slide my tongue inside her mouth Fallon makes a sweet little sound and whispers, "I love you so much."

Oh God. I trip over the arm of the sofa, Fallon falls onto her back, and I rip open the top button on my pants as she giggles up at me.

"You can't say that when I'm already excited, baby," I pant. "I won't be able to last."

She gives me a naughty smile and says, "But you're so good at making it up to me, over and over and over again."

She's got me there. I try to bite back my smirk as I pull the condoms out of my pants pocket. I keep one between my teeth as I toss the others onto the coffee table, and then I lower my body on top of Fallon's, heat pulsing in my abdomen.

Fallon leans up and gently bites the other side of the wrapper, making my irises black out as I release my hold on it.

"Jesus Christ," I murmur, as I gently pinch the foil between my fingers, easing it back so that Fallon can slowly tear it open. My chest pumps heavily as I slip the condom from her lips, discarding the wrapper on the floor and rolling the rubber down my length. I lean one arm over her head, gripping the sofa for extra leverage, before I knock her knees further apart and spank her heat with my rigid cock.

"I love you," I grunt as I slowly slide it inside, groaning hard when she pulls me down so that she can reach me for kissing.

I kiss her back, slow and deep, wanting to take all of the time in the world with her.

It's an early Friday morning but we're going to treat it like a lazy Sunday.

She whimpers into my mouth so I roll my hips a little harder, telling her how much I love her with my body, a million promises in each kiss.

"You like that?" I ask, as I push both of her thighs up against the couch, feeling fucking feral over how deep this angle is.

"Yes, yes, yes," she says quickly, her brow arching when I thrust it in to the hilt.

"Jesus," I murmur, dropping my eyes from her beautiful face.

Her cheeks are flushed pink and her eyes are all sparkly, and it's making it damn near impossible to not spurt my load already.

I look down at her body and my abdomen tightens, because Fallon's soft bouncing breasts are going to make me blow.

"How'd you get to be so cute and sexy at the same time?" I grumble, releasing one of her thighs so that I can hook my forearm beneath her neck. Her throat arches back and I groan loudly as I lick her warm skin. "Perfect," I murmur. "You're so damn perfect. Little angel face with those big sexy tits."

The heels of her feet dig into my shoulders as she moans, and I laugh against her throat, murmuring, "Fucking adorable."

"You're adorable," she mumbles, and now I'm really laughing.

I sit up on my haunches, grip my hands around her waist, and then I shove her hard down on my dick, my chest doubling in size as I watch her take it.

"What'd you call me?" I ask, grinning victoriously when she laughs and shakes her head. "Huh? What'd you just call me, baby?"

To show her just how *adorable* her man can be, I pull out, roll her over, and then press my bodyweight into her back, slapping my dick against her pussy before thrusting hard back inside of her.

"I didn't mean it, I didn't mean it!" she pants between her laughter, moaning when I slide my hands underneath her body and start massaging her breasts.

My body tenses as I accidentally shoot out another pump of pre-come and, high on the pleasure of release, I grunt against her neck, "I think it's time to make that baby."

She giggles and squirms, her body bouncing underneath mine. She looks back at me over her shoulder and warmth rips through my chest.

Prettiest fucking girl in the world.

"You have s-such beautiful eyes," she whispers to me, and I suddenly jerk a little rough because that was the last thing that I imagined she would say right now.

I'm pounding her like an animal and she still manages to say the sweetest shit.

"Thanks," I manage. "Our babies will have 'em too."

"*Hunter.*"

I bury my face in her neck as I thrust us to the finish line, palming her soft tits with big eager hands.

"You gonna spend the summer being my girl?" I ask her

breathlessly, kissing at her throat as she squirms beneath me.

"Yes," she pants quickly, arching up to help me thrust.

"And when you're back at college in the fall, you'll let me come visit?"

"*Yes*," she says again, releasing a whimper.

"And then, when you graduate, I'm gonna be all yours and you're gonna be all mine."

This time it isn't a question, it's a fact that I want to hear her affirm, and I kiss her as sweet as I can manage as my body swells with its impending release.

I press a peck to her little dimple and she laughs prettily, making me feel like the luckiest guy in the whole damn world.

"I'm gonna be all yours and you're gonna be all mine," she repeats, smiling as she entwines our pinkies and kisses me back. Her voice is a tiny happy whisper as she murmurs, "I promise."

ABOUT THE AUTHOR

Sapphire is a writer who specializes in New Adult and contemporary romance stories. She has a First Class Honours Bachelor of Arts degree from Durham University and a Master of Philosophy degree from Cambridge University.

She loves love.

You can find out more about the author on her website: www.sapphireauthor.com

For more updates, Sapphire can be found on TikTok and Instagram: @sapphiresbookshelf

P.S…

Thank you to every reader who has ever sent me a wonderful message, comment, bookish edit, review and DM! Your kind words mean more to me than you will ever know.
Love always,
Sapphire

Printed in Great Britain
by Amazon